The Art of Us

a novel

Teri Wilson

The Art of Us

Print Edition

The Tule Publishing Group, LLC

ISBN: 978-1-944925-19-2

Dedication

For Cameron and Hannah

And in honor of the Combat Paper Project, bringing healing through art.

"I feel that there is nothing more truly artistic than to love people."
—Vincent Van Gogh

Acknowledgements

Thank you to my friends at Painting With a Twist in San Antonio, Texas, the inspiration for Harper's Art Bar. I am also indebted to Sue Healey for her support, as well as for fielding all of my Boston-related questions. As always, I have endless gratitude and affection for Elizabeth Winick Rubinstein. And I owe a special thank you to Jane Porter for being such an amazing mentor and source of encouragement to so many authors, myself included.

Chapter One

When Harper Higgins first had the idea to adopt the little one-eared dachshund from the Boston Humane Society, she didn't think much about how he'd need to be walked even if it was raining outside. Or snowing, which it did six months out of the year in Boston. Sometimes seven or even eight.

Rain or shine, sleet or snow. That was reality with a dog. Not unlike the postal service.

When she first saw him on one of the local morning news shows, wearing his little yellow *Adopt Me* vest, Harper didn't think much about any of the technical aspects of owning a pet. All she saw was that ear, or lack thereof, and she knew he was the dog for her.

Rembrandt had owned a dachshund. So had Picasso. And Andy Warhol, Jackson Pollock, and David Hockney. According to rumor, Leonardo DaVinci even had a dachshund. Allegedly, her name was Mona, and he often discussed his art with her. But that was unsubstantiated, so it didn't count in Harper's eyes. As an art historian, she was a stickler for that type of thing. History and legend were two very different things. One was steeped in reality and the other in fantasy. Harper lived in reality. Her feet hadn't strayed from that territory since she was ten years old.

She liked it that way. So long as she lived in reality, she couldn't have the rug swept out from under her again. *Work hard, become independent, learn to take care of herself.* Those were her ideals. Oh—and adopt one-eared dogs. That was a new one.

How could she not, though?

She was a bona fide expert on Vincent Van Gogh. He was her favorite artist. She couldn't have adored his work more if he'd had two ears, or three, or four, for that matter. He was a genius. So the dog's lone ear, plus the fact that he was a dachshund sold her on the idea.

She would have called it a sign, if she'd believed in that sort of thing, which she didn't. But she'd taken one look at the dog, grabbed her keys, and driven straight to the animal shelter.

And now here she was—huddled beneath a tiny umbrella in the cascading rain—waiting for Vincent to select the precise blade of grass on which to pee.

"Come on, Vincent. It's getting late." She cooed, when what she really wanted to say was, *"Any day now."*

Walks in the rain aside, she really did love the little guy. She simply had no idea what she was doing. She'd never had a dog before. Not even as a kid. Someone who knew more about dogs probably would have told her to stop walking around and to stay in one spot and wait for Vincent to do his business. Continual movement just meant new smells, new distractions. Someone who knew more about dogs also probably wouldn't have let Vincent's leash slip through her fingers when Vincent tore after the guy carrying the enormous basket of flowers.

One minute Harper was standing ankle-deep in rainwater

with a leash in her hand and the next, that leash was trailing after Vincent like the tail on a kite as he ran headlong into trouble.

"Vincent, wait!"

Vincent didn't wait. He didn't even hesitate. He threw himself directly into the path of the man carrying the flowers. There was a loud thud. And a splash. And then the sky rained purple blooms in and among the raindrops.

"*Vincent!*" Harper ran after him.

The dog was standing on the center of the flower man's chest, tail wagging, lone ear flapping in the wind of the storm, while the man lay flat on his back on the cobblestoned walkway. Harper dropped her umbrella and scooped him into her arms at once. The dog, not the flower man.

"Are you okay?" she asked, bending over the fellow and looking into his eyes to check for consciousness.

He frowned. Deeply enough to guarantee that yes, he was awake. And no, he was not a happy camper at the moment.

"I don't know."

Surrounded by pretty purple flowers, a frowning man had never looked quite so ethereal. They encircled him completely. Lying there in the water, with blooms scattered all about, he reminded Harper of Sir John Everett Millais' famous painting, *Ophelia*. Except the subject of *Ophelia* was dead in a river. And this man was very alive—and by all appearances very grumpy—in a puddle of dirty rainwater.

Wincing, he pushed himself to his feet. "Damn it."

"Are you hurt?"

"My ankle. I must have twisted it." He looked down at his right hand. There was a trail of blood by his thumb. It mixed with the rain, thinning and lightening. If it had been oil paint, it would have been carmine red. "And I have a cut on my hand."

"But you're upright. That's an improvement."

He glared at her.

She glared right back.

She probably should have apologized on behalf of Vincent. But the truth was, she didn't want to. *I'm sorry* were words that had never come easy to Harper. And this guy's attitude was beginning to grate on her nerves.

She glanced at the flowers that lay at their feet. Violets.

Such a modest flower. Pretty enough. But lacking the colorful drama and splendor of the irises, sunflowers, or poppies that Van Gogh painted. She wondered if Van Gogh had ever painted violets before. Not to her knowledge. And if anyone in this day and age would know, it would have been Harper.

With her free hand, she took her wallet from her purse and pulled out a twenty. She glanced back down at the ground, the upended basket, and the wet, ruined, trampled violets ground into the cobblestones. The delicate petals had taken on the quality of crushed grapes on the pavement.

For good measure, she pulled out another twenty-dollar bill. "Here. Will this cover all of them? How much do you usually charge?" She offered the money to the man.

He made no move to take it, but rather scowled at the bills and then at her. *So much for going the extra mile.* She should have stuck to just the one twenty-dollar bill.

"What is that for?"

She waved the money around a bit. Bait. She wished he would go ahead and take it. She felt like an idiot just holding it like that. And it was getting all wet.

"For your flowers. I'm not sure what you charge for them. Will this be enough?"

His eyes narrowed. Piercing blue eyes, framed with tangled, wet, dark lashes. When he aimed his gaze directly at Harper, she had to remind herself to breathe for some strange reason.

"I wasn't selling them." He spat.

"Oh." She blinked.

What on earth was he doing with a giant basket of violets? It wasn't the sort of arrangement a man might give a woman. She'd just jumped to the logical conclusion that he was selling them. Was that really such a horrible thing to assume?

Judging by the look on his face, yes. Yes, it was.

His square jaw was practically throbbing with tension. And those blue eyes of his were so frosty a shiver ran up her spine. Or maybe the shiver was due to the fact that she was soaked to the bone.

"Is that what you think—that I sell flowers out of a basket on the street corner?" He made it sound like it was one step up from begging for spare change.

"Calm down. I thought you sold flowers. I didn't say you were a panhandler." She couldn't help but cast a wry look at his clothes.

He was a mess. Enough of a mess to suggest he'd been a mess even before Vincent had knocked him down. Grass stains on the legs of his jeans, mud caked on his hiking boots, and a plain white t-shirt, soaked and transparent.

She had to give credit where credit was due though and, in this instance, it was due somewhere beneath that dampened t-shirt that clung to muscles the likes of which she wasn't sure she'd seen on an actual living, breathing man. Unless Channing Tatum counted as human, and she wasn't entirely sure he did. He was more of a mythical creature. Like a unicorn.

The man standing in front of her was looking more like a mythical creature himself with each passing second. Only not a unicorn. More like a dragon. A dragon of the fire-breathing sort.

"No, you didn't think I was a panhandler. You just thought I hung around on the street corner selling violets. For your information, I'm not a flower girl."

She willed herself not to look at his biceps, straining the sleeves of his t-shirt. But mid-blink she found herself sneaking a glance at them again. He was right about one thing. He most definitely was not a girl. Not a flower girl or any other variety.

"It was a simple misunderstanding." She jammed the money back into her wallet.

Great. Now all of her other money would be drenched as well. And her wallet. And the inside of her handbag. If he thought she was going to apologize for jumping to a completely rational conclusion, he was mistaken.

"If you weren't selling them, what were you doing with them?"

He stared at her impassively and said nothing. Her question hung there in the space between them, not unlike the soggy dollar bills had just moments before.

Super.

"Fine. Don't tell me." She rolled her eyes, half at him and half at herself. She sounded ridiculous.

Get it together, Harper. He's just a man that your dog knocked over.

He crossed his arms. This time Harper managed to avoid ogling them.

"I wasn't planning on it."

Who cared why he had all those violets? Harper certainly didn't. But, of course, the fact that he refused to tell her caused her to wonder all the more. Anyone would wonder. Her wondering didn't have a thing to do with that soaked white t-shirt he was wearing. She chalked it up to simple human nature. And she was, after all, only human. No one had ever confused her with Channing Tatum.

"Who are you anyway?" she asked.

She was certain she'd never seen him before. Granted, a lot of people lived in the South End. But she was sure he was new to the area. One, he didn't have an accent. And two, well the biceps. Surely, she would have noticed those hanging around. Dating wasn't high on her list of priorities. Actually, it didn't make an appearance anywhere on the list. She didn't have time for dating. She had a career to worry about, but she wasn't blind.

He gave her a tight, one-hundred percent nongenuine smile. "Who am I? Not a flower girl."

That narrowed it down, didn't it? "Yes, I believe we've established that already. I'm Harper Higgins. *Doctor* Harper Higgins. And you are?"

SHE DIDN'T REMEMBER.

Tom could tell, simply by the blank expression on her face.

For three days in a row, they'd gotten their morning coffee

at the same coffee shop. Not the South End Starbucks. Hell, not Starbucks.

It was a tiny local place, with sizes called *Yes*, *Yes Please* and *Oh, God, Yes* instead of small, medium, and large. He'd seen her come in every morning and order the same thing each time—a vanilla soy latte with one Splenda and whip.

Oh God, yes.

He wasn't stalking her or anything. He just had a knack for remembering things. He'd been trained to notice things, after all. Boxes. Soda cans. Animal carcasses. Seemingly ordinary things to find among roadside trash in Iraq, but deadly when they contained homemade bombs.

He'd noticed Dr. Harper Higgins. Blonde hair. Pretty green eyes, constantly glued to her cell phone. And the combination of Splenda and whipped cream, which was somewhat unique. She'd stuck with him.

Clearly nothing about him had stuck with her.

"Tom Stone." Tom extended his bloody hand, thought better of it, and drew it back. "You're a doctor? Good. I think I might need stitches."

"Oh. I'm not exactly that sort of doctor." Her cheeks flushed pink in the semidarkness. Tiny droplets of rain had collected, undisturbed, in her hair. They glimmered in the moonlight like stardust. If she hadn't been such a snob, Tom would have likely thought her beautiful.

But that was an awfully big *if.* An *if* of epic-sized proportions. She'd looked right through him three straight times, and now she thought him a street peddler.

"What sort of doctor doesn't stitch people up? Even dentists give stitches."

Her flush brightened a shade. Her dog squirmed in her arms. Mischief on four dripping legs.

"I'm not a dentist."

He ventured another guess. "A podiatrist?"

There had been dueling doctors in Iraq—a foot surgeon and a podiatrist. The battles they often engaged in made the actual war look like a lazy Sunday afternoon picnic.

"No." She tightened her grip on the dog and blew out a sigh. A raindrop fell from the tip of her nose.

"Oh, God. You're not a shrink, are you?" That was the absolute last thing Tom needed. He'd seen more shrinks than bullets over the course of his final tour.

She lifted her chin, giving him a better view of those bewitching eyes. They glittered, dark in the moonlight, like dangerous emeralds. "The proper term is psychiatrist."

He'd hit the nail on the head.

Marvelous.

No wonder she seemed so nuts. He jammed a hand through his soaked hair.

"And, no. I'm not one." For some reason, her denial didn't usher in the surge of relief it should have. "If you must know, I'm a doctor of philosophy."

He blinked. *Doctor of philosophy?*

It took him a minute to decipher what she was saying. Doctor of philosophy. A PhD. She was an academic. She wasn't a doctor at all. Not one that had a place anywhere on the physician spectrum, at least. Certainly not one who could stitch up his hand.

"I see. So you're not a real doctor." He would have laughed if his hand weren't throbbing so badly. "What does a philosophy doc do all day? Sit around contemplating the great mysteries of life, like what came first—the chicken or the egg?"

"It means I have a PhD. And it most assuredly is real." Her voice rose an octave, and her dog's one ear drew back on his tiny head.

Tom had seen a lot of things in his life but a one-eared dog wasn't one of them. One-eared dogs? No. PhDs? Of course. "Relax. It was a joke. And I know what it means. I'm not an idiot."

Did she really think he was that stupid?

Judging by the haughty twinkle in her eyes, yes. She did.

"I think it's best that we just end this line of questioning. And perhaps this conversation altogether."

"Fine." His jaw clenched.

So tightly a ribbon of pain wound its way from his jaw to his temple. The rain had eased up, though, coming down as a fine mist rather than droplets. That was something to be grateful for.

"Fine." She echoed, lifting her chin.

Ample blonde curls tumbled over her shoulder and her back, weighted down at the ends from the rain. In the pale light of the moon, all that teeming hair made her look like a mermaid. Or an angel.

Oh, the irony.

"Just answer one question for me," he said.

She nodded. "That's acceptable."

That's acceptable. Who talked like that? "If a tree falls in the forest and there's no one around to hear it, does it still make a sound?"

He was antagonizing her. Intentionally. He wasn't sure

why, other than the fact that he was enjoying it. And it had been a long time since he'd enjoyed much of anything.

"You're not as funny as you think you are. My PhD is in fine art, not philosophy."

He tried mightily not to let his shock show in his expression. "You're an artist?"

Weren't artists usually laid back? If not quite laid back, then at least human?

"A professor." For the briefest moment, there was a crack in her perfect composure.

Tom blinked, and she was once again appraising him with that cold stare of hers.

"Look, I'm sorry about what happened. I should probably get Vincent home. Can I call someone for you?"

That damned cell phone of hers.

"No," he said darkly, his answer carrying a bit more bite than he intended.

She glared at him, unafraid. "Suit yourself. Can I least give you a ride? I may not be a real doctor, but I'm not sure you should be walking on that foot."

He would have told her she should be more careful. She had no business offering rides to strange men. Even strange men who had just been accosted by her terrorist of a dog. Getting in a car with a man she knew nothing about was dangerous. And just plain stupid. But it didn't take a PhD to know that those words would have fallen on deaf ears.

He shook his head. Water flew off his hair, like a wet dog after a bath. "No need. I live right here."

"Here?" She looked over her shoulder at the row of waterfront cottages that Tom would never be able to afford.

"Not there. Here." He hitched a thumb toward the row of boats bobbing in the harbor.

She frowned. "You live in Boston Harbor?"

"Don't look so horrified. I live in a boat, not an inner tube."

"Sorry. It's just..." She shook her head and readjusted her grip on her crazy dog. "Never mind. I'm sorry. Let's just leave it at that. I'm sorry."

Tom wasn't sure he'd ever set eyes on a more uncomfortable woman. She looked almost as though apologizing caused her actual, physical pain.

Try having a knot on your ankle the size of a baseball. Then we'll talk.

"Fine. See you around, Doctor Higgins." He turned toward the boat that was his. The one closest to the small yellow building with white trim that served as the marina office.

"Do you ever get seasick?" she said to his back.

He turned around, astounded that she would want to keep the conversation going. They were both drenched head to toe. She was even shivering.

"What?"

"On the boat." She glanced at the water.

It looked black in the darkness. As black as a raven's wing. The moon was nothing but a sliver, casting the barest of light on the surface of the water. The harbor was full of shadows tonight. Shadows and rain, falling like tears.

"Do you ever get motion sickness? Doesn't all that constant bobbing around bother you?"

She'd been so businesslike during their entire exchange, the last thing he'd expected was for her to ask him anything remotely personal. The question caught him off guard.

Did the movement of the boat bother him? No, not at all. After years of sleeping in a desert tent, with sand filling his every pore, he welcomed the water. Not just welcomed it. *Craved* it. He craved it like a dying man craved oxygen. He didn't even mind being out here in the rain. At least, he hadn't until his legs had gone out from under him.

At night, the sound of the water lapping quietly against the boat's hull was like music. The most exquisite lullaby he'd ever heard, playing softly in the background as the boat swayed in the harbor. It was like being rocked to sleep in the hands of angels.

And none of that was any of Doctor Harper Higgins' business.

He shook his head. "No."

"No? That's it? Just…no?" She blinked.

She had lovely eyes. Warm and green, like a field in summer. Too bad they were looking at him as though he were some kind of miscreant. Or a flower girl.

"Just no." This time he said it firmly. Firmly enough for her to know the topic was no longer up for discussion.

Then he turned his back once again on Harper Higgins—*Doctor* Harper Higgins—and her wet, unruly little dog, and he limped off in the direction of his boat.

Chapter Two

THE NIGHT AFTER Vincent's ill-fated run-in with the surly sailor, as Harper had come to think of Tom Stone, a drunken marriage proposal gave her a whole new appreciation for the blueness of Pablo Picasso's Blue Period.

She wasn't the object of the marriage proposal in question. Obviously. Hers was a life carefully crafted to avoid exactly this sort of humiliation. She had no desire to be on the receiving end of any marriage proposal, be it drunken or stone-cold sober. She'd witnessed her mother being proposed to more times than she could count. All of which had ended in marriage, none of which had lasted more than a matter of months. Harper had made her share of romantic mistakes, one that stuck out as particularly notable, but at least she'd stopped short of marrying the man.

Just witnessing such a spectacle nowadays was its own unique form of torture, even when it had nothing to do with her. The events leading up to the highly intoxicated groom-to-be dropping down on a bent, paint-splattered knee were rather tortuous as well.

"Okay, everyone, I'd like you to pick up your biggest brush." Standing at the front of a room lined with tables covered in white butcher paper, which held rows of tabletop easels and paper plate paint palettes, Harper faced her students.

Students might have been a stretch. Most of them had come to the Boston Art Bar to have a good time, sip some wine, and go home with a piece of art they could claim to have painted, even if Harper intervened with a few corrections at the end of the night. They weren't serious art students, like the sort of pupils Harper had always imagined herself teaching. The sort Harper had once been. Then again, that type of dedication to learning was a rarity. Harper was hard-pressed to find such love for learning, even among the art history students she taught twice a week at Boston College of Art.

Tonight's class was the very opposite of serious, which would have been somewhat frustrating on any given night. But on this night, less than twenty-four hours after having to defend her doctoral status to a total stranger—a total stranger who, for some reason, she was having trouble forgetting—her patience was running thin.

Even Vincent looked annoyed, inasmuch as a sleeping dachshund could express any sort of visible emotion. He was curled on his dog bed, right next to the raised platform where she stood at her easel at the head of the class. And his eyes were closed. But there was a crease in his tiny doggy brow, as if he was worried about something. The forgotten location of a buried bone, maybe. Or the fact his mistress was at her wit's end.

Harper repeated herself, this time speaking loud enough to be heard over the raucous laughter and wine-soaked conversation that appeared to be of more interest than recreating one of Picasso's finest masterpieces. "Let's try and stay on track, folks. We're halfway through class, and we still have a lot of work to do. Please pick up your largest brush."

"You mean big daddy?" the seemingly unsuspecting bride-to-be asked, waving her largest paintbrush in the air with one hand and gripping a juice box in the other. Except it wasn't technically a juice box in that it contained nectar of the fermented variety. Wine. In a silver pouch with a straw stuck in it. Classy.

Inwardly, Harper cringed. She might have done so outwardly as well. She didn't mind the juice box so much. There was an entire cooler of them setting smack dab in the center of the room. It was the paintbrush's nickname that she found particularly difficult to stomach.

"Yes. Big daddy."

Four years of undergraduate studies, six years of graduate work and a two hundred-page dissertation on *A History of Dutch Painters from Rembrandt to Van Gogh,* and here she was—talking to a room full of adults as if they were kindergarteners. Legitimate descriptions for paintbrushes such as round or flat, and sizes such as triple zero or ten, were apparently too difficult to grasp. Peyton Winslow, the owner of Art Bar and consequently Harper's boss—at least for this one of her two jobs—insisted she give the brushes cutesy names. So big daddy it was. Along with his friends, hot mama and baby bear. Somewhere in Westerkerk, Amsterdam, Rembrandt was no doubt spinning in his unmarked grave.

Harper glanced at the clock. 8:30 pm. Only an hour and a half remaining of class. Time to get down to business or she'd be here all night. "Does everyone have big daddy ready? Good. Now dip one corner of your brush into your white paint and the other corner into the darkest blue..."

"Which one? My paper plate has nothing but blue." Mac Coleman, one of the regulars at Art Bar, gestured toward his palette with big dad...er...his largest brush.

Mac, their one and only octogenarian client, habitually enrolled in every single class that Harper taught. And he was no less afraid of touching the blank canvas with the smallest dab of paint than he'd been on day one.

Harper pasted on her most saintly smile. "The darkest blue." What was so difficult about that?

"This one? Or is this black?" he asked, pointing at a pool of inky black paint.

"That's black. We'll use it at the very end of class." Assuming they ever made it to the end. "The darkest blue is right beside it."

"Can I trade my paint for another color?" Juice Box frowned at her canvas, thoroughly covered in various shades of blue. The completed background of the painting.

She'd actually done a surprisingly good job, Harper noted. Sweeping brush strokes, with just the right amount of paint. And she'd managed to avoid the most common mistake—overworking the canvas and thereby muddying things up. All the various colors of blue were still visible, just as they should be.

"I'm sorry. I don't understand. You want a different color blue?" Harper was pretty sure she'd made use of the entire spectrum of blue acrylic on hand.

And she always had her students mix colors as well. So they had at least twelve shades of blue at their disposal. Probably more. Picasso himself had likely only used half that many.

"No. I want pink." Juice Box smiled brighter than a tube of

cadmium yellow paint.

Harper released a sigh. Vincent opened one eye.

"Why would you want pink? The name of the painting is *Blue Nude*. It's from Pablo Picasso's famous Blue Period." Hence the blue background, blue foreground, and all over blueness.

Aside from the black outline of the female figure and a single, exquisite swath of yellow highlighting her shoulder blade, blue was the only color visible in Picasso's famed masterpiece. It was painted in 1902, during the second year of a four-year period when Picasso sank into a deep depression. Blue tones dominated his paintings from this time, and his subjects were often those on the fringes of society. Beggars. Street urchins. The blind.

Blue Nude was one of the most popular classes that Harper taught at Art Bar. People loved it. They thought it romantic with its cool shades of blue and its lovely view of a bare, curved, feminine back. In actuality, the woman Picasso painted was likely a prostitute. Harper never told her students this, of course. Peyton would no doubt fire her if she did.

What was it with artists and prostitutes anyway? They went together like tubes of paint and brushes. The women made convenient models, of course. But so many times, it seemed to be more than just a business arrangement. Van Gogh had even fallen in love with the prostitute he painted most often. Her name was Sien, and he'd been completely enamored with her, even living with her after the birth of her baby boy. His family had been horrified, of course. Harper often wondered how differently things would have turned out if only Van Gogh hadn't bowed to family pressure and left his mistress. Could they have been happy? Probably. By most accounts, Sien was the love of Van Gogh's life. But he left. And both their lives had ended in suicide.

But Harper really needed to stop thinking about Sien and concentrate on her class. She was already skating on thin ice after refusing to dress as Bob Ross for Halloween. Dearly departed Bob Ross, the host of PBS's *The Joy of Painting* for a decade and painter of "happy trees." Bob Ross, with his larger-than-life brown afro. Harper had taken one look at the wig Peyton expected her to wear and flatly refused. She'd donned a peasant dress and penciled in a Frida Kahlo unibrow, and Peyton had been mildly appeased. But she would never forgive Harper if she ruined a date night cash cow like *Blue Nude* by blowing the lid off the painting's less-than-romantic truth.

But that didn't stop Harper from wanting to at times. Times when no matter how hard she tried, she couldn't seem to impart her love and appreciation for the rich history of art unto the gathered inebriated masses. Times like this one.

Juice Box smiled. Oblivious. Her teeth were stained slightly purple from all the red wine that had been consumed during the first hour of class. "I like pink. It's my favorite color."

Then why didn't you choose one of the classes based on Picasso's Rose Period?

Harper gritted her teeth. "I'm sorry, but we need to stay on track together so we can all finish our paintings by the end of class."

"But it's just so very...*blue.*" She made a face.

Her date shot Harper a dirty look. "Give her some pink." He barked.

Charming. If Harper had known at the time that he was

about to propose marriage, she would have issued some sort of warning to Juice Box. Something along the lines of, *"Run!"* The naïve girl may have been misguided in her attempt to alter one of the most significant paintings of the 20th Century, but that didn't mean she deserved to be bound to someone so unpleasant until death do them part.

"She's right. It's awfully blue. I wouldn't mind if we added some pink," another of the classmates said.

Mac Coleman nodded. "Or what about purple? That might look nice."

Now, not only was Rembrandt rolling in his grave, but Picasso was rolling right along with him. And possibly Henri Matisse and Paul Cezanne, along with the rest of the Modern Art movement.

Harper jammed her free hand—the one that wasn't holding big daddy—on her hip. "We're not changing the painting. We can't layer pink on top of our blue background. The pink would be too transparent."

A room full of blank faces stared back at her. Clearly nothing she was saying was getting through. How could she put it so everyone would understand? "Your paintings would end up looking ugly."

No sense in mincing words. There were enough empty wine pouches and actual bottles scattered about that Harper doubted anyone would remember the next morning if she'd been overly stern. But a hideous painting would be a permanent reminder that she'd let things get out of control.

And besides, altering history was just plain wrong. Even art history.

Especially art history.

"Oh." Juice Box seemed to deflate on her painter's stool.

It wasn't until that moment that Harper saw the bedazzled pink phone cover on the cell phone that sat next to her easel. Along with her pink handbag. She probably should have seen this coming.

An awkward silence fell over the room for a moment. Harper pretended not to notice it. "Now. Let's regroup. Is everyone holding big daddy?"

A voice she'd heard only once before, but was certain never to forget, pierced the quiet. "Big daddy?"

No. Please God, no. Not now.

Not him.

The paintbrush in question slipped from Harper's grip and went crashing to the floor, sending white and blue paint flying in all directions. In an instant, the floor of Art Bar resembled a Jackson Pollock drip painting. Before Harper could make a move to clean it up, she heard the skittering of Vincent's doggy toenails on the tile floor. The next thing she knew, the dachshund was trotting through the wet paint, leaving alternating blue and white paw prints in his wake.

In an instant, it appeared as though there were hundreds of them, and they all led in one direction—directly toward Tom Stone.

"Vincent, no!" Harper scrambled down from the platform, her easel's little stage, as quickly as she could, which wasn't quickly at all given that she was slipping and sliding in the puddled remains of Picasso's Blue Period. "Vincent, come."

He didn't come.

His flagrant disobedience came as no surprise to Harper, considering she'd never gotten around to teaching him that command. But it had sounded good coming from her mouth. Firm. Authoritative. It had been worth a shot.

Tom glared at the tiny dog and backed up, bumping into one of the tables in the process. Six canvases swayed on their easels while students struggled to right them without letting go of their wine glasses.

"Sorry." Tom moved away from the table, directly into Vincent's path.

Vincent launched himself at Tom as though he were a long-lost friend, which Harper supposed he was. Sort of. Vincent never forgot a face. Or in this case, a pair of legs.

The little dog danced around Tom Stone's feet, slipping and sliding on its paint-drenched paws. Harper noticed Tom had a big black air cast on one of his feet. A result of the previous night's events, she supposed. Just looking at it made her cringe. But not quite as much as the way Tom cringed when he looked at Vincent. Vincent…who was now balancing himself on his hind legs and pawing at Tom's shins. For all practical purposes, her dog was busy making the canine equivalent of a finger painting on the surly sailor's legs.

Tom scowled, living up to the nickname he knew nothing about. Yet. "You need to do something about this dog. There are things that could help."

Harper had never been one to take orders well. The fact that he had somewhat of a valid point was irrelevant. "Since when is my dog your business?"

He didn't say a word. He simply lifted an angry brow and aimed a pointed look at the legs of jeans, smeared with messy paw prints from the knees down. Messy paw prints that would not wash out. Didn't Harper give the same *this-paint-will-stain-*

your-clothes lecture at the beginning of each class she taught at Art Bar?

Okay, so he had a teeny, tiny point. Harper would never concede, though. He looked smug enough already. Besides, she wasn't completely in the wrong. Why was he even there, interrupting her class, in the first place?

She crossed her arms and did her best to pretend that her dog still wasn't trying to create a canine artistic masterpiece on Tom's shins. "Vincent never would have gotten paint all over you if you hadn't snuck in here and surprised me."

He ignored her and squinted at the painting on her easel. "Wow, that's a lot of blue."

Again with the blue.

"I wanted to use pink, but she won't let me," Juice Box said, sounding a little too accusatory for Harper's taste.

Tom had been standing in her classroom only a handful of minutes and already he was turning her students against her.

"Really?" He frowned. "How does this work? You're all painting the exact same thing? In the exact same colors?"

"Yep," Mac said.

Yep. A single syllable? After months of art classes, that was all Mac could muster in her defense?

She jammed her hands on her hips. Vincent trotted past her, blue toenails clicking on the blue floor. Too bad. At the moment she was thinking Tom's jeans could have used a few more paw prints. "There's more to it than that, really. We're recreating a master work of art. *Blue Nude.* Perhaps you've heard of it?"

He shrugged. If it bothered him that she'd successfully one-upped him, he hid it well. "Doesn't ring a bell."

She allowed herself a triumphant smirk. "Pablo Picasso. Does his name sound at all familiar?"

He nodded. "Sure it does."

"Then, surely..."

Tom rolled his eyes. "Picasso's a hack."

A *hack*? Was this guy for real? "He's one of the most renowned artists of the twentieth century."

"A lot of his paintings look like cartoons. Eyes all over the place, faces cut in half." Tom glanced at Mac. "Agreed?"

Harper gave Mac the same look she'd given Vincent when she'd commanded he come to her. Unlike Vincent, Mac obeyed. He kept his mouth shut.

She turned her attention back to Tom. "They're not cartoons. It's called cubism, and it's a genuine art form. However, what we're doing tonight is not cubist. *Blue Nude* is a lovely figurative piece."

Once again, she kept the prostitute part under wraps. Tom Stone didn't need to get anywhere near that can of worms.

"All done in blue. One color? That's it?" He scowled at her easel. He scowled an awful lot.

She wondered if that was normal for him, or if she brought it out in him. She almost hoped for the latter. He didn't exactly cater to her good side, so it seemed fair. "For the most part. Yes. It's a monochromatic painting. Does that sound more appealing than a 'cartoon'?"

She made air quotes around the word cartoon. Harper never used air quotes. Why she was doing so now was beyond her.

"Honestly?" He cocked his head, as if waiting for her to tell him whether she was truly interested in his honest opinion.

She had the distinct feeling she wasn't.

"Sounds a little boring to me."

Juice Box threw up her hands. "Exactly."

"Boring. *Boring?*" Over the course of history, there had been countless words to describe Picasso's work. Not all of it was flattering, but Harper doubted anyone, anywhere, at any time had dared call his paintings boring.

"You asked. I answered." Tom's eyes remained frosty, and he smiled.

Well, not really. But his lips moved in a manner that suggested he was thinking about it. In a sardonic way, no doubt. A Tom Stone version of a smile, apparently.

Juice Box bounced up and down on her painter's stool. "Now can we use pink?"

Harper pretended she hadn't heard the question. She remained facing Tom, thinking how nice it would be to dump paint on his shirt so he'd match head-to-toe. "What are you doing here, anyway? Aren't you a little out of your element?"

"I didn't come to see *you* if you that's what you're thinking." Tom's blue eyes grew even frostier, if that was possible.

As cold and judgmental as they were, they were nice eyes. Somewhere, deep down—way, way deep down—they had a dreamy quality about them. Like a Monet painting.

A Monet painting? Really, Harper?

She cleared her throat and injected as much sarcasm into her tone as possible. "I'll try and control my overwhelming disappointment."

"Ouch," Mac said, his bespectacled gaze darting back and forth between Harper and Tom. "This is getting more and more awkward by the minute."

A few of the other students snickered.

Tom didn't even flicker an eyelid. "Aren't *you* a little out of your element, *Doctor*?" He crossed his arms and made an excruciatingly slow scan of the room.

Harper took a long blink before following his gaze. She spent so much time at Art Bar she'd grown accustomed to the surroundings. Now, however, she was forced to look at everything through fresh eyes. And she'd never been more aware of the mediocrity of the setting—the poster depicting famous master paintings with kitschy kittens randomly inserted in the scenes here and there, the bumper sticker adorning the front door that asked, *"Which barnyard animal is a famous painter?"* Answer: *Vincent Van Goat.* And of course the wine bottles, anywhere and everywhere.

Art Bar hardly resembled an academic classroom. She knew it. And so did he.

"You told me you were a professor. You lied." At last, a smile tipped his lips. It seemed he had no problem smiling when he was laughing at her.

Harper's face grew instantly hot. "I did not lie."

She hadn't lied. She was a college professor, just as she'd said. Granted, it was only a part-time position, which was why she taught four nights a week at Art Bar. But as far as she was concerned, she was a professor who moonlighted as a recreational art instructor. *Not* the other way around.

In any event, she hadn't lied. She would drag him out to her car and show him the faculty parking sticker on her windshield if he refused to believe her.

Tom's sardonic smile widened and he nodded at the framed photograph from Halloween that hung above the cash register. It was the only picture from October thirty-first that

Harper hadn't managed to confiscate, the sole shred of photographic evidence of her humiliation. And humiliating it was. Her image. Her face. In all its penciled-in unibrowed glory. Oh God.

Damn you, Fridà Kahlo.

At least it wasn't the brown synthetic Bob Ross afro. Although at this point, she wasn't altogether sure that would have been any more mortifying.

She met Tom's hard gaze full-on, giving him her best professorial look. The one that conveyed authority and intelligence. Except it didn't seem to be working. He didn't look the least bit intimidated or impressed. Not that she cared what he thought of her. Harper Higgins didn't waste time worrying about other peoples' opinions, unless those other people were on the faculty board at Boston College of Art.

A trickle of sweat ran down her spine. Why was it so warm in here all of a sudden?

Tom smirked in the direction of the Halloween photo. "Nice eyebrows. Very scholarly."

Laughter skittered through the room. Even Mac couldn't hide his amusement. Loyal Mac.

That did it.

Harper was going to set this guy straight. Not because his opinion of her fake unibrow carried any weight whatsoever, but because he'd disrupted her class. And he was just plain annoying.

"For your information, I am an adjunct professor at the Boston College of Art."

His expression remained unchanged.

The laugher in the room died down for the most part.

Harper supposed she should have been relieved, but the quiet of the room only seemed to make this conversation more awkward. If that was even possible.

"There's an assistant professor spot opening up in six weeks, and I expect to be promoted." And she *would* be promoted. So long as Lars Klassen didn't get in her way.

Tom was beginning to look the slightest bit bored. Clearly, he wasn't getting it.

"I'll be on the tenure track. Do you understand?" Why, oh why, was she wasting her time explaining this to him?

"I think so. One question, though—do you call your paintbrushes big daddy at your fancy art college?" Once again, everyone in the room snickered.

Everyone, that was, except Tom Stone.

Chapter Three

DO YOU CALL your paintbrushes big daddy at your fancy art college?

Harper ignored his asinine question and busied herself dabbing at the mess on the floor with a wad of paper towels. She didn't have time for this. She really didn't. The clock was still ticking away and the paintings weren't any closer to being finished than they'd been twenty minutes ago.

Peyton had already been hinting that Harper's classes were too advanced. Harper's boss would have preferred her to paint originals instead of reproducing master paintings. But that would have been a waste of Harper's education. Besides, she no longer painted originals. Ever.

"Everyone, let's take a short break." It wasn't like they could do anything until she got this mess cleaned up. Maybe if they were on an official break, the students would find something other to do than watch her make a fool out of herself in front of Tom Stone. Again. "Class will resume in exactly five minutes."

Tom crouched down beside her. "Here, let me help you."

"That's really not necessary." It came out a little more curtly than she intended.

But really, she was a little too rattled at the moment to worry about pleasantries. And the fact that she was rattled only rattled her more.

This man made her nervous.

No one made her nervous. She couldn't say why Tom was an exception. But she didn't like it. Not at all.

"You know, a little exercise would go a long way," he said, ignoring her words of protest and scrubbing at the spilled paint with a few paper towels he took from her roll. There was a bandage on his hand. Collateral damage from the night before.

"Excuse me?" She sat back on her heels and looked at him, incredulous.

"The mischief maker. Your dog, remember? The one responsible for this mess." He lifted a brow at Vincent.

Seemingly satisfied with the artistic rendering he'd left behind on the studio floor, the dachshund had returned to his dog bed and was sprawled belly-up, bright blue paws pointed skyward.

"Exercise would go a long way in combating his boredom."

The dog. Of course. He'd been talking about Vincent.

Why was she still sucking in her stomach? "I have a lot on my plate at the moment, in case you haven't noticed."

Two jobs. And the upcoming art show she was curating at the college. She barely had time to sleep. But the art show was the feather in her cap, her only advantage over Lars Klassen, the key to securing the promotion to full-time, tenure track staff. The promotion that she and Lars each wanted. The promotion that only one of them would get.

She'd managed to secure a world-famous political graffiti artist as the main exhibitor for the show. Lucky for her, the date of the show's opening in two months aligned perfectly with the faculty board's deadline to choose a candidate for the assistant professorship. Not that Harper believed in luck, necessarily. She believed in hard work, in creating one's own success. In any rate, she didn't have time to put Vincent on a physical fitness regimen. Not now.

"He's not bored. Look at him. He gets to come to work with me. How many dogs can say that? Most have to stay home alone while their owners are off making a living." Vincent released a sigh that belied his tiny size and plopped his chin on the raised edge of the dog bed, looking…not bored, exactly. Definitely not bored. Reflective. Yes, that was it. He looked reflective.

Tom cut his eyes at Vincent and then back at her. "Hire a dog walker. It would make both your lives a lot easier. And mine, if we're destined to keep crossing paths."

Destiny? It was a notion that belonged to painters, poets and dreamers. Not art history professors. Even if Harper did believe in such romantic ideas, which she didn't, crossing paths with Tom wouldn't play into her idea of destiny. Crossing paths with any man wouldn't.

Sure, she'd dated since Rick. Some. A little. A very little.

Dinner or a movie here and there. But she was always careful to keep things carefully compartmentalized. She wasn't about to let her heart get in the way and ruin her future. Hadn't she learned from watching her mother make that very mistake? Over and over and *over* again? And hadn't the way things ended with Rick taught her romantic notions such as love were about as practical as selling paintings on the street?

But why was she thinking about such things now, when she was kneeling in paint alongside the surly sailor? She scrubbed at the floor with greater force. "You really do enjoy giving me orders, don't you?"

"It wasn't an order. It was a suggestion." Tom's scrubbing arm went into overdrive as well.

Either he was just as frustrated with this whole encounter as she was, or he was trying to hurry and beat her at cleaning up the spilled paint. Both scenarios were equally aggravating.

"A suggestion from the man with a cast on his foot and a modern art painting on his jeans, both compliments of your dog."

Someone in the room cleared his throat rather loudly, tearing Harper's attention away from Tom. "While we're taking a break from painting, there's something I'd like to say."

Harper looked up. It was Juice Box's oh-so-charming boyfriend. The guy was slurring his words. Who knew what was going to come out of his mouth?

She stood. "You know, we've just about finished cleaning up. I think we can get started now."

"No. I've been waiting all night. It's time." He sank down on one knee in front of Juice Box's barstool.

Harper felt sick all of a sudden. She could see what was about to happen. Who couldn't? The entire scene had all the cheesy trappings of a public proposal. Men only knelt at women's feet for one purpose. Even a non-romantic like Harper knew that much. She watched in horror as he reached into his pocket and produced a tiny velvet box.

Juice Box was bobbing her head, nodding her agreement before he'd even gotten the words out. With each little movement of her head, Harper's chest grew more and more tight. She wished she could say something. Something to make Juice

Box slow down and think about what she was doing. *Should* she say something?

Of course not. She barely knew the girl. It was none of Harper's business, anyway. Things were probably going to be fine. Not all men just upped and abandoned their families without any warning whatsoever. Then again, some of them did. Like Harper's father.

Harper found herself wondering what kind of education Juice Box had. Did she have a job? Could she support herself and maybe even a few kids later on down the line? Or would they end up living with friends, dependent on the kindness of others until she found someone else to marry?

These were the thoughts tumbling through her mind as the groom-to-be popped open the velvet box to reveal a gold band sporting a modest sized round stone. "Lori, sweetheart, will you marry me?" he said.

At least he'd gotten right to the point. Harper didn't think she would have been able to take a long soliloquy. Then again, the intended groom didn't seem the type to wax poetic.

"Yes!" The bride-to-be jumped off her barstool and threw her arms around him, thoughts of defacing *Blue Nude* with streaks of pink clearly forgotten in her moment of bliss.

The room exploded in cheers and well wishes. Whatever slim degree of control Harper still had over the class was immediately and irrevocably lost.

Super. Just super.

She rolled her eyes.

"What's the matter? You're not a believer in wedded bliss?" Tom's voice dripped with every bit as much cynicism as Harper felt.

Still, she couldn't help but notice his posture—kneeling on one knee, directly at her feet, peering up at her in expectation at the question he'd asked. Body language as old and traditional as time itself.

It was horrifying. And even though she knew good and well Tom Stone wasn't about to propose to her, seeing him there like that caused a sheen of sweat to break out on her forehead. Not simply because it was him, although she'd be hard-pressed to think of a less suitable prospect. He could have been any man on bended knee, and she would have had the same sickening reaction.

She took a giant leap backward, stumbling over her own feet in her haste to get away from him.

"Careful there." He stood and offered his hand to help her steady herself.

She refused it. "I'm fine."

"Of course you are." He glowered at her and dropped his hand back to his side. It seemed he was always glowering. "As thrilling as this has been, I think it's time for me to go."

"Of course." *Finally.*

"Try and keep your beast away from me, if you don't mind, Doc." He jammed his hands on his hips, glanced at Vincent and raised a single, irritated eyebrow.

Doc? Was that supposed to be funny?

She was a real doctor, damn him.

Without even thinking about what she was doing, she grabbed the closest juice box, pierced it with a straw and sucked down a mouthful of wine. "Don't worry. Neither Vincent nor I have plans to cross your path anytime in the near future."

Or far off future. Or future in general.

"I should be able to sleep at night, then. Good luck with your blue painting." The corner of his mouth lifted in a half-grin.

The sight of it infuriated Harper. A lecture on the importance of Picasso's contribution to the art world danced on the tip of her tongue, but she held it in check. Her words would be wasted on the likes of Tom Stone. She took another massive sip of wine. As massive as she could get from a tiny straw. Her head spun a little. "Good bye."

"Bye, Doc." He winked, and to Harper's utter mortification, that wink sent an electric zing flying in her direction.

Butterflies swarmed in her belly, not unlike the time she'd seen Vincent Van Gogh's *Starry Night* in person for the first time.

Her mouth grew dry.

It was the wine. That had to be it. Because she sure as heck couldn't be attracted to a man like him. He thought Picasso's paintings were cartoons. He had no respect for her work. He thought she was a fake doctor. He wasn't even nice.

He was a Neanderthal.

She turned away, wordless, lest her face betray the storm of confusion swirling away in her consciousness. The last thing she needed was Tom Stone to think she found him attractive. Because she didn't.

It wasn't until after he was gone that Harper realized she had no idea why he'd even stopped by Art Bar in the first place.

TOM CLOSED THE door on the mayhem that was Art Bar and

guided his steps back in the direction of the harbor. He had a bit of a limp after the fiasco with the dachshund—the *first* fiasco with the dachshund—but the air cast seemed to be helping.

Good. To say not being able to walk would be an occupational hazard would be beyond an understatement.

He shook his head and shoved his hands in the pockets of his newly paint-spattered jeans. There was a cool breeze blowing off the water tonight, unusually cool for the beginning of autumn. October had barely dawned. The leaves hadn't even begun to turn and change in preparation for their twisting, falling dance to the ground. Flowerpots and window boxes in Boston were still overflowing with vibrant, plentiful blossoms. Winter should still be a frosty, distant dream.

At least that was what Tom hoped. The boat wasn't ready for winter. In its present state, it wouldn't be livable in the gentlest of snowfalls.

One step at a time. He wasn't going to get all worked up about winter when he had more pressing things to take care of. Like his foot. And his hand. And his clothes. Tom grimaced. Why did everything on that list seem to have something to do with Harper Higgins?

Doctor Harper Higgins.

She sure was hung up about that title. Tom had never been one for titles, even when he was enlisted. A man was a man. A soldier was a soldier. On the battlefield a soul was a soul. Just like any other.

He'd treated his superiors with the necessary respect, of course. That had been one of the core lessons his father had passed down to him in the intermittent times he was between deployments during Tom's childhood. By the time Tom was eighteen, the number of days he'd actually spent with his dad had totaled less than five years. He'd been more of a mythical figure than a real person, a man who wore fatigues and lived in places like Germany, Japan and Iraq.

Iraq. Like father, like son.

He might be a soldier and the son of a soldier, but Tom knew the real measure of a man wasn't the number of stripes on his uniform. He'd learned the hard way what made a person a decent human being. Having a father more devoted to country than family and a mother who he'd never known had been all the schooling he needed in that department.

Life lessons.

A real education. Infinitely more valuable than whatever could be taught in an ivory tower.

He couldn't help but laugh when he thought of what Harper would have to say about that. Clearly, she'd spent more than her fair share of time in a classroom. She was probably smart as a whip. And she wasn't suffering from any shortage in the confidence department. But had she really lived? Judging by her obliviousness about how to deal with her own ten-pound animal, he doubted it.

He hadn't expected to see her tonight at Art Bar. That was for sure. Not that he'd known ahead of time exactly what he'd stumble in on. Was it a bar? Was it an art school? Both, he guessed. Or neither. He was having a difficult time putting his finger on it. He just knew it definitely wasn't what he was looking for. Even without the added headache of adding Harper Higgins and her troublemaking dog into the mix.

When he reached the end of the street where the cobblestones gave way to the smooth sidewalks flanking the harbor and the creaking, worn wood of the dock, he made a left instead of turning right toward his boat. He followed the curve of the sidewalk around to a nondescript green warehouse with thick plastic sheeting over the opened door.

"Knock, knock." He called as he pushed the plastic aside and crossed the threshold.

As always, the fragrance of fresh flowers hung heavy in the air. An intoxicating cocktail of blossoms—roses, lilies, irises, hydrangeas, orchids, and who knew what else. Tom was no flower expert. He asked for pretty much the same thing every time.

"There you are." Frank Southard, owner of Southard's Wholesale Floral Supply, came around the corner clutching a fistful of pink carnations, their jade colored stems dripping a trail of water in his wake. "I thought you might not come tonight."

"I'm here. I'm a little later than usual, that's all." He hadn't planned on his side trip to Art Bar being such an eventful and lengthy ordeal.

Frank motioned toward his cast and frowned. "What happened to your foot?"

Tom shrugged. "I had a run-in with a wild beast."

He didn't elaborate. Frank didn't expect him to. That was why the two of them got along as well as they did. Frank had been the first person Tom met when he'd gotten out of the hospital and moved to the harbor three months ago. Over the course of those months, they'd come to know both everything and nothing about each other.

Tom knew Frank had served a year in Vietnam from August of '67 to November of '69. He'd lost his left leg below the knee when he stepped on a landmine in the Tet Offensive. He had *Purple Heart* tattooed on his right forearm, along with the name of his closest friend, who he'd lost in the incident. A loss that had proven more painful than the loss of his leg.

Frank knew Tom had done two tours in the Middle East—twelve months in Afghanistan and another fifteen in Iraq. He'd managed to keep all his limbs, but that didn't mean he hadn't been brutally wounded. As had been the case all his life, he carried his losses on the inside. Invisible, but very much real.

Tom knew Frank was married to a woman named Sarah, but he'd never laid eyes on her, and he didn't know how many children they had, if any. Frank didn't know if Tom was married or single.

That was how it was. Everything and nothing.

Tom liked it that way. It kept things simple. He needed flowers, not a father figure. He'd done well enough without one all this time.

"I'm guessing you want the usual?" Frank's gray eyebrows rose.

"Yep." Tom nodded.

"Alright, then. A bundle of the day's cheapest offering. Pink carnations this go-round. Will these work for you?" He nodded at the carnations, now laid out on the counter next to the cash register.

Tom nodded. "Thank you."

"No problem. I hold out hope, though, that you'll come in here one day and ask me for two-dozen long stemmed roses. Don't get me wrong. It's nice that you bring your lady flowers five days a week. All flowers are nice. But trust me. Every woman loves a rose. It's the flower of romance."

Tom responded with nothing more than a smile. There was no woman. That was not what the flowers were for.

Frank told Tom how much he owed, and Tom handed over the money, dropping a dollar in the tip jar. He watched Frank prepare the flowers as he did every evening. It was a ritual Tom never grew tired of witnessing—the drying of the stems, the trimming of the leaves, the sight of Frank's big sausage fingers handling the blossoms with such delicacy and care they could have been spun gold. Or stardust that might slip through his fingers if he didn't treat them with the proper respect. There was a reverence about the way he wrapped them in green tissue, gently nudging the petals to make sure each flower was properly showcased. No shy blossoms.

"Here you go." He handed Tom the wrapped flowers as though he was handing over a newborn infant rather than a bundle of cheap carnations. "How did the violets work out for you yesterday?"

The violets.

Tom pasted on a grin. "Very well."

"Good. Glad to hear it." Frank wiped his hands on the small red towel he always kept tucked into the front pocket of his vinyl florist apron. "Well then, it's back to work for me. I'll see you tomorrow night."

"Bye, Frank." Tom waved, holding the carnations in the crook of his elbow as he ducked back through the plastic sheeting and into the moonlight.

Then he grasped the flowers with both hands, just to be extra careful. And perhaps to make atonement for the sad, wilted demise that had befallen the violets. It would have broken Frank's heart to see those purple petals ground into the cobblestones. The blood of a florist, spilled onto the pavement.

The wind had picked up while he'd been inside. He walked into it, tucking the carnations into his jacket and ducking his head. Somewhere above, a gull cried. And then another. Dueling birds of the sea. They swooped in the sky, dropping down so close that Tom could hear the whip of their wings in the wind, and then rising back up, following him, circling him until he reached the boat.

Gunner's ears were visible even in the twilight, two triangular points, dark against the backdrop of the setting sun.

Woof.

"Hey there, buddy." Tom hopped down into the boat and ran a soothing hand over the German shepherd's head.

"I'm home." He said the words aloud as he did whenever he returned.

He wasn't quite sure who he was trying to convince, himself or the dog, that this was home. This boat. This city. This country. Sometimes, it still felt foreign to him. He wasn't quite sure where he belonged anymore.

Hell, who was he kidding? He'd never been sure where he belonged. When he'd been a kid, he'd slept on sofas at various relatives' home as often as he'd slept in his own bedroom. He supposed that was what his short-lived marriage had been about—an attempt to fulfill a craving for a place, a person to call home.

He looked at the carnations, really looked at them. He wouldn't have chosen pink, probably. But with the sky awash in fiery red, orange, and luminescent pink as the sun fell and dipped into the harbor, they took on new life. They seemed pinker now, more vibrant. Perfect.

Time to get started.

Chapter Four

By the time Harper was finished at Art Bar, she'd completely given up on the idea of an umbrella. The rain had relented for the most part, although a fine, grey drizzle still swirled in the foggy breeze coming off the harbor. Since she obviously needed to keep a tighter grip on Vincent's leash, she was left with only one free hand. And after the evening she'd had, she preferred to keep that hand busy holding what remained of her juice box of wine.

A pleasant warmth coursed through her, despite the cool mist on her face. And her head felt rather fuzzy. It was a welcome relief. After the surprise marriage proposal, her class had turned into an engagement party. Paintbrushes and canvases were practically forgotten, which meant she'd pretty much completed all the paintings herself. Party or no party, she couldn't let everyone go home empty handed. At the end of each class, she always took a group photo of all the students with their paintings for the Art Bar Facebook page. She couldn't very well post a photo of twenty students showing off their plain blue canvases.

So she'd finished them herself while everyone else danced the night away. Literally. As Harper had put the last touches on the final *Blue Nude*, the blushing bride had been busy teaching

Mac Coleman how to do the Beyoncé "Single Ladies" dance. He was shockingly good at it.

Twenty Picassos. In one night. She'd probably be seeing *Blue Nude* in her sleep for days.

Fine. That will be a nice change from dreaming about Tom Stone.

She tripped through a rain puddle when she realized that she had indeed dreamt about him the night before. He'd waltzed right through her imagination carrying that mysterious basket of violets. And he'd looked far more virile than any basket-wielding man should.

She took a generous swallow of wine from the straw poking out of her juice box. The dream had completely slipped from her memory until now. She must have blocked it out somehow. Well, she wouldn't be dreaming about him again. That was certain.

He'd called her *Doc.*

Her blood boiled every time she thought about the condescending smirk he seemed to have on his face every time he said it. Not that she'd thought about it much.

Well, maybe it had crossed her mind a few times.

She squeezed her juice box dry and then tossed it in a nearby trashcan. It missed. By a mile. She bent to pick it up and nearly tripped over Vincent in the process. The dog let out a yip and skipped in an excited circle.

"Sorry, Vincent." She gave him a scratch behind the ear and stood back up. Her head spun. "I think I might be a little intoxicated."

Vincent yipped and took off again, pulling the leash tight. Harper stumbled after him.

As much as she hated to admit it, Tom Stone had been right. Something needed to be done about the dog. The trouble was, she had no clue what to do. How did people do this all the time? Other people adopted dogs left and right with seemingly no trouble at all. How were there not dogs running wild and knocking down men carrying flowers all over the place?

"Vincent, slow down."

The dachshund's lone ear gave a twitch, so she knew he heard her. But he was too busy trying to yank her arm out of its socket to look back.

"Vincent, please." Her tongue felt thick, and unless she was hearing things there was a slight slur to her words.

Good grief, she was definitely drunk. After only two juice boxes. Three, max. Harper couldn't remember the last time she'd been the slightest bit tipsy. She rarely drank. She much preferred being in control of her faculties.

She blinked into the mist, wondering exactly when the night had gotten away from her. Had it been the nauseating marriage proposal? No, things had already begun to slip from her grip before then. Right about the time Tom had strolled into Art Bar.

Ugh. Stop thinking about him. You're never going to see him again.

If only she could clear her woozy head before she and Vincent got home and she fell into bed. She very much wanted to forget about that man before she accidentally dreamed about him again. *If* she happened to dream about Tom Stone tonight—and that was a mighty big *if*—it was sure to be a nightmare. The kind of nightmare that caused people to wake up screaming.

Coffee. That was what she needed. Wasn't that how people always sobered up in the movies?

Harper shook her head. She didn't want to think about how long it had been since she'd sat down and watched a movie in its entirety. Probably about as long as it had been since she'd had a glass of wine, until this evening, obviously. She was usually far too busy working to indulge in such luxuries. Maybe it was time to start thinking about getting a life.

No. That was the trio of juice boxes talking. She had a life. A perfectly fine life. And once she secured her promotion to assistant professor, it would be an even better life. What she most needed now was a jolt of caffeine.

She hastened her steps and headed toward the coffee shop where she usually stopped in the morning on the way to campus. She'd never been there at night before. Not once. She had a schedule she liked to stick to, and stopping for coffee fit neatly into a morning slot. She had no idea if the place would even be open this time of night.

She scooped Vincent into her arms and pushed through the door. The stillness of the interior was a shock. The shop was completely empty, save for a lone employee wielding a mop.

"Sorry, we're closing." The young man in the apron glanced up at her. "And no dogs allowed inside. On the patio only."

He took a closer look at Vincent, and his expression softened. Likely because of the dog's missing ear. Harper had noticed its absence seemed to have that effect on people.

"Just one cup? Please?" She stood up a little straighter, trying mightily to look professorial. Or at the very least, sober.

The young man sighed. "Okay, but all I've got is plain coffee. I can't make your usual, Miss Higgins."

My usual.

And he knew her name. Harper certainly didn't know his, even though he wore a nametag pinned to his apron.

She glanced at it. "That's fine, Marshall. Wonderful. Thank you very much."

He moved behind the counter, filled a cup and handed it to her.

Harper took a sip, closed her eyes and sighed. "Oh, yes."

Marshall frowned. "Don't you mean *Oh God, yes*?"

Oh God, yes. She'd forgotten about their ridiculous sizing. It was almost as bad as naming a paintbrush big daddy. She felt a sudden dash of empathy for poor Mitchell. Or was it Marshall?

"How much do I owe you?" Vincent squirmed in her arms, and her coffee sloshed in its cup.

Marshall cast a worried glance at his freshly mopped floor. "Don't worry about it. It's on the house."

Harper wanted to insist that he let her pay, but memories of the paint-splattered floor of Art Bar came rushing back. She really didn't want a repeat of that disaster. The evening had been eventful enough as it was. Perhaps it was best to keep a firm grip on Vincent rather than digging around in her handbag.

"Thank you," she said, making a mental note to give him a generous tip tomorrow morning. "Very much."

"No problem. See you in the morning."

Then just as she turned to go, her gaze landed on the community bulletin board behind the cash register. A flier for someone's lost kitty took center stage and was surrounded by advertisements for an outdoor festival at Union Park, a jazz concert at Wally's Paradise, and a million other things Harper would never attend.

She glanced down at Vincent, still squirming in her arms, and back at the bulletin board. "Can I ask you something, Marshall?"

"I suppose." He gave her an odd look. This was already the longest conversation they'd ever shared.

"Is there a business card or flier for a dog walker somewhere up there?" She gestured toward the bulletin board with her coffee cup.

"Actually, I think there is." He turned and sifted through the layers of papers held in place with thumbtacks. "Here we go."

He offered her a tiny square of blue cardstock that said simply *DOG WALKER*, with a local Boston number scrawled in pencil. It was exactly the sort of unprofessional looking thing Harper would have completely ignored if she weren't so very desperate. She took it from him and stared at it for a second before tucking it in her pocket.

A number. That was it. No name. Nothing. Just the number.

But with any luck, whoever was on the other end of that number would change everything.

TOM SAT STARING at the canvas in front of him as he absently swirled his brush in a cup full of clear, clean water. Pigment rose from the bristles, moving through the water in gentle swirls of red and white until the liquid ran nearly as pink as the carnations he'd spent the past hours recreating in bold swipes of acrylic.

He removed the paintbrush, dabbing the bristles clean on a towel, taking great care to wipe them in the proper direction. Every time he completed a painting, no matter how late the hour, he was meticulous about the cleaning up process. He found the routine soothing—washing and patting dry the brushes, tightening the screw-top lids of his tubes of paint, scrubbing away any stray paint splatters. There were always paint splatters. Sometimes when he finished, he stepped back from the canvas and looked around, stunned to see paint everywhere. On his clothes, on his skin, on the floor. Sometimes even on the dog. It always took him by surprise, as if he'd been in a trance during the creative process, unaware of anything and everything other than the movement of color on canvas.

But that was the whole point, wasn't it? To lose himself for a few sacred hours.

He'd been skeptical at first. Four months ago, when the art therapist had walked into his room at the military hospital in DC with a blank canvas in one hand and a caddy full of paint and brushes in the other, he'd thought she was nuts. He'd known nothing about art. He still didn't for that matter, other than the fact that the therapist had been right. Painting was relaxing. Like a mental vacation. And to his complete and utter astonishment, it made him forget.

When the therapist had first shown up, he'd been unsuccessfully chasing forgetfulness from his hospital bed for a month. Even his dreams had remembered, oftentimes far more vividly than his waking consciousness. He hadn't agreed to give art therapy a shot on that first day. Nor the second. He should have. This truth, like so many things, was crystal clear in retrospect. He'd turned her down flat. But she kept coming back. Day after day, week after week, always with that paint-splattered caddy in her hands.

And then one day, the caddy had vanished. She'd stood at the foot of the bed with a handful of ribbons in her hand, not saying a word. Aside from the missing caddy, she'd looked as she had every other day—tattered apron in a red, white, and blue print over a flowing skirt that skimmed the floor, a Wounded Warrior Project pin fastened to the scarf wrapped around her flowing hair, salt and pepper, with bright pink tips. Betsy Ross with a Bohemian streak. Tom had reached the point where he'd begun to look right through her. But something about those ribbons had captured his attention. Upon closer inspection, Tom had realized they weren't ribbons at all, but strips of fabric. Fabric in an all too familiar pattern of desert camouflage.

His gaze had snagged on the shredded khaki material. Just for a beat, but long enough that it didn't escape notice.

"Well, now. It seems I've finally gotten your attention." The art therapist's grin had been downright triumphant. "I'm Sue, by the way. We haven't officially met."

"Tom Stone." He'd grunted in response, his eyes focusing once again on the long strips of camo. His head had throbbed as he'd looked at it. Then again, his head had throbbed continually back then. One of the many blessings of post-concussion syndrome.

Tom had seen a lot of uniforms in his time with the military. From the pristine, starched DCUs of new recruits, to those that were no longer khaki, but stained a deep, bloody burgundy. He'd seen BDUs that had been so blown to bits there'd been nothing left but a spaghetti tangle of thread. But he'd never laid eyes on a uniform that had been deliberately cut to pieces. That had been a new one.

"Come with me," Sue had said, disappearing down the hall with a wink, so sure he'd follow she'd never looked back.

She'd let ribbons trail behind her, a flutter of memories drawing him from the bed, beckoning him. He'd fallen for it, of course. He'd pushed himself out of bed and chased her down the hall like a puppy. A puppy with an excruciating headache.

The god-awful smell in the room where they'd ended up had only made the pounding in his head worse. It was an odor he'd not been familiar with—some ripe combination of vinegar and good Swiss cheese. Or not. In reality, it had been paper pulp. Paper pulp made from camo ribbons just like the ones Sue carried.

"What is this?" He'd asked, as his gaze had scanned walls covered with ragged edged sheets of rough-hewn paper.

Paper in every hue imaginable, covered with poems, drawings and silhouettes of tanks, helicopters, and explosions. Subjects he knew intimately. But, somehow, standing there in that hospital room-turned paper factory, Tom had felt as though he was seeing it all for the first time. The colors and the delicacy of the handmade papers had transformed images that haunted him at night into something entirely different. Something compelling and striking. Beauty from ashes.

"What is this?" He'd asked again, the unexpected emotion in his voice scraping the inside of this throat.

"This is the Combat Paper Project." Sue, hands still full of her tragic bouquet of camouflage ribbons, had given him a wistful smile. A smile of understanding.

And that had been the day he'd fallen in love with art.

Tom still had the project he'd made that day. It was the only thing nailed to the wall inside his boat. Back when he was stationed in Kirkuk, if anyone had told him he would one day live in a boat with an Army uniform hanging on the wall, he would have thought them insane. But he didn't think of it as camo anymore. And the boat thing...on some level he knew it wasn't exactly a normal living arrangement. But it was what it was.

He stood and stepped away from the easel, his foot throbbing slightly as he put weight on it for the first time in a few hours. Gunner rose to his feet, ears pricked forward, fur rising slightly along the ridge of his spine, on high alert in response to his master's movements. Ever aware. Ever vigilant.

"Good boy," Tom murmured, and the shepherd relaxed a bit.

He gave his paintbrush a final swirl before tossing the water overboard. He always painted outside, either on the deck of the boat or on the dock. He liked the freedom of it—the briny smell of the harbor, the salt in the air.

He took one last look at the row of boats bobbing against their moors in the black water as he lifted the newly finished painting from the easel and carried it inside. As he propped it on the corner table, he spotted his cell phone. A message flashed across the screen indicating he'd missed a call.

He frowned at the display. He'd been so caught up in his painting that he hadn't even heard it ring. He set the phone to speaker and accessed his voicemail while he stared at the cotton candy puff of pink flowers on his canvas. The brush strokes looked good. And the flowers seemed to pop off the linen, just the way he liked.

"Yes, hello? Hello?"

Tom froze, forgetting about the painting altogether.

It can't be her. It just can't.

Oh, but it was her. Her voice at least. Right there in the cabin of his boat.

"This is Dr. Harper Higgins."

Tom rolled his eyes. She sounded a fair bit more relaxed than usual. In fact, she sounded sloshed. But he doubted there was enough alcohol in the world to make her forget to use her *doctor* title.

She went on. "Marshall from the coffee shop gave me your number."

Interesting. Tom would have bet money that she didn't even know Marshall's name.

"I need a dog walker. I mean my dog needs a dog walker. But you probably knew that's what I meant."

Drunk. Definitely. Tom smiled to himself.

"I'll be at the coffee shop in the morning if you'd like to meet me to discuss things. 8:00 sharp. I hope to see you then."

The line went dead.

8:00 sharp. God, she was uptight even with a few drinks in her.

He should forget the message. Just because she'd called him didn't mean he was duty-bound to come to her beck and call. But he could use a new client. Even a new client with a dog intent on maiming him. Money didn't grow on trees. There was already the hint of a nip in the air, and he wasn't even close to having enough money to winterize the boat.

The opportunity to look her in the eyes while he gloated over the fact that she'd actually taken his advice and called a dog walker was an added bonus.

The message ended, and the display on his cell phone went dark. The boat seemed exceptionally quiet all of a sudden, a nonsensical turn of events that left Tom equal parts mystified and irritated.

"Come on, Gunner. Time for bed." The dog scrambled to his feet as Tom flipped off the lights and headed toward the sleeping cabin.

Carnations and acrylic paints forgotten, it was Harper Higgins' pretty face that he saw in his dreams. Her luminous green eyes. The wavy blonde hair, as lush as a wheat field during harvest. And, against all odds, he slept like a baby.

Chapter Five

"GOOD MORNING, MITCHELL." Harper smiled, despite the early hour and her excruciating headache. The coffee house was packed as it always was this time of day, and the constant buzz of chatter wasn't helping to alleviate the pounding in her temples.

"It's Marshall." He pointed at his nametag.

Dang it. She'd been so pleased with herself for remembering, too. "I'm sorry, Marshall."

"It's okay, Dr. Higgins. Here you go. Your usual." He handed her a paper coffee cup with a cardboard sleeve wrapped around it.

Harper took her latte and shoved two dollars in the tip jar. "Thank you, Marshall."

Maybe she was overdoing it with the name thing. But she was still grateful for the free coffee the night before. She'd all but stumbled into bed last night. Who knew what kind of trouble she could have gotten into without a jolt of caffeine? When her alarm had gone off at 6:30 this morning, she was still facedown, fully dressed, on top of the covers. Vincent had been curled up smack in the center of her pillow, and she still had the crick in her neck to prove it. Along with the headache and a mouth that felt as if she'd swallowed a bucketful of sand.

Harper refused to call it a hangover, even though that was precisely what it was.

It was mortifying to even think about. She'd gotten drunk. At work.

She took a deep breath as she found a seat at one of the tables by the door. This was a new day. She had her latte and her briefcase. She was meeting the dog walker. Everything was perfectly lined up for the day to be productive and professional. No one had to know about last night.

And no one would get engaged today while she was at her real job. Thank goodness. She'd experienced enough engagements and marriages vicariously through her mother. After Harper's father had packed up and left the day before her tenth birthday, she and her mother had been virtually penniless. Her mom, having dropped out of high school to get married at seventeen, had no education to speak of and no way of supporting herself, not to mention a ten-year-old daughter. And forget child support. No one could find Harper's father, much less squeeze a nickel out of him.

So, Harper's mother had settled on someone else to marry. And when that didn't work out, she found husband number three. And so on, and so on. If there was one thing Harper knew about marriage, it was that it didn't last. And when it ended, it left nothing but devastation in its wake.

It almost reminded her of what had happened to Sien after she'd fallen for Van Gogh. Family, friends, and patrons all turned their backs on him after he'd chosen to live with her and her baby boy. Eventually, he had to leave in order to get back in the good graces of the people who supported him. Once he was gone, Sien married another man out of desperation. Just like

Harper's mother. Three years after marrying, Sien drowned herself in the Schelde River. Not exactly a glowing endorsement of wedded life.

Anyone in Harper's position would have indulged in a juice box of wine or two after being forced to witness a bended-knee marriage proposal. And, of course, having to do so alongside Tom Stone was just icing on the cake. Every time she remembered the mocking tone that had come out of his mouth when he'd called her *Doc*, a fresh jolt of pain shot to her temples. And the fact she'd noticed just how particularly attractive his sarcastic mouth was only worsened the pain.

Without a doubt, it was a lovely mouth. Nice lips. Kissable, if she was being honest. Quite kissable. She would have liked to paint those kissable lips. If she still painted original work, which she didn't.

Harper forbade herself to give Tom's lips another millisecond of thought, sipped her coffee, and checked the time on her cell phone. 8:09. She frowned. She was certain she'd told the dog walker 8:00 in the voice mail she'd left. And she'd received a confirmation text at some point in the night. It had been right there on her phone's display screen when she'd managed to drag herself out of bed.

C U in the morning.

How could she forget that? So eloquent.

She glanced at it again just to make sure she hadn't been mistaken.

"Good morning, Doc."

She looked up. Him. Of course. No one else had ever called her that in her life. And, God willing, no one would again.

Why was he here? At *her* coffee shop. Had she somehow

conjured him simply by reminiscing about those lips? Her gaze instinctively zeroed in on his mouth. Kissable indeed. Goodness, it had been a long time since she'd been kissed.

She blinked and looked away.

"You again," she said.

The cell phone slipped through her fingers and clattered to the ground. Why was she always dropping things around him?

They both reached for the phone at the same time. He got to it first. "Looks like you've got a text. 'C U in the morning.' Hot breakfast date, Doc?"

Her cheeks burned and she snatched the phone from his hand. "A business meeting."

"A business meeting? Really?" He smirked. Naturally. "That sounds important."

Why had she called it that? The dog walker would probably show up any minute now with half a dozen dogs in tow and make her look like a liar again.

"It is. Important, I mean." Truer words were never spoken. Tom was still limping a bit. And he still had a cast on his foot and bandage on his hand.

He had nice hands. Big. Capable-looking. Her gaze lingered on them, interlaced casually on the tabletop. Wait. Why had he sat down?

"What are you doing?" she asked.

He shrugged. "Sitting."

She stared at him, waiting for a more thorough explanation. None was forthcoming. "What are you doing here?"

"I come here every morning. You mean you've never noticed?" He clutched at his chest in mock heartbreak. "That wounds me, Doc."

She rolled her eyes. "You do not come here every day."

An espresso machine hissed behind the counter, and the line for coffee stretched almost all the way to the front door.

"Sure I do. I can prove it." He pointed at her coffee cup. "Vanilla soy latte with whip. Oh, and a Splenda. Can't forget that."

It wasn't possible. This was some sort of trick. She would have noticed him before. Surely.

She shook her head. "No."

"Oh God, yes."

Harper blinked. She wasn't sure she'd ever heard those salacious words come from such a gorgeous mouth before.

"The size." He pointed to her cup again. "Of your regular drink. *Oh God, yes.*"

The stupid sizing again. That had to be changed. Maybe she should start a petition or something.

"Assuming you do indeed come here every day, which I'm still not convinced you do, why are you here now…sitting at my table? I told you I'm waiting for someone." She glanced at her phone again. 8:19. A vague sense of unease began to crawl up her spine.

"I have an appointment." Tom grinned, looking altogether pleased with himself. "I suppose you might call it a business meeting."

The coffee cup in Harper's hand paused midway to her mouth. A wave of nausea washed over her. She swallowed it down.

She wasn't quite sure if it was from the hangover or his words. "A business meeting?"

"That's what you called it, right?" He winked.

A wicked wink just like the one he'd given her the night before, the one that had set her insides on fire.

Her neck grew instantly hot.

She told herself she wasn't attracted to him. Of course, she wasn't. He was an ass. A handsome ass, but an ass nonetheless. That wink could ignite an inferno in any woman. It was a matter of simple chemistry. Science. Nothing more. It didn't mean a thing.

What do you know about science? You're an art historian.

She took a deep breath. *Don't look at his mouth. Or his eyes. Or his arms.* She had a bigger problem than chemistry to tackle at the moment—it appeared Tom Stone was Vincent's new dog walker. It couldn't possibly be true. It just couldn't.

"Cat got your tongue, Doc?" Mischief danced in those Van Gogh blue eyes of his. God help her, if he winked again she would spontaneously combust.

She cleared her throat. "How long do you plan on calling me Doc?"

He shrugged. "Forever. I know how much you value that doctor title. And seeing as you're my client now, I aim to please."

So it was true. Harper's head throbbed with fresh intensity. "You're the dog walker."

"At your service."

She slammed her coffee cup down on the table. A splash of latte flew out of the little hole in the lid and landed on the arm of her blazer. Her favorite blazer. Grey. Armani.

Everything had been going so well only five minutes ago.

"So that whole speech you gave me last night about needing to hire a dog walker was a trick to get me to hire you?"

"A trick?" He raised a single, incredulous eyebrow. "Doc, if I'd been offering you my services, I would have given you a business card."

"You have business cards?" She highly doubted that, considering his pencil-scrawled phone number she still had folded into a square in her wallet.

"Of a sort." He shrugged. "Is that really so important?"

She supposed not. "The point I'm trying to make is that you should have told me."

"Why? Would you have hired me on the spot?"

"No, of course not."

"I rest my case, Doc." He crossed his arms.

His muscular, manly arms.

Harper's head spun. "I don't think this is a good idea."

"Because you don't like me."

She squirmed in her chair. "I wouldn't say that."

His gaze was perfectly impassive. "I would. You don't like me, and I don't like you."

Could he be any more blunt? She was beginning to long for the time when he stared sullenly and didn't say anything. "Then you see my point."

He shook his head. "Actually, no. I'm not walking you. I'm walking your dog. And your dog likes me. A lot."

He had her there. Vincent did indeed seem to carry a torch for Tom Stone. It was the dog's only serious flaw. Harper considered it far more disturbing than the missing ear. Or his rambunctious streak. "He might like you. A little."

"Most dogs do. That's why I'm a dog walker and not a flower girl."

Oh, geez. Again? "If I'm even going to consider this arrangement, you're going to have to let that go."

He completely ignored the statement and instead began digging around in his pocket. He pulled out two white, oblong pills. They rolled around in his palm with, no doubt, a pocketful of germs. "I almost forgot. Here, I brought you a present. Consider it a peace offering. Ibuprofen."

If he thought she was going to swallow those, he was insane. She crossed her arms. "No, thank you. What makes you think I need ibuprofen, anyway?"

"I can only assume you're hungover since you drunk-dialed me last night."

Oh, my God.

Harper wanted to crawl under the table. Was it her imagination, or was every set of eyes in the coffee shop turned her way? She glanced around. From his spot behind the counter, Marshall was grinning a mile wide.

She fixed her gaze back on Tom. "Could you please keep your voice down? And I did *not* drunk-dial you."

"You sure about that? Because I saved the voice mail." He pulled his cell phone out of his pocket. Apparently he kept other things in there besides unsanitary pharmaceuticals. "I could play it for you on speaker."

"Don't you dare," she said through gritted teeth.

Her head was pounding harder than ever now. She looked longingly at the pocket-ibuprofen. No, she couldn't. Surely, she wasn't that desperate.

She'd wondered why he'd been so pleasant. So chatty. He'd been mocking her the entire time. The ibuprofen captured her attention again. She was one dose of anti-bacterial gel away from swallowing them.

"Admit it. You were drunk." He gave her a perfect-lipped grin.

Harper swallowed. "I was not."

"Plastered."

"No." Really, it hadn't been that bad, had it?

"Shit-faced."

Harper rolled her eyes. "Charming. Can we stop now?"

"Sure. As soon as you admit it." He grinned again.

No way. She could barely admit it to herself, much less him. "Why do you even care?"

His grin faded a bit. "I'm not sure, actually."

An awkward silence ensued. The hum of the coffee shop even seemed to settle down. Harper waited for Tom to say something else. Anything.

When it became apparent that he intended to remain mum, she spoke up. "I might have a had a tad too much wine. It was a stressful evening." Then, so he wouldn't think she'd attributed too much importance to his visit to Art Bar, she added, "You know, with the marriage proposal and everything. It kind of threw the night into an uproar."

"I can imagine. Proposals have a way of doing that, don't they?" His eyes darkened to midnight, like the shadow in a Vermeer painting.

And something about that haunting hue caused Harper to soften toward him. Just a little.

TOM SHIFTED IN his chair. He'd suddenly become distinctly uncomfortable. Then again, Harper didn't look any more at ease than he was.

How had the conversation come around to romance?

Tom watched her lift her coffee cup to her lips. He was sure that cup was empty by now. She seemed to be at a loss over what to do with her hands. She set the cup down and drummed her fingernails on the tabletop.

He should say something. Although why he felt the need to put her at ease was a mystery. Guilt, probably. He'd given her an awfully hard time thus far. Not that she didn't deserve it.

He sat up a little straighter. "For the record, I'm not a fan of the institution either."

"Institution?" She dragged her gaze back to meet his and licked her lips.

Tom was held spellbound for a second by the slow slide of her crimson tongue against her upper lip. He had a sudden inexplicable craving for cherries. "Marriage. We were talking about marriage."

"Are you?" she asked. "Married, I mean? Do you have a wife living with you on that boat of yours?"

She just had to make a crack about the fact he lived in a boat.

Tom's jaw involuntarily clenched. "No."

Her gaze narrowed ever so slightly. "Have you ever before?"

The specificity of the question caught him off guard, and the answer slipped out before he'd even realized it. "Yes, for a very short time."

His jaw clenched again. His personal life was none of Harper's business. Besides, he never talked about his marriage. With anyone. Not that there was much to tell.

Four months was nothing. His ex-wife had probably spent

half of that time penning the Dear John letter she'd sent him in Iraq, ending it all. A blip in the radar of his bachelorhood, buried five years in the past when he'd still been naïve enough to believe in love and forever, it hardly counted as a marriage.

"A very short time. Right." She grabbed the pills and tossed them back, choking a little when she tried to wash them down with the dregs at the bottom of her coffee cup.

"What about you? Have you ever been married?" he asked, more than ready to remove himself from the spotlight of this particular conversation.

"No. Absolutely not." She shook her head so hard that Tom thought it might snap right off her neck. "Never have and never will."

So it seemed he and *Doctor* Harper Higgins had something in common after all—a mutual hatred of marriage. Interesting. Although he couldn't help but wonder what she could possibly know about marriage since she'd never taken the plunge.

He couldn't stop the ironic smile that came to his lips. "It's settled then."

"What's settled?"

He leaned a bit closer. Close enough to discover she smelled of flowers. Not sweet, tame flowers, like roses. Something wilder and more exotic. Orchids, maybe. Tom found that profoundly odd, given her rigid personality. "You and I will never marry one another. Obviously."

She let out a huff of laughter. "*Obviously.*"

Her face flushed bright pink, and it brought to mind the carnations he'd painted the night before. Those lush, feminine blooms.

Why did she look so irritated? And why did he feel the

same?

He sat back in his chair, away from her intoxicating fragrance. "Perhaps we should stick to talking about your crazy dog."

She raised a single, uptight eyebrow. "I think that would be appropriate, don't you?"

There. Right there. That was the Harper he knew. The one who'd knocked him down in a rainstorm and gotten so righteously offended when he'd called her out, making him believe she was a real doctor. Rigid, cold, concerned about what was and wasn't appropriate. A snob of the highest order.

"Absolutely."

"And since you're going to be Vincent's dog walker, I want you to stop calling him crazy."

Tom was beginning to wish he'd saved those ibuprofen tablets for himself. Harper didn't just give him a headache. She *was* a headache. And now that he'd agreed to walk her dog, she was *his* headache. "Afraid I'm going to hurt his doggy feelings? Do you have a PhD in dog psychiatry as well as art history?"

"Very funny. Look, I just don't think it's very nice to talk that way about your clients." She lifted her pretty little chin. "Even if they are dogs. And he's not crazy. He's just spirited and bright. Like a pop art painting."

Tom said nothing. He suddenly found himself at a peculiar loss for words. She was sitting there comparing her wild dog to an art movement. It was nuts. And well, sort of sweet.

Hell.

He was envious of the damn dog. Not jealous. Definitely not jealous. But envious, perhaps. To have that kind of woman on his side would be soul-stirring. A woman who would see nothing but the good in him. A woman who would stick by him and defend him, even when it didn't make sense. Who wouldn't want a champion like that?

Not him. Obviously. As sweet as she could be to her wacky dog, she irritated the hell out of him. He'd just as soon mock her as kiss her. Not that he had any plans to kiss Harper Higgins. *Doctor* Harper Higgins.

Too bad. Her ripe cherry lips looked so kissable at the moment. But Tom knew better. Give the woman five minutes and she was sure to open that lush mouth and say something infuriating. About her education. Or the fact that he lived on a boat. Or her superiority over him in general.

Under the table, his fists clenched. His gaze wandered to her lips again. So red. Like a shiny satin bow.

What a waste.

Chapter Six

THE MOMENT HARPER entered the art history hall at Boston College of Art, she ducked into the bathroom to dab at the coffee stain on her sleeve with a wet paper towel. The last thing she wanted was a souvenir of her encounter with Tom Stone emblazoned on her arm for the remainder of the day.

You don't like me, and I don't like you.

She would have thought he'd been flirting if he'd had the slightest smile. He hadn't. In fact, he'd looked even more like he'd been on the verge of a murderous rampage than he usually did.

It was true, of course. She didn't like him. Not at all. And it was pretty obvious he didn't like her either, so the statement shouldn't have come as a surprise. And it didn't. But something about hearing him say those words aloud made her feel oddly vulnerable. Which was patently ridiculous.

The door to the ladies' room swung open, and the department secretary, Lindsay, rushed inside. "Here you are. I've sent you three texts. Where have you been?"

Harper looked up from the stain, which somehow seemed to be getting worse with her efforts to eradicate it. "I had a breakfast meeting."

Yes, she was still thinking of it as a meeting. It surely hadn't been a pleasure cruise. Or, God forbid, a date. "My phone was on vibrate. I'm not late, am I?"

"No." Lindsay rolled her eyes. "You're never late. The department meeting doesn't start for another eighteen minutes."

Eighteen minutes. An appreciation for such precise detail was one of the reasons Harper and Lindsay got along so well. "Then why the panic?"

Once Harper tore her attention away from the latte stain and directed it squarely on Lindsay, she saw the worry lines creasing her forehead. And she was doing the rapid blinking thing she tended to do when she was stressed.

"It's bad. Really bad." Lindsay's eyelashes fluttered like hummingbird wings.

Harper's stomach turned. And this time, it truly didn't have a thing to do with her hangover. "Please tell me this is in no way related to the show."

"I'm afraid it is." Lindsay squeezed her eyes closed.

Apparently the problem was of such magnitude, it went beyond blinking.

Which could only mean one thing.

"Lindsay, please don't tell me Archer is pulling out. Anything but that." Archer was the artist whose work the entire show was centered around. Personally, Harper didn't much care for him.

For starters, he insisted on going by that pretentious name. Like Sting. Only Sting was a musician, and plenty of musicians went by one-word names, even monosyllables. Serious artists did not. Even Picasso had a first name, for crying out loud.

Harper probably could have overlooked the name thing,

though, if she'd believed in his work, which she didn't. Not completely, anyway. How could she? He was a graffiti artist who'd been classically trained in portraiture at the Sorbonne in Paris. His chosen medium was spray paint and his canvas, public buildings. His subject matter, however, was riveting. He wasn't simply an artist, he was a political activist. His themes ranged from anti-war to anti-fascism to anti-poverty. He was *anti* a lot of things.

And for all of this, he was an international darling of the art world. Everyone loved Archer. So much so that law enforcement tended to turn a blind eye to his antics.

Sometimes, he painted on free-standing brick walls rather than actual buildings, as Harper had arranged for him to do for her gallery show. But he felt that showcasing his work "on the instruments of capitalism" made more of a statement. She wondered if that was what this hiccup could possibly be about.

Maybe she could convince the university to let him spray paint the exterior of the student union.

Right. That should go over well.

Whatever the problem was, she would fix it. She had no choice. Without him, there would be no show.

No show, no promotion for Harper.

"He emailed this morning and canceled." Lindsay let out a massive sigh.

No.

No, no, no, no.

Harper could feel the latte coming back up her throat. She was going to be sick.

She clutched her stomach. "He can't cancel. He just can't. What did he say? Is he running out of time? Because we can send someone there to help him finish his pieces if necessary."

Harper would do it herself if she had to. She'd pack up her things, drive to New York and live out of her car for the next two months if it meant the exhibition would take place as planned. Archer was controversial. Some thought him pretentious. And some thought him absurd. But everyone had an opinion about him, which was why securing him for the show had been such an enormous feather in Harper's academic hat.

She had her classes to worry about, plus teaching at Art Bar. But if Archer needed her in New York, she could figure something out. Maybe she could commute. It wasn't entirely unheard of.

Lindsay's eyelashes began fluttering again. Ominous butterfly wings. "The email wasn't from him exactly. It was from his assistant."

His assistant. Since when did guys who wore holsters filled with cans of spray paint have assistants? Something was profoundly wrong with the world.

"He cancelled via his *assistant*?" Harper grabbed her briefcase and slung her handbag over her shoulder. "This is not happening. I'm getting him on the phone right now."

Then Lindsay dropped the biggest bomb of all. "You can't. He's in jail."

Harper's briefcase hit the bathroom floor with a thud that echoed until her ears rang. "Jail."

She could barely breathe. In her imagination, she sank cross-legged to floor. In reality, she remained upright. Because that was what strong women did, even when they were dying inside. "For how long?"

"Six months." Lindsay eyed her with concern. "You don't

look well at all. Are you okay?"

Hysterical laughter bubbled up Harper's throat. She was far from okay. She wasn't sure she'd ever been quite so far away from anywhere before.

If it had been anything else—*anything*—she could have worked around it. Heck, he could have been dead and she would have been in a better position to pull art magic out of her hat. At least then, she could have displayed whatever he'd completed, and the art world would have eaten it up. If there was one thing an art critic loved, it was a dead artist.

Not that she wished Archer dead. Although, the thought of wringing his neck had a certain appeal.

"I'll be fine. Everything will be fine." Her voice sounded tinny and strange, completely at odds with what was coming out of her mouth.

But that was part of being strong and independent, wasn't it? Believing in oneself, even when the odds looked impossible? Or, as in the present case, pretending to believe?

She'd believed in herself once. Really believed. She'd believed in art and paint and beauty. And then with just a few lines from his typewriter, Rick had eradicated that belief.

The paintings of Harper Higgins aren't bad. They're not particularly good either. They simply are. And that makes them forgettable.

Why had she ever thought it was a good idea to date an art critic?

Never mind all that. It no longer matters. You have a genuine career now, one based on facts and professionalism.

Unfortunately, at the moment, her career was also based on a certain pretentious artist who was sitting in jail in an entirely different state.

Lindsay unspooled a generous portion of paper towels from the dispenser on the wall and ran them under the faucet. She twisted them until only a few fat droplets of water fell to the floor while she pressed the paper towels to Harper's forehead.

The cool provided some much-needed temporary relief to her aching head. Harper watched the drops fall on her blazer in dark water spots. She glanced at the latte stain. Still there. As soon as she got home from work, this fake Armani was going straight in the trash.

"What happened?" She heard herself mumble, as she watched her dreams fly right past her.

The prestigious show she was supposedly curating, the promotion she'd wanted so very badly…

"He was charged with destruction of public property."

"I suppose that shouldn't come as a complete surprise. He's a graffiti artist, after all." Harper glanced up and saw herself reflected in Lindsay's glasses.

Good grief, what was she doing letting the department secretary act as a nursemaid to her emotional breakdown? Granted, Lindsay was Harper's friend. But she was also a business colleague. And this was hardly professional behavior, even for a professional who'd just been dealt a deathblow to her career.

She took the paper towels from Lindsay's hand, tossed them in the trash and stood ramrod straight. "Thank you for giving me a heads-up before the department meeting. I'm fine. Everything is going to be fine."

Lindsay regarded her through narrowed eyes. "Um. How exactly is everything going to be fine?

"I don't know. But I know it will."

Harper glanced at her watch. She had seven more minutes to figure out how to make that happen. She could do it. Nothing was more important.

As Van Gogh himself once said, *I am seeking. I am striving. I am in it with all my heart.*

AN EXCESS OF flowers was a constant in Tom's life. As problems went, it was a nice one to have. It beat the hell out of worrying about getting shot by an insurgent or driving over an IED.

Sometimes, when the harbor was bathed in a particularly colorful sunrise, he fed the flowers to the water. Stem by stem, he would toss them over the side of the boat and watch them float away. As if by that simple action he could paint the whole world and color it with beauty in the broken places.

Other times, like this morning, he chose a more practical means of disposing of the subjects of his paintings.

"Flowers again? You really shouldn't, Tom." Mrs. Bell, the manager of the marina, scolded him as she always did. And then, again as she always did, she smiled brightly enough to light up a night sky. "Thank you, young man. But I do wish you'd find a nice, young lady to share all these flowers with."

"You're welcome." He handed her the carnations. "And I'm fine on my own. Thanks."

"You live on a boat. You walk dogs for a living. You spend too much time alone. There's got to be someone you'd rather give flowers to, other than me."

A memory of Harper, those red lips of hers pursed in irritation, flashed through his mind.

"Nope. No one." He shook his head a tad more firmly than necessary.

"Well, thank you. It's been an eternity since this one gave me flowers." She nodded toward her husband, who was busy filling a vase with water at the small sink in the corner.

The older man shrugged. "I don't need to bring you flowers now that Tom is here."

"What's your excuse for the past thirty-eight years, then?" Mrs. Bell winked at Tom.

He'd seen these two in action enough to know it was only good-natured teasing. How they'd managed to stay married to one another while also working together day in, day out, was a mystery.

Togetherness. It was what had been lacking in his own marriage. His ex-wife had loved him once. She'd fallen as swiftly for him as he had for her. They'd met at the library, and his heart had tumbled as hard and fast as the books that had fallen from her arms. In the beginning, she'd looked at him the way every man dreamed of being looked at by a woman. But distance had a way of blurring love's vision. Each day he'd spent in Iraq, the memory of her eyes had faded. By the time her letter arrived, he'd forgotten what it had felt like to look into their fathomless blue depths.

And she'd forgotten him altogether.

He couldn't imagine such a thing happening to the Bells. Their marriage seemed as intact as the marina.

The marina was something of a fixture on Boston Harbor, yet small and simple enough to be a two-person operation.

With less than seventy-five slips, it was one of the smaller ones there. About ten percent of those slips were occupied by boaters who lived aboard their vessels as Tom did. He wondered if that number would decrease when the weather grew colder.

"I'm glad you stopped by, Tom." Mr. Bell handed the vase to his wife, who began arranging the carnations one stem at a time. "I need to find out when you're moving out."

Tom frowned. "Moving out? Maybe there's been some kind of misunderstanding. I'm not moving out."

Mr. Bell shook his head. "You're not planning on staying on that boat for the winter."

Tom's frown deepened. "Actually, I am. That's one of the reasons I chose this marina. I was told residents could remain on their boats year-round."

"They can, yes."

Tom relaxed ever so slightly. "Is there another problem?"

"Yes, son. Your boat." He waved toward the window, where the bow of Tom's vessel was barely visible in its slip at the far end of the dock.

Even from this distance, Tom could make out Gunner's triangular ears standing at attention as he waited for his master. Like Batman. In dog form.

"Your boat isn't near ready for winter. Do you have any idea how cold it gets in Boston? Really cold. Really, really cold. And just when you think it can't get any colder, guess what happens."

Tom raised his brows. "It does?"

"Yep. It does. You need to winterize her. Soon."

He knew this, of course. But he figured he still had a good

month or two until things got critical. "I plan to. I know I need to shrink-wrap her in plastic, and the engine and water lines will need to be heated."

"You'll need to do more than that when the temperature drops below freezing."

This was news. Tom had thought his list was pretty much comprehensive. "As in?"

Mr. Bell flopped into the ancient red leather chair behind his desk. "I'd recommend adding a good diesel fireplace, in addition to your heaters. It will make a world of difference in a snowstorm. You'll be warm as can be in there. Life aboard is beautiful when it snows, but not if you're shivering. You'll also need a smoke and carbon monoxide detector."

Shrink-wrap.

Winterizing the lines.

A diesel fireplace.

A heater.

A smoke and carbon monoxide detector.

The list was growing longer. And exponentially more expensive.

He'd spent every penny of his combat pay on the boat itself. He did okay with the dog walking, certainly well enough to get by. But he wasn't exactly rolling in hundred dollar bills.

Mr. Bell shrugged, oblivious to Tom's money issues. "Don't worry, son. I'm sure it sounds like more than it really is. With a little help, you could probably get it all done in a weekend."

Tom didn't have a little help. He didn't have any, actually.

He could probably ask Frank to lend him a hand if he grew desperate, assuming he could get away from the flower business.

Of course, the idea of asking a man over thirty years his senior who only had one leg for help with anything physical might not be the best idea Tom had ever had.

He crossed his arms. "And if I don't have help?"

Mr. Bell shrugged again. "You could always hire it out. That's what a lot of the old-timers do."

"Old-timers. He means people our age." Finished arranging the carnations, Mrs. Bell carried the full vase to her desk, which was pushed up against her husband's so that they faced each other.

So now Tom was an honorary old timer. He wasn't sure how to feel about that.

"Here. I've got a brochure. These people can fix you right up." She opened a drawer and pulled out a glossy, rectangular flier.

Tom took it, glanced at the price list and willed himself not to let the shock show on his face. "Thank you. I'll give this some thought."

Mr. Bell leaned over and began digging through the massive metal toolbox he kept behind his desk. He pulled out a wrench and wagged it at Tom. "You do that, son. But don't think about it too long. Time is running out. If your vessel isn't properly prepared by the time true winter rolls around, I'll have no choice but to ask you to leave."

Tom nodded. "I'll take care of it. You have my word."

"All right. We'll see you later, then."

"Thanks again for the flowers," Mrs. Bell called out as Tom slipped out the door.

Her words barely registered. His head was still reeling from the dollar amount on the brochure in his hands. And as he whistled for Gunner, zipped up his leather jacket and began walking toward his first client's home, he wadded the flier into a ball and tossed it in the nearest trashcan.

Chapter Seven

HARPER WONDERED IF she could possibly be developing a split personality syndrome. On the outside, she appeared as she always did at the weekly art history department meeting. She nodded at all the proper times and paid close attention to every word Dr. Martin, the department head, uttered. She laughed politely at the cringe-worthy joke he made about Henri Matisse. And it was truly awful. *What did the artist say to the dentist? Matisse hurt!*

She typed copious notes into her tablet, just in case Lindsay missed something important.

But as together as she appeared on the outside, she was coming apart on the inside. With each minute that ticked by, she was getting closer to the moment when Dr. Martin would ask for an update on the Archer exhibit. And she still wasn't at all sure what she would say.

She glanced up at Dr. Lars Klassen seated directly across from her. Her nemesis.

Maybe not a nemesis in the strictest sense. It was not as if she and all the others sitting around the conference table were superheroes and villains. And Lars wasn't necessarily evil. He was just after the same job that Harper so desperately wanted. They were the only part-time professors in the department.

And the one edge she had over him was sitting in a jail cell in Manhattan.

Lars narrowed his gaze at her from across the oak expanse of the conference table. She smiled sweetly back at him. He looked away. It was almost scary how she could pretend nothing was amiss.

"And now I'd like to discuss the curriculum committee's report." Dr. Martin nodded at Lindsay, and she rose from her spot beside Harper to pass out a stapled list of classes to be offered during the academic year.

Dr. Martin cleared his throat. "As you can see, we will be offering the same core courses. At the advanced levels, Ancient Art and Architecture will be merged with Medieval Art and Architecture. This new combined course will be a four credit-hour class and will be taught by Dr. Christian."

Harper's fingers flew over the keyboard of her tablet, even though on the surface this change really had nothing to do with her. On the other hand, Dr. C was probably old enough to teach Ancient Art and Architecture from personal experience, so one never knew. Things happened. Last year Harper had been called to take over a class for another professor who'd been fired in scandal after it had been discovered he'd been sleeping with a student. Hellenistic and Roman Art. It wasn't her area of expertise at all, but she was game for anything that kept her from dressing up as Frida Kahlo and painting a unibrow on her forehead.

"If you'll flip to the back of the packet, you'll find a list of new courses still being evaluated. Of the five listed, two will be added to the course catalog." Dr. Martin held up two fingers for added emphasis.

Harper looked at the list, and there it was—her dream class, spelled out right at the top. *Advanced Seminar on Vincent Van Gogh*. And right next to the course title was her name. *Dr. Harper Higgins.*

It was almost too much to hope for. The odds were against her. Two in five. But if she got promoted, her course load would double. She was fairly certain her Van Gogh seminar would be a *go*. Pun intended.

Of course, Lars had a proposed course on the list as well. *Advanced Painterly Seminar—Man Ray*. Harper had to give him credit for creativity. Man Ray was best known in the art world for his photography. Choosing to study his paintings instead was a bold move. Creativity aside, she had no intention of letting that class end up in the final course catalog.

"Moving on." Dr. Martin tossed his handout on the table and directed his gaze at Harper. "Dr. Higgins, can you give us an update on the Archer gallery show?"

Beneath the table, Harper's left leg began to shake.

"Ouch." Lars backed his chair away from the table. "Somebody kicked me."

"Sorry." Harper pasted on a smile. If she had to kick someone, at least it had been Lars. "An update on the show. Yes."

Every pair of eyes was on her, including Lindsay's, which had begun to blink like crazy again.

Dr. Martin frowned. "Well? Is everything in order?"

"Actually..." *Say it. Just say it. Archer has been arrested. There will be no show*. "I've had a change of heart."

"A change of heart? What is that supposed to mean?" Lars. Naturally.

"Well..." *Say something. Something brilliant.* "Um."

Um? Surely you can do better than that.

"I'm no longer sure Archer is the direction we should go." She took a deep breath and waited for whatever chaos was sure to come.

There was no chaos. Instead, there was just a long, awkward silence, which was even worse.

"It's a little late to rethink an entire show, Dr. Higgins," Dr. Martin said in an eerily calm voice. "Even if you were to go in a different direction, I doubt you could find anyone of Archer's celebrity at this late date. Two months is not sufficient time for most artists to put together an entire exhibit. There's a reason Michelangelo took four years to paint the Sistine Chapel."

There was so much wrong with that statement that Harper didn't know where to start. Although, a good beginning point would have been that Michelangelo undertook that project over 500 years ago. And really, the fact that he'd mentioned Archer and Michelangelo in the same breath was alarming on multiple levels. She had to clamp her mouth closed so she didn't say something terrible, because as nuts as Dr. Martin sounded at the moment, he was still the head of the department. And the fact that he'd invoked the name of Michelangelo meant he was dead serious.

Serious enough to pull the show from her altogether if she admitted the truth. But she couldn't outright lie and say she was currently curating an art show minus the artist.

She glanced across the table, where Lars was watching her with a definite look of triumph in his eyes.

He smirked and directed his attention fully at Dr. Martin. "I have someone we can use."

We? Since when was there a *we* in the equation? She was curating this thing.

Dr. Martin lifted a Michelangelo-loving eyebrow. "Do you? Tell us more."

It was in that moment that Harper flung herself into the dangerous place known as the point of no return. "I've already got another artist lined up."

She had to physically grab her knee to stop her leg from jiggling. It was shaking so hard that it was banging against the underside of the conference table. And the wind coming off Lindsay's rapidly blinking eyelashes nearly knocked her out of her chair.

"You've replaced Archer? Unilaterally? You can't do that," In the span of Harper's hastily uttered sentence, Lars had gone from ultra-cool professional to whiny, spoiled child. "Can she do that, Dr. Martin?"

Dr. Martin released a long, measured exhale. "Dr. Higgins is the show's curator."

Harper grinned victoriously, even though the very concept of victory was ridiculously out of reach right then.

I've got another artist lined up. Small detail…this artist is imaginary.

"The curator is the overseer of the exhibition, the one ultimately responsible. That being said, I would love to hear more about this replacement you've come up with." Dr. Martin stood, indicating the meeting was over. *Thank God.* "First thing in the morning, Dr. Higgins. Clear your calendar, would you?"

"Yes, sir," she said, not knowing whether to celebrate the fact that she'd bought herself more time or scream in agony, Edvard Munch-style, at the enormous lie she'd just told.

What have I done?

HARPER ARRIVED AT work at Art Bar that evening to find Peyton dabbing a big daddy-sized brush at one of the most ridiculous paintings she'd ever seen. She wasn't even altogether sure what it was. A panda maybe. Or a polar bear. Or possibly the Pillsbury doughboy.

"Hi, Peyton." She averted her eyes from the disaster on the easel and unclipped Vincent's leash.

He trotted over to his dog bed and flopped onto it with a Great Dane-sized sigh.

"Oh, hello," Peyton said absently as she scrutinized her painting. "You're early tonight."

"Just a bit." Harper slipped a painting smock over her head and wrapped the tie around her waist.

She'd been going stir crazy sitting at home, waiting for the class she was teaching tonight. She couldn't stop thinking about the mess she'd made for herself at work. At her *real* work.

"Do you know the final head count for tonight? I thought I'd go ahead and get the supplies ready." She reached for the stack of paper plates, or as they were known at Art Bar, artists' palettes.

"Twenty." Peyton dipped her brush into a pool of white paint. Just when Harper thought it couldn't get any sillier, it did.

Peyton began adding wings to the marshmallow-esque creature, making its identity even more ambiguous. An angel-panda-doughy-man? Who in the world would want to paint that, much less hang it in their living room?

Harper suppressed a shudder and began counting out paper plates. "Twenty. That's a rather small class, I suppose."

"Yes, it is." Peyton dropped big daddy in a cup of water.

The painting must be complete. Thank God. Harper had been afraid she might add something else, like bunny slippers. Or possibly antennae.

Peyton swiveled on her barstool to face Harper. "We need to have a chat about that."

Harper looked up. "We do?"

Peyton's expression was rather serious all of a sudden. Far too serious for someone who had just painted something that pushed every known boundary of whimsical. "Yes. You've got to start choosing simpler paintings for your classes."

She wasn't altogether surprised to hear this. Peyton had mentioned it once or twice before. Tonight's class was a study in surrealism. Salvador Dali. Far from simple. But profound. A painting that really made people think.

Harper scrolled through her mental catalog of master works. "I can pick something a bit easier for next week. Monet, maybe?"

Monet. Always a winner. People swooned over those dreamy lily pads.

Peyton shook her head. "Think simpler."

"Simpler." Perhaps this wasn't the moment to mention that she'd been working on a reproduction of the Mona Lisa that she hoped to add to next month's schedule. "Okay. Let's see. What about Picasso's Flowers of Peace?"

It was hardly a painting. More of a line drawing, really. Two penciled hands, holding a very simplified cluster of colorful daisies. A child could probably paint the flowers. "The hands would be the only part people might have trouble with. I could pencil in some guidelines for everyone to follow. We could probably do that one in two hours instead of three."

Peyton shook her head. "Even simpler."

Simpler than a line drawing? With guidelines drawn in place?

"Umm..." Harper was at a loss.

The only thing she thought might be simpler was a Jackson Pollock-style drip painting, but Peyton would never go for it, with good reason. The mess would be astronomical.

Peyton lifted a brow. "You're not getting the hint, so I'll just come out and say it. I need you to do some original paintings. Very simple. Very fun."

Harper shook her head. "But I don't do that."

Peyton knew she didn't paint originals. Those days were over. Once upon a time, she'd dreamed of selling her original paintings in galleries, or even just on the sidewalk. Anywhere, so long as she could paint for a living. But the reviews from her first solo exhibition had put an end to those notions. Not just Rick's. The others, too.

Shallow. Lacking any depth. Devoid of feeling.

The assessment had devastated her. It still did. Hadn't he known? Couldn't Rick see how hard it had been for her to place even the smallest amount of trust in a man? All her life, she'd watched men walk right out the door. There was a reason she didn't walk around with her heart on her sleeve or paint it in crimson on her canvas for all the world to see.

She hadn't painted a single original piece since the day she'd read those words. And she was fine with that. Who went to school and studied art history for nearly a decade to sell paintings on the street, anyway?

Someone who loves to create art even more than studying it.

Peyton sighed. "Look, I know you have the whole perfectionist thing going on. But I assure you, I'm not asking for perfect. I'm asking for cute. Light. Playful. Something like..."

Don't say it. Do not say it. Please.

"...this." She nodded at the winged monstrosity she'd just painted.

She couldn't be serious.

Harper did her best not to wince. If she were to paint something all her own, it would not resemble what was on that easel in the slightest. She had too much respect for the paint, the brushes, the canvas, and for art itself to make something without meaning. Art should say something.

"Peyton, you know that's not me." She chose her next words very carefully. "And well...I have to wonder how many students would want to sign up for something so...so...quirky. I mean, it's so unique..."

She was really putting her foot in it. But Peyton either didn't notice, or she didn't care.

She grinned at Harper. "Forty-two."

"Forty-two? That's an oddly specific estimate." Harper looked at the painting again and tried to imagine it hanging in forty-two homes, on forty-two walls, on forty-two nails in Boston.

"It's not an estimate. I painted it the other day and put it up on the online calendar. The class is full, with a waiting list as long as my arm. I had to paint another one because someone off the street came in to buy the original." Peyton beamed.

Harper was happy for her. She really was. She was also completely mystified. "Wow. That's...impressive."

"I know, right? That's what I'm trying to tell you. Just whip up something adorable. I'm going to have to cut back on your master reproduction classes. We can't keep offering those night after night if this is the kind of thing that will pack the room. Understood?"

Harper understood, all right. She understood that she probably wouldn't have a job at the college after her meeting with Dr. Martin in the morning. She understood that her position at Art Bar, which had always been her plan B, was in all likelihood about to become her only plan.

She looked at the flying marshmallow again. This was what she was going to be doing for the rest of her life while Lars Klassen got tenure.

"I understand."

TOM TOOK A deep breath and considered his next words carefully. What he was about to say was important. From the moment the two of them had laid eyes on one another on that rain-slicked cobblestone street a few nights ago, things had seemed to spiral out of control.

He didn't like it. Not one bit. And he aimed to fix it. If they were going to be seeing each other on a regular basis, he didn't want any lingering awkwardness between them.

"Look, I know we didn't start off on the right foot," he said, pausing for a reaction.

Silence.

A thick blanket of fog had descended on the harbor, swallowing the two of them in a puff of grey. Their own private cloud.

"I'd like to be friends." He continued, "Or at the very least, get to the point where we can treat each other with mutual respect."

More silence.

"So." Here came the tricky part. "I'm going to have to insist that you calm down. Stop drooling at the sight of me. And most importantly, stop throwing yourself all over me every chance you get."

Woof!

The subject of his lecture sprang toward him, banged into his shins and twirled a frantic dance on his tiny hind legs. Tom had never heard of anyone ever being literally smothered to death by dachshund affection. But Vincent was giving it a go.

Tom sank onto one of the park benches along the harbor walk and let the dog launch himself into his lap.

"I suppose my little speech has fallen on deaf ears." Vincent's one ear twitched, and Tom winced. "Sorry, I forgot. Deaf ear. Singular."

Vincent pushed his little brandy-colored face within a centimeter of Tom's and licked the tip of his nose. The dog had no boundaries. None. But his affection was certainly easier to take when sitting down, fully prepared for the onslaught.

Gunner sat on his haunches, watching the display with detached interest. The shepherd was the very epitome of devotion. He'd literally risked his own life to keep Tom out of harm's way. More than once. That dog knew more about him than any person ever could. They'd walked in one another's footsteps a world away, in a land of sand-covered strife. But Gunner wasn't one to demonstrate his loyalty with a face full of slobbery kisses. His devotion was of the quiet sort.

It struck Tom that he and the shepherd were alike in that way. And he wondered if this quality that was so invaluable in a dog, in a soldier, was perhaps less than ideal in a human being. In a lover.

Not that it mattered. Love, the kind of love that danced in the night, the love that the poets had written of, with ink-dipped feather quills, was not something Tom was anywhere near capable of. Whether or not he'd ever possessed the ability to taste such affection before his time in the Middle East was debatable. His ex-wife would surely have something to say on the subject, and Tom doubted it would be complimentary. Hence her hasty retreat.

In the four months they'd been married, they'd spent one night in the same bed. He'd spent the other one hundred twenty one nights in a tent in Iraq, loving her the only way he knew how. By providing for her, fighting for his country, living the life of an honorable man. It was the only life he'd ever known.

Like father, like son.

He'd thought she would wait for him. He'd thought wrong.

And any capacity for love he'd once had was no longer present. It had died on those bloody fields of battle, the far-off place where his heart and soul lay scattered in crimson tatters. He hadn't needed the army psychiatrist to tell him that he'd come home a broken man. It was painfully obvious, even to himself. His brothers had come home in boxes. Tom's body had become a box. A box that contained nothing but shards of a soul. A box full of shattered remains was no more capable of loving than it was of being loved.

End of story.

Gunner gave Tom's leg a nudge with his muzzle, prompting him to glance at his watch. 8:45. Time to head to Art Bar and catch up with Harper. He'd walked Vincent the full length of the Freedom Trail. Two and half miles, which seemed like a fair distance for a dog with legs that measured approximately four inches tall and a dog walker who still had an air cast on his foot. According to the arrangements he'd made with Harper when he picked the dog up, he was to return when her class ended at 9:00. And God forbid he arrive at 9:01.

He returned Vincent to the cobblestones and directed his steps southward, a slow smile creeping its way to his lips. When he'd gone to Art Bar a few hours ago to collect the dog, Harper had been setting up for her class. There had been four rows of tabletop easels, five to a row. Each had a paper plate set in front of it with identical pools of brightly colored acrylic paint arranged in a perfect circle. The whole affair had Harper's pristine fingerprints all over it. A place for everything, and everything in its place.

While she'd given him a laundry list of instructions pertaining to Vincent—as though he'd never walked a dog in his thirty-two years on the planet—Gunner had meticulously sniffed the perimeter of the room and Tom had snuck a glance at the painting on Harper's easel. It had looked vaguely familiar. Tom was pretty sure he'd seen something like it before. A beach, with three clocks that looked as though they were melting. Weird as all get-out. Next to it had been a perfectly simple painting of an angelic polar bear. It may have been a little on the saccharine side, but much less frightening to look at day in and day out. He'd wondered what would possess a room full of people to want to paint something like the melting clocks instead.

Then again, maybe they didn't. Maybe there'd be another uprising among the ranks, as there had been the night before. Maybe he'd return to find Harper sucking on another juice box full of wine, her lush lips stained with burgundy merlot and that luxurious blonde mane of hers tousled, as though she'd just gone for a walk in a windstorm. Or rolled out of a soft, warm bed.

Doubtful.

The reality of the situation lay somewhere between those two scenarios. When he opened the door, he was hit in the face with twenty identical paintings. If his math was correct, that made sixty melting clocks. And they'd all been painted in the same blue-brown-gold color combination. Kudos to Doc for keeping everyone in line.

Except none of them looked finished. None of the clocks had hands yet. Or numbers, for that matter. But maybe that was how it was supposed to look. What did he know about melting timepieces?

"Okay, who else needs help finishing up? Raise big daddy in the air so I can see you, and I'll come give you a hand." At the front of the room, Harper craned her neck to see how many hands were raised.

All of them. Every big daddy in the room was pointed skyward.

She was going to paint the faces on sixty melting clocks?

We're going to be here all night.

Tom frowned.

Not we. *She.* She's *going to be here all night.*

He'd been hired to walk the dog until 9:00. And a glance at the clock on the wall—a real, non-melting clock, complete with numbers—told him it was 9:02. He wasn't one to get that specific, but Harper sure was.

This was not his problem. The students seemed happy enough, sitting on their stools, sipping wine from straws. He should just go. For once, Vincent was behaving. The leash wasn't even taut. He stood at Tom's side as if he were a completely normal dog. It was amazing what a little exercise could accomplish.

"Come on, boy," Tom whispered, so as to draw as little attention to his odd trio as possible.

He would have thought a man with a cast on his foot, who was flanked on either side by a German shepherd and one-eared dachshund, would have caused more of a commotion. But he managed to walk along the far right wall and up to the front of the room without much of a fuss. Harper had already abandoned her teaching easel at the head of the class and was busy helping one of the students. He wasn't even sure if she'd noticed his arrival.

He bent to unclip Vincent's leash, and the dog flopped on his bed with a weary sigh. Before Tom even stood up, he was snoring at a volume that belied his diminutive size.

Tom turned to go.

It only took a few steps for him to realize that something, or rather someone, was missing. Gunner. Tom turned to find him sitting calmly beside Vincent, as if guarding the small dog.

Or more accurately, guarding everyone present *from* Vincent.

Tom put his hands on his hips. "Gunner, your work ethic is killing me here."

He was ready for bed. Today hadn't been the best of days. Since he hadn't managed to win the lottery over the course of the past eight hours, he still wasn't sure what he was going to do about winterizing the boat. And before Vincent, he'd had his usual round of clients. Three dogs in the morning, and four more in the afternoon. He typically walked his clients in groups, but he wasn't quite ready to trust Vincent in such a scenario. Call him crazy.

All told, he'd probably walked a dozen miles or so, dragging the big air cast on his sprained foot with him all the while. That in itself wasn't a problem, though. He liked the freedom of being outdoors, feeling the crunch of his feet on gravel. He loved walking, even in the rain. Especially in the rain. And he rarely used an umbrella, preferring instead to feel the drops splat against his skin, run down his face, his neck, his arms. He wondered if it would ever end, this ceaseless craving he had for water.

The difficulty with today had been getting out of his head. No amount of rain or miles spun under his feet had done the trick. He was mentally exhausted, and certainly in no shape to tangle with the likes of Harper.

He stood with his hands on his hips in a sort of standoff with his dog. Gunner would have abandoned his duty and gone home with Tom if he insisted. Of course, he would. But the shepherd's instincts were spot on, as usual. Leaving now didn't feel right.

Damn it.

Tom sighed. "Fine. We're staying. You." He pointed at Vincent. "Stay put."

Vincent's only response was a drowsy twitch of his paws, as if he were dreaming. Chasing rabbits in his sleep.

"You." Tom turned his attention back to Gunner. "Make sure Vincent stays put. Got it?"

Tom turned, seeking out Harper. She was still on the front row, easel number two, squinting at the canvas. Fine. He'd start at the back of the class. It was probably better she didn't see him.

He took a final glance at the completed painting on her easel at the front, making note of the placement of the numbers and the way the black arms of the clocks threw blue-gray shadows on their melting faces. There was a sign tacked to the tray of the easel with the painting's name—*The Persistence of Memory* by Salvador Dali, 1931.

The Persistence of Memory? Perfect. Just perfect. The persistence of memory was something Tom was all too familiar with. He could only shake his head at the irony of it as he made his way to the easel in the far back corner of the room and got to work.

The students barely noticed him. They'd flung themselves into full social mode while waiting for Harper to finish their paintings. A few glanced at him when he sat down on their stools and touched brush to canvas, but once they saw he wasn't ruining their cookie cutter masterpieces, they simply shrugged and carried on.

He was on the seventh set of clocks when Harper finally got around to him. His shoulders tensed, and he braced himself for a berating. Oddly enough though, he didn't sense the usual waves of tension rolling off her.

He slid a glance in her direction. She wasn't even looking at him. In fact, she hadn't even noticed he was there. She only had eyes for the painting.

"Nice work. Very nice work." There was an unmistakable note of surprise in her voice, with the barest hint of awe.

And for a moment, just a moment, as she stood a heartbeat away without realizing it was him, he caught a glimpse of a Harper he'd not yet seen. Hair piled haphazardly on her head, with a few wayward, blonde locks tumbling free, grazing the gentle curve of her neck and collarbone. Cheeks flushed from the rush of creativity. Voice breathy and relaxed. This woman didn't give a damn about the initials after her name. This woman wasn't a doctor. She was a painter.

She pointed the end of her reed-thin paintbrush at one of the clocks on the canvas. "I love your shadow detail. It's exquisitely done."

Then she turned to look at him, and the magic spell was broken. "Tom?"

He watched as her features seemed to rearrange themselves before his eyes. And he was once again looking at that carefully put together woman who'd thought he was a flower peddler. The lovely painter he'd caught only a glimpse of vanished, like a wisp of smoke.

"Doc," he said flatly.

She glanced at the painting, and her gaze seemed to linger on the clock faces before she turned toward him again. "What are you doing here?"

He shrugged. "I'm returning your dog. It's after 9:00."

"That's not what I'm talking about. Why are you *here*, sitting on this stool?" She pointed at his hand. "Holding a paintbrush?"

He set the brush down with exaggerated calmness. "It looked like you could use some help."

"Wait." The guy who rightfully belonged on the stool raised his hands in surrender. "I thought he was your assistant or something. Should I have not let him finish the painting? I mean, he did all the others. I thought it was okay."

"The others?" Harper's eyes narrowed—her lovely eyes that looked even greener than they ordinarily did here in the brightly lit art studio.

"Uh, yeah. He did all of these." The guy waved a hand toward the back row of students, all busy chatting, sucking down wine from their straws like there was no tomorrow and snapping cell phone photos of their completed paintings.

Harper walked from one painting to the next, bringing her face within an inch of the canvases. Inspecting. Studying.

Tom rose from the stool and motioned for Gunner to follow. He wasn't about to stick around and wait for the fallout. She was angry. He should have known. She was prickly like that. But hell, he'd done her a favor. Not that he'd expected any thanks for it. Harper was hardly the type to express her gratitude. But that was fine. He enjoyed painting, and it had been nothing, really. Nothing at all.

That didn't mean he was going to let her berate him.

He pushed the door open, holding it wide for Gunner to slip through. Then the grey mist of the harbor swallowed them as Tom left Art Bar, those ever softening clocks, and Harper Higgins behind.

Chapter Eight

"WAIT!"

The cobblestones spun under Harper's feet as she searched for Tom in the fog. He'd walked out. Just like that. Without even saying goodbye.

And she'd impulsively run right after him, leaving Art Bar to manage itself. Something she'd never before done, even for a moment. There was no telling what might happen. There was enough wine and paint between those walls for a group of twenty unsupervised students to create a disaster of epic proportions. If Peyton knew Harper had walked right out the door, she would kill her. Fire her, certainly. A possibility that frightened her even more than death at the moment, since her job at Boston College of Art was suddenly hanging by a most precarious thread. She needed Art Bar now.

It was a sobering realization. But that didn't stop her from going after Tom Stone.

"Tom, wait. Please." Her voice echoed in the darkness.

She wasn't even sure which way he'd gone. So she headed toward that fateful street corner where he'd been carrying the flowers the other night. The night the sky had rained violets.

And there he was, standing with a huge German shepherd at his side. She didn't even know he had a dog. Then again, she didn't know he could paint either.

"Tom." She slowed to a stop.

Tom Stone had sat down and put the final touches on ten reproductions of a Salvador Dali painting. She was out of breath, more from the stunning turn of events than from chasing him down.

Breathless.

She blinked, at a sudden loss for words.

He stood there looking at her impassively, probably waiting for her to say something other than just his name.

Her heart pounded away like mad. "Why didn't you tell me?"

His eyes narrowed. "Tell you what?"

"That you could paint." She threw her hands in the air.

He was being so evasive. She didn't know whether to kiss him or strangle him.

Strangle him. Obviously.

"Why didn't you tell me?" She repeated. This time her voice had a slightly sharper edge to it.

It didn't escape Tom's notice. He glared at her. "Whether or not I could paint isn't on the list."

"The list?" She glanced at his dog sitting still as a stone at his feet and couldn't help but marvel at his perfect behavior.

"The list of things you and I are allowed to discuss with one another. Remember?"

She tore her gaze from the dog and aimed it back at Tom. It all came back to her—the conversation from this morning, when she'd been so nauseatingly hungover. *Perhaps we should stick to talking about your crazy dog.*

And her hotly issued response. *I think that would be appro-*

priate, don't you?

He'd called Vincent crazy. But she was willing to overlook that at the moment. "Never mind the list."

He crossed his arms. "Okay, but if we forget the list now, then it's out the window altogether. No limits on what we can and cannot discuss."

That runs both ways, Mr. Undercover Dali. "Fine."

He nodded, but appeared no happier than he usually did, which wasn't happy at all. "Fine."

They stood there facing one another in the misty moonlight. Harper felt bashful all of a sudden, which she had difficulty understanding after she'd chased him halfway to the harbor. She had no idea what to say, but whatever it was, it seemed important that she say it. Thanking him seemed like a good start.

"Thank you for what you did back there. It was a big help." She nodded in the direction of Art Bar.

His gaze softened a bit. "I thought you could use a hand. You would have been there half the night finishing up. It was nothing."

It wasn't nothing. It was most definitely something, which was why she was standing out here with her arms wrapped around herself in the cool indigo night.

"Your numbers and dials were remarkable." She wasn't flattering him. They were perfect. As fine and thin as a single strand of hair and executed with such a graceful hand. The paintings he'd finished were better than those Harper had completed by far. She could scarcely wrap her mind around it.

In true Tom Stone form, he said nothing in reply.

"And your shadows were beautiful." She smiled, thinking

about the smoky blue color he'd used. He'd mixed it himself. There wasn't a color close to being that subtle on any of the palettes in Art Bar.

"There's nothing beautiful about a shadow," he said skeptically.

He couldn't be more wrong. "Paul Cezanne once said that shadow is a color, just as light is. That sounds like beauty to me."

Tom regarded her blankly. "Am I supposed to know who this Paul guy is?"

She hoped he was joking. She really did, or the idea that had begun to take root somewhere in the back of her head would never come to fruition. "Seriously? Paul Cezanne. He's a French Post-Impressionist. He's really quite famous."

"Sorry, Doc. Maybe we should stick with talking about the dog after all." He sounded mad. Great.

Clearly, she was going about this the wrong way. "Where did you learn to paint, Tom?"

There was a long pause before he finally said, "The army."

It was the absolute last thing she'd expected him to say. "Are you joking?"

"Do I look like I'm joking?"

"No, actually. You don't." It wouldn't kill him to crack a smile once in a while.

Maybe he wouldn't make her so nervous if he looked the least bit happy to be talking to her. Who was she kidding? The butterflies swarming in her belly would probably go into overdrive if that were the case.

She was a nervous wreck, and this time it wasn't solely because of Tom's broad shoulders and that bone structure that would have made Michelangelo weep. She couldn't quite shake the notion that had popped into her head the moment she'd realized he could paint. It was preposterous. It was dishonest. It dangled there in her mind like a ruby red apple. Forbidden fruit.

Stop thinking about it. This whole idea is absolutely absurd. Even if he can paint better than Rembrandt himself, it would never, ever work.

But what other options did she have?

She swallowed. "I didn't realize the army was in the business of giving art lessons."

He didn't elaborate, not that she'd expected him to.

Time to stop beating around the bush. "I need to know what else you can do. Do you paint often?"

"Every day." He shifted his weight from one foot to the other. His hurt foot. She'd forgotten all about it. "Why the third degree, Doc?"

She wasn't about to tell him now. He'd think she'd lost it. Or possibly that she was drunk again. Besides, she needed to see what he could do first. "I need to see your work. Your paintings."

"My art isn't like what you do in there." He shot a look over her shoulder, toward Art Bar. "It's personal."

Personal was good. Very good. "Please, Tom. This is important."

"It's important for you to see my paintings?" The beginnings of a smile took form on his lips.

Harper wasn't so sure that was a good sign. She had a feeling he was on the verge of laughing at her. "Yes. Very. I'm serious, Tom. I need to see them."

He jammed a hand through his hair. Dampened by the fog, it stayed slicked back, giving Harper an even finer view of his steely eyes. "Okay. Fine. Maybe you can come by the boat sometime and I'll show you a couple canvases."

A sense of triumph swelled up inside her and danced in time with the thrill of danger she'd begun to embrace. A heady combination, which she found altogether unfamiliar. She felt drunk with it.

As light on her feet as she'd been the night before. "Tonight."

He began to protest. "No…"

She wasn't about to let him finish. "Yes. Yes, tonight. It has to be tonight. Right now."

TOM WASN'T SURE what to make of Harper's fervent interest in his art. And he was almost afraid to ask.

He stole a glance at her, strolling beside him along the harbor walk. Against his better judgment, he'd gone back with her to close up Art Bar so he could show her the paintings. Tonight. She still hadn't explained the urgency, and he was beginning to feel too tired to care.

Vincent's leash was wrapped around one of her slender, elegant wrists, and in the opposite hand she carried a silver juice box. It said Capri Sun on the outside of it, but he highly suspected it contained juice of the fermented variety.

What had gotten into her? Energy rolled off of her in waves. She'd been somehow transformed into some dark, dangerous beauty, green eyes shining bright in the darkness.

Electric. He half expected sparks to come shooting from her fingertips.

She didn't utter a word the entire way to the boat yard, which made him all the more curious. She was laser-focused. A woman on a mission. A mission that somehow involved his paintings.

"This is it," he said, slowing his footsteps as they approached his boat.

It sat perfectly still in the dark water. The harbor was uncommonly calm tonight, the water as black and ominous as the moon during an eclipse.

Harper's eyes widened the slightest bit. "Um, okay. How do we get on it?"

Tom reached for the stern line and gave it a good tug. The boat slid through the calm water like a hot knife cutting into butter. When the edge of the boat's port side kissed the weathered wood of the dock, he reached a hand toward Harper. "Ready?"

"Yes." She scooped Vincent into her arms and placed her hand in his.

He lifted her over the thin strip of water and then followed her on board. Gunner sprang in after them, landing on the boat in a whisper of footfalls.

Harper smiled. "Wow, I guess he's used to being on the water."

"He's adapted to it remarkably well." Tom studied her for a moment. "You look nervous. Is it the boat?"

Or me?

She lifted her chin. False bravado. "I've actually never been on one before."

"You've never been on a boat? Ever?" Tom couldn't keep the shock from his voice.

If ever there was a person who needed to experience the serenity of gliding over a mirror surface of crystal water, it was the woman standing on front of him.

"Never." She shook her head.

He popped open the storage compartment where he kept the flotation devices. "Do you want a life jacket? I've got one."

She stared at the row of bright orange life vests. "Are you ridiculing me right now?"

"No, I'm being perfectly serious. I want you to be comfortable here."

Why? Why on earth did it matter? It wasn't like this mysterious visit was destined to become a regular thing. Neither one of them wanted that. That much had been established this morning over coffee.

"Can we please just take a look at the paintings?" She bounced on her toes, on the verge of jumping right out of her skin.

He really needed to figure out what she was up to before he let her start rifling through his artwork. What had seemed inconsequential before, when she'd been standing in a swirl of fog imploring, insisting that he bring her here, now felt oddly intimate. As though he were showing her more than paint on canvas. Those paintings felt like pieces of himself all of a sudden.

And she was here. At his home, his sanctuary on the water, with her hair moving in the gentle breeze and drizzle shining like diamond dust where it gathered in her golden tresses.

She looked absolutely beautiful. Wherever it had come

from, this newfound looseness suited her.

Tom found it unsettling. He almost had to remind himself who she was. His client. A snooty academic. Someone he had nothing in common with whatsoever. Because the way the moonlight played on her marble white skin made him forget all about the initials that followed her last name.

"Where are they? In here?" She slipped right past him and jiggled the knob on the door to the cabin.

He pulled his keys from his pocket, his eyes never leaving her. "Why do I get the feeling that's not actually Capri Sun and that there's a drunk dial in my future?"

"Taste it." She shoved the silver foil pouch in his face.

He held up a hand. "No, thanks. I'm good."

"I'm serious. Taste it." She inched it closer, until his eye was in serious jeopardy from the little yellow straw.

He grabbed it, took a tentative sip and winced as the sickly sweet concoction hit his tongue.

She grinned triumphantly. "Told you."

"Okay, Doc. You've proved your point. But I don't feel any better about this. Why the urgency to see paintings?" he said as he slipped the key in the lock.

"I'll tell you," she said as he stepped aside so she could slip in front of him. "After you show them to me."

And with that she crossed the threshold. Into his boat. His home. His life.

Why did he get the feeling he would come to regret the intrusion for a long, long time?

BEING IN A boat was different from what Harper expected. She'd anticipated ceaseless motion and a feeling of being trapped inside a bottle, bobbing to and fro. The cabin was larger than it looked from the outside. She could easily stand upright. There was plenty of room for her, Tom and the two dogs. There was a sofa, a television, all the normal things she'd see in a living room on land. Vincent lay curled in a ball on the couch, as though he'd lived on the water his entire life, watching Gunner methodically sniff every square inch of the baseboards.

Harper waved a hand at the shepherd. "What's he doing? Does he smell something?"

"No." Tom shook his head. "If he smelled something you would know it. This is just what he does when he enters a new space."

"But this isn't a new space. You live here."

Tom lifted a brow. "I thought we were here to look at paintings, not discuss my dog."

Grumpy, as always. But she wasn't about to complain. Not now. This was far too important. "We are. Most definitely."

"Wait here," he said and headed toward a slender doorway that seemed to lead to the back of the boat.

The bow? The stern? She had no idea. But she had to admit his boat was rather homey, with a surprisingly artistic flair. There was even an easel in the corner. Its legs and tray were paint splattered with colorful drops of pinks, reds, violets and blues. Tom Stone was apparently a man who liked color.

The movement inside the boat was minimal. But what really surprised her was how quiet it was. So quiet, the silence felt weighted.

But that was probably just her imagination. Her anticipation was so palpable she could barely breathe. The only sound she could hear was the familiar tune of canvases sliding against one another, coming from the room where Tom had disappeared. His bedroom, she presumed.

Back when Harper had been a painter—of real paintings, not the simplified versions of masterpieces that she did now for Art Bar—she'd loved the smooth, barren white of a blank canvas almost as much as a finished painting. The linen pulled tight across wooden frames had always spoken to her of infinite possibilities. Sort of how she felt now.

She shook her head. What was she doing?

It's not too late. You can walk right out of here. You could leave without even seeing the paintings. Run from temptation.

She wouldn't. She couldn't. Any and all doubts about this absurd plan, she'd left somewhere along the harbor walk. Her misgivings, her uncertainties lay among the cobblestones, as forgotten as the many feet that had walked along that same path. Whatever happened was no longer up to her. She'd made a deal with fate. If his paintings were good, she'd go through with it. If not…

Well, if not, she would simply watch her career take an enormous step backward tomorrow morning in that meeting with Dr. Martin. But they were going to be good. She knew they were. She could just feel it. Or maybe she'd simply reached a point where desperation was making her delusional.

She paced back and forth across the room and as she did, her gaze fell on the sole piece of art that hung on Tom Stone's walls. She paused in front of the framed image and stared. It wasn't at all what she'd expected, and yet at the same time it was.

It wasn't a painting at all, but a large sheet of what appeared to be hand-crafted paper with an image silk-screened onto the pulp—a black military tank, rolling over a field of red flowers. A shiver ran up and down Harper's spine. The simplicity of the image somehow strengthened the impact of its message. She couldn't quite take her eyes off it.

She wondered where he'd gotten it. Handcrafted paper art wasn't exactly commonplace.

Stick to business. This isn't a social visit. You're here to see his paintings.

"Do you need any help in there?" she called and sat down on the sofa.

Tom reappeared in the narrow doorway between the two rooms, two canvases in each of his hands, still hidden from view. "In my bedroom? No."

Her face flooded with heat. She was blushing. She never blushed.

A rare smile danced on Tom's lips. "Don't tell me that's what this is all about. A 'let me see your etchings' type of thing?"

He was poking fun at her again. For once, she didn't mind. Not when those canvases were right there, less than three feet away.

"Hardly." She rolled her eyes. "And you've got it all wrong. It's 'do you want to come up and see my etchings,' not 'hey, let me climb aboard your boat and see your paintings'."

"Fine. I'll just put these away then." He turned around.

"Wait." She hopped off the sofa and grabbed at his sleeve, mistakenly getting a handful of firm bicep.

Her brain told her fingers to let go. Her fingers, in turn, blatantly disobeyed. "Don't put them away. Please."

"I was only joking." He waited a few full seconds, then looked at her hand still clutching his arm. "You can let go of me now, Doc."

"Oh." She jerked her hand away. "I'm sorry."

She was even more nervous around him than usual. Maybe the close quarters were to blame. Either that or his relentless teasing.

Yeah, right. You know exactly why you're nervous.

Tom was a handsome man. She'd admitted as much to herself from the very beginning. But somehow the realization that he was an artist made him infinitely more attractive. And intriguing. She couldn't help but wonder what else he was hiding...

Stop. This has nothing to do with attraction and everything to do with your future.

Even if she had any interest in allowing a man into her life—which she most definitely did *not*—she could never be with someone who'd never heard of Paul Cezanne. It would have been like a vegetarian marrying a butcher.

Her stomach roiled at the thought of marriage, however brief.

How did people do it? Let another person so wholly into their lives? Open up their homes, their hearts, their minds, their pasts, presents, and futures like open wounds? Every time she'd seen another man walk out on her mother, a layer of scar tissue had formed over Harper's heart. Now she could scarcely feel its beat.

She crossed her arms. Time to get down to business. "Let

me see."

He gave her the sort of look she gave Vincent when he was misbehaving.

She sighed. "Please. Let me see, *please*."

"Okay, since you asked nicely." He brushed past her.

It took superhuman effort not to sneak a look at the paintings before he got them set up. Part of her wanted to crane her neck for even the tiniest glimpse of color, but another part wanted to cover her eyes and hold her breath so she could experience it all in one, overwhelming, all-consuming rush. The best way to experience art.

He walked over to the sofa and smiled down at Vincent. He had endless smiles for her dog all of a sudden. None for her, unless they were of the sardonic variety, but smile upon smile for the dog.

"Vincent." One word. That was all he said, and Vincent hopped off the sofa and stretched out the floor with his front legs shooting straight forward and his hind legs behind. Superman-style.

What was it with her dog's blind adoration for this man? It was baffling. And somewhat nauseating.

Tom lined the canvases up one by one on sofa. Harper forbade herself to look at them, fixing her gaze instead on Tom's broad shoulders, his muscular back. Because he was there, after all. Right in front of her. She had to look at something.

"Here they are," he said, jamming his hands in his pockets and stepping aside.

Harper closed her eyes, took a deep breath and sent up a silent prayer to every dead artist who'd ever walked the face of the planet.

Please let them be good. Please.

Her lashes fluttered open, and her breath caught in her throat.

A garden lay spread before her on Tom Stone's sofa. A cotton candy shock of pink carnations, hydrangeas as pure and lily white as clouds against a robin egg sky. Daffodils like drops of liquid sunshine. Bleeding heart poppies.

And lastly, violets. Those violets he'd been carrying the night they met. He'd apparently gathered them from the rain-soaked pavement, taken them home and stroked them back to life with his paintbrush. Innocence and beauty, crushed by the world. Crushed but not destroyed, the humble purple blooms somehow even more lovely in their imperfect state.

The paintings weren't good. Not by a long shot. They were brilliant.

Later, in the many moments when Harper relived what happened next, she would blame her actions on the beauty of those brushstrokes, the breathtaking swirl of color, those pinwheel flowers painted with such abandon that if she'd closed her eyes, she was sure she would have inhaled the sweet smell of carnations warmed by the summer sun. Those paintings had sung to her, and their song was one of her future. Of hope.

But in that moment, she wasn't thinking of the art show, Dr. Martin, or Archer, sitting in his jail cell down in New York. She wasn't even thinking of Lars Klassen waiting in the wings to steal her promotion right out from under her. She wasn't thinking about Rick and how she'd never felt quite good enough for him. She wasn't thinking about her father or all the other men her mother had brought home. A laundry list of men who'd let Harper down, time and time again.

Her thoughts centered around one man, and one man only. The man whose hands had created those gorgeous paintings. The man standing beside her, watching, waiting, with those unreadable frosty eyes of his.

Then she let her thoughts go. For the first time in her life, Dr. Harper Higgins acted on impulse rather than according to a carefully crafted plan.

She rose up on tiptoe, cradled Tom's beautiful face in her hands and kissed him good and thoroughly, right on his artistic lips.

Chapter Nine

ONE MINUTE TOM was thinking how awkward this little scenario felt—watching Harper stare at his paintings, wondering what the hell was going on in that obstinate head of hers. And the next, *awkward* was the last thing he felt.

In one heartbeat swoop of desire, his mouth was captured by hers. Seized. Taken. In every possible sense. She was a huntress, and he'd become her star-crossed prey, caught in her snare of swirling want. And, by God, was it ever a turn on.

He wasn't sure he'd ever been kissed like that. And the blood boiling pleasure of it was only enhanced by the fact that Dr. Harper Higgins would have been the last woman he would have ever expected to create such a surge of instant arousal in him. The sensual trail of her fingertips sliding through his hair, the sweetness of her candy tongue, the exquisite softness of her rose petal lips, all combined to nearly drag him to his knees.

He was hard as a rock. He'd become granite the instant Doc had touched her lips to his.

What the hell?

She pressed into him, like a hothouse orchid leaning toward her first glimpse of natural light, and he decided to stop questioning whatever was happening. Not that he could have managed to douse a flame like this one. For that, there wasn't enough water in all of Boston Harbor.

As stirring as it was being kissed like that, Tom wasn't one to be dominated. Quite the opposite actually. In a single, swift move, he backed her up against the wall, pressing her against the hard wood, savoring the surprised squeak that came from somewhere deep in her throat. And savoring even more the way she gave in, her body going boneless, their kiss growing deeper and more urgent.

Just as he was thinking of sweeping the canvases to the side, sending them clattering to the floor in a rain of acrylic petals and leaves, and laying Harper down beneath him on the narrow sofa, a sharp pain pierced his ankle.

It startled him more than hurt him. He pulled away from Harper's kiss. "Ouch."

Okay, so maybe it actually hurt him more than it startled him.

"What's wrong?" Harper's eyes were deliciously heavy-lidded, her pupils dark and dilated. "Oh, my God, did I bite you?"

She brushed her swollen lips with trembling fingertips. "I did, didn't I?"

"No."

In fact, she had. She'd sunk her teeth right into his bottom lip. He could taste the barest hint of blood, but he wasn't about to complain about it.

"But your dog is doing a number on my ankle."

They both looked down at Vincent, latched onto Tom's sock with a death grip of dachshund teeth.

"Oh, my gosh." Harper straightened, pushed the hair from her eyes and cleared her throat.

But it was the look in her eyes more than her mannerisms that told Tom the wanton creature who'd kissed him within an inch of his life was fading away. He watched her vanish, not sure how to keep her there, or why he really wanted to. Then it was too late. The professor had returned.

"Vincent, stop it. Right now," she said.

The dog gave no indication that he'd heard her.

Tom bent down to pick him up. "Let go, you monster."

He half-expected Harper to order him not to call Vincent names. She wisely kept her mouth shut. The dog was Dracula disguised as a one-eared dachshund.

He tucked Vincent under an arm and stood back up. He'd barely gotten situated upright when Harper started talking, her voice as crisp and professional as ever.

"I apologize."

"For?" He knew perfectly well what she meant.

But he wanted to hear her say it. He wanted to hear her confess out loud that she'd kissed him, because if she didn't admit as much right now while her lips were still bee-stung swollen, she never would.

She lifted her chin a fraction, the way she always seemed to do when she was arguing with him. Not a good sign. "For kissing you."

Irritation took the edge off his arousal, leaving good old-fashioned sexual frustration in its place. So, she was sorry she'd kissed him, was she?

"I'm sorry, too."

Wait. He wasn't sorry.

Was he?

Yes, he was. Of course, he was.

"It won't happen again." Harper's voice dripped certainty.

The logical, left side of Tom's brain told him to agree. Kissing Harper had disaster written all over it. Prime example—her sudden change in personality. And the squirming dog in his arms.

The right side of his brain, the side where art and passion lived, thought differently. Right-brained Tom thought left-brained Tom was, in fact, an idiot.

"Agreed. Although, I'm not the one who started it."

Mature. Really mature. Neither side of his brain knew where that response had come from.

He breathed out a sigh. "It's getting late. Why don't we call it a night? I'll walk you home."

He grabbed his keys off the coffee table and started toward the door. Gunner roused himself and was on Tom's heels in an instant.

Harper, however, remained stubbornly rooted to her spot. "But we haven't talked about the art yet."

The paintings. The reason she'd come here in the first place. Tom had completely forgotten. "You wanted to see them, and now you have. What's left to discuss?"

"I want your paintings for a show at the college where I teach," she blurted.

Tom blinked. Surely he hadn't heard her right. "What?"

"I'm curating a show for work, and the artist I had lined up is in jail. I needed someone else." She bit her lip, and he had even more trouble concentrating on what she was saying. Not that what she saying made any sense whatsoever.

Nothing about this situation was sensible. Three months ago, he'd been living in a tent in the desert. Now he was standing in his boat holding a one-eared dog and talking about art shows.

He shook his head. "But I'm not an artist. I'm a…" Dog walker? Soldier? Wanderer? He wasn't even sure how to finish that thought. "I'm no artist."

"You are, Tom. You can really paint." She sat down in the red leather chair opposite the sofa and began studying the paintings again. Clearly, she wasn't leaving anytime soon.

He tossed his keys on the countertop between the galley kitchen and the living room, then set Vincent gently on the floor. "Doc, I don't paint these things to hang them on walls where people can gawk at them. I do it for other reasons."

"Such as?"

To remember. To forget. "I learned in the hospital. It's like therapy. I told you—it's personal."

He couldn't think of anything less personal than having pieces of soul hanging in a college somewhere for all the world to see. It made him uncomfortable enough to watch Harper gazing at them like she did.

"Don't you see? That's what makes them good. They're about flowers, but at the same time they're not." Her eyes went slightly misty again, almost like they had in the moment before she kissed him.

He shook his head. "They're flowers, Doc. That's all. Plain and simple."

"Where do you get them? The flowers?"

It was a question he hadn't expected. "Why do you want to know?"

She shrugged. "Just curious. You don't have to tell me."

"I get them from a flower guy. Frank Southard. He's a

friend." Not that it was any of her business.

"Oh." She stood, walked toward the sofa and picked up the painting of the violets. "Well, we'll have to come up with a theme for the show. Warrior Artist, maybe?"

Good God, she was stubborn. And delusional. "No way in hell."

Warrior Artist?

He didn't feel like either of those things.

"Tom." Her bottom lip gave a bit of a wobble.

A crack in her armor, the smallest glimpse of vulnerability, nearly as achingly beautiful as the woman who'd kissed him only moments before.

"Please."

"I said no. I'm sorry." He couldn't do it. Not if she planned on billing it as a soldier's homecoming dripping with paint. Wasn't he already having enough trouble leaving the past in the past?

"I'm going to be honest with you. I'm kind of desperate. I need someone by tomorrow morning." She blinked up at him, and the desperation she spoke of was written all over her beautiful face.

"Doc, this is crazy. Even assuming I wanted to do it, which I don't, I wouldn't begin to know how to prepare for something like this." He sank down on the edge of the sofa.

One of the canvases beside him slid into the other one, and Harper jumped up to separate them, handling the paintings as if they were made of gold. It was surreal.

"We would need a good number of paintings. Twenty or so. We could do that in a month, right?" Her casual use of the word *we* was alarming.

"Twenty paintings is a lot." A lot. But doable. Doable if he didn't have other things on his plate like winterizing the boat.

Then, as if she could read his mind, she added, "There could be money, you know. The paintings could be offered for sale. The college would take a commission, but the lion's share of the money would go to you."

It was the one thing that could make him consider this nonsense. "How much money are we talking about?"

There it was again. *We.* Coming from his own mouth, as though he and Harper were a team. His head was starting to hurt.

"A few hundred dollars per painting, I imagine. So long as they sell, of course."

Tom didn't need to do the math to know that was a lot of money. Thousands. More than he needed. "So what's the hook here? What aren't you telling me?"

There had to be more. Wasn't there always?

"Well, like I said, we'd need a theme. Something that sets you apart and makes your work extra-special. The artist I had lined up for the show is quite famous." She paused, and Tom could see the wheels turning in her head. He dreaded hearing whatever was about to come out of her mouth. "And since you don't seem to like the warrior artist idea…"

"Don't go there, Doc."

"Okay, okay. I won't. But I can't walk into my meeting tomorrow and tell my boss that I've fired Archer in order to show the work of a total unknown without any formal training who's just started painting. He would think I'd lost my mind."

"That's what I'm trying to tell you. I'm not an artist." He waved his arms around the boat, as if to emphasize his point.

But maybe real artists lived on boats. He didn't even know.

"What if we made you into one?" There was a dangerous sparkle in her eyes.

Be afraid. Be very afraid. "What are you suggesting?"

"A new identity. We can manufacture a past. You trained in Amsterdam, in the Van Gogh tradition. I can teach you everything you need to know in order to pass for a classically trained artist."

"That sounds like lying." Probably because it was, in fact, lying.

"It is. Technically." She frowned.

"And don't you think a simple Google search would tell these academic friends of yours that I'm not, in fact, classically trained?"

"Google. Right." She blew out a sigh. "Okay, so we can't lie about your qualifications exactly. But I'll think of something. Some other way to set you apart. You know, besides the military thing."

He glared at her. Hard.

"Not that, I promise. Something else. I don't like lying either, but it's the only way. I've already thought about it, and I know we can do this."

He lifted a brow. "But you only just found out I could paint. How could you have possibly given this any thought?"

"I've thought of nothing else since the minute I saw what you did at Art Bar." Her gaze wandered to his mouth for the briefest of moments.

So brief that Tom almost thought he'd imagined it. He was willing to bet there'd been one thing that had crossed her mind besides this ludicrous plan that sounded like something out of a bad sitcom. The kiss.

The kiss that still lingered somewhere in his marrow. The kiss that had come out of nowhere. The kiss that possibly outranked the scheming and lying as reasons he should turn her down flat.

Everything in his consciousness screamed at him to say no. Aside from the inherent wrongness of it, they'd never get away with fooling Harper's people into believing he was a real artist. It was a disaster waiting to happen. Spending a Boston winter on the harbor in his unprotected boat was a safer proposition.

He sighed. "I'll think about it."

HARPER LINGERED AT the coffee shop the next morning as long as she possibly could, hoping to run into Tom. She smiled politely at everyone. She called Marshall by name, and got it right on the first try. She even gritted her teeth and uttered the words *Oh God, yes* when placing her order.

She was doing everything possible to get the universe on her side so that Tom would agree to be her artist for the show.

I'll think about it.

He'd uttered those words less than twelve hours ago, and since then, she hadn't heard a peep out of him. Nothing. No text. No phone call.

He knew about the meeting she had scheduled with Dr. Martin this morning. It was due to begin in exactly half an hour, and she still didn't know what in the world she was going to tell her boss.

Her last ditch hope was that he would be here this morning, waiting for her. To tell her yes.

As an act of desperation, she'd even ordered a coffee for him. It sat untouched in the center of the table where she waited. The same table where they'd just had coffee the previous day.

So much had happened over the course of the past twenty-four hours. Archer. The show. Finding out Tom was a dog walker, then discovering he was an artist. What next? Was he an astronaut, too? Was he orbiting the moon right now when he should be here, agreeing to save her career?

But somehow, even though there was so much hanging in the balance—her job, her life, basically—that kiss overshadowed everything. The phenomenal kiss.

She gripped her coffee cup. Oh. God. Yes.

It was an aberration. It had to be. She'd been kissing the art, not the artist. She'd been pressing her lips to those lovely brushstrokes. And, by gosh, could those brushstrokes ever kiss back.

Forget about it. You have far more important things to be worrying about right now besides a silly kiss.

Silly kiss. Right.

It had been anything but silly. Who would have thought she would have been so completely aroused by being pinned against a wall? She was a strong woman. Strong women didn't go for that sort of thing. Or so she'd thought.

Stop thinking about it.

She glanced at her cell phone again. Five minutes. She had less than five minutes before she had to leave for work. And still no answer from Tom.

She spent them alternating between commanding herself

not to think about the kiss and then thinking about it. When she didn't have a moment left to spare, she got up and tossed her empty coffee cup in the trash. She lingered for a moment, unsure what to do with the coffee she'd bought for Tom.

In the end, she left it right there in the center of the table. Beneath the cardboard cup, she left a note that simply read *Please.*

Lindsay was blinking up a storm when Harper arrived at work later than morning. Harper couldn't really blame her. She was on the verge of a stress-blinking spree herself.

"Good morning." Harper smiled through gritted teeth, trying mightily to pretend that nothing was wrong. A sort of mini-rehearsal for the meeting with Dr. Martin. "Is he here yet?"

"Yes." Lindsay nodded. "He wants to meet you in the conference room at nine."

Harper glanced at her phone for the umpteenth time. 8:55 and still no word from Tom.

"I suppose I should get ready, then." She set down her briefcase, grabbed her tablet, and straightened her pencil skirt.

Everything seemed to be moving in slow motion all of a sudden, like the air was weighted down with the death of her dreams. Her ears roared. Lindsay was talking, but it sounded like a blur. Harper could only pick out random words here and there. Words like *plan, Lars,* and *fired.*

Harper wondered if she might be on the verge of fainting. She'd never fainted before, but surely this is what it felt like—straddling the dual realms of reality and a nightmare.

She wasn't going down without a fight. She headed toward the conference room, nodding at whatever Lindsay was saying, acting as if everything was normal. And just as she was about to step over the threshold, her phone vibrated.

She'd been clutching it like a child holding a teddy bear. Her last vestige of hope. But its sudden vibration still startled her. And immediately snapped her out of her panicked trance.

Please, please, please.

The word was a monosyllabic mantra in her head as she glanced down at the display.

Thanks for the coffee.

Her heart sank into her shoes. That was it? He was thanking her for the coffee?

Well, that was that, she supposed. She should have known he'd let her down. Just like Rick. Just like all those fathers.

She gave herself a good, mental kick for allowing herself to think for even a moment that he would have been different. Tom Stone didn't owe her anything. Why would he want to help? She was on her own, just as she'd always been. And now it was time to sit across from her department chairman and face the music.

She felt a sudden affinity with Sien, which was absurd. Harper was a professor, not an artist's muse. And surely not a prostitute. But at the moment, her sense of desperation was pretty intense. Not quite throw-herself-into-a-river intense, but close.

Poor Sien. Harper rolled her eyes. *Poor me.*

The department chair glanced up at Harper when she walked in, already frowning, as if he knew what was coming.

He nodded. "Dr. Higgins, good morning."

"Good morning." She smiled one of those wooden smiles she'd been practicing all day.

Her legs shook as she sat down. Surely, Dr. Martin could

hear her knees knocking together under the table.

She cleared her throat, suddenly anxious to just get it over with. "About the show. There's something I need to tell you."

"Yes?"

And then, her phone vibrated again. A tiny buzzing noise that to Harper's ears sounded more like a choir of angels.

"Um, as I was saying…" She glanced down as discreetly as possible.

Two words, comprised of only four letters. But they were more than enough.

I'm in.

Chapter Ten

HARPER SOMEHOW MANAGED to survive the meeting with Dr. Martin, even though her heart seemed to pound harder and harder with each lie she told.

She was sitting across from her boss pretending that her dog walker was a serious artist who'd learned to paint on the streets of Amsterdam. Did Tom even know where Amsterdam was?

Don't be ridiculous. He does. He was in the army. He's probably been all over the world.

Right. Because Amsterdam was such a hotbed of wartime activity.

She was losing it. The odds of actually getting away with this farce were slim to none. But it was too late. Random facts about a person who didn't exist were flying out of her mouth.

He's heavily influenced by Post-Impressionism, and his current body of work is reminiscent of Van Gogh's sunflower series for the Les Vingt show in Brussels in 1890.

His work has never been seen in a juried exhibition, but he's been approached by several galleries in Europe.

He's had no formal training, but his knowledge of fine arts is encyclopedic. He's a genius. Truly.

Where was she coming up with this stuff?

Tom Stone? A genius with an encyclopedic knowledge of

art? If she hadn't been so nauseous, she would have laughed out loud.

As it was, she practically had to clamp her mouth closed with her hands. The only thing that forced her to stop talking was the faint memory of an Oprah episode where she'd heard that people often gave too many details when they were lying about something.

Stop talking.

She sat back in her chair, and interlaced her hands on the tabletop to keep them from shaking.

Dr. Martin nodded thoughtfully. "Tom Stone certainly sounds intriguing."

You have no idea. "There's a rawness about his paintings I love. An aching quality."

At least that part was true.

Dr. Martin frowned. Harper's stomach churned. Frowning was not good. Not good at all. *Do something.*

What she should have done was tell the truth, or, at the very least, let Dr. Martin go ahead and turn the show over to Lars Klassen. Instead, she did the exact opposite. She told the biggest lie of them all.

"There's something else about Mr. Stone you should know." *He's a dog walker, not a painter. And despite the fact that I loathe the very sight of him, I kissed him last night.* "He's a descendent of Vincent Van Gogh."

Oh. God.

What had she done? She'd gone too far. Absolutely too far, but—

"I beg your pardon?" he said. But his frown suddenly disappeared.

Bingo.

"I'm sure you remember that Sien mothered a child when she lived with Van Gogh," she said.

"Yes, but wasn't she already pregnant when they met?"

"According to most accounts, yes. But there's speculation that Van Gogh himself was the father of the child." This was true. Sort of. At least Harper thought so. She remembered reading a blog somewhere that had proposed such a scenario. At the time, she'd dismissed it as nonsense. "A boy. Tom Stone's great-grandfather."

"I'm assuming this can't be confirmed."

"It can't. DNA testing wasn't around in Van Gogh's day." *Thank goodness.*

Dr. Martin nodded. "And you say he's talented? This Tom Stone?"

"Absolutely." Harper's voice had stopped shaking.

It was almost as though she believed the rubbish she was spouting. Not all of it was rubbish, though. Tom had the talent to pull this off.

"Okay, then," Mr. Martin said. "The department will certainly support your decision. I very much look forward to seeing what this young man can do."

You're not the only one. "I'm sure you won't be disappointed."

"I should hope not. It's quite unusual to switch gears like this so late in the game. What did Archer have to say about the change in plans? Do we have anything in writing with him? Because we absolutely cannot risk any kind of legal action. There's not an attorney involved is there?"

"I can promise you that our art show is nowhere on Archer's attorney's list of concerns." Surely, he had other things to worry about. Like parole. "The artist was quite cooperative regarding the change. In fact, he's planning on taking an extended break from his art for a while." Like until he retires his orange prison jumpsuit.

"Very well." Dr. Martin stood. "Thank you for your hard work on this, Harper."

She rose to shake his hand. "You're quite welcome, sir."

Her feet itched to run back to her office. She forced herself to go slowly, to put one foot calmly in front of the other as she made her way down the long corridor.

She was nearly home free, just ten feet away from her sanctuary—where she fully intended to shut the door and breathe into a paper bag until she came to terms with this strange new person she seemed to be turning into—when the last person she wanted to see poked his head out of the office opposite hers. "Harper."

"Lars." Was it her imagination, or was he looking at her strangely?

He knows.

Ugh. She was being ridiculous. How could he possibly know?

"How was your meeting with Dr. Martin this morning?" His eyebrows crept up his forehead.

So, this was a fishing expedition.

She smiled in a way she hoped was natural looking. "Fine, thank you."

"Everything in order for your show? Because if you need an artist..."

"I've got an artist. Everything is right on schedule." *Not that it's any of your business...*

He said something else, but Harper wasn't even sure what it was. She disappeared into her office before she might have to give him Tom's name. The last thing she needed was Lars poking his nose into Tom's imaginary background. That could get her into very real trouble.

Once inside, she leaned against the door, closed her eyes and tried to catch her breath.

"So?" someone called out, this time from inside her tiny office.

Harper's eyes flew open. "Lindsay. Gosh, you nearly frightened me to death."

"Sorry." Lindsay blinked. Once. Twice. Three times. "Tell me what happened. I'm dying here. Did he fire you?"

"No. Of course not." Harper straightened her pencil skirt and took a seat behind her desk.

"Did he take you off the show? Is Lars curating it now?" Lindsay glanced in the direction of their nemesis's office.

"Everything's great." Great. Really? "I mean, fine. I explained to Dr. Martin that I decided to change the direction of the show, so I replaced Archer."

"I know. You told him that yesterday. But there is no other artist." Lindsay was talking with exaggerated slowness, as though Harper were a five-year-old. Or suffering from some sort of mental break, which wasn't too far from the truth.

"*Was* no other artist," Harper corrected. "I have one now."

"You found a new artist in less than twenty-four hours?"

"Shhh. Please keep your voice down." She could just see Lars out in the hallway with a glass pressed against her door. "No one knows that part. And no one knows that Archer is in jail."

Yet. He was a celebrity of sorts. It was bound to make the news sooner or later. Another detail to contend with.

"Who's the artist?" Lindsay asked.

"His name is Tom Stone." *He paints in the Van Gogh tradition. In fact, he might even be an actual descendent of Vincent's. We're so lucky to have him.* "He's my dog walker."

WITHIN LESS THAN ten hours of sending Harper that fateful text message, Tom realized he'd been in no way prepared for what he'd gotten himself into. He'd expected days and nights of painting. He'd known he was going to have to look important people in the eye and lie to them about who he was, what he was.

But he hadn't quite been prepared to be schooled. Literally. And most thoroughly.

He'd had his ass on a stool at Art Bar for over two hours. Facts were flying from one end of the studio to the other. And he was being tag-teamed. Granted, the colleague of Harper's, who'd come along to help whip him into proper artistic shape, wasn't quite as intense as the good doctor. But, really, was that even a possibility?

"Where was Van Gogh born?"

"Where did Van Gogh die?"

"What is his most famous painting?"

"How many days did it take him to paint the first four paintings in the Sunflowers series?"

His head swiveled back and forth between the two of them

as he rattled off the answers. "Zundert, Netherlands. Auvers-sur-Oise, France. *Starry Night.* And four sunflower paintings in six days."

Tom's head was about to explode from the sheer amount of information that had been crammed into it by Harper and her cohort—someone named Lindsay who worked with Doc at the art college. Apparently, his transformation into an actual artist was going to be such an enormous undertaking that it required a team.

"Very good, Tom." Lindsay smiled and blinked a few times. He'd noticed she had some sort of eye tic problem. "Don't you think we can call it a night, Harper?"

Harper shook her head. "No. We haven't even begun to scratch the surface of Van Gogh. And we've got Boudin, Cassatt, Degas, Forain, Gauguin…"

"Stop." Tom held up a hand. "Just stop."

He had no idea what she was even saying. It sounded like a French ABC lesson. And he couldn't take any more.

He shifted on the stool where he'd been sitting. Harper had been pacing back and forth the entire evening, which made this feel more like an interrogation than an education. They'd begun at 9:00, when the class she'd taught at Art Bar had ended. Outside, the sky had grown darker, the shadows of night sliding further down the walls of the studio. Tom glanced at the clock. Midnight.

"We're done," he said.

Harper shook her head. "No."

Lindsay's eye tic kicked back into gear.

"Yes." He stood. "I already know more about Van Gogh than I do about myself. That's enough for one night, Doc."

"There's just so much ground we need to cover." She crossed her arms.

Tom felt like maybe he should back up a few steps before she started beating him with a ruler or something.

"Harper, he's right. We can't teach him everything in one night. We've gotten a good start, though. He'll be fine." Lindsay gave him another smile. "I've already planted blog posts and articles online suggesting Tom could be Vincent Van Gogh's great-great-grandson. We're good to go."

Harper shook her head. "But I told Dr. Martin that he's got an encyclopedic knowledge of classical art. *Encyclopedic!*"

"Harper, we can do this," Lindsay said. "But not all in one night."

At least someone seemed to believe he could pull this off. He'd begun to wonder. "I'm finished. I have nine dogs to walk tomorrow, including yours." He aimed a pointed look at Vincent, splayed belly up on his dog bed, snoring loud enough to peel the paint off the walls.

"Fine," she said in a tone that indicated it was anything but fine. "But you're free tomorrow night again at nine, aren't you?"

He started to make a crack about having a life in addition to walking dogs, painting, and this crash course in art history, but, in truth, he didn't. Besides, she was right. If they were going to pull this off, he had a lot to learn. Far more than he'd thought. "Sure. I can be here."

"I can't. Sorry." Lindsay looped a light grey scarf around her neck a few times and picked up her purse.

Harper frowned. "Wait. What do you mean you can't be here tomorrow?"

"I can't." Lindsay yawned. Gunner, tucked into a ball beside Vincent's dog bed, followed suit. "I have a date tomorrow night."

"A date?" Harper blinked in what looked like disbelief. "Can't you cancel?"

Now she was just being ridiculous. "Doc, be reasonable."

"I'll see you at work tomorrow, Harper. Tom, it was a pleasure meeting you." And with that, Lindsay bolted before Harper could ask her to sacrifice something else on the altar of his education.

Within seconds of her exit, the air in Art Bar grew thick with tension.

Tom shook his head. He was probably imagining things.

Then Harper glanced at him and quickly glanced away. Her authoritative persona seemed to have scooted out the door behind Lindsay. Tension. Definitely.

"Are you ready?" he asked. "Or do I need to regurgitate Van Gogh's shoe size in order to get out of here?"

"Very funny. You can go ahead and take off. I have a few things to clean up around here." She glanced around the pristine art studio and wrapped her arms around her waist.

What exactly was going on here? He highly doubted she had things to do. He'd watched her scrub every drop of paint off every surface in this place once her class had ended. He'd done a good part of the cleaning himself. He'd even gotten a glimpse of the cabinets where she kept the art supplies—row upon row of tubes of paint, each facing the same direction, labels lined up just so.

Tom shook his head. "You can't walk home alone, Doc. It's after midnight."

"I'll be fine. Really. Besides, I've got Vincent. He can fend off any attackers." Her stubborn streak was going to be the death of him over the course of the next two months.

He breathed out a sigh. "While that's probably true, I'm still not letting you walk home alone."

She picked up a neatly folded, white towel from the tray of her teaching easel and began wiping down one of the tables. Tom had eaten off dirtier surfaces. He watched her, wondering how long she was going to keep up this charade. Every so often he caught her stealing a glance at him. And when she tripped over one of the table legs, it dawned on him what was going on.

He took a step closer to her. She backed up three. Bingo.

"Doc, are you trying to avoid being alone with me?"

"What?" She sputtered. The towel slipped from between her fingers.

Tom couldn't help his thoughts straying to how much it looked like a white flag of surrender as it fluttered to the floor. And how, despite the fact that she drove him to the brink of insanity, he very much liked the idea of Harper Higgins' surrendering.

Again.

Don't go there.

He ground his teeth together. He'd never be entertaining such thoughts if she hadn't kissed him. Would he? No. Definitely not. Probably not, anyway.

But it was tough to shake the memory of their kiss. The warm, wet wonderland of her mouth. How quickly she'd melted against him when he'd pressed her against the wall. It would take more than a lingering case of post-concussion syndrome to make him forget something like that.

Her gaze darted all over the room—the colorful paintings hanging on the walls, the sleek, pine skeletons of the empty table easels, the rows upon rows of jewel-toned wine bottles. She looked at anything and everything other than him.

He waited, until finally she aimed a nervous glance in his direction.

He lifted an amused brow. "You appear to be avoiding being alone with me."

"Don't be ridiculous." Her words were confident, but the nervous tremor of her voice was not.

"That's what this is all about, isn't it? Your refusal to let me walk you home…pulling Lindsay into our little circle of trust…" He bent to pick up the towel.

She reached for it at the same time and their fingertips collided in a storm of sparks.

She jerked her hand back and stood. "I had no choice but to include Lindsay. She's the secretary in our department. She's the one who got the email from Archer's assistant."

"Who is Archer?" Tom folded the towel into a square and offered it to her.

She reached for it with tentative fingers and took it before their hands could touch again. "Archer is the artist whom you are replacing in the show."

"Ah. I suppose it's only a matter of time until I'm learning his shoe size as well."

She laughed, and Tom realized he hadn't heard her laugh often. If ever. Too bad. She had a great laugh.

"Not his shoe size. Just being aware of his existence is sufficient as far as Archer is concerned. And the fact that he's an aerosol artist."

"Aerosol artist? Like hairspray?"

Her brow furrowed. "Spray paint."

"That was a joke, Doc."

"Oh." She laughed, and at the sound of it, Tom realized that was what he'd been aiming for. Making her laugh again. "I can't believe it. Mr. Serious made a joke."

"Mr. Serious? Is that what you call me when I'm not around?"

"No." She smirked. "My pet name for you is actually the surly sailor."

Tom's jaw clenched. She thought that highly of him, did she?

"For the record, I prefer Mr. Serious. So long as those are the only two options."

She nodded. "Duly noted."

"And also for the record, you can relax. I'm not going to kiss you." He looked pointedly at her mouth.

"Kiss me?" The towel trembled in her hands. She was shaking.

Good. He'd done a fair bit of trembling himself when he'd thought back on their little encounter in his boat. It was nice to know he wasn't the only one who'd been shaken up a little.

A little? Who are you kidding?

She let out a fluttery, nervous, butterfly laugh. "Who said anything about kissing?"

"Nobody." He shrugged. "But you were thinking about it."

"Don't be ridiculous." She rolled her eyes.

Then her gaze settled on his lips and lingered there. A spike of arousal shot through him. And she'd done nothing but look at his mouth. God, he was in trouble. Of all the women in the world, why her?

"You thought about it when you left the boat last night. You were thinking about it tonight, before I even mentioned it. And you're thinking about it right now." He took a step closer, wondering if she'd back away.

She didn't.

Her gaze shifted to meet his and her lips parted. Ever so slightly, just enough to tell him she wanted his mouth on hers again. She wanted that kiss just as badly as he did.

He grinned down at her. "I'm not going to kiss you."

She swallowed. He traced the movement of it up and down the slender column of her throat. God, her neck. Lily white and perfect.

"You're not?" She breathed.

He shook his head and tried not to think about how her eyes had darkened with desire. Deep forest green, the perfect place to get lost for a while. "No, I'm not."

"Why not?" She blinked. "I mean I'm glad, of course. Because it would be inappropriate."

"Inappropriate." He echoed. "And why is that exactly? Other than the fact that we don't like each other."

He reached for a strand of her silky blonde hair and wrapped it around his fingers.

She licked her lips and her breathing grew shallow. Tom could see it in the quickening rise and fall of her breasts.

"We're working together now. It would be unprofessional. If anyone in my department found out about it, I'd be a laughing stock. I'm curating your show. It's an obvious conflict of interest. And, as you mentioned, we don't like each other."

"And that's exactly why I'm not going to kiss you." He gave

her hair a little tug. When she gasped, he released it. "Besides, you'll kiss me again in due time."

"Ha." She swatted him with the towel in her hand. "Don't flatter yourself, Mr. Serious. Last night was an accident."

"An accident? Is that what we're calling it?" He lifted a brow.

She turned three shades of red. Tom felt himself growing hard again. Why her flustered state affected him like this was a mystery he wasn't sure he wanted to examine.

She made a move to back away, but bumped into a stool in the process. So she crossed her arms and stayed where she was, mere inches away. "There's no *we,* okay? Other than our professional association. Understood?"

Understood?

He understood plenty.

He understood she was afraid to be alone with him because she didn't trust herself not to kiss him. He understood it was only a matter of time until he had her pinned against the wall again. He understood Harper Higgins wanted him.

What he didn't understand at all was why he wanted her just as badly.

He stared at her for a long, silent moment. He could feel the heat coming off her, could smell the wild orchid scent swirling around her upswept hair. When he saw her in this environment, surrounded by paint and creative energy, something inside him came undone. The art goddess in Harper Higgins was going to be the death of him.

Perhaps it was a good thing she kept that part of herself well under wraps.

He took a long, measured inhale. "Understood. Now get

your things together, Doc. It's time to go."

She lifted her chin. "I'm the one in charge around here, remember?"

"Whatever you say, Doc."

He could follow orders all day long. He was good at that. He could study, recite facts about all the artists she loved so much, and paint flowers until the sun came up. He'd given her his word to be ready for the gallery showing. And that was her baby. She was the boss, as far as that was concerned.

But if she thought either one of them was in charge of whatever heat there was simmering between them, she was sadly mistaken.

I'm the one in charge here, remember?

Right. *We'll see about that.*

Chapter Eleven

TWO DOZEN GIGGLING preteen girls, wearing tutus and hopped up on sugar, were somehow easier to control than Harper's usual roomful of twenty tipsy adults.

Tonight's art lesson was a private party rather than an ordinary Art Bar class. The party was a celebration of the twelfth birthday of Tiffany Webster, aspiring ballerina. So, naturally, Harper had chosen one of Edgar Degas's classic ballerina paintings as inspiration. She'd selected one of the paintings in his Dancers in Pink series, and had narrowed the image down to just the figure in the foreground—a ballerina dressed in a long, fluffy pink tutu, with her back to the artist. Perfect, really, because that meant the most challenging thing the girls had to paint was the back of the dancer's head. Peyton should be happy as a clam.

And she was. Happy, and more than a little frazzled.

"How in the world can you keep an eye on all these kids, much less their paintings?" Peyton rubbed her temples and ducked as a cupcake whizzed past her head.

Harper caught the cupcake midair. "Oh, come on, it's not so bad."

In truth, she loved the chaos. For one thing, her students were genuinely excited about what they were painting. There had been squeals of delight when she unveiled the completed model canvas. And as soon as they'd filled in the pink tutus with swirls of color, they'd all started posing for selfies beside their easels. It was awfully cute.

But even better than cute, it was a wonderful distraction from the fact that in exactly eighteen minutes, Tom would stroll through the door with Vincent in tow. And this time, Lindsay wouldn't be there to chaperone their tutoring session.

Harper inhaled a shaky breath, despising how just the thought of being alone with him somehow completely unraveled her. "Girls, it's time for the finishing touches. Everyone pick up baby bear."

She waved her smallest brush in the air and for once didn't give any thought to the silly nickname. Baby bear and his friends were the least of her worries. She showed the girls how to fill in the slim black choker around the dancer's neck and glanced at the clock again.

Sixteen more minutes.

Right. Like he would return with Vincent right on time. Not that it mattered. She didn't care if he was late this time.

"Harper, can you wrap things up here on your own? The blow dryers are all plugged in along the back wall. I've got to get out of here. I can't take another minute of Justin Bieber." Peyton winced.

Harper glanced at the iPod docking station on the sales counter. "Actually, I think that's One Direction, not the Biebs."

Peyton frowned. "I'm too old for this. How on earth do you know that?"

"This isn't my first ballerina party, remember?" Harper

dropped baby bear in a cup of water and wracked her brain for an excuse to get Peyton to stay a bit longer. Or possibly all night. "Do you really have to go? I can turn the music off. We're almost finished here. Stay." *Please.*

"Why? I don't think you need my help. You've done a great job tonight."

Everything within Harper told her to just drop it. Peyton had just given her a nice compliment. Finally, something was going her way at one of her jobs. Why push it?

Because I so desperately do not want to prove Tom Stone right.

He'd been so smug the night before—invading her personal space like that, bending ever so slightly, just slightly enough so she'd thought he was going to kiss her. She'd wanted him to kiss her. Every cell in her body wanted it. Waited for it.

Only he hadn't. He'd told her he knew how much she'd thought about it, how much she wanted it, that she would kiss him again in due time. He'd stood there with that tempting mouth of his, lit the match of her desire, and simply watched her burn.

It was wholly unsettling. Undeniably arousing. And one hundred percent unacceptable.

"Peyton, why don't you stick around for a while? Just for fun." *Yes, won't it be a rocking good time, keeping me from jumping my dog walker's bones?*

"Aren't you tutoring your private student tonight?"

Harper nodded. She'd told Peyton about Tom. Sort of. It had been a matter of necessity. She'd needed a place to conduct their lessons, and, for obvious reasons, neither her house nor his boat were viable options. So she'd asked permission to use the studio for a private tutoring project. "Yes. You can help. It'll be fun!"

Fun. Why did she keep saying that?

"As tempting as that sounds..." Peyton rolled her eyes. "I've been here all day. But you enjoy yourself."

"Will do." She pasted on a smile.

Enjoying herself was precisely what she was worried about. Perhaps she was fretting over nothing. Tom had been business as usual when he'd come to collect Vincent. In fact, he'd barely looked at her as he'd quietly walked into the studio with that ever-present cast on his foot and Gunner following obediently on his heels after he'd done his habitual sniff inspection of the entire studio. Goodness, that dog was like a robot. If these daily walks transformed Vincent into a dog that was one-tenth that calm and collected, they'd be worth every penny.

She sighed and asked the ballerinas to raise their hands if they needed any help with finishing touches. Only a handful wanted her assistance, so by the time Tom returned with Vincent—only two minutes late this time—he had to fight his way inside against a flow of exiting tutus and damp canvases.

He held the door open until all the girls had filed out, each of them giving Gunner and Vincent dozens of pats and hugs along the way. Gunner accepted all the attention with distinguished civility, while Vincent squirmed, writhed, and flopped on his back in ecstasy.

Once the parade of tulle had come to an end, Tom stepped inside and closed the door. Gunner immediately began sniffing the baseboards, sweeping from one end of the studio to the other in business-like fashion.

"Hello." Harper busied herself cleaning up a cupcake that had been ground into the floor, working more slowly than was necessary, scrubbing the tile until it gleamed. Anything to avoid looking Tom in the eye.

Really, Harper? Get a grip. You can't go the entire night without looking at him.

"Finished already, Doc?" he asked, his feet visible in her periphery. One was clad in a well-worn combat style boot and the other in his walking cast. "It's a little early, isn't it?"

"No, actually. It's 9:03." This was just silly. She stood up and leveled her gaze at him. Surely, she could look at the man without wanting to kiss him. "You're late."

She was nitpicking and she knew it. Anything to put some much needed distance between the two of them.

He glared at her. "Three whole minutes. I suppose a good flogging is in order."

"No, just a quiz." She placed the cleaning supplies neatly on the proper shelf in the supply cabinet and made a mental note they needed more 409. She spun back around to find Tom frowning at her. As per usual.

"A quiz?" he said flatly.

"Yes. I need to see if any of this information I've been throwing at you is sinking in." She picked up her ubiquitous legal pad, the one with the never-ending list of things she thought Tom should know. By the time this was over, she was going to need another pad. Or three.

"It's sunk. Trust me." He shook his head, exasperation written in every one of the fine lines near the corners of his eyes.

Why did laugh lines look so appealing on men? Better yet, how had Tom acquired any when he hardly cracked a smile?

He crossed his arms. "I don't need a quiz."

Was she imagining things, or did he seem unusually tense tonight? Great. That made two of them. "Well, you're getting one."

"Doc." He blew out a frustrated breath. "Let's just get started. Surely, you have three thousand or so facts all lined up for me to memorize tonight. The sooner we get going, the sooner we can get out of here."

She should have been pleased to realize he wanted to get this over with as much as she did. So why did she find his attitude so irksome?

"You're not afraid of a tiny pop quiz, are you?"

"Hardly." He lifted a challenging brow. "You're talking to the man who remembered you from the coffee shop back when you thought I sold flowers on the side of the road."

That again. "Okay then, hotshot. Let's see you put your money where your mouth is."

He looked at her for a long moment, until the irritation in his eyes began to smolder. "If you insist on quizzing me, we should at least make it interesting."

Alarm bells began going off in her head. But wasn't that what he wanted? For her to back down? *I don't think so.*

"What are you suggesting? A wager?"

The smolder in his gaze turned positively wicked. "A wager. What a great idea."

She fiddled with her notepad. Why were her hands shaking all of a sudden? "And what do you suggest for our terms?"

"Let's keep it simple." He glanced at her throat, her waist, her legs, leaving a hot trail of want in every place his gaze traveled. "An article of clothing for each question."

The notepad slipped from Harper's fingers, landing on the

tile floor with a splat. She told herself to bend down and pick it up. There was no need to get all flustered. He wasn't serious, of course. He was just teasing her, as usual. He'd never actually go through with it.

She couldn't seem to make herself move.

Tom collected the legal pad from the floor and handed it to her. "You know what they say about all work and no play, Doc. Or would you rather forget the pop quiz altogether?"

So that was what he was after. He wanted to run the show. Well, that was *so* not happening. She didn't have anything to worry about, anyway. She was still wearing her artist's smock from class. She had socks, shoes, earrings, jeans, and a shirt beneath her sweater. More importantly, she had a list of ten rather difficult questions. She would win this thing hands down. And when she did, would it really be so awful to get a glimpse of what was going on under that t-shirt of his?

She studiously ignored the fact this was exactly the sort of thing she'd been worried about when she realized they would be alone together all night.

But she had the upper hand here. Didn't she?

She nodded and stuck out her hand. "Deal."

ONLY HARPER HIGGINS would want to shake over something so ridiculously close in theory to strip poker.

Tom glanced at her outstretched hand and noticed a faint tremor. Always so nervous.

"You sure about this, Doc?"

He'd been joking. Obviously. Simply giving her a hard

time. He'd had no intention of really going through with it. He knew she wouldn't have either.

Except that it appeared as though she did.

"One hundred percent, unless you've changed your mind." She leveled her gaze at him and gave her petite chin a haughty jerk upward.

He'd been more than willing to back down and let her off the hook until that snooty little gesture. It was time for the good doctor to get what she had coming.

He reached for her hand, letting his fingertips slide against hers ever so slowly, torturously, until her palm came to rest in his. "Let's do this."

"Yes, let's." She nodded, a slow, mesmerizing move of her beautiful head.

Like it always did, Tom's attention fixated on the locks of hair that had escaped from her bun. Spun gold, just begging to be wrapped around his fingers. "Doc?"

"Yes?" She was breathless, as though she could read his mind.

Tom had never been gladder that she couldn't, and he would have given his left arm to know what was going on in her head at the moment. "Are you going to ask me a question now?"

"Oh." She dropped his hand as if it was on fire. "Yes. Yes, of course."

He sat on the closest stool and waited.

She cleared her throat, then consulted her scribbled-upon legal pad that she carried around everywhere, flipping from one page to the next to the next.

She was wound tighter than he'd ever seen her before,

which was saying a lot. "Any day now, Doc."

She slammed the notepad down on the table. "All right. Since you're so anxious."

Then she sauntered off across the room, leaving Tom to wonder exactly what she had up that academic sleeve of hers. He sat back and watched as she plucked her freshly painted canvas from her easel, walked back toward him and came to rest standing just a few feet away with the painting between them. An exquisitely rendered barrier of color, form and composition. Art.

He glanced at the picture—a ballerina with porcelain shoulders, upswept hair, posing in a fluffy pink cloud of a dress. Pretty. Very pretty.

Harper moved the canvas a fraction closer. "Tell me what you know about this painting."

So this is how she was going to play it? *I don't think so.* "That's not a question."

She shrugged, but her cheeks glowed pink. She knew perfectly well what she was doing. "Sure it is."

"It's too open-ended. There's no definite answer. Don't be a cheater, Doc." He knew that would get her.

Sure enough, it did. Her pink glow intensified, until her complexion matched the color of the ballerina's dress in her painting. *Pretty as a picture.* "Fine. Name the artist of the painting that inspired this reproduction."

He could have answered that question in his sleep. Did she really have so little faith in him? "Hmm. That's a tough one."

"Prepared to give up"—she glanced at his chest—"your shirt?"

Oh, this was going to be fun. "My shirt? Going straight for

the jackpot, are we?"

"Like you wouldn't do the same." She pursed her lips. "If you knew the answer, which apparently you don't."

He shook his head. "A shame. And to think you would have been willing to shed your shirt."

"That's how the game is played. And, as I said before, I'm no cheater." She smiled.

So pleased with herself. So confident. So very, very wrong.

"I suppose I should at least venture a guess." He crossed his arms and pretended to study the canvas as Harper tapped her foot happily against the tile floor, gloating already. "Let's see. This is just a stab in the dark, mind you."

"Stop stalling or lose your shirt." Her smile was exaggeratedly sweet, oversolicitous. He was about to wipe it right off her face.

He glanced at the canvas for a fraction of a second and then fixed his gaze back on her. "Edgar Degas. French Impressionist. *Dancers in Pink.* Or in your case, *Dancer in Pink.* Singular. You've eliminated the other dancers—four, also dressed in pink, in the foreground, plus two wearing blue in the background. The exact date is unknown, but historians guess it was painted sometime during the 1880's."

He watched as the blood drained from her face. Her eyes grew wide, brighter than ever before, like a verdant, green forest of memory. For a moment, he thought the painting might slip right out of her hands. And when those cherry lips of hers parted and then abruptly closed again, Tom realized he'd done the impossible.

He'd rendered Harper Higgins speechless.

Chapter Twelve

HARPER COULDN'T BELIEVE her ears. She might as well have been listening to a robot. An art scholar robot with Tom Stone's glorious Renaissance physique—the physique she'd thought she was about to get a good look at, up close and personal.

What had just happened? Tom should be standing there with a chest as bare as Michelangelo's David right now.

"Doc?" He angled his head.

His gorgeous head, which suddenly seemed more gorgeous than ever, now that she knew he had a catalog of art facts floating around in it. Or at least Degas-specific art facts.

"Yes?" She blinked, her mind awhirl. And then the shock of his perfect answer began to wear off, and she realized if he didn't have to take off his shirt, it meant she did. "I mean no. *No.*"

"No? You're not trying to tell me I got the answer wrong, are you? Because I'm fairly confident in its accuracy." He smiled. It was maybe the first genuine smile she'd ever seen cross his lips.

Fairly confident, my foot. He'd known exactly what he was doing all along. "You tricked me."

"I did no such thing. I got the answer right, fair and square.

Six times over, by my count. And now it's time you paid the price." He wrapped his hands around hers and slipped the painting from her grasp.

She watched as he returned it to its place on the easel at the front of the classroom, wrapping her arms around herself. A not-so-unconscious reaction to the thought of disrobing in the glaring studio lights of Art Bar. She felt a sudden, sharp stab of sympathy for every nude model who had posed in her figure drawing classes back in art school.

God, why in the world had she agreed to this nonsense?

Because you thought you would win.

Because you never back down from a challenge.

Because you thought Tom Stone would be standing here half-dressed right now.

He strode back toward her. Slowly. Deliberately. His footsteps were so quiet neither Gunner nor Vincent stirred the slightest bit when he walked past them. They were far away in dreamland. How Harper envied them.

Tom closed the remaining distance between them, coming to a stop less than a foot away.

"Harper," he said, his voice uncharacteristically tender.

A lump formed in her throat. Hearing him say her name like that—her *real* name—coupled with the soft sea of blue in his eyes as he looked at her, made her feel more naked than if she'd stepped out of every stitch of clothing on her back.

She unwound her arms from around her body, slipped the paint-splattered artist smock over her head and dropped it on the floor. Her heart thumped so hard that she wondered if he could hear it, pounding away like thunder. Van Gogh's familiar words danced in her memory, only this time they pirouetted with new life. No longer a comfort or reassurance, but a call to adventure. Wild, chaotic, colorful adventure. Like a Jackson Pollock painting come to life. Fearless.

I am seeking. I am striving. I am in it with all my heart.

Without taking her eyes off Tom's, she reached for the hem of her sweater. Just as a cool shock of air hit the bare skin of her tummy, he stilled her hands with his. His fingers were warm, so warm. And his hands as big and strong as those of a Rodin sculpture. Yet his touch was somehow reverent as he pulled the hem of her sweater back in place.

He cupped her chin in one of his big hands and murmured, "I've a mind to start elsewhere, Doc."

Before she could even begin to imagine what he had up his sleeve, he reached up and slid the paintbrushes from her hair—the ones she always used to hold her bun in place. First one and then the other. Harper gasped as her chignon came loose, and her hair tumbled over her shoulders, cascading down her back. Then Tom's hands were in her hair. And the slow, graceful slide of his fingertips against her scalp, coupled with the way he was looking at her—as though she were a work of art—was unquestionably the most sensual moment of her entire life.

He twirled a lock of hair around his finger and gave it a gentle tug before whispering a single word. "Beautiful."

For once, that was exactly how she felt. Beautiful. Free. Like a creature of desire. Like art.

So she really couldn't help herself. Even though she'd vowed not to, even though she knew she'd come to regret it later, she did the one thing she'd been trying so desperately to avoid. She kissed him.

Again.

This time he seemed to know it was coming. As she pressed her wanting lips to his, his hands immediately slid back into her hair. And it felt so good, so perfect, that she sighed into his mouth. Purred like a kitten. To her recollection, such a noise had never escaped her mouth before. Then again, she'd never been kissed by the likes of Tom Stone.

He'd turned the tables at once. She was no longer the one doing the kissing. It was all him—his seeking mouth, his probing tongue, the warmth of his firm body pressed against hers as he backed her into the studio wall.

And she was grateful for that wall, because without it there to support her, she likely would have melted into a pool of liquid desire right there on the tile floor of Art Bar. Tom's quiet demeanor, his brooding seriousness Harper found so unnerving most of the time had only hinted at the man behind the mask of indifference. This was a kiss that bespoke of power. Pure, masculine power.

All her careful control, all her cherished independence was no match for the concentration of desire swirling in her mind and body. She gripped at his shirt with needy fingers, fingers she scarcely recognized as her own. Fingers that yanked his shirt up and over his head, so at last she was looking at his muscular, bare chest. Exploring his perfect form with her gaze and her touch, dipping her fingertips in the grooves between his abdominal muscles.

God, he was perfect. So perfect she wanted nothing more than to bend down and lick his sinuous form. But just as she dipped her head, Tom's fist tightened around the hair at the nape of her neck and pulled. Not so hard as to cause pain, but firm enough so her head fell back and she found herself looking up at him in astonishment.

He'd pulled her hair. She shouldn't have liked it. It definitely shouldn't have aroused her. But she did, and it had. Oh, how it had.

Another purr escaped her. It rose up from her soul and passed through her lips where it was instantly swallowed by Tom's hungry mouth. Harper's knees buckled. She slumped against the wall, and Tom's free hand—the one that wasn't wound in her hair—wrapped around her waist, hauling her upward so their lips never parted. The kiss remained unbroken, eternal. She was drowning in it, being dragged under by a torrential flood of desire. And there was no kicking against the current, no struggle to find her breath. There was no burning in her throat and lungs, other than the hot sting of sudden, overwhelming longing. She got the sense if she opened her eyes, she would find she was on the bottom of the ocean, looking up at the surface of the water. Heavy with desire, weighted down, and perfectly accepting of her fate.

Tom broke the kiss and stared down at her, his eyes ablaze with cool, blue ice-fire. "God, Doc." He breathed, resting his forehead against hers.

"I know, I know," she whispered, raising her mouth for more, her thoughts snagging only briefly on the irony of her words.

I know…I know.

She knew nothing. She didn't know why she'd reacted to him like she had. What was it about this man? She'd known plenty of artists before. She'd kissed other artists. But it had never felt like this. Never. Not with Rick. Not with anyone. The one thing she did know, the most important thing of all, was that somehow Tom felt it, too.

This kiss was different. It was a masterpiece, a work of art that outshone anything Harper had ever before seen, felt, painted, or experienced.

His mouth came crashing down on hers, and with sweet, tortured relief, she tasted him again. Minty warmth. A slight hint of vanilla. He ground into her, and she felt the hardness of his arousal pressing against her belly. She leaned into it, drawing a moan from him. Her body was no longer her own, no longer controlled by all her rules, all her rigid expectations. No amount of thinking could stop her from giving herself to him in that heated moment. There was nothing that could stop what was about to happen.

Save for one thing—her boss's sudden, shocked howl. "Harper?!"

AS INTRODUCTIONS WENT, it was memorable.

Tom was shirtless and hard to the point of pain, but he did his best to pretend everything was as normal as could be while he shook hands with the woman who'd brought an abrupt end to the most erotic tutoring session in the history of art education.

"Tom Stone," he said through a clenched jaw.

He hadn't foreseen being interrupted when he was on the verge of taking Harper Higgins against the wall. He hadn't foreseen *anything* about this night.

"Peyton Winslow." Her gaze flitted briefly to Harper, who'd somehow managed to rearrange her features back into her doctor persona, then back at him. "Why does your name sound familiar?"

Harper cleared her throat. "I told you about Mr. Stone, remember?"

Tom raised an incredulous brow. *Mr. Stone?* That was a first. Once again, they'd grown simultaneously closer together and farther apart.

"He's my student." Harper smoothed down her hair.

Tom did his best not to stare. He could still feel the silky smoothness of those luxurious blonde waves as he'd wrapped them around his fingers. A phantom touch. A memory that would no doubt stay with him when he lay alone in his bed tonight.

She looked at him, and he wondered if she would allow herself to remember. Somehow he doubted it.

"Tom, Peyton owns Art Bar."

Which made her Harper's boss. Great.

He nodded. "Nice place you've got here."

It was perhaps the dumbest thing that could have come out of his mouth. Definitely the dumbest, if the look on Harper's face was any indication. Could she cut him an ounce of slack? To say the turn of events had caught him off guard would be an understatement.

"Thank you, Mr. Stone." Peyton bit her lip, no doubt to keep from laughing.

He wished she would. All three of them should be laughing right now. This wasn't high school. He and Harper were consenting adults, after all.

He glanced at Harper. She definitely didn't appear to be on the verge of laughter. In fact, she looked mad. Downright pissed off. "Tom is the student I've been tutoring."

"Obviously. It appears you've been working really hard," Peyton said drily. "What happened to your foot, Mr. Stone?" She gestured toward the air-cast.

"I was attacked by a crazy dog." He glanced at Harper. Pissed off. Definitely. "Sorry. I meant I was attacked by a spirited and bright dog."

Vincent barked in his sleep.

Peyton turned her attention back to Harper. "I'm sorry to interrupt the education of Mr. Stone, but I forgot my purse." She walked toward the front counter, presumably to fetch her forgotten bag.

Harper was hot on her heels. "Peyton, this is not what it looks like. I assure you."

Isn't it? Tom reached for his shirt and pulled it over his head.

"Harper, it's after hours. What you do on your own time is your business." Peyton glanced at Tom.

He was beginning to feel like an oddity, an abstract painting on a wall of old school portraits.

"That being said, this is still my studio," Peyton continued.

"Yes, I know." Harper nodded. "And I assure you that this will not happen again."

Tom tucked his shirt in with more force than necessary.

"There's no need to make assurances. But I might expect you to make other concessions..." Peyton crossed her arms and stared pointedly at the canvas on display by the cash register. A white winged cartoon character. Kinda cute actually.

"Oh." Harper released a weary exhale. "I see."

"Good." Peyton beamed. "I suppose I'll be going now so

you two can get back to work."

"Not necessary. We're finished here." Harper grabbed Vincent's leash off the counter and clipped it onto his collar.

The little dog yawned and climbed out of his dog bed. Gunner's ears pricked forward as he looked at Tom and waited for instructions.

"Come on, boy. Time to go home," Tom said.

He wasn't altogether sure what had just transpired, but whatever it was had put an end to his tutoring session, an end to Harper's pop quiz and perhaps worst of all, an end to that phenomenal kiss.

HARPER WALKED SIDE-BY-SIDE with Tom toward the harbor while the dogs trotted out in front, tails wagging and paws falling on the cobblestones with soft nighttime whispers. So far, the walk had been a silent one, and for that she was grateful.

My boss just walked in on me on the verge of having sex in the workplace.

Granted, it wasn't her real job. It was just Art Bar. But if things didn't go as planned with Tom's gallery show, Art Bar might become her real job. Her *only* job.

And now, all because Peyton had caught her in a most compromising position, she was going to have to break down and paint some originals. Hearts, flowers, marshmallow people. What was next? Dogs playing poker, maybe?

How had this happened? It was like she'd somehow become another person. Another person who did things like play art-themed strip poker at her place of business and passionately kiss a man she didn't even like.

Except she sort of did like Tom now, didn't she?

She snuck a glance at him walking quietly beside her. They hadn't said more than two words to one another since leaving Art Bar. Twenty minutes ago, she'd been sighing into his mouth and now it was as though nothing had ever happened.

But that was for the best, wasn't it?

She didn't want to become one of those women. Women like her mother. The ones who were dependent on men. And right now that would be all too easy, considering her career was currently in crisis. Not to mention the fact there was too much riding on this charade to risk any kind of romantic entanglement.

They had work to do. A lot of it. So much that it frightened her when she thought about it seriously. She'd spent the afternoon in her office at the college making a list of anything and everything that Dr. Martin or the rest of the faculty might ask Tom at the art opening. It had filled her entire yellow legal pad. He might know everything there was to know about Degas's *Dancers in Pink*, but that didn't mean he was ready to impersonate a descendent of one of the most famous artists in the word. Or a man with an encyclopedic knowledge of art. The amount of information he had to learn was staggering. And tonight had suddenly become a complete and total loss.

They would start over again tomorrow. Everything would be fine. Lindsay was free tomorrow night, so there was no way Harper could accidentally kiss Tom again. It was too late to get any more work done tonight anyway.

The moon had risen to the very top of the starry sky. The fog from the previous few nights had lifted, leaving the night as smooth and black as velvet. Walking under such a clear, dark sky, Harper was reminded of a rhyme she'd first heard in art school.

Black is the color of colors, and yet the color of none. When all the colors mix together, the color left is the one farthest from the sun.

She'd always found a certain beauty in pure, unadulterated black. Like the utter stillness of outer space. To Harper, it was a quiet, soulful color.

She glanced at Tom again, strolling beside her in the shadows of the harbor walk, and thought about all the colorful drops of paint that littered his easel.

She should say something to him. The silence between them was starting to feel awkward. "Do you have any questions about Degas? Van Gogh? Anything that we've gone over so far?"

He gave her a sideways look. "Just one, if you don't mind my asking."

"Ask away."

"Why are you doing this?" he asked.

The question caught her off guard. She'd meant questions about Van Gogh or any of the other ten thousand things they'd been studying. "I told you. Archer is sitting in a jail cell in New York. I needed someone else."

"But why not find a real artist?"

She wished he'd stop thinking of himself that way. Granted, he didn't know a Picasso from a kindergarten painting. But soon he would. More importantly, he had an artist's eye. And she suspected underneath all that brooding disinterest, he had an artist's soul. He couldn't paint like he did if he didn't.

Stop. This is the kind of thinking that keeps getting you into trouble.

She cleared her throat. "There wasn't time. If I didn't come up with someone immediately, I would have lost my chance to curate the show. I'm competing with another adjunct professor at the school for the promotion next fall. His name is Lars Klassen, and he had an artist that was available. The department chair would have given Lars the curatorial job, and I would have been out of the running."

"And this promotion is that important?" His voice was quiet in the night. Calm, as though part of the darkness. The dogs didn't even swivel their heads at the sound of it, but kept walking out in front.

"Of course it is. Who knows when I'll get another shot at tenured faculty? And if I get this job I can teach full-time." When *I get the job. Not* if. *When.*

"But you do teach. At Art Bar." He didn't get it. Not at all.

"That's not teaching." It was more akin to babysitting. Even more so, now that most of her classes would no longer center around master reproductions.

Tom shrugged. "It looks like teaching to me."

Looks sure could be deceiving. "Well, it's not. Not real teaching, anyway. Most of the people who come into Art Bar aren't serious about art. They don't care about the history of the painting they're reproducing, or why the artist created it in the first place. They just want to paint a pretty picture and have a good time."

"And what's wrong with that?"

"Nothing, I suppose." It just wasn't what she'd trained for. And it certainly wasn't a serious career.

They rounded the corner where the coffee shop stood. Its lights were turned off, the window shades pulled down. She could see Tom's boat from here, and her little cottage was only a block away.

"What is the purpose of art, Doc?" Tom glanced at her again. In the dim light of the streetlamps, she could see glints of gold in those Monet blue eyes of his. "Remembering the past, or looking for the beauty of the present?"

Harper's throat grew tight all of a sudden. He had a point. A rather eloquent one at that.

Tom Stone, you are just full of surprises.

"The purpose of art is a topic that's been hotly debated for centuries. I'm not sure there's a clear-cut answer on that one." Off the top of her head, Harper could think of six different theories.

"Good. That's one less thing I have to memorize in addition to Van Gogh's shoe size." Tom gave her a sardonic grin.

Another joke. Would wonders never cease? "I know you're only joking about Van Gogh's shoes, but he painted them, you know."

Tom looked at his feet, one in a shoe and the other in its cast, then back up at Harper. "He painted his shoes?"

They'd reached her cottage. For once, Vincent wasn't in a massive hurry to drag her inside. Probably because the object of his devotion was standing in the middle of the street instead of heading for the front porch.

"Yes. Several times. Worn, beat up shoes. Shoes that had seen a lot of miles. One of his fellow students in Paris said he bought the first pair of shoes he wanted to paint at a flea market, but still thought they were too pristine to paint. So he wore them on a long walk in the rain, and only then were they fit to be painted."

Tom actually looked interested, which was shocking considering the late hour and all the surprising detours this unusual night had taken. "So, Miss Van Gogh Expert. Why do you think my 'great-great-grandfather' only wanted to paint beat-up shoes?"

Miss Van Gogh Expert. Sarcastic as that was, she much preferred that to being called Doc. Although not quite as much as that tender moment when he'd actually called her by her name.

"Critics say the shoes were a symbol of the struggle of the day laborer, but I tend to disagree. I like to think his intention was broader, more universal. Maybe what he was really trying to say was that things that have been damaged by life can still be beautiful."

"I like that, Doc. I like that a lot." Something about the way he studied her made her overlook the fact that he'd switched back to calling her *Doc*.

She shifted her weight from one foot to the other, suddenly anxious to get inside. This was beginning to feel almost pleasant, and that sort of interaction needed to stop. Immediately.

She dug around in her handbag and pulled out her keys. "Thank you for walking me home. It wasn't necessary, but thank you."

"Yes, it was. And you're welcome." He gave a casual wave and turned to go.

She had the sudden urge to say something before he left. Something about his art. "You know, Tom. Your violets are like Van Gogh's shoes."

His footsteps slowed and he turned back to gaze at her

quizzically. She tried mightily to ignore the way the double luminaire of the old-fashioned streetlights bathed him in a mystical, warm glow. Like candlelight.

"My violets?" His brow furrowed.

"Yes." There was an unusual tightness in her throat all of a sudden. "Your painting—the one you did the night we met. The way you made those flowers look so lovely, even though they were damp and wilted. Damaged but beautiful. That painting is what convinced me this would work. And it will."

His work possessed what hers had always lacked—depth. Meaning. She was beginning to wonder if all those critics had been right when they'd called her shallow. She wasn't sure she'd ever really poured herself into a painting like he did. Hers had been technically perfect, but all those emotions that she tried to keep so firmly under wrap had never made their way onto her canvas. As much as she hated to admit it, Rick hadn't been completely wrong in his assessment. The fact that it had come from someone who'd supposedly cared about her at the time still didn't make it any easier to stomach.

She'd thought she and Rick had been the real thing. But looking back, he'd never cared about her as much as she had about him. She would have never dreamed of saying a word to hurt him, even if it had been true. But what did she know about love that was real? She'd never seen real love, much less felt it in her soul.

Life should be simpler. People should be able to tell when something was real and when it wasn't.

Harper swallowed around the lump in her throat. "You're a real artist, Tom. You are."

He shook his head. "I'm not, Doc. I'm just a guy who

paints because he can't sleep at night."

Then he did walk away, and the darkness that Harper had found so poetic only minutes before seemed to swallow him up. By the time his words had reached her, he and Gunner had begun to fade. Two ghosts in the night.

Chapter Thirteen

"I SEE THERE'S been a significant change in your life." Frank wiped his hands on the front of his florist's apron and looked Tom up and down.

He wasn't quite sure how to respond to that. His first thought was that maybe all the facts Harper had been drilling into his head over the course of the past two weeks had begun to spill out. Perhaps there were dates, names and tiny little paintings falling out of his ears. "A change?"

"Your foot." Frank gestured with a pair of dangerously sharp-looking scissors.

Oh, right. The air cast, or rather the absence thereof. "Yeah, it's pretty much healed."

"Good for you." Frank grinned. "I just got a new shipment in this morning. Some really beautiful flowers. Tell me I can sell you something special for your lady this time. No bargain basement flowers. Just this once."

Tom shook his head. "Sorry. Just the usual again. Give me the cheapest you've got."

Frank sighed. "All right, all right. But someday you're going to come in here and I'm going to sell you the flowers that will sweep your girl off her feet."

He was going to have to say something. It was starting feel

wrong letting Frank believe he was in love or something, when he so clearly wasn't. "There's no girl."

"Sure there is." Frank waved a dismissive hand at him as he stepped into the big, walk-in cooler. He returned carrying a bundle of blooms in his arms.

Tom spied a glimpse of yellow swirled with orange nestled among the tissue paper, but he couldn't tell what kind of flowers they were. "There's not. I assure you."

"There's always a girl. Trust me. You live long enough, you know these things." Frank opened the tissue paper to reveal a generous pile of tulips.

They were yellow, tipped with bright orange, as if they'd been kissed by flames. More than a little wilted, but that would work. *Damaged by life but still beautiful.*

Plus, they were Dutch. Straight from the land of Van Gogh. Harper would no doubt swoon over that particular detail.

Frank picked up the scissors and began removing about a quarter inch from the ends of the tulip stems. "There's either a girl in your arms or one who you wish was there. So which is it?"

Tom was starting to regret he'd said anything about the nonexistent girl. "Neither."

Frank shrugged.

Any other florist would have probably asked why he bought so many flowers. If he wasn't giving them to a sweetheart, just what was he doing with them? Not Frank. And that was why Tom liked Frank. He didn't ask a bunch of questions. Not usually, anyway. Today was somewhat of an exception.

Tom had been answering a lot of questions lately. Harper

and Lindsay had really been putting him through the paces. On the rare occasion when Lindsay couldn't make it, things were even more intense. Harper was all business. Gone was the woman who'd risen up in flames the moment he'd touched her, the woman whose fingertips had explored him as if he were a gift she'd waited for all her life, the art goddess he'd found so enchanting.

And, God, did he miss her. More than he should have. Far more.

Not that she was anywhere close to being relaxed when Lindsay was around. But in her absence, she seemed even more meticulously precise than usual, ticking down the list of things on her yellow legal pad with unrelenting scrutiny. She also bumped into things an awful lot on those evenings. Once she'd dropped a stapler on his foot. Luckily, he'd still been wearing the air cast at the time so it had just bounced off and he'd escaped without further injury.

"Will these work for you, then? They're a week old." Frank gestured toward the tulips. "You can have them for seventy-five percent off."

"Yes, thank you. I don't think I've ever seen multi-colored tulips before," Tom said, running one of the long green stems through his fingers.

"They're not as common as the other colors, but we get them on occasion. I was surprised to see them this time of year, though, what with winter coming early." Frank continued cutting. *Snip, snip, snip.*

Tom let the flower slip from his fingers. "Winter's coming early?"

"Yep. And it's supposed to be a bad one."

Great. He'd been so busy studying art history, art present, and art future that he'd pushed the winter problem to the back of his mind. He was in a race against nature, and this race was the reason he'd signed on for the crazy art scheme to begin with. Selling those paintings was the only way he could get ahead of this thing. "How bad of a winter exactly?"

"Bad. They're predicting record lows and a much earlier freeze." Finished trimming the stems, Frank wrapped the flowers in a fresh, crisp layer of green tissue paper and tied the bundle with a string.

Tom handed him a few dollar bills from his wallet. "Good to know." *Not that I can do anything about it yet...*

"Tulips are clever, though. They're known for blooming early and outsmarting the winter in tough years. Always prepared, tulips."

Always prepared. Like the boy scouts.

Too bad Tom had never been much of a boy scout.

"Thanks, Frank." He slid his wallet back in his pocket and took the wrapped bundle of flowers.

"See you tomorrow." He held up a hand. A stationary wave. "Just so you know, those variegated tulips have a special meaning."

Tom was almost afraid to ask. Did these particular tulips mean he'd freeze to death by Halloween? "And what is that, exactly?"

"They mean *beautiful eyes.* So tell your girl how pretty her eyes are when you give them to her." The lines around Frank's eyes creased deeper as he smiled.

"There's no girl, Frank."

Frank slid a vase of flowers to the center of the counter and reverently plucked away a few dried petals. Only hands that had seen the unfathomable horrors of battle could worship the simple beauty of a flower like that. "Like I said before, there's always a girl."

Tom shook his head. He knew better than to entertain notions of inviting someone into the mess that was left of him. If he couldn't make a marriage work for longer than a handful of days back before all the pain, all the loss, how was he supposed to hold one together now? He lived on a boat. The only meaningful relationship in his life that he'd successfully maintained was with a dog. He couldn't even sleep through the night. And now, he was living someone else's life—one of a person who didn't even exist. He had nothing to offer this hypothetical girl Frank spoke of.

Funny how the thought of that hypothetical girl brought back memories of being kissed by Harper Higgins. Then again, those were memories that Tom had found difficult to shake. Just when he'd thought he'd pushed it as far back in his mind as he could, she would do something; move in the subtlest of ways—tuck her hair behind her ear, exposing her lily white neck, gesture toward a picture of a painting with one of those hands that she'd so elegantly run over his body with tremulous longing—and it all came rushing back.

By all appearances, she'd forgotten about their trysts. On the surface of things, it was as if their lips had never touched. She still looked at him in disbelief and exasperation half the time they spent in one another's company. But every so often, usually when he showed her a new painting he'd been working on for the show, he would catch a glimpse of whatever ran deeper. And in the rarest of moments he could see. She remembered. No matter how much she didn't want to.

Some memories were like that. They lingered. The more one tried to forget them, the more demanding they became. Sometimes they changed, taking on new forms and shapes. But they were always, always there. Like the melting clocks in that painting. *The Persistence of Memory.*

"Bye, Frank." He backed away from the counter. Gunner sprang to his feet to follow.

Frank cast a final glance at the tulips in Tom's arms. "Beautiful eyes. Don't forget."

Tom just shook his head and kept walking.

Beautiful eyes.

If Harper's eyes were the ones that came to mind, he preferred to believe it was because she was the female he'd been spending the most time with lately who didn't have four legs and a tail. Besides, he had bigger problems than Harper, her haunting, emerald eyes, and the most persistent memory of her mouth at the moment.

A sudden chill bit through his jacket as he pushed through the heavy plastic coating of the doorway and out onto the creaky wooden walkway lining the harbor. A seagull sat on a nearby wooden post, its feathers rippling in the wind. The churning water appeared frosted, tipped with whitecaps dancing and leaping over the edge of boats filled with shivering tourists. The flag on the Congress Street Bridge by the Tea Party museum shuddered, wrapping itself completely around the flagpole.

A foreboding shiver coursed through Tom.

Ready or not, winter was coming.

HARPER SAT BESIDE Lindsay on the park bench and watched as her napkin blew away in a whirlwind of brisk, salty air. Before she could even think of running after it, it had disappeared from view. "Goodness, it's windy today."

"And cold." Lindsay's teeth chattered. "The leaves have just started to change. It shouldn't be this cold yet."

If Harper had realized a cool front was blowing in—literally—she wouldn't have suggested this picnic lunch. They had things to discuss. Things they definitely could not talk about at the college. But she could have found someplace warmer, someplace where her sandwich wasn't about to blow right out of her hands.

"So, what do you think of Tom? Be honest." Harper took a nibble of her PB & J and stuck the remainder of it back in her canvas lunch bag.

She was too nervous to eat. Too nervous to do much of anything.

So long as she was actively working toward the success of the show, she was fine. Of course, that basically meant that any time she wasn't tutoring Tom or looking at his paintings, she was a wreck. Not convenient, to say the least.

"I like him." Beside her, Lindsay was inhaling a Tupperware container full of tuna salad. Clearly she wasn't suffering from the inability to eat. But her career wasn't the one on the line, was it? "Don't you?"

Yes. No. Maybe. "It's not about liking him. It's about if you think he can pass as a real artist?"

Lindsay eyed her over the rim of her plastic bowl. "How

would I know? You haven't let me see any of his paintings."

That again.

Lindsay had been anxious to see Tom's art since that fateful day he'd agreed to play the role of artist in the melodrama that had become Harper's life. She wasn't entirely sure why she was keeping them under wraps, other than she wanted everyone to see them properly. As a collection. Hung with care on smooth white walls to best show them off. A canvas for the canvases, in a way.

Because that was how they deserved to be seen.

If she was being completely honest with herself, she had to admit that she also liked the idea of being the only one who'd seen them thus far. As if they belonged to her in some tiny way. Logically, she knew this wasn't the case. Logically, she also knew she needed to stop thinking of those brushstrokes as anything other than what they were. Paint on linen. Nothing about the show was personal. This was business.

But that was the trouble with art, wasn't it? It had always been inherently personal, even to Harper. Art was the one thing that could reach over the walls she'd so carefully constructed around her heart.

And that was exactly what made Tom Stone so very, very dangerous.

Those walls were there for a reason—self-preservation. And they had the troubling tendency to crumble to the ground around Tom. Especially when they were alone together.

Two nights ago, when Lindsay was off on another date and Harper was forced to tutor Tom by herself, he'd been spouting off facts about Cezanne, and Harper had become hypnotized by the movement of his mouth. That glorious mouth of his. She couldn't seem to take her eyes off of it. And every time she looked at it, she remembered the taste of it, the searing warmth of it, and she had to stop herself from kissing him all over again.

To prevent herself from making that mistake yet again, she'd played a little game wherein she'd imagined what colors she would use if she were going to paint those lips she couldn't seem to stop thinking about. She would ask him a question and instead of listening to his answer, she'd mix colors on a fantasy palette in her head. Alizarin crimson, titanium white, burnt umber. A touch of cadmium yellow light, and for that lovely shadow right beneath the swell of his lower lip—ultramarine blue. Then she'd stared at that shadow until she'd lost herself in it. She'd all but disappeared in that cool blue, sultry curve. Cezanne had been right. Shadow was indeed a color, and it was beautiful.

And here she was again, thinking about Tom's gorgeous mouth when Lindsay was sitting there waiting to find out when she would see one of his paintings.

"Don't you want to wait and see Tom's work when it's hung properly, with the correct lighting and framing? As a collection?" *Yes. Say yes.*

Lindsay shrugged. "You have a point. It always looks better that way. Still, I'm just so curious."

"Trust me. You won't be disappointed." Harper gazed at the boats bobbing in the harbor. Row upon row of masts, stretching skyward, like something out of a Renoir painting. Only this was real life, not a painting. And one of those boats belonged to Tom. "It's not the art that I'm worried about. It's him."

There was a long pause as Lindsay stabbed at her tuna salad with her fork. "Well. He's come a long way."

He had indeed come a long way. His capacity for memorizing details was staggering, but every day Harper seemed to remember something else to add to her list. She hadn't realized what an enormous undertaking it would be to cram years of art history into two months' time.

"You don't think he can pull it off, do you?" she asked, giving voice to her deepest fear.

Lindsay sighed. "I honestly don't know. If it weren't for Lars, I'd say yes. But he could be a problem. I mean, we've planted a few articles online. But Lars is sure to do some digging into Tom's background. At least there were thousands of illegitimate children running around back in the day. We've got that going for us. And it's not like Lars could actually prove that Tom *isn't* related to Van Gogh. But the more he knows about art, the better."

"I know." The bite of PB & J that Harper had eaten sat in her stomach like a rock. She felt sick again. "Listen, no matter what happens, I want to thank you for all your help. I hate that you've been dragged into this. Without you, I wouldn't even have a chance of getting that promotion."

"You're welcome. It's been fun, actually. And I don't like Lars any more than you do. He pretends not to know how to use the coffeemaker so I'll get his coffee. I can't imagine if he were around full-time. I'd probably be sharpening his pencils, too." Lindsay replaced the lid on her plastic container and stowed it away in her giant handbag.

"I suppose we should get back to the office." An unexpected wave of wistfulness hit Harper all of a sudden. Or maybe it was just exhaustion. The charade was beginning to take its toll.

Five more weeks. You can do this.

Lindsay pulled a face. "Yes, I've got to get back. Lars might be thirsty."

Harper wanted to laugh, but she couldn't.

Lindsay smiled. "Hey, listen, it was only a joke. Don't worry. Everything is going to work out just fine."

"Do you think so?" She didn't know why she was asking. Lindsay didn't have a crystal ball.

Harper supposed she simply wanted to rid herself of the worry that nagged at her every time she thought about the show, which was pretty much all her waking hours. And a few of the sleeping ones as well.

"Yes. Tom's not ready yet, but we've got time. Plenty of it. He can do this. *We* can do this. Try not to worry."

"Plenty of time," Harper echoed. "Thank goodness for that."

LARS WAS WAITING for them with empty coffee cup in hand when they returned to the college. Harper took a deep breath as she pushed through the double glass doors into the reception area where he paced back and forth in front of Lindsay's desk.

What now?

"Harper. I see you've decided to return from your long lunch. Wonderful." He gave her a smile that wasn't really a smile. More like a forced curvature of the lips.

Harper gritted her teeth and reminded herself she had the

advantage here. At least for the time being. She had no reason to be intimidated by Lars. "Not long. Just regular."

He made a grand show of looking at the watch strapped around his wrist. Behind his back, Lindsay rolled her eyes.

Good grief, they'd been gone less than forty-five minutes.

"Is there something you need, Lars?" This was odd behavior, even for him. He might be annoying. And competitive. But he didn't typically lay in wait like this.

"Actually, yes. I have an invitation for you." He pulled a thick, cream-colored envelope from his pocket and handed it to her.

"An invitation?" She stared at her name printed on it in elegant script. Harper Higgins, PhD.

Her first thought was that it must be a wedding invitation, which she'd want to drop in the nearest trashcan even if it had nothing to do with Lars. The fact that it did made her doubly anxious to rid herself of it.

"Yes." He nodded. "I'm hosting a cocktail party and lecture next Friday, on the effect of Dadaism on Contemporary Art. I do hope you can make it."

"Oh." She flipped the envelope over, and saw the Boston College of Art insignia at the top, which meant the party was an official department event. And this was the first she'd heard of it. Interesting. And somewhat alarming.

She shot a quick glance at Lindsay. Lindsay shrugged almost imperceptibly.

Something was definitely wrong if the department secretary didn't know anything about an event that was scheduled to take place in less than ten days. Did that mean Lars had printed his own invitations?

A million different warning bells went off in Harper's head. "I'm surprised I haven't heard about this before now."

"It's somewhat impromptu. An old classmate of mine is visiting from Paris. I thought it would be a shame not to take advantage of his expertise while he's here all the way from the City of Light. Don't you agree?"

Now she knew she wasn't being paranoid. He was up to no good. Since when did Lars ask for her opinion on anything? Especially Dadaism, a field that was a world away from her expertise.

"It sounds very nice. I'll definitely be there." She actually had a class scheduled at Art Bar that night. *The Son of Man* by René Magritte. One of her last master reproduction classes before she began painting glorified caricatures when the news schedule started next month. Oh well. There were only a handful of people signed up for the class. She'd have to reschedule. Either that, or Peyton would be teaching people how to paint a man with a giant green apple for a head all on her own.

"Excellent." Lars's smile turned more genuine now. Genuinely evil. "And I was wondering if you could deliver this for me."

He reached into his pocket for another envelope. Without even looking at it, Harper feared she knew whose name she would find on the front.

Her gaze darted to the white parchment square. Sure enough, there it was.

Mr. Tom Stone.

She couldn't even bring herself to reach for it. *This cannot be happening.*

Lindsay stepped between them and grabbed it for her. She needed a raise. A big one. "Is this for me?"

Lars frowned as the invitation slipped from his grip. "Actually, no. It's for Harper's artist. Why would I ask Harper to deliver an invitation to you when you're standing right here?"

"Sorry. Silly me." Lindsay shrugged. "Here you go, Harper. Did you hear that? Your artist is invited to Dr. Klassen's party next week. Isn't that wonderful? Everyone from the department will get to meet him. *Everyone.*"

Now that the shock had abated somewhat, she was able to reach for the envelope. "I'll certainly pass this along, but I don't know. I doubt he'll be able to make it."

"You doubt it? He's local, isn't he?" Lars's eyes narrowed.

"Yes, but he's busy preparing for the show. He signed on late, remember? Plus, he's rather reclusive." *That's right. Go ahead and make up more random facts about Tom's fictitious person. Because that's exactly what we need—more falsehoods to keep track of.*

Lars crossed his arms. His empty coffee cup dangled from his pointer finger. It annoyed Harper to even look at it. She vowed to get the man to stop having Lindsay get his coffee. It was the least she could do to repay her for all the help she'd given her.

"Reclusive. That's unfortunate," he said. "While you were at lunch, I took the liberty of discussing the matter with Dr. Martin."

Of course he did.

"And he thinks it would be the perfect opportunity for us all to get to know your Mr. Stone." Lars gazed at her expectantly.

What was she supposed to do now? "I suppose I'll have to talk to Tom, er, Mr. Stone, and see what I can arrange."

His gaze turned triumphant. "You do that."

She didn't like the fact that he was so clearly pleased with himself. He wanted Tom there for a reason. And whatever that reason was, it couldn't be good. "I will."

He whistled as he walked back to his office, and Harper realized he'd never filled his empty coffee cup. Apparently, that had just been a prop. Coffee wasn't what he was after. He'd wanted to make sure she would serve Tom up for inspection, and it looked like he'd gotten his way. If she didn't bring him, it would look like she had a reason to hide him.

Maybe because she did.

Chapter Fourteen

TOM BENT TO unclip Vincent's leash and watched Gunner nose at the little dog's heels, herding him in the direction of his dog bed. He'd walked them at least two miles, but the air was brisk, with leaves swirling everywhere. Dogs tended to love such weather. Their coats were cool to the touch, as if they'd been standing in front of an opened refrigerator. Usually a walk in the cold riled a dog up. In Vincent's case, that wasn't such a good thing.

Harper sat on a stool in front of a canvas saturated in color. Cornflower blues, whisper pinks and innocent spring greens, colors that Tom usually thought of as light and delicate. But the way they'd been applied to the canvas in such lush, sweeping caresses of a paintbrush made them appear anything but dainty.

She turned away from the painting and pointed the bristled end of her brush at the canine duo. "That's awfully cute. When did you train Gunner to herd Vincent?"

"I didn't."

"Then how does he know what to do?"

Tom shrugged. "He's intuitive that way. Military dog." Right on cue, Gunner began searching the perimeter.

"Oh." Harper's eyes shined with unasked questions.

Maybe it was the vague sense of unease gnawing at him over what he was about to do, the guilt at the thought of disappointing her, but she seemed even prettier than usual tonight. Her hair was twisted in its usual knot, secured with those crisscrossed reed-thin paintbrushes that screamed out for his fingertips every time he saw them. A tiny dab of blue acrylic had come to rest on her cheek. He was sure she didn't realize it was there, and he wasn't about to let her in on the secret. He found this colorful dash of imperfection most charming. She was at her most radiant when she was painting, and the fact that she seemed oblivious to this little detail only added to her allure. Sitting there in front of that vibrant painting in the soft light of Art Bar, she looked like his art goddess again. The muse he'd been searching for without ever realizing it.

Reaching to brush the paint from her face with a swipe of his thumb wasn't so much a conscious decision as it was an instinct. A reaction beyond his control.

It was the first time he'd laid a finger on her since Peyton had walked in on their kiss. The sensation of skin on skin was as much of a shock to him as it was to her. She gasped at his touch, but to his great relief didn't shy away. Until Lindsay walked in.

He shoved his hand in the pocket of his jeans as Lindsay breezed past the two of them and dropped a stack of books on the closest table. Art books, no doubt. For his ongoing education. "Hi, you two. Have you started without me? I haven't missed anything, have I?"

"Missed anything?" Harper's fingertips fluttered against her face in the place where the pad of his thumb had just been. "No. No, of course not."

She glanced at him. He looked away.

"Has she told you yet?" Lindsay asked, blinking as if she were running against the wind.

Neither of those things could be good. Tom didn't know which to worry about more—the fact that her nervous tic was back, or that Harper needed to tell him something.

"No, she hasn't." He leveled his gaze at Harper.

She gave him a tight smile. "We need to talk."

"Yes, we do." Whatever it was she had to say, it was going to have to wait. He needed to get his news out of the way first.

Her smile faded. "I know. That's what I just said."

He'd been determined to get to Art Bar once her class was finished and get this conversation over with as soon as possible. When he'd come by at the beginning of class to pick up Vincent for his nightly walk, she'd seemed even more tense than usual. Which was pretty damned tense. He hadn't expected to find her looking so calm afterward. Painting relaxed her. He wondered if she realized that.

"Tom, wow. Your leg." Lindsay pointed at his cast-free foot.

He wasn't sure whether to be glad she was there or not. He probably should have spoken with Harper in private about his change in plans, but having a buffer wasn't without its advantages.

He glanced at Harper. "Yeah, that's actually part of what I need to talk to you about."

"We need to talk about your foot?" Harper's gaze flitted to his feet.

"In a way, yes." He sighed. She wasn't going to like what he had to say, no matter how loudly or how many times he said it.

But he didn't exactly have a choice. Neither did she.

"Well?" she asked.

"Now that I'm out of the cast, I'm going to need to walk more dogs."

Her expression remained neutral. "Okay."

She hadn't grasped the extent of the situation. Obviously. "A lot more dogs. It's going to be taking up a serious amount of hours."

"What are you saying, Tom?" She spoke very slowly. With great care. As if she could slow down time until it went backwards and the words had yet to leave his mouth.

"I need to cut back on the time we spend preparing for the art show. I can't keep doing this. I'm sorry." And he was sorry. But really, they'd made so much progress already. It couldn't hurt to cut back just a little. Could it?

Harper shook her head. "No. No, no, no, no."

With each *no*, her voice grew incrementally shriller. Tom half expected the paintings to start falling off the walls. "Look, I said I'm sorry. It can't be helped."

"You're *sorry?* Are you *kidding* me?" Harper jammed her paintbrush in a cup of water. As she did so, to Tom's utter astonishment, her bottom lip quivered.

He hadn't expected this to go well, but the last thing in the world he anticipated was that he would make Harper Higgins cry.

He'd never been good with tears. Womanly tears, in particular. Battlefield tears he was okay with. He ignored them. That was what he was supposed to do. The appearance of womanly tears, on the other hand, was usually a whole different sort of field. A minefield. Particularly when the woman with the shiny, tear-kissed eyes was someone like Harper. Strong. Strong to the point of being annoying. Past that point, if he was being honest.

He'd never seen his wife cry. Not once. He'd always told himself it was because she wasn't the crying type. But everyone broke eventually, didn't they? If he'd been around to see her tears, maybe they would have lasted. If he would have loved her—really loved her—he wouldn't have been able to stay away. Then the tears would have been as few and far between as he'd thought they were.

Seeing Harper vulnerable like this made his chest hurt. A real, physical ache. He didn't want to be the cause of her tears. In his weaker moments, he thought it would be awfully nice to be the cause of her each and every smile.

"Damn it, Doc." He jammed his hands on his hips. "Please don't cry."

"I'm *not* crying." A big, fat tear slid down her pretty porcelain cheek.

Tom's arms itched to wrap themselves around her. He knew without a doubt that would an unwelcome move. It was one thing to wipe away a little paint from her face, but embracing her, pulling the length of her body against his, was another entirely.

He crossed his arms to prevent himself from completely losing his mind and acting on the impulse. "Doc, I'm still in this. I just can't keep spending quite as much time studying. Between that and painting, I don't have any extra slots to add more clients. And now that the cast is off my foot, that's a necessity."

Harper sniffed. Another tear slid down her cheek. Thank

God Lindsay was here. Who knew what he would have done if they'd been alone together.

"It's almost winter," she said in a voice he'd never heard come out of her mouth before.

She was taking this awfully hard. Something wasn't right here.

"Exactly," he muttered.

Lindsay cleared her throat. "Listen, let's all calm down for a minute. Harper, why don't you tell Tom about the party? I'm sure he'll reconsider once he knows what's going on."

Not likely. "What party?"

Harper took a deep inhale. One long breath. That was all it took, and suddenly she sat up ramrod straight. The tears vanished and once more, she was all business. Just like the times she'd kissed him within an inch of his life and then acted as though nothing had happened.

It was downright eerie how she could turn her emotions on and off like that.

She looked at him coolly, her face an unmoving mask. "The department at the college is having a cocktail party next week in honor of a visiting expert on Dadaism."

Tom lifted a brow. "Dadaism? Is that a real thing?"

Harper threw her hands in the air. "Of course it's a thing. A very important thing. A thing you should know all about if you're an artistic genius and Van Gogh's great-great-grandson."

"Take it easy, Doc. What does Dodoism have to do with adding more dogs to my schedule?"

"*Dadaism.*" Again with the shrillness.

It was a welcome relief after the tears. Never had two teardrops torn him up like that. What was the matter with him?

"You said it wrong on purpose, didn't you? Just to irritate me."

Guilty. And it had worked. She didn't appear to be anywhere close to tears now.

"Don't be silly. It was an honest mistake. Dodoism." He winked.

Her cheeks flushed pink, and for a second Tom thought he glimpsed the beginnings of a smile. *Smiling through her tears.* Again, not an image he'd ever think to associate with Harper.

Then he blinked and any faint trace of smile had disappeared.

She crossed her arms. "The department chair wants you at the party."

He shrugged. "Fine. When is it? I'll be there, even though I'm not exactly a party guy."

Harper's hands shook. She was probably on the verge of wrapping them around his neck and strangling him. Again, better than tears. "You don't get it. This isn't a party. It's a test."

Funny, he could have sworn she'd called it a party two seconds ago. "What kind of test?"

He shot a questioning glance at Lindsay. As usual, she deferred to Harper.

"One of the other professors in the department wants to use a different artist for the show. He's the one who organized this little shindig. I'm not sure what he's up to, but it can't be good."

He wasn't liking this. "Is this the Lars guy you told me about before? The one who wants your promotion?"

"Yes." She tilted her head.

A lock of hair fell from her haphazard bun and danced along the delicate line of her collarbone. Taunting him. Why he was thinking about burying his hands in her hair and running his tongue along the fine length of that bone when she was clearly exasperated with him was a mystery.

"You remember that?"

He remembered a lot of things. *The persistence of memory.* "Yes, I do."

"Harper was hoping you'd be willing to spend extra time studying so that you'd be fully prepared for the party," Lindsay said, her head swiveling back and forth between the two of them.

He had no reason to feel guilty about this. None at all. Being paraded around at a party wasn't part of the original plan. He'd already spent more time on this charade than there were hours in the day. And he was doing just fine. He might not have heard of Dadaism—and he still harbored doubts about its authenticity—but he'd recognized the swirling lily pads on Harper's canvas at first glance. Monet.

Three weeks ago he'd never heard of Monet.

He shouldn't feel like he was letting her down. And he didn't. That uncomfortable sensation gnawing at his insides was something different. It had to be. Indigestion maybe.

This isn't about her. It's about you. And the little luxury of having a roof over your head. "Look, I don't have a choice, okay? I'm going to get kicked out of my home if I don't winterize the boat. And that takes money. Money I don't have."

His statement settled between them, wrapped in an uncomfortable silence.

"So that's what this is about? Money?" Harper said.

"Yes." Tom's head was beginning to hurt.

He was more than ready for this to be over. Not just this conversation. All of it. The studying. The show.

The feeling that he was letting her down.

He'd had enough of letting people down. He wanted his life back. His quiet, lonely life. *Not lonely. Alone. There's a difference.* Part of him wondered if he even knew what that difference was.

"Let's not panic." Lindsay's fluttering eyelashes said differently. "Maybe there's another option here. Harper, could you get him an advance on sales from the show?"

She shook her head. "No. I can't ask for something like that. It would be a huge red flag."

Red flag or not, that wasn't happening. "I wouldn't take it if you could. I don't want money I haven't earned."

Lindsay let out a laugh. "You've earned it. You've been working your ass off. Right, Harper?"

"Yes. Yes, of course. If there were a way to get an advance on sales without jeopardizing everything, believe me, I would. But with Lars watching us as closely as he is, I can't. It would raise suspicions, and that's the last thing we need." It was high praise coming from the likes of Harper. "I wish I could do something to help."

He wished that, too. He wished a lot of things.

"Wait a minute. I've got it!" Lindsay clapped her hands, prompting both dogs to stir with excitement. Furry tails beat against the floor of the studio in synchronized thump-thump rhythms.

She seemed way too excited all of a sudden. The hair rose on the back of Tom's neck, as if his body knew something that his mind didn't. "Got what?"

"The solution. It's so simple," Lindsay said.

Harper's expression was a wary as Tom felt inside. "Then please share."

"Tom needs to walk more dogs because he won't be able to stay on his boat if it's not ready for winter. But if he's going to be ready for the party, he needs to spend even more time preparing. Don't you two see? The answer is so obvious."

Not obvious enough apparently. He and Harper exchanged curious glances.

Harper sighed. "Lindsay. Please. Spit it out."

"Tom doesn't need to take on any more clients. He can move out of his boat and stay with you until the show. Once the show is over, he'll have all the money he needs. Until then, you'd have plenty of time together for tutoring." She grinned as if she'd solved all the great mysteries of the universe at once.

She hadn't.

She'd gone insane.

Tom couldn't even bring himself to look at Harper to gauge her reaction. He couldn't imagine she'd go for it. She probably thought it was even a worse idea than he did.

He and Harper. Living together. Under the same roof.

Day and night.

No. God, no. Just...no.

"Problem solved." Lindsay gave them simultaneous pats on their backs. Tom thought he saw Harper wince as her hand came down between her shoulder blades. "You're welcome, roomies."

HARPER COULDN'T HAVE heard Lindsay right. Surely she hadn't just suggested that Tom move into her house.

Tom Stone, of the moody blue eyes. Tom Stone, of the broad Michelangelo-esque physique. Tom Stone, of the pinned-against-the-wall, swollen lipped kisses.

Every bit of blood in Harper's body rose to her cheeks. She stole a glance at Tom. He looked equally horrified at the prospect, which definitely did not hurt her feelings. Or possibly it did in the smallest conceivable amount.

She cleared her throat. "Thank you for the suggestion, Lindsay. But I really don't think that's such a great idea."

Lindsay's eyelashes fluttered. Great. Her feelings were hurt. "It's a perfect idea."

Tom shook his head. "Not perfect. Definitely not perfect."

Lindsay frowned. "Sure it is. You'd have a nice, warm place to stay without having to take on more clients. And the two of you would have loads of time together. Harper could drill you for hours."

Oh, my God. Stop talking. Stop talking, please.

Tom snickered. "You might want to rephrase that."

Lindsay's eyebrows crept naively up her forehead. "What?"

"*Never mind.*" Harper leaped off her stool. She couldn't seem to sit still. Not now that Lindsay was trying to move Tom into her house. "Let's think, okay? Surely there's another way to handle the situation. Lindsay, you know how tiny my house is. It's not even a house, really. It's a cottage. It's got less than a thousand square feet."

Lindsay glanced at Tom. "The man lives on a boat. I'm sure he'd be okay in a corner of your cottage."

Nobody puts Baby in a corner.

Clearly, the stress of the situation was getting to her. She was quoting *Dirty Dancing* in her head.

"Please. Talk about me like I'm not here," Tom said. "I love that."

"I don't even have a spare bedroom. He'd have to sleep on the sofa." Tom Stone, stretched out on her sofa. All six-foot-three of him. Or thereabouts. It was not like she'd measured him or anything.

Regardless of his exact dimensions, he was tall enough his feet would hang off the end of her little red couch. She couldn't imagine waking up, strolling through the living room on the way to walk Vincent, and finding Tom's bare feet staring her in the face. His sleeping body, rising and falling languidly with each breath.

Or maybe she could imagine it. Maybe she already *had* imagined it. That in itself was a problem.

Lindsay's eyed widened. Her mind was churning again. Good grief, when was she going to run out of crazy ideas. "You have your studio. Couldn't he use that? You don't work on your gallery paintings anymore."

Tom narrowed his gaze at Harper. "You painted? For galleries?"

God, she'd bet he looked amazing with bed head.

She swallowed. "A long time ago, yes."

"The studio would be perfect. He could use the space to paint, and I've got an air mattress you could borrow. A twin. I'm sure it would fit." Lindsay smiled.

She made it sound so easy. Like Tom was a rescued kitten or something.

Harper couldn't think of anyone less warm and fuzzy. "Do

you really think he wants to sleep on a blow-up mattress?"

"Once again. I'm right here." Tom raised his hand. "Does anyone care to hear my thoughts on the subject?"

Only if you think it's as horrid of a prospect as I do. "Of course."

"What happens if I don't sell any paintings at the show? What then? I just keep on living in your studio until spring?" He shook his head. Harper was pretty sure she was shaking hers even harder. "No. I'll just stick with my plan of doubling up on clients."

"And stop tutoring for the time being? In that case, you might not even need to worry about the show." Lindsay shot Harper a worried glance.

The truth was that Lindsay's idea really was sort of genius. *In theory.* But even the best theories weren't without faults, right? Like that one about the earth being flat—it probably seemed like a great theory back in the day. Until no one managed to sail off the edge of the map and the whole theory went kaput.

Concentrate. Her mind was wandering all over the place, like it always did when she was stressed. *Focus, Harper.*

"I'm quite sure Tom doesn't want to live with me. I mean, not that he would be living with me in a romantic sense. We wouldn't be *living together.* Not like that. We would be roommates. Platonic friends. Not even friends, actually. Business associates." What in God's name had just come out of her mouth? "Business associates." She repeated. "If we decided to do it, but we're not."

She clamped her mouth shut before she said something even more mortifying.

Lindsay regarded her through narrowed eyes. "Are you okay?"

Harper snuck a glance at Tom. That sardonic grin of his was on the verge of making an appearance. She could tell by the amused gleam in his eyes.

She wanted to die. "I'm fine. I just don't think it's the best idea for Tom to move into my house."

"Yeah, you pretty much made that clear," he said.

Lindsay shook her head. "I think you two are being ridiculous. It's the perfect solution. Give me one legitimate reason why it's not."

His mouth. His hands. His eyes.

And, oh God, the paintings. If he lived there, that meant he would be painting there. Harper would have to walk around blindfolded so she wouldn't fling herself at him again.

"Um," Harper stammered, struggling to come up with a reason she could actually admit to aloud. "Well..."

"What?" Lindsay threw her hands up.

"I think what the good doctor is trying to say..."—Tom's gaze slid over her, and she felt the touch of that look every bit as much she'd felt the unexpected thrill of his thumb against her face earlier—"is that she's afraid to be alone with me."

"Afraid?" *Yes. Very much so.* "Don't be absurd."

"Why would you be afraid to be alone with Tom? He's a perfect gentleman. It's not like he'd attack you or anything." Lindsay rolled her eyes.

Actually, quite the opposite. Harper closed hers and wished she could somehow time travel out of this moment.

"I suppose the two of you can come up with a better idea?" Lindsay asked.

Harper opened her eyes and glanced at Tom. He smoldered back at her. Whether that was a serious smolder or whether he was poking fun at her, she had no idea. Her face grew hot all the same.

"Wait a minute. What's going on here?" Lindsay looked at Tom. Tom looked at Harper. Harper looked at the floor. "Oh. Ooooh."

Her eyes widened. She looked like she couldn't decide whether to be shocked, thrilled, or horrified. Probably some warped combination of the three. "So you two..."

"No!" Harper shook her head.

"No." Tom shook his harder.

Gunner's ears flattened. The nos were flying so fast and furious that even Vincent heard them. He cowered on his bed.

"Right. Obviously there's nothing going on." Lindsay snorted.

"There isn't. Truly." This was getting ridiculous.

The last thing she needed was anyone from the college thinking she couldn't keep her libido in check. Because she could. Of course she could.

She didn't want to end up like her colleague who'd been fired for sleeping with a student. He'd been a full-time, tenured professor. He'd had the academic world at his feet and he'd thrown it all away by losing control over his impulses. That would not happen to her. Granted, Tom wasn't a student at the college. But he was the artist in an exhibition that she was curating. A sexual relationship, or any other relationship that went beyond detached professionalism, was strictly out of the question.

No more kissing. Period.

Assuming she could stick to that rule, Lindsay's argument about the extra time they would have to prepare was a valid one. But that was an awfully big assumption.

"Maybe we're all getting ahead of ourselves here. It's not winter just yet. Surely there's a compromise to be had." She glanced outside and saw the green awning of the pub across the street flapping in the wind. Okay, so maybe there was a stiff breeze. But it was not like they were going to get snow any time soon. "Why don't we proceed as planned, just until the party? If the weather becomes a problem, we can revisit the living arrangements as needed."

"Revisit the living arrangements?" There was a world of danger in Tom's arched brow.

"The party is in one week. Please, please, don't take on any new clients until after next Saturday. We need every spare minute this week to get ready." She took a deep breath, not quite believing what she was about to say. "If you get kicked off your boat before then, you can stay with me."

There was nothing to worry about. How far could the temperature drop in one measly week? It was still October, for crying out loud. It never snowed in October.

Lindsay nodded. "That actually seems like a good compromise. There's no way it will snow before next week."

Tom's jaw clenched. An emphatic *no* was on the very tip of his tongue. Harper could feel it.

She would beg if she had to. There was really no choice. "Please, Tom. Please. Seven days. That's all I'm asking."

"Seven days." He repeated through gritted teeth.

She nodded, afraid she might cry again if she spoke. She could feel the tears gathering behind her eyes and blinked hard to keep them in check.

Tom stared at her for a long moment, his gaze softening ever so slightly.

He exhaled a weary sigh. “Fine.”

Chapter Fifteen

"SEVEN DAYS." TOM stared out his window at the layer of misty vapor swirling over the black water of the harbor. Not fog this time. Snow. Twirling masses of it. Everywhere. "Try two."

The earliest snowfall in the history of Boston, according to the meteorologist on the evening news. This was the same meteorologist who'd failed to predict the surprise weather phenomenon, so what did he know, really?

It sure was pretty, though. Tom couldn't deny the beauty of the flurries drifting through the night sky. The most delicate and holy of angels. He was particularly struck by the sereneness of it all. It was like watching a silent ballet.

A silent ballet that was forcing him onto Harper Higgins' sofa.

"You ready, son?" Mr. Bell stood in Tom's living room with an armful of canvases.

Tom turned his back to the window and tossed one last pair of socks into his duffle bag. "Yep. I think that's everything. Thanks for the help."

"No worries. I feel badly about this. I do." Mr. Bell glanced at the snow swirling against the windows and shook his head. "I thought you had more time. I certainly didn't expect this."

"None of us did." Tom zipped the duffle bag closed. Gunner rose to his feet, prepared to follow him. Anywhere and everywhere.

"These are good, you know." Mr. Bell nodded at the canvases in his arms. "Really good."

"Thank you." A thought occurred to Tom as he watched the marina manager regard his paintings—he couldn't tell the Bells about the show at the gallery. Nor Frank.

Tom wasn't one to form attachments. He never had been. Growing up sofa-surfing with various relatives while his dad was deployed sort of cemented the deal on being a loner. But seeing Mr. Bell look at the flowers he'd painted, Tom realized that Mrs. Bell would have probably liked to see all those flowers he'd given her, preserved in forever brushstrokes, hanging on whitewashed walls.

And Frank. Frank, who treated each and every stem as if it were the embodiment of lost innocence. Pure, perfect treasures. If anyone should see those paintings, it should be Frank.

But it just wasn't possible, was it? The name that was to be printed on the gallery wall might be *Tom Stone*, but that man wasn't him. That man was a lie.

It felt wrong all of sudden.

He'd known well enough what he'd been getting into. A lie was a lie, plain and simple. But he hadn't given much thought to how far-reaching one lie could actually be, how many lives it could affect. He didn't like it.

Too late. You made a promise. You're in this for the long haul.

The long, long haul all the way to Harper's sofa.

To add insult to injury, he literally couldn't afford to have a crisis of conscience at the moment. Homeless. On top of everything, his participation in this charade had left him homeless. Why in hell had he let Harper talk him into waiting until after the party to take on additional clients?

Because she gets to you.

That was going to stop. It had to, for a multitude of reasons. Firstly, he loathed the idea of not having a home of his own. He'd slept on enough sofas, air mattresses, and cots over the course of his lifetime, thank you very much. If he'd had any idea that the weather would change so suddenly, he would have never agreed to wait to increase the number of dogs he walked per week. He should have known, though, or at the very least been prepared for anything. Starting right now, he'd be prepared for whatever came his way, including tears falling from Harper's lovely, emerald eyes. He couldn't fall prey to those tears again.

Because now they'd be roommates. They were going to be near one another day in, day out. If he let her every gesture, every hair toss, every diamond tear she shed, get to him like a punch in the gut, he'd never survive living under her roof. He'd have her in bed in half a second, and that would only complicate things tenfold. A hundredfold. A thousandfold. And weren't things complicated enough already? The lines were already so blurred he was beginning to forget what was real and what wasn't.

Will the real Tom Stone stand up?

He scowled and heaved the duffle bag onto his shoulder. "I'm ready."

"Let's head out." Mr. Bell smiled, as if the reason for the speedy packing was a vacation. Or a trip to Disneyland.

Disneyland. Why did that word conjure an image of Harper tangled in colorful bed sheets atop a four-poster bed rather than Mickey Mouse or a rollercoaster? He could see her there, as real as real could be, all that blonde hair fanned out over the pillows, her fair skin perfectly offset by sheets of scarlet. Or violet, perhaps.

Stop. None *of this is real.*

He scowled harder, trying his best to make small talk with Mr. Bell as they walked the short distance to Harper's cottage. They covered the usual topics—the weather, the Red Sox, the weather, the Celtics, the weather.

Tom was grateful when they reached the walkway to Harper's cottage. He wasn't sure he could take any more talk about the snow, as he blamed it for his miserable predicament. Well, mostly he blamed himself, but the snow was a close second.

"This is it," he said, letting his gaze linger on her home.

Cozy.

He'd seen it before, of course. But for some reason the little house seemed softer now, more welcoming. Another thing to blame on the snow, perhaps. She had a fire going in the fireplace, as evidenced by the plume of dove-gray smoke twirling its way from the chimney toward the night sky. Snow had begun to gather in a thick layer on the picket fence that surrounded her front yard, smoothing out its edges. Warm, golden light beckoned from the windows.

Cozy. Definitely.

This is her home, not yours. He didn't need the reminder. He wasn't a little kid anymore. He knew better than to allow himself to get comfortable only to find the rug swept out from under him again. Just as he'd been beginning to grow accustomed to a new pillow, a new school, his father would come back for a short-lived stint on American soil, or his relatives would decide it was time to shuffle him around again. That was a pattern that didn't need repeating. He'd fallen for it again when he'd been married. No more. Enough was enough.

"Are we going to go in, or stand here in the snow all night?" Mr. Bell shifted the canvases in his arms.

Harper would have a fit if they got wet. He couldn't put off the inevitable any longer. He unlatched the gate on the picturesque white fence and tried not to think about the fact that he felt like he was walking into a scene from a Christmas card.

"Let's go," he muttered.

HARPER WAS BAKING cookies. She never baked.

At least these weren't homemade. They were slice and bake, from one of those rolls of cookie dough that she sometimes nibbled on after a particularly long day. Or every day maybe. Things had been a little tense around campus lately, but that would change. As soon as she got her promotion, everything would fall beautifully into place.

She opened the oven door a fraction and took a peek inside. The cookies looked perfect, or so she assumed. She'd never made actual cookies from one of those logs before. Why bother baking when the dough was perfectly delicious?

Things were different, of course. She couldn't very well say *dig in* and hand Tom a spoon and a hunk of cookie batter.

Oh God, she was baking him cookies. What was she thinking? This wasn't a slumber party. They weren't two teenage girls about to paint their nails, watch the Kardashians, and gossip about their friends.

They were adults. She was a woman, and he was a man. Was he ever a man…

She'd been nervous when he'd texted her and said he was on the way over. She'd been a wreck since the first snowflake had drifted down from the heavens. Since when did it snow in October?

Since you started telling lies to get your way.

So this was karma. Now she was going to have to put her money where her mouth was and let Tom sleep in her house. And eat in her house. And *shower* in her house, which she could only assume he would do naked, seeing as that was how most people showered.

She felt hot all of the sudden. Were the cookies burning? She peeked at them again. They looked perfect. Too perfect. Since when had she turned into Betty Crocker?

She should throw them out. They sent the wrong message. In her nervous frenzy, a welcoming gesture had seemed like a good idea. Now it seemed a little over the top, like she'd been sitting around praying for the temperature to drop so he'd have to move in with her. *I've been waiting for you! Welcome!*

The doorbell rang. Vincent erupted into a barking fit that could wake the dead and scrambled to the front door, his feet sliding out from under him along the way on the slick wood floors.

Dang it.

Too late. She wouldn't be able to throw the cookies away. She'd simply have to act like she did this sort of thing all the time…baking. *Right, and maybe you should pull out some knitting needles while you're at it. Totally believable.*

She tossed her oven mitts on the counter and headed for the door. Her heart thumped like mad as she reached for the doorknob. *Get a grip on yourself.*

She swung the door open and found Tom, customary scowl firmly in place, standing beside an older man she'd never seen before. His presence threw her for a moment. Tom didn't seem like the type to have many friends. Then again, she wasn't the type to make cookies. At least the mystery man was smiling, whoever he was.

"Hello. Please come in. I'm Harper Higgins."

"*Doctor* Harper Higgins," Tom corrected, without so much as cracking a smile. Gunnar stood beside him, calm, cool, and collected, as always, despite the fact that Vincent was running frantic circles around him. "And this is my friend, Mr. Bell."

A friend he called mister?

"Oh, a doctor!" The friendly Mr. Bell smiled as he crossed the threshold carrying an armful of Tom's art, none of which had been packed away in wooden crates like any other gallery artist would use, particularly in this sort of weather.

But that was why they were here, wasn't it? Tom wasn't any regular gallery artist. His work was so beautiful, she sometimes forgot.

"Let me take those for you." She returned Mr. Bell's smile and unloaded the paintings from his arms one at a time.

She arranged them on the dining room table, and instantly the room was transformed into a garden of lilacs, poppies, pansies, and daisies. Harper had to remind herself to breathe while looking at them. Goodness, they were stunning. The one thing Tom didn't need to worry about with regard to the show was the actual painting. She couldn't improve upon his artistic ability if she tried.

"Nice, aren't they?" Mr. Bell motioned toward the paintings. "I didn't realize Tom painted."

She glanced at Tom. His arms were crossed, eyes downcast, his face expressionless. He shifted his weight from one foot to the other and sighed. Loudly. Harper wasn't sure she'd ever seen a more uncomfortable looking man. That was something they'd need to work on. He would need to grow accustomed to hearing people discuss his work. "Neither did I, until recently."

"Thank you for your help, Mr. Bell. I'm sure you probably want to head home before the snow gets bad," Tom said.

He ignored Tom's intended dismissal, which was right about the time that Harper decided she liked Mr. Bell. A lot. "So how do you two know one another? If you don't mind my asking."

"Um...well..." She glanced at Tom, unsure what to say.

Well, you see, I ran into him the street and now we're involved in a complicated scheme to defraud my boss into giving me a promotion so I can get ahead in my career and Tom can raise the money he needs for his boat. You know, the usual.

"I see." Mr. Bell's sudden grin made the Cheshire cat look like he needed powerful antidepressants.

Clearly, he didn't see.

Tom slung an arm over Mr. Bell's shoulders and guided him toward the door. "Thank you again for your help. Don't you think that Mrs. Bell might be worried about you out in the snow?"

"No worries at all. I'm glad to help. And you're right. I really should be going." He turned toward Harper. "Dr. Higgins, I can't tell you how delighted I am to meet you. Thrilled, really."

"It was a pleasure meeting you," she said, studiously ignoring the daggers that Tom's stare was busy tossing her way. "Good night. Be careful out there."

Tom stepped outside with Mr. Bell and closed the door behind him. Gunner pawed his way to the door and fixed his unwavering gaze on it, as if he could see through the wood to his master on the other side.

Harper shook her head. That dog was really something. "Gunner, he'll be right back. He's not leaving you here alone. I promise."

The shepherd glanced at her for a split second and then went back to staring a hole in the door.

"Okay. Stay right there if it makes you feel better," Harper said.

She didn't even want to contemplate what Vincent did when she walked out the door. Pining for her didn't seem like a likely scenario. Chewing on the furniture was a more realistic possibility.

She went to check on the cookies while Tom was outside. At least that was what she told herself, because *checking the cookies* had a much nicer ring to it than *hiding in the kitchen.*

As hiding places went, it was a poor one. Within ten seconds of sliding the cookie sheet from the oven, her tiny kitchen was full to bursting. Gunner and Vincent entered, their noses upturned and quivering at the aroma of freshly baked cookies. Tom wasn't far behind.

"What were you thinking, answering Mr. Bell like you did? You hesitated. You stammered. You blushed," he said through clenched teeth. "He's got it in his head that we're a couple now."

"I'm sorry. He caught me off guard. I wasn't sure what to say." She poked at one of the cookies with the corner of her spatula.

Tom threw his hands in the air. "How about the truth?"

"No. Absolutely not. Are you crazy? We can't go around telling people what we're doing." She pointed the spatula at him. "Wait a minute. You didn't tell him, did you?"

"I didn't utter a word. When I mentioned the truth, I was talking about the fact that I'm your dog walker. Remember that small detail?"

"Oh." That was right. He was her dog walker. She'd completely forgotten. She glanced down at Vincent, who looked annoyed, inasmuch as dogs could express annoyance. "I didn't even think about that. Sorry."

Tom pushed her spatula aside so it was no longer aimed at him, then noticed the cookies. He frowned down at them. Honestly, how grumpy must a person be to frown at cookies? Especially fresh-from-the-oven-cookies.

"I think there are enough lies floating around without adding to them, don't you?"

She agreed, of course, but she didn't particularly like the way he'd said it. "I didn't force you into this, you know."

"No, you begged."

"I did *not* beg." Except she sort of did. "Maybe I begged *a little*, but you agreed. Now is not the time for a crisis of conscience."

His mood was worrying her. They were far too invested in to give up on things now.

Now is not the time for a crisis of conscience.

She wasn't sure if she'd said those words for his benefit of hers.

He glared at the cookies again. "Did you actually *bake?* For me?"

She crossed her arms and shoved the spatula out of sight. If only she could make the cookies disappear as easily. "No."

"Then what are those?" He pointed at the offensive cookies.

Gosh, they smelled good. She refused to look at them. "Nothing."

"Nothing?" He snorted.

Attractive. Seriously. Who knew it was possible for a man to look that good while snorting?

Good grief. This was exactly why she hadn't wanted him here. Tom had been under her roof for less than ten minutes, and they were already arguing. That was better than kissing, she supposed. Unfortunately, if past history was any indication, arguing typically led to kissing. That, in and of itself, was baffling. And more than a little disturbing.

"Fine. They're cookies." She rolled her eyes. "But I didn't make them for *you*. I bake all the time."

"Do you now?" He lifted one of her pristine oven mitts from the countertop and examined it. The price tag still dangled from a corner.

She started to say she baked so often that she'd worn her old oven mitts out, but then she remembered what he'd said about lying. He was right. They were both neck-deep in untruths at this point. She was beginning to have trouble remembering what was real and what wasn't.

"Fine. I made them for you." She waved a hand toward the cookies. "They're yours. And there's milk, too. I felt badly that

I talked you out of increasing your dog walking load and now you've been forced out of your home. You could say this whole arrangement is my fault."

His lips—those glorious lips—twitched, and an almost-smile found its way to his mouth. "Maybe because it *is* your fault."

"Do you want the cookies or not?" She picked up the spatula again, this time with the vague notion of using it to clobber him over the head.

He frowned again, as if life and death hung in the balance instead of a little butter mixed with sugar, flour and chocolate chips…or whatever the Pillsbury doughboy put in that log.

She slid one of the cookies onto the spatula and held it toward him. "Take one. It won't bite. On the contrary."

He looked at it for a prolonged moment, and just when Harper was about to give up, he picked it up and took a bite. Then another and another, until the cookie was gone.

"Have some more," she said, wondering why she felt so ridiculously pleased all of a sudden. She hadn't technically done anything but slice up some dough. "You like them, don't you?"

He shrugged and took another. "They're decent."

Decent. Right. "It wouldn't kill you to admit that you liked them, you know."

"They're fine." He tossed the second one back on the cookie sheet. "Why don't we just skip the welcome wagon, and you can show me where I'm sleeping. It's getting late."

"Sure." She nodded woodenly.

So this was how it was going to be? They were going to simply tolerate one another for the duration of his stay? Fine. It was for the best, really. They should keep things professional. It was less confusing that way. She had no real reason, no real right to feel disappointed.

So why did she?

TOM FELT LIKE the biggest jerk in the universe as Harper led him out of the kitchen, through the living room, and to the room she called her studio.

"This is it," she said. "I know it's small. I hope you'll be comfortable in here. I borrowed this bed from Lindsay."

A bed. She'd borrowed a bed and had somehow moved it here herself, without asking for a bit of help. Not asking for assistance shouldn't have surprised him. This was Harper Higgins, after all. Superwoman. The fact she'd done it all on her own wasn't the shocking part.

It was the thoughtfulness that got him. The bed. Not a cot, not an air mattress, not a sleeper sofa, but a real bed. She'd gone and moved a real mattress and box springs into her home, all by herself. For him.

And the cookies. The damned cookies.

"I'm sure the room will be fine. The bed looks great." It was a twin and looked to be a few inches shy of the length of his body, but it was a bed. He'd slept on far worse. Many, many times.

"Okay, well. Good." She stood awkwardly beside him, as if unsure whether she should stay or go.

Go, he wanted to say. *Just leave.*

Except he didn't really want that, which made the leaving all the more necessary.

She turned toward the door, and right before she reached it, he managed to say something. "So this is your studio?"

Brilliant. What a riveting conversationalist you are.

"Yeah. I don't use it much anymore." She glanced at the easel in the corner.

Its tray was empty, and there was a stack of pristine white canvases leaning against the wall behind it. Art waiting to happen.

"Why not?" he asked.

"Oh, you know..." Her voice trailed off.

There was a story there. One she didn't want to tell. And weren't those always the best kind?

Leave it alone.

"No, I don't know. That's why I'm asking," he said, apparently incapable of leaving things alone where the good doctor was concerned.

She sighed, and her red ribbon lips curved into the saddest of smiles. She shook her head. "Honestly? Because I'm terrible at it."

So there was something she thought she couldn't do? Interesting. Very interesting, considering that particular something was painting, and he knew good and well how much art meant to her.

"I wholeheartedly doubt that," he said.

She was wrong. He'd seen what she could do when she painted at Art Bar. Granted, those were reproductions. But they were soulfully done. Art lived inside Harper. It was so obvious. Didn't she know?

She crossed her arms. "Trust me. I have a file full of newspaper articles detailing precisely how horrible I am."

"Newspaper articles?" That was a new one.

"You know…critics and the like." Her gaze dropped to the floor.

Then Tom remembered something she'd said about critics a while back, something about dating one. "You don't mean…"

She gave him a slow nod. "Yes, that's exactly what I mean. It was a long time ago, though, and I'm fine. Obviously. I'm more than fine."

Except that she no longer painted.

"Doc, there's nothing more subjective than art. It can't be judged. Not by anyone."

"Unless it's someone's job." She wrapped her arms around herself, and she looked so uncharacteristically vulnerable that Tom felt like running to the kitchen and eating every last one of the cookies she'd made. Anything to make her smile. "Rick wasn't the only one. None of the reviews were good. It wasn't personal."

Tom decided his next order of business after eating all the cookies should be hunting down this Rick character and pummeling him into the ground. "Bullshit. There's nothing more personal that creating something from nothing."

"Well, it doesn't matter anymore. Painting is my past. Besides, once I get my promotion, I won't have time for anything else."

Painting was her past. Tom wasn't sure whether or not he was buying that. He knew all too well how the past had a way of rearing its ugly head. "Not even Art Bar?"

She rolled her eyes. "*Especially* not Art Bar."

He shook his head and sighed.

"What?" she asked, clearly baffled.

She didn't get it. He wondered if she ever would.

She was a painter. She may not realize it, but she was happier with a brush in her hand than she was teaching art history. To anyone who'd seen her paint, it was obvious. Maybe he should line the walls of Art Bar with mirrors.

"What?" She repeated.

There was no use trying to explain something she wasn't ready to admit. Tom knew good and well how the past shaded things in impossible hues to eyes that were colorblind.

He shrugged. "Nothing."

She lingered silently in the doorway, halfway between staying and walking away. Tom felt the push and pull of her spirit as much as he felt his own.

She'd given him something tonight—a piece of herself. Even after he'd been such a jerk earlier.

"I'm sorry," he said.

She narrowed her gaze. "For what, exactly?"

"For earlier, about the cookies. They're good. They really are."

"They're slice and bake. I'm not exactly Suzie Homemaker, Tom." She laughed, but her eyes still carried a hint of sadness.

Suzie Homemaker. A pang hit him right in the center of his chest. "It's just staying here…the cookies, the bed…"

"Look, I know you don't want to be here, Tom."

He was botching this. Royally. "That's not it. I grew up being shuffled from one house to the next while my dad was away. I've slept on my fair share of sofas."

"I see." She nodded, and her sharp academic edges softened a bit.

But she didn't see. Not really, because he hadn't explained

anything. "The whole concept of home is a bit vague for me. I thought I'd created one when I got married, but that didn't work out either. Not that I blame my wife for leaving. I was never there. I guess in some ways, I'm my father's son."

"Oh, Tom." She touched her hand to her mouth, and she was looking at him in that way that he'd always hated—sympathetic, kind. But seeing that look on Harper's face was less excruciating than he'd expected.

It was nice. Almost.

"So if I was rude about the cookies, I'm sorry. I'm not accustomed to that sort of hospitality. I find it difficult to accept, even under the best of circumstances." God, could this be any more awkward? It would have been less painful if he'd cut open an artery and bled out all over the floor of Harper's studio.

"Apology accepted." Her pretty mouth curved into a wistful smile. "No more cookies."

He smiled back. "No more cookies."

"Good night, Tom." She fluttered her fingers in a butterfly wave and disappeared.

"Good night," he whispered in her wake and reminded himself once again this wasn't his home, no matter how unexpectedly pleasant he'd found it.

This wasn't his home, and it never would be.

Chapter Sixteen

3:55 *P.M.*

Five more minutes left of Harper's afternoon office hours. She shoved the books about Dadaism she'd checked out from the college library in her briefcase and prayed that a student wouldn't come rushing in at 3:59. She'd already had two show up from her Van Gogh seminar begging for her to change the grades on their mid-term papers, because it was *totes* important that they both got "A"s.

She'd given them both an extra credit assignment, a gesture she thought was more than generous. Their crestfallen expressions had indicated the students thought otherwise. No doubt they expected her to change their grades simply because they'd asked. Not going to happen.

Sometimes she wished she could dispense with giving grades altogether. They were all her students thought about, when what she really wanted to impart on them was a love for art, its history, and its place in the world. She liked to think if grades were taken out of the equation, they would all still come to class just to learn.

You totes live in a fantasy world.

She glanced at the time again. One more minute, and not a student in sight. Perfect. Lars's party was in less than forty-eight hours, and there were still so many things to go over with Tom. Even with him living at her house, there still didn't seem to be enough hours in the day to talk about art.

And art was pretty much all they'd talked about in the three days since he'd moved in. Harper wasn't sure which one of them had made the decision to avoid any more personal revelations—most probably, both of them. In any case, it was better this way. They weren't friends, after all. Certainly not lovers. They'd shared a few steamy encounters in recent weeks. No big deal.

No big deal at all, other than the fact she couldn't seem to shake the restlessness those encounters had stirred within her. It was fine, though. That restlessness was easy enough to ignore when they stuck to business. All business, all the time. It was quite productive and absolutely appropriate.

It was also positively maddening.

Tom would be sitting there talking about Jackson Pollock, and she would nod, smile, and suddenly imagine Tom flinging paint over her naked body. He, the artist. She, the canvas, covered in wanton abandon like one of Pollock's drip paintings.

He'd stop whatever he was saying and stare at her until she'd snapped out of her trance, face hot, a little breathless.

"Everything okay, Doc?" he'd ask.

Everything was not okay. Clearly.

"Dr. Higgins?"

She snapped to attention, blushing at the thought of Tom and of cold, wet paint dripping on her skin. What in the world had gotten into her?

"Dr. Martin," she said, averting her gaze from his art-themed tie. Jackson Pollock. *Of course.* Her neck grew ten degrees warmer. "How can I help you?"

"Have you seen this?" He tossed a newspaper on her desk.

She glanced down at it. The Arts Section of *The New York Times*, with a boldface headline that shouted *Avant Garde Artist Archer Jailed Following Destruction of Public Property Charges.* Beneath her desk, one of her legs started bouncing uncontrollably. She tried to swallow, but her mouth had grown too dry.

Relax. All he knows is that Archer is in jail. You knew he would hear about it eventually. Nothing has changed. "Yes. Yes, I did. A shame, really. Don't you agree?"

She forced herself to look her boss squarely in the eyes. He frowned. Her chest seized. Sooner or later, all of this lying was going to give her a heart attack.

"Interesting timing, don't you think?" he asked.

"Interesting timing?" She repeated, stalling so she could think for a second. He sounded suspicious. What could she possibly say? "Oh, the show! Of course. It's a good thing we've switched gears. Can you imagine if we were all set to put on a show, and we didn't have an artist?"

Dr. Martin shook his head. His Pollock tie moved back and forth. "No, I can't imagine."

Harper could. She could imagine it all too well, seeing as it had actually happened. "Well, like I said, everything is fine. We're moving along, right as scheduled."

Distraction. It was the only tactic she could come up with. She would ignore Archer's dilemma altogether and simply talk about something else.

"Mr. Stone's paintings are lovely. I think you'll be very pleased with the collection." She willed herself not to look at the newspaper even though she felt as if it might burn a hole through the surface of her desk.

"You didn't know about this, did you, Harper? When you decided to change directions for the show, I mean." Dr. Martin tapped his index finger on the headline. *Tap, tap, tap.*

So much for her attempts at redirection.

This was it. This was the moment she could put a stop to all the lying. If not all it, then at least some of it. She could simply admit that yes, she'd known, and she'd done what she did in order to save the day. Would Dr. Martin understand?

No. Of course he wouldn't. He'd demand to know why she hadn't been truthful upfront. He'd want know why she hadn't come to him immediately. And he'd be more curious than ever about exactly where she'd found Tom.

As appealing as it was, telling the truth, or even a version of the truth, simply wasn't possible. It was a pipe dream.

She shook her head. "No. I just heard about Archer's legal troubles recently. Like I said, what a shame."

She dropped her gaze to the newspaper again, and that was when she saw it—the subscription sticker with the addressee's name on it. *Dr. Lars Klassen.*

Her blood boiled. That misogynist, coffee-swilling jerk. He'd seen the article and run straight to the department head. Wasn't it enough he'd thrown together the ridiculous Dodo party?

Dada. For goodness sake, don't say Dodo. Don't even think it. Not in front of Dr. Martin.

"I suppose it's a good thing you replaced him when you did. We dodged a bullet, didn't we?" He refolded the newspaper and tucked it under his arm, probably so he could return it to that snake, Lars.

Ugh. "Totes."

"I beg your pardon?" Dr. Martin tilted his head as if he were hearing things.

Oh, how Harper wished that were the case. *Totes?* Seriously? She was losing it. One hundred percent losing her mind. "I mean yes. Yes, we certainly dodged a bullet."

"Well, then, good work, Dr. Higgins." He turned to go.

Just as Harper allowed herself to exhale, he spun back around. "You and Mr. Stone will be in attendance at Dr. Klassen's event Saturday evening, won't you? I'm looking forward to a nice chat with your artist."

She nodded. "Absolutely."

My artist. Mine. Why did those words make her forget all about Archer, Lars, and *The New York Times*?

Losing it. Most definitely.

Totes.

TOM STOMPED THE snow off his boots as he pushed through thick plastic sheeting and into the floral warehouse with Gunner on his heels. A blast of lukewarm air hit him in the face, but it was barely enough to shake the chill from his bones.

He'd walked three dogs through a foot of snow over the course of the morning. A few of his clients had opted to have him pay home visits to their dogs, letting them out briefly and spending a few minutes playing with them indoors rather than braving the cold. But dogs were dogs, not people. Most of them preferred being outside, snow or no snow.

He couldn't blame them. There was a certain freedom to

being outdoors that even a sky full of swirling snow couldn't abate. He rather liked it himself. So did Gunner. It was a welcome change from being hit in the face with blowing sand.

It had been odd at first, seeing the snow blowing across the pavement like a dancing phantom. When he'd peered out the windows of Harper's living room that morning, it had looked exactly like the desert sands. For a moment or two, he'd imagined he was back in Iraq, watching sand skitter across the roads of Kirkuk. His senses had automatically gone on high alert. But then he'd stepped outside, and instead of the sticky hot sting of sand, he'd felt the gentle kiss of snow on his cheeks.

It had been a moment of sublime retribution. Nature reversing itself. He'd stood there on Harper's front walkway with his arms spread wide, face upturned, until the flurries had settled in a fine layer on his clothes. Soldier turned snowman.

Frank gave him a onceover as he walked in. "Is it still coming down out there?"

Tom pulled his thick wool beanie off, ran a hand through his hair and ordered Gunner to sit. "Pretty much, yeah."

"And you walk dogs in this weather?" Frank shook his head. "Crazy."

"They like it." He shrugged and glanced at his dog panting softly, his long shepherd muzzle stretched into what could pass for a happy grin. "I like it, too."

"Crazy," Frank muttered again, this time under his breath.

"How are the flowers holding up?" Tom took a look around at the colorful blossoms surrounding him.

A rainbow of perfumed petals. Just as he was about to turn his attention to Frank again, his gaze snagged on a handwritten sign above a bucket of lilies.

Picasso Calla Lilies.

Picasso—a name that had once been vaguely familiar. Once upon a time, Tom had associated it with images he'd thought cartoonish. Now of course, he could recite Picasso's life story, his list of most influential paintings and his famous last words. *Drink to me, drink to my health. You know I can't drink anymore.*

Tom even knew the man's eye color.

"Oh, the blossoms will be fine. The secret is not turning the heat up too much. They don't need to freeze, but we don't want the petals sweating, either." Sweating petals. It was an image only Frank could conjure. "Wait here, I've got your flowers in the back. Some nice miniature tea roses. A week old."

He put down the spool of green floral wire he'd been winding and headed toward the walk-in cooler.

When he'd gone, Tom took another look at the Picasso flowers. They were like nothing he'd ever seen, much less painted. The center of each bloom was deep, dark purple, gradually fading into a creamy white outmost edge. Their perfect wrap-around petals indeed looked as though they'd been kissed by the paintbrush of an artist. They were breathtaking. They were eye-catching and exotic. They were also six dollars per stem.

He calculated how much a generous bundle of them would cost. A lot. More than what he usually spent on flowers in an entire month.

"Here we go." Frank returned, cradling a bouquet of miniature white roses. They were perfectly lovely. Pretty.

Ordinary.

"What do you think?" He held them up for Tom's inspection, a ritual that had become routine. Tom had never turned down one of Frank's modestly priced offerings. He couldn't afford to.

He cleared his throat.

Picasso Calla Lilies. Wouldn't Doc get a kick out of those? He wondered if she'd ever heard of them before.

He had no business buying her flowers. None whatsoever. And yet...

They'd been walking on eggshells since the cookie incident, which was one hundred percent his fault. They'd been cookies, not love letters.

Not flowers.

"Well? Shall I wrap the tea roses up for you?" Frank peered at him from over the top of his glasses.

He should get the roses. They were perfectly fine.

"Not yet," Tom said. "Not just yet."

HARPER HAD READ every bit of media coverage on Archer's arrest, searching for something, anything that could clue Dr. Martin in on the fact that she'd known about it when she'd made the decision to replace him with Tom. Other than the obvious detail of the date of his arrest being the same as the date that she'd announced her plan to switch gears, there was nothing. Surely her boss wouldn't remember the exact date she'd told him about changing artists for the show. He was a busy man. He had more important dates to keep track of in that academic head of his.

I hope so, anyway.

The door to Art Bar swung open. Harper's stomach flipped

in rebellious anticipation at the prospect of Tom's arrival, which was ridiculous when she thought about it. Good grief. She was living with the man now. Day in, day out. It was time to get over her nonsensical infatuation.

I am not *infatuated with him.*

She looked up from the copy of the *Washington Post* that was spread open on the table in front of her, carefully arranging her features into a mask of indifference. But it was a wasted effort. Tom wasn't the one strolling through the door at all.

"Peyton. Hi." Even she could hear the barest note of disappointment in her own voice. Pathetic.

"Hello." Peyton heaved two enormous cardboard boxes of wine onto the table.

Boxed wine. Rosé. With garish orange stickers that screamed *clearance* stuck all over the cardboard. Classy. Harper forced herself not to sigh.

"What's with all the newspapers?" Peyton picked up the *New York Times*, gave it a cursory once over and dropped it back on top of the pile. "Are you planning on teaching a paper mâché class or something?"

Paper mâché. Seriously? She was still trying to wrap her mind around the marshmallow panda painting. "No. I was just reading up on something."

"Couldn't you do that online and save a tree, or perhaps an entire forest?" Peyton frowned at the pile of newsprint. *The Boston Globe, USA Today, the Times, the Post, the Guardian, the Daily Telegraph.* All the heavy hitters.

Maybe Harper had gone a little overboard. Paranoia tended to do that to a person. "The online versions don't always have the complete story."

Peyton shook her head. "No, they don't. Then again, sometimes they have even deeper coverage. More pictures, more opinion pieces in their blogs, that sort of thing."

Well, wasn't that great news? Harper might have to ask Lindsay to give the virtual newsstands a perusal. "Super."

Peyton straightened the stack of papers. "Don't throw these out when you're finished with them. I'm sure we can use them for some sort of project."

We. Right. That *we* had Harper's name written all over it. She could see herself now, elbow-deep in paper mâché paste.

"Speaking of new projects." Peyton smiled, and Harper knew exactly where she was headed. "Have you whipped up any new originals? I'd love to see what you've been working on. I am so ready to cut back on my hours around here. I'm telling you, Harper, I'm not sure how much longer I can do this."

Harper's gaze dropped to the *Times.* She'd been hoping against hope to avoid this topic. She'd made Peyton a promise and, especially once she'd been caught kissing Tom up against the wall of Art Bar, it was a promise she intended to keep. The trouble was, she couldn't seem to be able to paint.

She'd tried. Several times. Every time she'd sat before her easel at home, nothing happened. She couldn't even make herself paint the simple marshmallow bear. It was as if her hands had forgotten how to paint.

Reproductions? Now, those were a different story. She could paint those all day long, even the most difficult ones. The Mona Lisa's subtle smile? No problem. John William Waterhouse's Pre-Raphaelite women of Arthurian legend? Piece of cake. She could even manage a passable variation of Georges Seurat's *A Sunday Afternoon on the Island of La Grande Jatte.*

That was a tricky one, made up of countless teeny, tiny dots. Pointillism.

Still, she didn't like the idea that she couldn't make herself paint even the simplest of original paintings. She should be able to come up with something. A unicorn. An ice cream cone. Anything. But the moment her paintbrush touched the canvas, her hand began to shake and then…nothing.

Tom had come home from walking dogs on two different occasions and found her sitting there, staring at her plain white canvases. She was sure he probably thought she was crazy. Sometimes she was inclined to agree with him.

"Well, did you bring anything to show me?" Expectation glimmered in Peyton's eyes.

"Actually…" Before she could finish, for once, fortune smiled down on Harper.

The front door opened again. Tom. Since she hadn't had the proper time to prepare herself for the assault of his devastating good looks on her senses, butterflies took flight in her stomach the moment she saw him. Thousands of them. Maybe even millions.

"Hello." He didn't smile, exactly, but his usual grim expression relaxed ever so slightly.

Flutter, flutter, flutter.

"Mr. Stone." Peyton's grin could have lit up Boston Harbor in a midnight blizzard. "How nice to see you again."

"Thank you. It's nice to see you, too." Tom smiled.

At least this time everyone was fully clothed. That didn't seem to make things any less awkward, though.

Peyton looked pointedly at the green tissue-wrapped bundle in his arms. Flowers. No doubt they were for Tom's next painting, which of course piqued Harper's curiosity. She strained to get a glimpse of what lay beneath the green tissue, but he held them even closer to his chest.

Peyton glanced back and forth between the two of them. "If you're here for another tutoring session, you're a few hours early. Harper is teaching class tonight."

"Actually, he's here to pick up Vincent. Tom is my dog walker." Harper sat up a little straighter. She wanted Peyton to forget all about what had happened the other night. She wished she could forget it herself.

Sure you do.

"Your dog walker?" Peyton's eyebrows rose. "And your private tutoring student? Interesting."

Harper shook her head. "It's not that interesting. Really, it isn't."

The less said about their warped relationship, the better. She wanted to keep things as professional as possible.

Tom aimed a pointed stare at Harper. "We're actually roommates, too."

Every butterfly in Harper's belly came to a standstill. "Um…"

"Roommates?" Peyton blurted. "This is certainly news."

Harper shook her head. If she shook it any harder, her brain would have rattled. "No. We're not roommates. Absolutely not."

Tom lifted a brow. Harper knew good and well what that eyebrow meant.

No more lies.

She sighed. "Well, we are, but it's not how it sounds. And it's temporary."

"Very temporary." Tom nodded. Thank goodness he'd deigned to corroborate her version of events.

Harper could have kissed him. Wait. No. That was how all this mess had gotten started in the first place. "As temporary as it can possibly be."

Peyton snorted. "It sounds like you two need to get your story straight."

Harper glared at Tom. As per usual, his smile seemed to grow in direct proportion to her irritation.

"Whatever you two have going on, just save it until after class, okay? Mac Coleman is signed up to paint tonight. The man is eighty years old if he's a day. He would have had a heart attack if he'd walked in on what I saw the other night." Peyton picked up the boxes of wine and headed toward the storage room.

Harper wanted to die. She wanted to drop dead right there in Art Bar surrounded by all that bad art and cheap wine. But first she wanted to murder Tom Stone.

She crossed her arms. "What was that?"

"I beg your pardon?" He smirked.

"You know what I mean. Why on earth did you announce to Peyton that we were roommates? She thinks we're a couple now, you know."

"As does my landlord. Remember?" He winked.

So that was what this was about. She'd embarrassed him, so he'd taken it upon himself to do the same to her. How ridiculously childish could he be?

"I hope you're happy."

"Oh, I am. Very."

"What I said to your landlord wasn't intentional. I spoke

without thinking." She tended to do that a lot around Tom. He never failed to bring out the worst in her, and at the oddest moments, the best. "You, on the other hand, appear to have your wits about you."

His sardonic grin widened. "Thank you."

Thank you? Honestly? "It wasn't a compliment."

"Thank you, regardless," he said.

Harper rolled her eyes. "You're impossible, you know that?"

"Impossible?" He glanced down at the tissue-wrapped bundle in his arms for a moment before pinning her with a look that had suddenly gone frosty. "I suppose I am."

"Finally, we agree on something." she said.

"At long last," he ground out. "You know, Doc. Before we met, I was a real person, with a real life. The Bells. Frank. Those are real people. Friends."

The air grew thick with tension. Harper was certain that even Vincent felt it, as evidenced by the way he'd swiveled his lone ear, laying it flat against his worried little head.

She wasn't sure what had happened. Somehow this exchange had become more of an argument than the playfully cutting barbs they typically traded.

Well, if he thought she was apologizing, he was in for a disappointment. He was the one who'd come gallivanting in here, giving Peyton the impression that the fact they were roommates meant he'd been spending every night in her bed.

Actually, the way you were kissing him the other night is what first gave her that impression.

Never mind. That was in the past. She sure wasn't about to kiss him now. And the scowl that had taken up residence on his face left no doubt he wasn't entertaining thoughts of kissing her either.

A change of subject was in order. Pronto.

She ventured another glance at the green tissue in his arms. "Are those flowers?"

"Yes," he said flatly.

"For a new painting?"

He looked at her without saying a word. The room was so quiet that Harper could practically hear the melting clocks ticking on all the Dali-inspired paintings hanging on the walls.

Finally, he said, "Yes. What else would they be for?"

She ignored his sarcasm. "Anything new and different? Let me guess…gerber daisies."

He shook his head. "No."

"Lavender?" That would be pretty. Unexpected, too. Although she liked the idea of the painting of the violets being the lone shock of purple at the show.

"No."

"You're not going to tell me, are you?" She craned her neck in an effort to get a peek.

He backed away. "Nope."

"You know I'll see them eventually, right? So you may as well show me."

"Let it go, Doc." He shook his head and stalked off, presumably to fetch Vincent for his walk.

She barely heard his final words.

"They're nothing special."

Chapter Seventeen

IN A CRUEL twist of ironic fate, Tom had been doing his best painting since he'd moved into Harper's home. Lord only knew why. It defied logic. He was in a foul mood more often than not, and he hadn't been quite so sleep deprived since the overnight missions he'd engaged in with his unit in Iraq. Sometimes an overnight would stretch into two or three nights at a time. Afterward, he'd return to camp with his ears, nose, eyes—every possible crevice—full of sand. Windburned, hungry, and so exhausted he'd sometimes hallucinate; he would drag himself to his cot and collapse until his growling stomach awakened him. Sometimes a matter of hours, other times a matter of days.

He was beginning to look upon those memories with fondness. At least then he'd eventually find some relief. As things stood now, there wasn't a sleep-filled night in sight.

He missed the boat. He missed the feel of the water beneath him in the quiet night. He missed the subtle sway as he closed his eyes and gave himself up to his dreams.

Here there were no dreams. There was no sleep. There was no movement, just agonizing stillness and an ache that had taken root the night Harper Higgins first pressed her lips on his. At the rate things were going, he wouldn't sleep a wink until all of Boston had thawed and he could go back to where he belonged.

Because he sure as hell didn't belong here.

Things with Harper had gone from bad to worse. She'd been in an awful mood when she'd come home from Art Bar. Tom didn't blame her, really. He'd given her a pretty hard time about Peyton and the whole roommate thing. But he'd been trying to prove a point, and that point was that she wasn't the only one whose life had been affected by their charade. He had a life, too. And pretending to be someone he wasn't had thrown a big, giant wrench in things.

He'd gone too far. Probably. Definitely.

But when Harper had been slamming cabinet doors in the kitchen after she'd come home, his name hadn't been the one she'd been mumbling about under her breath. It had been Lars's and, occasionally, Peyton's. He'd assumed her problem with Lars was the usual. He was her archenemy bent on destroying the entire universe. Or her little world, which, to Harper was tantamount to intergalactic destruction.

He wasn't sure what the deal was with Peyton, but he'd heard Harper muttering something about marshmallows and spotted unicorns and had decided it was best not to ask. He'd stayed out of her way as much as possible, which wasn't easy considering they'd had their usual late night studying session.

Harper had been more tense and anxious than ever about the party-that-wasn't-really-a-party, with good reason. They only had two days left to prepare, but she'd peppered him with only an hour's worth of facts and questions before excusing herself for bed.

Bed. The place where most people slept.

Tom hadn't even bothered. He'd just gone to his room and started setting up to paint. The first few nights he'd lain there, wrestling the sleeplessness. The passing hours had grown longer and longer until the night stretched before him in one unending yawn of desperate solitude. By the fourth night he simply couldn't take it anymore. At a loss of what to do at four in the morning, he'd given up and begun painting. With a brush in his grasp and the sensation of paint moving across linen beneath his hands, the hours had grown shorter, and the darkness less thick and the stillness not quite so lonely. By the time the sun had come up, bathing snowy Boston in soft watercolor hues of pink and lavender, a completed painting had sat on his easel.

He'd been reminded once again why he did this in the first place. Art as therapy. No, not therapy. It was even simpler than that. It was art as a way to get through the night.

So the next night he'd done the same. And the night after that, and so on. His art had become a glittering nighttime garden, like primroses that only blossomed beneath the glimmer of a setting sun. When Tom looked at those paintings, he imagined walking through a forest at night, the cool earth soft beneath his feet, the cry of an owl somewhere in the distance. While he and Harper had been breathing the same air, while she'd slept with only a thin wall of regret separating them, he'd painted a forest of blooming, tremulous flowers.

Tonight the calla lilies were coming to life on his canvas. Picasso's calla lilies. Flowers named after a master.

Tom had wondered if it would feel different painting flowers so different from those that he typically interpreted in his art. Lush flowers. Rich flowers. If he'd been at all hesitant, those worries had slipped away once he'd begun mixing the colors on his palette. The purple of those lilies was nothing short of majestic, with the most concentrated pigment located right at the center, the heart of the blooms. Purple hearts, like the ones that had been awarded to his fallen brothers.

At the first touch of that purple to canvas, he'd been spellbound. The sight of that glorious color blending with the purity of the white outer petals brought a rise of gooseflesh to his skin. It was a rush, painting something so exquisite—not unlike kissing a beautiful woman, the most beautiful woman whose lips he'd ever had the privilege of tasting. A woman who, in rare moments of inspired fervor, made his heart pump with the blood of creativity and vision. When she wasn't working his last nerve, that was.

"Tom? What in the world are you doing up at this hour?"

Speak of the devil.

He nearly fell out of his chair. What was *she* doing? Sleepwalking? She'd slipped up behind him as quiet as the night itself. He hadn't heard a sound.

He turned to face her and took a long, measured inhale while his heartbeat slowed back down to normal. Or as close to normal as it would ever get when he was taking in the sight of a sleepy Harper with just-rolled-out-of-bed hair. His gaze dropped to the expanse of creamy white flesh exposed by her delicate nightie. Collar bones that begged to be traced with his fingertips. Bare shoulders crying out to be kissed. This wasn't a doctor of any kind standing before him. This was living, breathing art.

He swallowed, with great difficulty, and wondered if she always slept in something so flimsy. The palest and sweetest of pinks. Like candy. It was almost as unexpected as it was alluring. He would have pegged her as the flannel pajama type, had he given any thought to what she wore to bed at night. Okay, so maybe it had crossed his mind. Once. Or twice. No more than twenty times, max. He blinked, and in the darkness behind his eyelids, he saw himself tearing that nightie right in two.

He opened his eyes and focused exclusively on her face. "Harper, what are you doing up?"

She tilted her head, and a wayward lock of hair fell gently across her face. "I asked you first."

"Couldn't sleep." He shrugged.

"How long have you been awake?" She peered around him, clearly angling for a glance at his canvas. "Don't tell me you've nearly completed an entire painting."

He moved to block her view, but she was too fast for him. She'd sidestepped completely past him and positioned herself between him and the canvas before he'd known what was happening.

He turned around. She was mere inches away, with her back to him, studying the painting, caught in the spell of color and composition, shadow and light. He could smell her shampoo—something floral. Sweet. Carnations, maybe? He leaned closer. Peonies. Definitely peonies.

She smells like one of my paintings.

At that thought, he went instantly hard. Was he dreaming? No. In order for it to be a dream, he'd have to be asleep. But this sure felt like one. Dreams were the place where muses walked off canvases and into real life with daisy chains in their tangled hair, drenched in the perfume of flowers. This was

Harper. She wasn't a muse. But at the moment, she sure as hell seemed like one.

Tom couldn't help himself. He reached out and touched her hair with the barest brush of his knuckles.

Soft. So soft. Like feathers.

"Tom, this is stunning." She shook her head and her hair swished out of reach.

He dropped his hand back to his side. "Thanks."

"I mean it. It's exquisite." She turned around.

She had that glassy-eyed look about her that she always had when she'd been immersing herself in art. As if she was drunk on color.

"But different from the others."

He frowned. "Different how?"

"Just different. The usual feeling of brokenness isn't there. This piece isn't about healing, as the others are. In this one, I see reverence. To me, it feels like the worship of beauty. What was your inspiration?" She blinked up at him, all wide-eyed wonder.

Tom could barely look at her. Had she forgotten that she was practically naked?

"I don't know." *Liar.* "Just the flowers, I guess."

"They're gorgeous." She walked over to the vase where he'd arranged the lilies and gently stroked one of the petals. "I've never seen anything like these before. What are they?"

"They're lilies. Calla lilies." He crossed his arms. "Kind of interesting, actually. They're called Picasso calla lilies."

"No, they're not!"

As he'd predicted, this news thrilled her. Her bow shaped lips spread into a wide ribbon smile. Undoubtedly, it was the most girlishly delighted he'd ever seen her.

That right there. That was the look he'd hoped to put on her face when he'd forked over the small fortune for those flowers.

He nodded. "They are."

Her gaze drifted to the flowers and lingered there, tracing the impossible beauty of the petals, the slender grace of the stems. Then she looked back at him. He saw an odd mixture of emotion in her eyes—the wonder was still there, but it was tempered with something else. She wrapped her arms around her midsection, as if she'd just realized how she was dressed, and it was then that he was able to put his finger on it. Fear.

That mask she always wore—the one that kept her hidden from the world, the one that made her seem so abrasive half the time—it was there to hide her fear. *Why are you always so afraid, Doc?*

He wanted to tell her there was nothing to be afraid of. But that was a lie, wasn't it? There was plenty to be afraid of. Life, pain, loss. He was the last person who could make her any kind of assurances.

"I love them," she said softly. "The lilies. They were a perfect choice."

Tell her. Tell her they're hers. You bought them for her, and they're hers.

His chest grew tight. He couldn't do that. It would change things. He knew it would. And she didn't want things to change. Neither did he.

He gave her a half-hearted shrug. "They were on sale. Frank's special of the day. I didn't choose them. They chose me."

"Oh. I see." Whatever was left of her smile faded. "I probably should be getting back to bed. It's late. I'm sorry if I bothered you. I saw the light on, so…"

"You didn't bother me. It's your house, Doc. No need to apologize. I'm just a guest remember?"

"A guest. Right." She cleared her throat. "Well, good night."

Then she brushed briskly past him, his ethereal muse gone, replaced with the good doctor he knew so well.

"Good night, Doc," he whispered in her absence.

His gaze fell on the painting. She was right. It was different than the others. There was nothing broken about this one. Because it wasn't real. It was a fantasy, just like the flowers, those lilies that looked as though they'd been touched by the brush of a revered Spanish painter who was long dead and buried. The painting wasn't about reality. It was an illusion. A hint. A glimpse at the glory of the way things could never be.

It almost hurt to look at it.

You don't want things to change?

You sure about that?

Chapter Eighteen

HARPER WOULD HAVE made a terrible spy.

She knew this much now. Between the anxiety over all the lies—which had grown so numerous she'd been forced to put them all on an Excel spreadsheet in order to keep up with things—and the general state of panic she'd begun to exist in whenever she was on campus, she was pretty much a basket case. How did Jason Bourne do it?

She was beginning to have an entirely new understanding for the pottery professor who kept a king-sized jar of Tums on his desk. She wondered if he had secrets, too. Or maybe lopsided bowls and throwing clay at moving pottery wheels carried hidden stresses that she just didn't appreciate. Either way, she could use a handful of those Tums right about now.

She stared at the computer on her office desk. Nothing. Just a bunch of nothing. For over an hour now, she'd been searching for information that was proving to be elusive. And she'd thought it would be so easy. Just a few clicks of a button. Isn't that what the Internet was for?

Bourne would never have these problems.

"Something wrong?" Lindsay stood in the doorway, frowning.

Everything. Everything is wrong. "No, nothing."

"Can I come in? I have some...*stuff*...to discuss." Lindsay bobbed her head toward Lars's door across the hall and blinked a few frantic blinks.

Lindsay wouldn't be signing up for a career in espionage anytime soon either, from the looks of things.

"Come on in. Shut the door." Harper waved her in.

She clicked the door closed behind her and sat in the chair opposite Harper. "Okay, I've finished looking at all of the online newspapers and I haven't found anything that even mentions Archer's participation in your show. So I don't think you have anything to worry about."

"Oh." Harper was at once both relieve and disappointed. Relieved, for the obvious reasons. But a little disappointed because she would have liked to think that the show she was curating was at least the tiniest bit newsworthy, that it meant something to someone, somewhere.

This was one of the key differences between painting and teaching. Paintings generally elicited some sort of reaction. Art made people feel something, even art that critics dismissed as shallow and lacking depth. Sometimes Harper missed that. She missed it a lot on days when she stood in front of a classroom of students who seemed more interested in the displays on their cell phones than they were in the power point presentation of the timeline of Dutch masterworks that she'd put together.

But there were more important things than feelings. More often than not, feelings spelled trouble. With a capital "T".

"Thank you for checking, anyway," she said. "I guess it stands to reason if there had been anything incriminating, Lars would have found it already. After all, he's the one who gave Dr. Martin the copy of the article in the *Times*."

"Right. But it hasn't changed anything. You knew in the beginning you'd never be able to hide the fact that Archer is in jail." Lindsay's eyelashes fluttered. "I mean, you knew that, right?"

"Yes, of course." Harper nodded.

She no longer had any idea what she'd been thinking at the outset of this mess. The only thing she knew for certain was that she'd never in a million years expected to meet a man on the street and only a matter of weeks later, wake up in the middle of the night to find him painting one of the most achingly beautiful pictures she'd ever seen.

Things were getting complicated. She didn't like complicated. She'd spent the better part of her life making things as logical and orderly as possible.

"What are you working on?" Lindsay nodded at the computer monitor with the Google search engine logo emblazoned across the screen.

"Oh nothing." *A whole lot of nothing.* "I'm just trying to find someone."

"Do you need some help? I've got a little time on my hands this afternoon."

Time. What a luxury. Harper no longer knew what it meant to have plenty of time. The days on the calendar had been whipping past in a frenzy of names, dates and images since she'd begun tutoring Tom. The harder they worked, the less time they had left. Only one day remained until Lars's party. One. Day.

She glanced at the computer. What was she doing embarking on a wild goose chase when she had plenty of more important things to be worrying about at the moment? Like where the local unemployment office was.

"Actually…" She looked down at the notes she'd scribbled on her note pad. Three words. Three words that had yielded nothing thus far.

Frank. Flower guy.

"Yes?" Expectation shone in Lindsay's eyes.

It would be so easy to just turn things over to her. Lindsay was perfectly capable of handling something like this.

But Harper had so liked the idea of doing it herself. "Actually, I'd like to take care of this on my own."

"Are you sure? Because you've got an awful lot on your plate right now. How are you doing, anyway? We've hardly had time to talk."

"Me? I'm fine. Everything is going great. Nothing to worry about at all." She pasted on a smile.

One more lie to add to the spreadsheet.

TOM TOOK ONE look at the photograph that Harper was busy waving in front of his face and laughed. Hard.

He'd needed a good laugh.

So had she, he could only imagine.

Things had not been going well. Since their initial moment of tenderness on the night he'd moved in, they'd been tiptoeing around one another. And that was fine. For the best, probably. Except things had been getting progressively more awkward, culminating in their late night encounter the night before.

It was exhausting.

He was tired. Tired of cramming facts into his overworked

brain every hour of the day. Tired of trying to become someone he so clearly wasn't. Tired of one sleepless night after another.

But most of all, he was tired of pretending not to notice how pretty Harper looked in the morning, all sleepy softness, with her hair in mussed disarray. He liked her best this way. Save for when she was sitting at an easel, mornings were the only times she seemed to let her guard down. She was at her most relaxed, most real then. Of course, until the night before, he'd had no idea what she'd been wearing beneath her fuzzy bathrobe. Now that he did, the pretending had become near impossible. There was really only so much a man could endure.

Tom had taken to "sleeping in." He stayed right there on his borrowed twin bed, eyes closed tight, body and mind tingling with awareness as he listened to her pad through the house. He could imagine the graceful flick of her wrist as she flipped on the coffeemaker, the elegance in her long limbs as she stretched like a cat, yawning and luscious.

God help him if he ever went in there and joined her. Not when she was all soft curves and grace, with night still clinging to her tumbling hair. He'd never be able to keep up the pretense that he didn't want her, didn't think about kissing her, or imagine her beneath him on that tiny twin bed every time he lay down in it.

Every damn time.

Now, it was easier to resist those impulses. It was evening. A half-empty pizza box rested between them—a pepperoni-scented barrier—while they sat on opposite ends of the sofa from one another. Harper had slipped into her professorial persona, the one she seemed to find most comfortable. The one he typically found most irritating.

He'd never expected her to make a joke. She never joked when she discussed art history. The topic was sacrosanct as far as she was concerned. But here she was, holding up a photograph of a urinal and trying to tell him it was one of the most important pieces of art from the Dada movement.

He laughed again and took a bite of pizza. "Good one, Doc."

"What's so funny?" She deadpanned.

"That." He nodded at the picture. Not only was it a urinal, it had the name R. Mutt scrawled on it in drippy black letters that looked as though a child had painted them. "Come on, Doc. You're pulling my leg. I know you are."

"I'm not. I swear." Her lips twitched.

He pointed at her mouth with what was left of his pizza slice. "See? You're about to laugh. There's no way this is real."

"It's totally real. Honest." A giggle escaped her.

"You can't even say it with a straight face."

She cleared her throat. "I promise. It's called *Fountain.* In 1917, it was submitted for exhibition in the Society of Independent Artists show. They rejected it."

He looked at the photo again and shook his head. "Of course they did. It's a *urinal.*"

"Its rejection caused quite a controversy. The rules of the show stated that every piece of art would be accepted from artists who'd paid the fee."

He fixed his gaze back on Harper. Face flushed from laughter, skin glowing, she looked happy. He hadn't seen her look this happy in days. He'd missed this look.

Stick to business. The "test" party is tomorrow night. "I'm guessing Mr. R. Mutt paid the fee?"

She lifted a brow. "You say mister like that's given. How do you know R. Mutt wasn't a woman?"

"At the risk of sounding repetitive, it's a *urinal.* Doc, you're killing me here." He snatched the photo from her and examined it.

"Actually, the identity of R. Mutt remains one of the art world's greatest mysteries. It was a pseudonym." She picked a pepperoni off one of the pizza slices and popped it into her mouth.

Tom looked up just in time to catch a glimpse of pink tongue. He immediately switched his focus back to the photograph. "You mean no one wanted to claim responsibility for this? Shocking."

"It was widely attributed to Marcel Duchamp. He did a whole series of replicas in the 1960s," she said.

"Replicas? You mean there are more than one of these?" He shook his head. He still wasn't altogether certain she wasn't pulling his leg. On the one hand, she seemed serious. And she was always serious about art. But it was so ludicrous he was having trouble wrapping his mind around it. "That's unfortunate."

"Replicas...oh, I know! I can teach this at Art Bar. Peyton's been after me to simplify my classes. It doesn't get much easier than this. I'll just put urinals in front of everyone and have them paint their names on them." She laughed. Loud and hard.

It was then that Tom realized they were having fun together, despite their mutual efforts not to. Fun was nice. Fun was fun.

Fun was also dangerous.

He thought about saying he was tired and needed to turn

in. He thought about all the shady truths floating between them and how the very simple fact that nothing they were creating together was real was reason enough to keep things professional.

He also thought about shoving the pizza box out of the way, pulling her against him, and kissing her senseless.

He could feel her heartbeat pounding against his, hear her gasp of surprise as he reached for her, see the sweet parting of her lips. God, how he'd missed those lips.

"Tom? Hello?"

She was talking to him. She'd likely been talking to him for the duration of his mental foray into forbidden territory. He wasn't entirely sure. Everything had kind of disappeared for a moment.

"Hello," he said, one foot back in reality and the other still firmly planted in the land of fantasy.

Come with me. Let me take you there.

Her gaze bored into his. And there it was—the delicious parting of lips. The subtle glimpse of candy tongue. Her green eyes glittered, as if she could read his mind. Or maybe, just maybe, her mind danced with the same imaginings.

"Tom, this is important. The party is tomorrow night. I need you to pay attention." Her voice had a breathless quality to it that he'd heard before on exactly two occasions. Both such occasions had ended with her mouth on his and his hands tangled in her hair.

"You've got my attention." His resistance was weakening. Who was he kidding? It had already left the building. "One hundred percent. Undivided."

She narrowed her gaze at him. Ever wary. Ever guarded. So

careful. God, how he longed to see her drop her defenses again. He'd walk barefoot over hot coals to see that kind of passion from her just one more time.

"Then tell me something," she said. "Since you're paying such close attention, give me one true fact. You can pick anything you'd like."

Harper and her quizzes. Tom was beginning to pity her students at the art college. He wondered if she tortured them the same way she did him.

Somehow he doubted it. "I want to be clear on the rules here. One true fact? Just one? About anything?"

She nodded. "Yes, anything from tonight or the past few days. Whatever you choose."

There were a million things to pick from. He could have waxed poetic about R. Mutt and his stupid urinal, because there was no way he'd ever be able to expunge that little morsel of Dada trivia from his brain. He could have talked about Salvador Dali's giant pet anteater that he led around on a leash and even took on the subway with him in New York City. But there were words that had been trying to leave Tom's mouth for hours, and they didn't have anything to do with *Fountain* or wildly inappropriate animals that had been kept as pets.

She stared at him. No doubt there were visions of slapping him with a ruler dancing in her head. "Well?"

One true fact. "The flowers are yours."

She sat perfectly quiet, perfectly still, like a Rodin sculpture.

For a minute, Tom wondered if she'd stopped breathing. "Doc?"

"What did you just say?" She was a bundle of intensity.

Every one of her nerves appeared to be on high alert and

pointed squarely at him. He wasn't altogether sure if this was a good or bad thing. For once, he couldn't get a read on what was going through her head.

He only knew that there seemed to be a lot going on in there at the moment. "I said the flowers are yours. The Picasso lilies. I didn't buy them so I could paint them. I bought them for you."

The change in her demeanor was slow at first, excruciatingly slow. It began with a slight movement of her lips, the tiniest glint in her emerald eyes. Tom was suspended in time. He was sure the clocks must have stopped while he sat waiting, waiting, waiting.

Then suddenly, in flash of blinding light, the rest of the change happened all at once. And she was there. Right there, less than an arm's distance away. His art goddess, come home. Except this time, the free-spirited smile on her face wasn't for a painting.

It was for him.

At last.

He'd been waiting for this moment for a long, long time. Probably since before he'd ever laid eyes on her.

"I know what you're thinking," he said as he picked up the pizza box and tossed it out of the way onto the coffee table.

Three seconds. That was all he was giving her to make up her mind before he wrapped his hands round her delicate waist and pulled her against him. Three seconds, which was more than generous considering he wasn't certain he'd last more than two.

"You're going to kiss me. Again." He touched her lips with his pointer finger and held her still. What he was going to say was important, and he needed her to pay attention. "This time it won't end there. Be sure."

He felt her breath hot against his fingertip, sensed the tremble in her lips.

"I'm sure," she said against his touch. "I've never been more sure."

His fingers slid down so he had a firm grip on her chin. She gasped and, with one hand holding her chin and the other burying itself in her hair, for the very first time, Tom Stone kissed Harper Higgins instead of the other way around.

Chapter Nineteen

BE SURE.

Tom hadn't needed to say the words. Harper had seen the seriousness in his gaze as he'd stared back at her, waiting for her to answer him as if she'd held the secret that made his flowers grow and his paint move across his canvases. She'd noticed the tension in the set of his jaw and known he'd been holding back, but had sensed his hold wouldn't have lasted much longer. She'd felt the insistence of his fingertip pressed against her lips and understood everything her body had ever wanted lay within the subtle assertion of that simplest of gestures.

Most of all, she'd sensed the change in the room—the way the walls seemed to ache and the air swirled with intention.

He wasn't playing around this time, and neither was she.

I'm sure. I've never been more sure.

In the span of a heartbeat, his mouth was on hers. One of his hands pressed at the small of her back, pulling her toward him with the force of an ocean swell. The other still held her chin firmly in place. She couldn't move her head. She could only feel. And taste. And dream.

That was what she liked best about kissing Tom—the touch of his lips unlocked the dreamer in her. Every time. This kiss was no exception. Hard, deep, forceful. As if he was swallowing every bit of her need, turning back time so she forgot what it was like to ever feel lonely or unwanted. It was so overwhelming she forgot to breathe. And then, just when her lips began to feel bruised and bee-stung, he pulled back. Not all the way, just a fraction. The world came to a screeching halt as Tom's movements slowed. The kiss changed, becoming gentle, languid as he touched her lips with just the barest brush of his. The sudden switch was excruciating.

She wanted more.

She needed more.

She struggled to lift her chin, but his grip remained firm. Not forceful, but insistent, preventing her from seeking what she so desperately wanted.

When she whimpered in frustration, he dropped his lips to her neck, trailing kisses all the way to her ear. "Problem?" he asked, his voice a slow, sultry whisper.

How could he be so calm? She was already frantic, and they'd done nothing but kiss. He'd barely touched her.

She opened her eyes. *I need you. I need this.* "Not at all."

"Good." He smiled. "This isn't one your art quizzes, Doc. You're not running the show anymore. We don't need to rush. I'm not going anywhere. Okay?"

I'm not going anywhere.

He'd left out an important word. *Yet.*

They hadn't made any promises about the future. They hadn't even discussed the here and now. Harper was glad for that. She wasn't ready to have that conversation.

She didn't know what was happening between her and Tom, only that it was something raw and powerful. And not something that fit within the bounds of reason.

This doesn't change anything. Everything can stay the same, just as it is now.

Even though Tom was kissing her again and she was rapidly losing all capacity for coherent thought, she knew this wasn't true. Sleeping with him…merely kissing him…would very much change things. It already had. And the thing it had changed most was her. She was changing right that very second.

Being with Tom frightened her. Not because she was afraid he would hurt her. She knew him better than that, and she would have never considered giving herself to a man she didn't trust. Her fear was rooted in her response to him. She didn't know what she was going to do from one minute to the next. It was the loss of control she feared. But even as she feared it, she craved it.

She wanted to be so consumed by desire she lost all sense of herself. She couldn't imagine what it would feel like to surrender, to give up the reins she clung to so tightly. Save for the times Tom had kissed her. When she was in his arms and her mouth was on his, she caught a tiny glimpse of the woman she could be. Unfettered. Unafraid. Free.

That was who she wanted to be. She just didn't know how to get there. But the way he made her feel gave her hope. And that was something she'd not had for a very, very long time.

"Harper," he whispered into her hair, "open your eyes. Look at me."

Her eyes drifted open. "Yes?"

"Get out of that head of yours. I want you. But I want you here. With me. All of you." With those words, he released his hold on her chin and let her go.

They sat facing one another, hearts racing, breathing quickened, eyes darkened by desire.

"I'm here." Harper breathed. "I am."

Tom stood, then he took her hands in his and lifted her off the sofa. Blood was pulsing through her veins with such force she grew a little light-headed. This was it. This was the moment she would lead Tom to her bed. The moment she'd thought about since the day he'd first moved in. No, that wasn't quite true. She'd been thinking about it longer than that, perhaps even since the night she'd first seen him lying on the rain-slicked pavement, surrounded by violets.

She turned toward her bedroom, her hands still entwined in his. He tugged on them, pulling her back.

She looked up, anxiety pooling deep in her stomach. She was more aroused than she'd ever been in her life. If he changed his mind now, she would die. Or worse, she might fall at his feet and beg.

His eyes implored her. He didn't look like a man who'd changed his mind. "Dance with me, Doc?"

They were the last words she'd expected to come out of his mouth. "You want to dance? Well, Mr. Stone. Aren't you full of surprises? Flowers and now dancing?"

"I'll take that as a yes." He pulled her close and settled her in a dance hold.

They'd been playing music while they studied, turned down low. Old standards like Dean Martin and Sinatra. Tom hummed softly in her ear as he spun her around the living room to those familiar refrains. His heart beat against hers and she could feel his arousal pressed against her. She leaned into his warmth, wanting to get closer to him, and closer still.

Without a doubt, it was the single most romantic moment of her life. She was dancing around a pizza box in her living room in her sock feet, but, in her mind, she'd traveled to some other faraway place. A place where nothing mattered but the music and the movement and the man who held her close.

They swayed together and her eyes drifted closed. Little by little their footsteps slowed. Tom's hands slid beneath the hem of her sweater. As he lifted it up and over her head, she stepped out her jeans until she was left standing before him in just her panties and a lavender lace bra.

"So beautiful," Tom murmured, reaching out to run a single, exploratory fingertip down her throat, between her breasts, over her tummy and ending at the lacy edge of her panties.

His eyes never left hers. She was nearly naked, while he remained fully clothed, watching her, gauging her reaction. She felt vulnerable, exposed, and more alive than she had in as long as she could remember.

"Kiss me," she whispered.

Somewhere in the fog of desire that had gathered in her head, his words from earlier drifted to the fore. *You're not running the show anymore.*

"Please," she added, "please, Tom."

He gave her what she wanted, leaning in and taking her mouth with his. At the same time, his hand pushed lace aside and he touched her, his fingers probing and insistent.

She melted against him, formless. Clay under the hands of an expert sculptor. She wanted him undressed, so she could feel the heat of his flesh against hers. She wanted him inside her before she collapsed from longing.

She wanted him.

NO MATTER HOW many nights Tom had lain awake wondering, wanting, the reality of seeing Harper bared for him was infinitely sweeter than anything he could have imagined. She was all lavender and lace. More feminine, more beguiling than he'd ever dreamed. To think that lacy bra, those barely there panties, had been there the entire time, waiting to be slipped off and abandoned in a puddle of satin at her feet was agonizing.

He bent to unfasten her bra and slipped its delicate straps from her shoulders. With a sigh, it fell to the floor, along with the final shred of Harper's resistance. He cupped her beautiful breasts in his hands, marveling at her softness.

Her fists gathered in the folds of his shirt. He knew she wanted him to undress, and he would. In due time. Right now he just wanted to see her and touch her before he lost his mind with need. Plus, there was something so sensual about having her wrapped around him, naked and yearning, while he was still fully clothed.

He dropped his mouth to her breasts and kissed them. She arched into him and made the kittenish noise that had haunted him since he'd first heard it when he kissed her against the wall of Art Bar, and any ideas he'd had about drawing things out into a slow, aching dance were instantly abandoned.

This was the Harper he wanted. The one she didn't show anybody. The Harper only he saw.

Even those times when she was peppering him with questions, her hair just so, her skin as white as an oleander against the severity of her crisp black blazer, he'd seen glimpses of this woman. She was there, with her watercolor eyes and paintbrush in hand, waiting. Waiting for someone to find her, to touch her, and tell her it was okay to give herself up to fate.

Didn't she know she couldn't control things, no matter how hard she tried? The walls she'd built around herself were paper-thin. There was no avoiding pain in this world. If anyone knew that, it was Tom.

Yet you do it yourself. You hide just as much as she does.

Maybe that was why he was the man who got to see her like this, the one privileged enough to taste and touch both her darkness and her light. The hard and the soft. The rough-cut diamond that everyone else saw and the feather on the wind they'd never noticed.

His lips moved from her breasts to her shoulder to her neck, and he whispered against the warmth of her skin. "Now, Doc."

She nodded, took him by the hand and led him to her bedroom. It was the only room in her house that he'd yet to set foot in. Steeped in shadows, he could still make out the paintings on the walls. They showed Boston street scenes from the South End. Snippets of everyday life, as seen through an artist's eyes. He knew without being told she'd painted them. Once upon a time, when she'd let her imagination out to play.

He followed her to the bed, mesmerized by the sway of her hips and the way her curves moved among the blues and grays of the darkened room. He remembered telling her once there was nothing beautiful about a shadow, and she'd corrected him. As always. But she'd been right. He wasn't sure he'd even seen anything more beautiful than her body as it was right now, like a monochromatic picture. *Blue Nude.*

When they reached the bed, she turned around and began

to unbutton his shirt. She gazed up at him, her eyes shining with want, and he let her undress him until they stood together clothed in nothing but the moonlight drifting in from the bedroom window.

He wanted to touch her everywhere, until there wasn't an inch of her perfect skin he hadn't kissed with his fingertips. He wanted to wind her hair around his fists and tug while he pressed his lips against hers until they bled, and at the same time, he wanted to make her giggle with the tenderness of butterfly kisses on her bare belly. He wanted to give her everything neither of them had ever had.

Her gaze traveled the length of his body, studying, memorizing, as if he were a statute in one of her books. She reached for him with a trembling hand and traced the muscles of his abdomen, exploring him with her touch until he didn't think he could take it anymore.

He caught her wrist in his hand, brought it to his mouth and kissed her fingertips, one by one. Then he laid her down on the cool white sheets of her bed.

And finally, as he'd imagined so many times, she was under him. His body hovered above hers and he kissed her as her hands found him and guided him home.

Home.

That elusive concept, the simplest and most complicated of words was the singular thought he had as he entered her. This woman who'd come into his life with all the drama of a rainstorm of flowers, this artistic enigma of passion and control who was arching up to meet him, to take him fully inside. She'd become home for him in the most intimate of moments.

He knew he shouldn't think of her in those terms. Whatever they had probably wouldn't last a day beyond the art show, when he would go back to being the real Tom Stone and she went on to follow her dreams. Dreams that would no longer have anything to do with him.

But he closed his eyes and allowed himself to believe in the illusion so long as he was buried in her depths, all the while reminding himself that it wasn't real.

His warrior heart refused to listen.

Chapter Twenty

HARPER HAD GONE straight from being in bed with Tom to standing on Lars Klassen's threshold. It seemed that way, anyhow.

She took a sideways glance at Tom. After last night, she feared looking at him full on. He was too perfect, too overwhelming. Like a rare, fiery, solar eclipse. If she focused every bit of her attention on him at once, it would surely burn her alive.

"Don't be nervous," she said, weighing the pros and cons of spontaneous human combustion.

He shook his perfect head. "I'm not nervous."

Harper wouldn't have believed him if he'd been anyone else. But this was Tom Stone, Mr. Cool Under Pressure, standing beside her. Lars Klassen and his evil plans to take over the world—or at least the art history department—might terrify Harper, but they were nowhere on the list of things that intimidated Tom. As far as she knew, no such list existed. If it did, it was surely on the short side. Microscopically small.

"Good." She nodded, and wished they'd gone over a few of the Dadaism notes one more time.

Who was she kidding? She didn't wish any such thing. Over the course of the past twelve hours, she hadn't thought about Dadaism once. She hadn't done any *thinking* at all.

She'd done nothing but feel. For the first time in her life, she'd abandoned all thought, all worries, all rules. It hadn't been a conscious choice. She'd been beyond choosing. Rather, she'd simply become. At Tom's touch, she'd been transformed into someone else entirely; a woman she'd never known existed. A woman she liked. A lot.

Unfortunately, that woman had no place at this party.

"Are *you* nervous?" His voice carried a hint of the tenderness it had in the early hours of the morning, the quiet hours when the lovemaking had been agonizingly slow and sweet. An aching whisper, as opposed to the primal scream of desperation that had finally brought them together the night before.

That gentle inflection somehow both soothed her and aroused her at once. Goodness, what was happening? She could *not* be aroused while standing on the front porch of Lars Klassen's home. That was just wrong on so many levels.

"No, of course not."

"Doc," he said, waiting quietly in the darkness.

She glanced at him for the briefest of moments. God, those eyes of his. Looking at them was like walking into the most beautiful painting she'd ever seen.

She let her gaze wander back to the door. It had a garish doorknocker in the center in the shape of an Egyptian cat. Very big, very gold, very Lars. In-your-face artsy. It looked like something that had been unearthed from King Tut's tomb.

"Doc, look at me." Tom cupped her face and turned her head toward him.

What was he doing, touching her here? They were at a university event. This could not happen. It was utterly unprofessional. If anyone saw them right now, she could kiss her promotion goodbye. She should tell him so. She *would* tell him so.

Just as soon as she could force herself to stop leaning into his touch and whimpering his name. "Tom."

"Doc," he whispered, running the pad of his thumb along her bottom lip. "Everything is going to be fine. We've got this."

We've got this. We've *got this.*

As if they were a couple. Which they weren't. Not by any stretch of the imagination. They were a team, not a couple. There was a difference between the two. A huge difference. A difference bigger and brighter than one of Monet's wall-sized water lily paintings.

"Everything is going to be fine." She repeated, not so much for his benefit as hers.

"Are you ready?" he asked, reaching for the doorknocker.

As ready as I'll ever be. She took a step away from him, so that they stood a respectable, professional distance apart. "Yes."

"All right. Here we go." He lifted the ring of the cat and knocked three times. While they waited, he muttered, "That cat knocker is a little creepy."

Laughter bubbled up Harper's throat. The fact that he could make her laugh at a time like this was a flat-out miracle.

The door swung open, and Lars greeted them with a smile decidedly creepier than the cat's. "Dr. Higgins, how nice of you to show."

"Dr. Klassen." She smiled. Or at least she hoped it was a smile. It felt more like she was grinding her teeth. "I wouldn't miss it."

He opened the door wider and motioned for them to step

inside. "Do come in, and please…introduce me to your friend."

Her *friend?* Was he trying to trick her or simply get on her nerves? If it was the second option, then mission accomplished.

"Lars, this is Tom Stone, the artist whose paintings will be showcased in the annual department art show later this month. Mr. Stone, this is Dr. Lars Klassen."

"Pleased to meet you," Tom said.

"The pleasure is all mine." Lars extended his hand. "It's not every day that I get to meet a descendent of Van Gogh. And an art expert, too."

"So you've heard of my great-great-grandfather, then?" Tom smiled, the perfect picture of calm.

They shook hands like two men who were about to walk twenty paces and then face off in a duel.

"There are so many people here who want to meet you, Mr. Stone," Lars said, leading them down a hall lined with bookshelves. Half of them looked like books that had gone missing from the college library.

Harper reached for one, but as her fingertips brushed its spine, Lars cleared his throat rather loudly. "This is Dr. Martin, the head of our department. Dr. Martin, may I present Tom Stone, Harper's artist."

Harper's artist. She rolled her eyes. He wasn't a possession to be owned. He was a person. And she should be introducing him to Dr. Martin, not Lars.

"Yes, of course." Dr. Martin nodded. "I've been looking forward to getting acquainted with you. Come with me. Let's have a chat before the lecture begins. Shall we?" He motioned toward a tiny study off the hallway.

It was so small that it only had room for a pair of red leather chairs and a round table between them. *Two chairs?* Where was she supposed to sit? On Tom's lap?

Her face grew hot.

"Harper, come along. You're going to miss the discussion on Shock Art as a means of fostering societal change." Lars looked at her expectantly, as if the prospect of a lecture on Shock Art would be too much for anyone to pass up.

She wasn't fooled by that look. He knew precisely what he was doing. The tiny room. The two chairs.

Divide and conquer.

Her plan had been to stay beside Tom all night, so she could intervene if things got dicey. She needed to be there, if anything to fill in the missing blanks of Tom's supposed background. She'd been so concerned with giving him the necessary information to make him sound like someone who was familiar with the finer nuances of art that she couldn't quite remember how thoroughly they'd gone over the specifics of his backstory.

She lingered in the hall, watching as Dr. Martin and Tom sat down opposite one another. Tom glanced at her. It was a sign of reassurance, and she tried her best to seize upon it. To believe in him. But it was so hard. She'd relied on no one but herself for a long, long time now.

"Harper, are you coming or not?" Lars's gaze narrowed.

Tom will be fine. It's you who's going to screw this up by acting like he needs a babysitter.

She turned away from the study where her future depended on what transpired between her boss and her dog walker. Her dog walker who she was currently sleeping with. How had she ever managed to get herself into this mess?

"Coming. Lead the way," she said.

Because really, what choice did she have?

"TELL ME ABOUT your art, Mr. Stone." Dr. Martin smiled at Tom.

Tom smiled back. He felt good about how this was going. So far, the discussion had centered around Harper, a topic he was more than qualified to discuss. The trick had been not giving away the extent of his qualifications.

"Dr. Higgins is a delight, is she not?" her boss had asked.

"A delight. Absolutely."

He'd tuned out for a second, remembering the taste of her skin, the feline way in which she moved beneath his touch—a cat stretching in the warm glow of sunshine, wanting nothing more than to be stroked, again and again.

Then he remembered where he was and that Harper was no longer wrapped around him in bed, but sitting in the next room worrying about what he was saying and doing.

Focus.

"My art?" Tom nodded. "I paint flowers."

"Flowers?" Dr. Martin leaned forward in his chair. "Go on."

Tom wasn't altogether certain how to proceed. What did he want, an itemized list? *Violets, carnations, hydrangeas…* "I guess you could say they're in the Van Gogh tradition. That's what Dr. Higgins seems to think."

That earned him another smile. "Will you be painting any sunflowers, then?"

"No, I don't think so. I see my great-great-grandfather as an inspiration, but I've no illusions that I can improve upon what he's already done with such beauty."

Dr. Martin tilted his head. "You don't find them pedestrian? Some feel that they've become so iconic that they've lost the luster of authenticity. I'm interested to hear a Van Gogh descendant's take on the subject."

Pedestrian? The first stab of worry found its way into Tom's consciousness. If this guy thought Van Gogh's work was bad, Tom's own paintings didn't have a prayer. "Not at all. But I've always believed that the value of art is unique to the person experiencing it. A thousand people can look at the same painting, and none of them will see the same thing."

"An interesting theory." Dr. Martin nodded. "And a reasonable explanation of how Henry de Groux could refer to them as 'the laughable pot of flowers by Mr. Vincent' while others saw a masterpiece."

Tom didn't know who this Henry de Groux was, but he sounded like a jerk. "Absolutely."

"Do you agree that he should have resigned? Or would art have been better served if he'd stood his ground?" Dr. Martin's eyes narrowed slightly.

Tom had no idea how to answer that question. Resigned from what? He was still trying to remember who the guy was.

He should know this. If he were really related to Van Gogh, he'd know exactly what Dr. Martin was talking about. "You know what they say about quitting. A quitter never wins, and a winner never quits."

He'd been aiming for a laugh. Or at the very least, to take the tension in the room down a notch. It hadn't seemed to work.

Dr. Martin frowned. "So you're telling me that you, a painter in the Van Gogh tradition, would have had Henry de Groux exhibit his paintings alongside Van Gogh's sunflowers at that first exhibition back in 1890, even after publicly disparaging them? That's an interesting point of view coming from someone such as yourself, Vincent's great-great-grandson, a man who has walked the same pathways as Van Gogh's famous shoes."

Van Gogh's shoes. Now that was something Tom knew about. Couldn't they talk about the shoes? "I've never been one to follow the crowd."

"I gathered."

An awkward silence fell over the room.

Tom wished he could get a read on the situation. Was he blowing this? He couldn't even tell anymore.

"What are your thoughts on Dadaism?" Dr. Martin nodded toward in the direction where Harper had followed Lars to the lecture.

This was tricky territory. Should he say what he really thought or what an art expert might have to say on the subject? He weighed the options. On the one hand, he may have already screwed things up. Falling in line with what he was expected to think might be the way to go.

On the other hand, there was no way he could pretend to like the urinal. He just didn't have it in him. "Not a fan. At all. *Fountain?* A joke. And the reproductions? Somewhere there's a men's room missing a whole row of urinals and we're supposed to think that's a good idea?"

Dr. Martin looked at him as though he'd just sprouted two

heads. Then, just as Tom was imagining Harper working at Art Bar and sucking on juice boxes for the rest of her life, he let out a laugh. Then another and another, until his face grew red and he bent in half, laughing uproariously.

Tom snickered. "I'm guessing you agree?"

"Wholeheartedly. Why do you think I've shut myself away in here with you instead of listening to Lars's guest?" He rolled his eyes.

"I'd gotten the impression it was to interrogate me," Tom said. It wasn't a joke.

Dr. Martin seemed to think otherwise. He laughed again. "I like you, Mr. Stone. I like you a lot."

"HE LOVED YOU." Harper could have floated all the way home rather than walking. Hearing Dr. Martin go on and on about how much he'd enjoyed talking to Tom had made every minute of sitting alongside Lars through the dreadful lecture totally worth it. "I mean, he really loved you. You nailed it."

"So, you're happy?" he asked.

"I'm more than happy. I'm thrilled." She looked at him walking alongside her in the lamplight of the harbor walk, and she felt an intense surge of gratitude to Lindsay for suggesting that he move in with her. She was happy he was going home with her. Happy he'd danced with her in her living room. Happy he'd been in her bed, all masculine warmth and desire, when she'd awakened this morning.

She was just plain happy.

"What in the world did you two talk about?" she asked.

He glanced at her. Snowflakes spun in the golden glow of the streetlamp, and they looked like stars falling all around him. "Lots of things, but I'm pretty sure the deciding factor was when I shared my thoughts on *Fountain.*"

She should have never shown him that photograph. "You did not."

He laughed. "Oh, I did. And I didn't mince words."

She could only imagine. "When have you ever minced words?"

"Not in a while," he said.

"I didn't think so."

"For the record, your boss shares my views on the work of R. Mutt."

She shook her head. It wasn't altogether surprising. Dr. Martin was a traditionalist. But he was also the head of the art history department. She'd never heard him denounce art of any kind. Ever. "He does, does he?"

"Definitely. He said given the opportunity, he'd piss all over it."

Harper stopped in her tracks. "Tom Stone, now you're making things up. Dr. Martin did not say that."

Tom grinned. "Oh, yes, he did."

All that studying, all that preparation, and when it came down to it, Dr. Martin's opinion of Tom was the result of a mutual dislike of a photograph of a urinal. Unbelievable.

"What else did you two discuss, or should I even ask?" A shiver ran up and down her spine.

The temperature had dropped even lower than what it had been over the past few days. Tom reached for her hands and warmed them with his. How was he so warm all the time, even out here in the cold? It made her want to bury her head against his shoulder.

"We talked about painting. And Van Gogh. And sunflowers."

She sighed. "All beautiful things."

"And we talked about one more beautiful thing." He gave her hands a gentle squeeze. "You."

She felt her smile fade. "Me?"

Tom's smile faded in turn. "Yes, you. Something wrong, Doc?"

"Yes. No." She shook her head. "I mean, maybe. What did you say?"

He shrugged. "That you were a delight."

"A delight? A *delight?* Please tell me you're joking." This wasn't happening. It couldn't be.

"I'm dead serious. Although I have to say, right now the adjective doesn't apply." He dropped her hands.

She crossed her arms. "You can't call me a delight to my boss. It's unprofessional. It makes me sound like…like…a dessert."

Tom's jaw hardened. "For your information, *Doctor* Higgins, those were your boss's words. I simply agreed."

"Oh." That was different, she supposed.

But still. Dr. Martin couldn't suspect they were romantically involved. It would ruin everything.

"He can't know we slept together, Tom. I would lose my job."

Tom was quiet for a long moment. Snow gathered on the shoulders of his coat while he stood there staring at her in the moonlight. "Your job. That's what you're worried about. Of course. It's what you're *always* worried about."

"Don't be angry. That's the whole reason we're doing any of this."

His eyes flashed. Clearly he was ignoring the *don't be angry* part of her comment. "And what if he thought we'd been intimate? What then, Doc?"

"I suppose I'd assure him it wouldn't happen again." At the rate things were going, it wouldn't. "It was a mistake."

"A mistake. Got it." He nodded slowly. "It was a mistake when you kissed me, and now you've made the mistake of sleeping with me. Those are two very big mistakes, Doc."

She wanted to take her words back and swallow them whole. "Tom, that's not what I meant."

"Yes, it was." He backed away from her, and somehow those few steps felt like a mile. "I'm going for a walk, Doc. I'll catch up with you at the house later."

"Tom, wait. Don't." Her teeth began to chatter. She'd never felt so cold before. "Come home."

"Home?" He shook his head.

"Yes, home. Come home with me." Even as the words left her mouth, she wasn't quite sure if she meant them.

They sounded an awful lot like begging. Like something her mother would have said once upon a time. And that was the last thing she'd ever wanted to sound like.

He stared at her and she could tell. She could see her own doubt reflected back at her in the cool, ice blue of his eyes.

"I don't think so, Doc. Not right now." He no longer sounded angry. He sounded hurt. Hurt, and very disappointed.

She wrapped her arms around herself, either to fend off the cold that was fighting its way into her bones or to hold herself together. She wasn't sure which.

He leveled his gaze at her before he walked away. "I'm saving us both from making another mistake."

Chapter Twenty-One

THE SNOW WAS relentless.

Tom stared at his boat on a sunny morning a week after the party, shrink-wrapped in plastic, sitting perfectly still in the harbor. The way the plastic shone through the layer of accumulated snow made it look like an ice cube bobbing in liquid. Except that there was no bobbing. Tom wouldn't have been surprised if the entire harbor was frozen solid. He peered into the water. No ice, just cold, black water.

One thing was certain, though. He wouldn't be moving back into the boat anytime soon. Not until it had been good and thoroughly winterized. Just looking at it sent a chill coursing through him.

Gunner didn't appear to be keen on the idea of returning to the boat either. He stood calmly at Tom's side, panting softly. Tiny icicles had already begun to form on the underside of his muzzle. On a day when his coat would have been warmed by the summer sun, the shepherd would have run ahead of Tom the moment he'd spotted the boat. He would have leapt aboard and begun his inspection without waiting for orders. The boat was home to both of them.

Not anymore. It had never looked so foreign. Tom supposed it made him feel better that Gunner appeared to share his opinion on the matter.

"Don't worry. We'll be back here soon enough. Not much longer." Tom gave the dog a pat on the head with his gloved hand before heading to his next client's house.

Not much longer. A week. A week was nothing. Seven days.

Seven days of wondering what was going on in Harper's head. Seven sleepless nights on his twin bed, surrounded by her paints and brushes, her art and books, all the things she loved. The things that made her the woman she was. Seven nights of knowing she was mere yards away, warm and wonderful, and he couldn't have her again.

It may as well have been a year. Or ten. Time in Iraq had moved faster. Nights spent in a desert tent, listening to far-off explosions that seemed to grow nearer and nearer had been less agonizing.

It was a mistake.

Damn right, it was a mistake. He should have never taken her to bed. He should have never touched her. Maybe he would have had half a chance at a moment's peace if he didn't know what it was like to have her beneath him, arching to meet him, eyes full of the life and fire that he'd always known she possessed somewhere deep inside. Knowing he'd seen such a magnificent side of her she kept so closely guarded was a powerful elixir. Like a drug. And he was teetering on the precipice of addiction. It was the only explanation for the way that night haunted him, because he couldn't be developing feelings for her. That just wasn't possible. Half the time, she still drove him crazy. Not the good kind of crazy, like the way she talked about her dog—"spirited and bright, like a Pop Art painting." Genuinely crazy. Certifiably, pull-his-hair-out nuts.

The way she sat and stared at that blank canvas for hours at a time made him want to scream. He'd never met another living soul so determined to control every aspect of life.

He squinted against the snow flurries hitting his face and pushed through the gate that led to the row of townhomes where his client lived. Buster, the Boston terrier.

Buster was somewhat of an institution in the South End. First, because he was a Boston terrier, the native breed of the city. Tom had noticed people in Boston lit up like Christmas trees whenever a Boston terrier was in their midst. It didn't matter if they were dog lovers or cat people. A Boston terrier sighting in Beantown was a reason to smile.

But there was more to Buster's claim to fame than simply the matter of his breed. His owner ran one of the most popular pubs in the South End. In the evenings, Buster could be found sitting atop the bar, occasionally trying to sneak sips of beer as pints were passed back and forth. On nights the Celtics played, Buster wore a green plaid bowtie. Last St. Patrick's Day, he'd ridden on one of the floats in the South End's parade.

He was undoubtedly Tom's most famous client. He was also a handful.

"Hello, there," Tom said after he'd let himself in.

From behind the baby gate that kept Buster locked in the kitchen when he was home alone, he bounced up and down and barked in response. In reality, the baby gate only worked about half the time. Today was one of those times.

"Imprisoned, I see. Well, no worries, I'm here to bust you out."

Gunner was waiting for them on the front porch, right where Tom had left him on a down stay. Buster's paws scrambled beneath him, trying to find purchase on the snowy ground as Tom locked the door behind them. Gunner looked at the terrier with thinly veiled disdain. If a dog could roll its eyes, Gunner probably would have done so.

"All right, you two. Let's go."

Walking Gunner and Buster together was always interesting, as they were as opposite as two dogs could be. Gunner, with his stoic dignity, walked calmly and quietly at Tom's side while Buster zigzagged his way down the sidewalk and threw himself in the path of every passerby. He was a lot like Vincent in that respect, except whereas Vincent's affection was aimed exclusively at Tom, Buster's was all over the place. Everyone was a target.

They'd gone all of ten feet when he accosted a baby stroller.

"Sorry," Tom muttered as he picked up the terrier and scooped him out of the way.

"Oh, it's okay." The woman pushing the stroller smiled. "Good afternoon, Buster."

Buster squirmed with glee. Tom kept a firm grip on him until they were safely out of stroller-range.

"Behave yourself," he said as he returned the dog to the pavement. Right. *If he could behave himself, you'd likely be out of a job.*

They managed to walk for a good minute or two before faced with the challenge of another pedestrian—a man in a black overcoat with his head bowed against the frigid wind. Tom wound Buster's leash around his hand a few times and lessened the slack, but the dog strained and pulled, dancing on his hind legs in an effort to greet the stranger.

The man glanced at the dog without slowing his steps.

Even with his hat pulled down low and a scarf wrapped around his face, he looked vaguely familiar. Then he met Tom's gaze and the memory came crashing down.

"Oh. Hello, Mr. Stone." The man loosened his scarf, exposing the rest of his face. It was him, all right. That jerk from Harper's department. The Dodo. Lars.

Tom forced himself to smile. "Hello. Dr. Klassen, right? From the party the other night?"

"From the party. Yes." He nodded slowly, and his eyes narrowed as his gaze traveled over Tom, Gunner and finally, Buster.

"This is the notorious Buster." Lars formed it as a statement, not a question that Tom could answer in the negative if he'd chosen to lie.

And as sick as he was of the lies, now was the time for one. "Yes, yes it is. The rascal."

Lars crossed his arms. "What are you doing walking Buster? Surely a prestigious artist with a show on the immediate horizon has better things to do than walk someone else's dog."

Tom had to give the guy credit. He didn't mess around. He cut right to the chase. "Just taking a break. Getting some air. Buster is a neighbor. Sometimes he comes along when I'm walking Gunner."

Lars glanced at the shepherd with indifference. "I see."

Tom shifted his weight from one foot to the other. Lars's breath hung in the air in a cloud of vapor. They stood there on the sidewalk facing one another in a silent duel, waiting for the other to say something.

Tom wasn't about to open his mouth. The less lies there were to keep track of, the better. He was already making mental notes about the fact that he supposedly lived next door the most famous dog in the city.

"Well, I must get back to the college. I have a class in half an hour," Lars said. "We're studying Hopper. Surely you're familiar with Hopper?"

"Of course." Tom nodded. Hopper…Hopper…yes, Edward Hopper, the American realist. "Like most people, I'm a fan of *Nighthawks*. But I actually prefer *Room in New York*. His use of color in that painting is outstanding, particularly the reds. Wouldn't you agree?"

"The reds. Yes." Lars scowled. Clearly he'd expected to trip Tom up.

No such luck. Although, he was beginning to long for the day when he would no longer feel like a Jeopardy contestant on call 24-7. "I'll let you get on to class then, Dr. Klassen."

"It was a pleasure seeing you again, Mr. Stone." He nodded before adjusting his scarf and moving on.

Buster spun a few quick circles, tangling himself in his leash. Tom sighed. *Yeah. A pleasure.*

EVERYTHING WAS WHITE.

Snow beat upon the windows, the yard was covered in a frosty blanket and the air was thick with snowflakes. But the whitest thing of all was the blank canvas staring Harper in the face.

Not again.

She exhaled a weary sigh. Yes. Again.

She'd been sitting at her kitchen table for the better part of an hour trying to come up with something to show Peyton.

Anything, just paint anything.

She couldn't wrap her mind around why this kept happening. Granted, it had been years since she'd put her own thoughts and feelings on a canvas. Her own soul, out there for the world to see. But this was different. Peyton herself had said that it didn't need to be perfect. She wanted cute. She wanted playful. She wanted a cartoon, for Pete's sake.

Just do it. Paint a polka dotted a unicorn. A monkey skateboarding. That marshmallow bear. Anything.

She dipped her brush in the puddle of pink paint she'd mixed together on her palette. Whatever she ended up painting, pink seemed like a good place to start. Was there a cuter color than pink? No, there wasn't. She got the bristles nicely saturated—not too wet, not too dry—and moved her hand toward the canvas. It stayed there, poised before the blank white linen, and began to shake.

The front door opened and she jerked her hand back. Paint flew from her brush and splattered her face, her neck, and her hair.

Marvelous.

Vincent came running from the other room, Tom's room, and made a beeline for the front door. Harper wasn't sure which was more alarming—the fact that she'd begun to think of her studio as Tom's room when he so obviously couldn't wait to move back to his boat, or that her dog had grown even more attached to him since he'd come to stay.

Would Vincent fall into a prolonged doggy depression when Tom and Gunner left? Would he lie around on his dog bed all day, pining for his lost love?

It's the dog who'll be doing the pining. Yeah, right.

She cleared her throat and turned her back on the accusatory blank canvas. Tom hadn't even removed his coat yet and already Gunner was busy searching, securing, protecting. Watching him do so caused a lump to lodge in her throat. She forced herself to look away.

"Hi," she said softly.

Tom looked up. "Hi."

She felt bad about what she'd said to him the night of the party.

It was a mistake.

She wasn't even sure if those words were true. On the surface, yes, it had been an awful mistake. They had work to do. Tom was living under her roof. She had no intention of giving her heart away again, only to have it returned, bruised and unwanted. Because Tom definitely wasn't looking for a relationship. When they weren't studying or talking about art, he barely spoke to her. He just watched her with those unreadable, fathomless blue eyes of his.

And yet, part of her had felt more like herself than she had in years when he'd undressed her. She'd felt wanted. She'd felt desired. She'd felt whole. It was almost like all her life she'd been an unfinished painting and the artist she'd been waiting for, the one she'd least expected, had come along and caressed her canvas with a final, perfect brushstroke.

Why couldn't she hold onto that feeling in the light of day?

"Have you been painting?" he asked, looking past her at the canvas standing on its table easel.

As he took in its empty state, his eyes glittered with a look all too familiar. Harper had seen that look on Rick's face plenty of times. Disappointment.

"I just sat down. I haven't gotten going quite yet." Another lie. For some reason, this one made her hate herself in a whole new way.

His jaw clenched. "I'm not judging you, Doc."

"Yes, you are. You should see the look on your face right now." She set down her palette and brush.

It wasn't like she was actually going to be using either one of those in the immediate future.

"This look has nothing to do with your art," he said, jamming his hands on his hips.

What art? She was a joke. She could copy things. She was no more an actual painter than Vincent was. The dog, not the Dutch master. "Is that so?"

"Yes. Look, we might have a problem on our hands."

She stood, then sat, then stood again. She'd always preferred to stand when getting bad news. It made her feel stronger somehow. "What kind of problem?"

He took off his beanie and jammed a hand through his hair. His face was red, windblown, and those lips she dreamed about in both her waking and sleeping hours were dry and cracked. Winter's toll. She pressed her fingertips to her own lips and tried not to think about kissing his back to life.

"I just saw Lars," he said.

The mention of Lars's name was enough to make her forget all about her artistic block. "Are you sure?"

"Yes I'm sure, Doc. I recently spent an entire evening being interrogated by the guy. I think I know what he looks like." He crouched down to greet Vincent, who'd been throwing himself against Tom's shins since the moment he'd stepped over the threshold.

How could he be so calm? "Did he see you?"

"Yes. We had a conversation." Tom stood, crossed over to the kitchen table and pulled out a chair.

"What did you discuss?" Harper sat down again. Their knees were a whisper away from touching. She scooted her chair backward a fraction.

Tom frowned at the space between them. "He wanted to know why I was walking dogs."

She dropped her head in her hands. "You mean he knows?" This was bad. This was really, really bad.

"Hey." He cupped her chin and forced her to look at him again. "I said we might have a problem. Emphasis on *might*. He doesn't know anything. I told him it was my neighbor's dog. I even threw a little art knowledge at him."

She regarded him through narrowed eyes. "You didn't mention *Fountain* again, did you? Because that might have been overkill."

He sat back in his chair and crossed his arms. "Have a little faith, Doc."

She rolled her eyes. "I have plenty of faith in you."

"Good." He winked, stood up and headed toward his room.

He was leaving? Just like that? Without telling her the rest of the story? "Where are you going?"

"To take a shower." He turned around and raised a challenging brow. "If you'd like to continue this discussion, you're free to join me."

If she hadn't already been sitting down, she might have fainted. She straightened in her chair. "In your dreams."

She wasn't going down that road again. She couldn't keep doing this with him, knowing there was an expiration date looming ahead. She was a mess. She couldn't paint. She could barely think.

He shrugged. "Suit yourself, but it might be a good idea. For someone sitting in front of a blank canvas, you've got an awful lot of paint on your face."

She grabbed the hand towel from her artist box and scrubbed at her cheek.

Tom stood watching her with a bemused expression that only made her more frustrated by the minute. "You can't stand it, can you?"

"I don't know what you're talking about." She did, naturally, but she wasn't about to play this game with him. If he thought she was going to beg him to tell her exactly what happened, he was going to be sorely disappointed.

"It's driving you crazy, isn't it? Not knowing." He gave her a rare smile, which only aggravated her all the more.

She wadded up the towel and crammed it back in her art box. "*Seriously,* what did you say?"

"Relax, would you? We talked about Edward Hopper. You know who he is, right? Realist painter. American icon." He winked again.

"Hopper." She nodded, and despite the fact that it always drove her mad when he teased her unmercifully, she grinned. "That was pretty genius. Lars is a big fan."

"So I discovered." His smile faded a bit. "You know, Doc. Things can work out, even when you're not trying to control them."

"*Controlling?* You think I'm controlling?" It certainly wasn't the most flattering opinion anyone had ever had of her but she couldn't quite feel offended, because even she knew there was some truth to it. More than a little.

"There are some things you simply can't control, Doc."

She lifted her chin. "And there are some things you can."

He aimed his gaze at her easel again. "How long have you really been sitting there in front of that canvas?"

She blinked. "A while."

He threw his hands in the air. "This is exactly what I'm talking about. You're too worried about what the finished product will look like. Let go. Stop trying to control the result and just paint, Doc. It doesn't matter what your brush ends up doing. Just paint. Paint whatever your heart wants. What does your heart want?"

He waited for a long moment for her to say something.

Harper knew what he wanted to hear, and those words danced on the tip of her tongue. Oh, how they wanted to spill right out.

You. I want you, Tom.

But she couldn't say them. She couldn't, any more than she could make herself paint.

"I see," he finally said, and then he walked away, leaving her alone with her paints, her brushes, and her smooth white canvas, ready and waiting for someone to bathe it in living color.

Chapter Twenty-Two

HE WOULD HAVE never have admitted it to Harper, but the encounter with Lars weighed on Tom. Something didn't feel right. The next day, the harbor walk felt almost haunted, as though he were being watched by some invisible ghost. He kept glancing over his shoulder expecting to see Lars walking behind him.

On the surface, everything appeared normal. There were no suspicious college professors lurking behind trashcans, spying on him. The snow still fell, the dogs still needed walking. But underneath it all, he couldn't shake the feeling that something was wrong.

Gunner felt it, too. He was hyperalert, ears pricked forward, nose quivering. Tom hadn't seen him this focused, this intense since they'd left the army in the rearview. The dog's demeanor did nothing to reassure him. Then again, the shepherd had most likely picked up on Tom's state of mind. Good working dogs were like that. Any change in the status quo was a signal, a sign that something could be wrong.

"Sorry, boy." Tom rested his hand on Gunner's head as they paused outside the door to Art Bar. The sun had just begun to set, casting shades of wisteria purples on the snow. Moving shadows stretched, closing in. *They're just ghosts.*

"Everything's fine."

He pushed the door open, fully expecting a lecture from Harper regarding the time. He was late. Looking over his shoulder all day had cost him in minutes. The first thing his gaze fell on when he walked in the studio was that familiar melting clocks painting. *The Persistence of Memory.*

Memories and time. Those ever moving hands of the clocks.

He shook his head and looked away.

"Hi, there," Harper said, counting out paper plates. Not the ones she ordinarily used for palettes. Pink ones, with cartoon ballerinas pirouetting around the border.

Another Degas copy sat on her easel. She must be doing another kid party tonight. Good. Those always seemed to put a smile on her face. At least one of them would be in a good mood.

"Hello." He bent down to greet Vincent, who'd come barreling toward his shins in his customary, over-the-top greeting. "Hello to you, too. Are you ready to walk?"

"Class might run long tonight. If you like, I can just meet you at home later." Harper glanced up at him and her cheeks went pink.

I can just meet you at home later. Like they were a family.

If she hadn't flushed, Tom may not have even noticed her phrasing. Being around one another all the time, the comfortable routines...somewhere along the line, it had all begun to feel nice. Normal. Real.

It's not any more real than those ghosts you've been seeing all day.

He cleared his throat. "That sounds fine."

Harper smiled, but her forehead creased with concern as she looked past him at Gunner sniffing the air, the baseboards, everything. "He's doing it again."

Tom finished clipping Vincent's leash in place and stood back up. "Yeah, he may be a while this time. He's been a little agitated lately." *Haven't we all?*

"Are you ever going to tell me what it is he's looking for?" she asked quietly.

Tom tensed. He didn't like where this was headed. He was surprised she hadn't figured it out. He forgot sometimes what it meant to be a civilian, to have never set foot in places like Iraq or Afghanistan. "Explosives."

"Explosives." Her eyes widened. "You mean bombs?"

"Improvised explosive devices. They're like bombs, yes. Homemade, thrown together with whatever is on hand."

The studio grew silent. The only sounds that could be heard were Gunner's footfalls as he swept back and forth, canvassing the room.

"Is this what you did in Iraq? You and Gunner?" she asked quietly.

Tom sighed. He thought for a moment about cutting her off, telling her to drop it, like she should have done when he'd been giving her a hard time about not painting. *But she didn't, did she?* "Yes. This is what we did. We would go in ahead of the unit and clear the area."

"Where were the bombs usually hidden?"

More questions. This was already the longest conversation he'd had on the topic with anyone who hadn't been there. Including his ex-wife.

She cares. Just answer her.

He shrugged. "Anywhere. Trash, animal carcasses."

"Animal carcasses? You mean there are dead animals lying around in the streets?"

"It's a mess over there, Doc. It's not like it is over here." Pictures moved behind his eyes. A blown-out building. A dirt road littered with paper. A pile of old tires. A plastic bag floating on the desert breeze. The urge to squeeze his eyes shut was almost overwhelming.

"Something happened over there, didn't it, Tom?"

She looked at him so closely he was sure she could see inside his memories. He wanted to rest his hands over her eyes like a blindfold. She didn't need to see those things. No one did.

A lot. A lot happened.

"We missed one. I got hurt and ended up in the hospital. Head injury." His voice sounded rusty, as if it hadn't been used for a century. "A lot of people were hurt that day."

"Oh, Tom." The look on her face crippled him.

The concern in her eyes, the sadness she felt for him, the understanding that the events of that day had changed things—everything. The tenderness with which she took it all in…real.

The door flew open and at least a dozen giggling girls spilled into the studio. There were balloons. And cake. Brightly colored packages and singsong voices filled with life and color, all of which stood in such stark contrast to the black and white film of Tom's memories that his head spun.

"Gunner." He called the shepherd to his side and turned to go.

"Tom, wait." Harper's voice reached him from across the crowded room. "You don't have to leave. Stay."

Stay.

He shook his head. "I can't."

He didn't belong here in this room full of innocent girls, of happiness and light. He wasn't sure where he belonged anymore. But as he left it all behind and stepped out into the darkness where the ghosts danced to their tragic melody, he wondered if he'd been the one playing the music all along.

Were they chasing him, or was it the other way around?

THE NEXT AFTERNOON, Harper stared at her misshapen marshmallow bear and shook her head. She honestly didn't know which fact she should find more disturbing—that she was actually painting this monstrosity, or that she couldn't seem to make hers look as good as Peyton's. *Good* being a relative term in this case, of course.

Peyton's panda was no masterpiece by any stretch, but at least it wasn't lopsided. And its edges didn't bleed into the background color. Harper's poor bear suffered from both these problems.

"Forget it." She removed the canvas from the easel, placing it on the floor, its bottom edge lined up against the baseboard.

Vincent, always fascinated with any change in his environment, sprung from his dog bed and trotted over to check things out. He stopped about two feet in front of the picture and stared at it for a few seconds, his soft brown eyes growing wide. His nose twitched, whiskers quivering at the end of his tiny muzzle. Then he sneezed. Not a tiny, miniature Dachshund sneeze. This was a sneeze of massive proportions. An elephant sneeze. And when it was over, Vincent looked pointedly at Harper before walking back to his bed and collapsing on it with a huff.

Everyone's a critic.

"I happen to know it's awful. There's really no need for such dramatics. I plan on gessoing over the canvas and recycling it, okay?"

She was explaining things to a dog. Oh, how the mighty had fallen.

She reached for another canvas from the stack she always had ready and waiting. As she placed it on the tray of her easel, she could see faint traces of the painting beneath the layer of gesso she'd used to cover it. Since she didn't consider the paintings she did for her Art Bar classes "real art," Harper never kept them. Other than the handful that Peyton hung on the walls of the studio for display, they were always painted over with gesso primer so the canvases could be recycled. Her canvases were like onions, covered in layer upon layer of hidden messages. Manet, Goya, Serrat and on and on.

She peered through the top layer of gesso on the canvas that she'd placed on the easel. She spied a rich green curve beside a sharp red angle and recognized the painting at once—Picasso's *Woman with a Book*, colorful cubism at its best. She'd taught the class about two months ago. Before.

Before of all the insanity that had become her life. Before the scheming, before the lies, before she'd had a man sleeping under her roof.

Before Tom Stone.

She picked up a brush, determined to get on with things. Yes, he was living with her. And yes, she'd slept with him. And yes, their futures had become ridiculously intertwined. But that did *not* mean she had to think about him constantly.

But it was difficult not to, especially after what she'd learned about him yesterday. It wasn't so much what he'd told her as it had been the look in his eyes. Hints of the past. His words had been few, but the voice with which he'd said them had spoken volumes.

She dipped her brush in the pool of cerulean blue on her palette and swirled in a generous portion of cobalt green. But even as she mixed the paint and began sweeping the background color over her canvas in broad strokes, Tom's advice invaded her thoughts.

Paint, Doc. Just paint. Paint whatever your heart wants.

Her hand began to shake, and her brushstrokes immediately suffered from it.

Damn it.

She dropped big daddy—*ugh*—her large brush—in her cup of water and stared at the blue green shadows on the canvas. When she'd been a real painter, this had always been her favorite part of the process. She'd loved nothing more than a canvas saturated in rich, vibrant color, but still absent of image. Colorfully, beautifully blank. Ready for her hand to give it shape and substance, to make of it whatever she wished. Art.

She blew a wisp of hair from her eyes. This wasn't about wishes. This was about work. Reality. And right now her reality was a little marshmallow panda that, for whatever reason, she couldn't seem to force herself to paint any more than she could come up with something on her own.

She squared her shoulders, reached for her smallest brush and dipped a corner of the bristles into titanium white. She really didn't need to add anything else. Peyton's panda was absent of dimension. In painting, white was rarely white. More often, it was subtle combination of blues, reds, greens and yellows, all working together to hint at the absence of color. Not so in this case. White was white was white.

She dipped the other corner of the bristles in her pool of carmine red.

What are you doing? Stop. You'll just end up starting all over again for a second time.

Before she could stop her hand, it guided the paintbrush to the yellow. Her fingers, the brush, and the paints seemed to be staging a mutiny. *Get out of your head.* Wasn't that what she was always saying to the students at Art Bar? *Relax and have fun. Just paint.*

It sounded an awful lot like Tom's advice.

She guided her brush to the canvas, and this time there was no tremble in her movements. Her hand was steady as a rock as it swept a curve of color onto the dead center of the canvas. Its shape was instantly familiar. Harper recognized it at once, even from that single swash of pigment that was no longer than her thumb.

A thrill coursed through her as she added another brushstroke, then another. A highlight here, a shadow there. The brush danced against the canvas, guided by hands that seemed to move of their own accord. The more the image in front of her began to take shape, the less Harper thought about the absurdity of what she was doing. The less she thought, period. She simply surrendered and allowed herself a rare moment of creating for the sake of creating. Not for work, not to make money, not to impress anyone. This was about taking the picture in her head, the image that danced behind her eyes when she dreamt, and capturing it like a butterfly in a net.

A butterfly, haunting and beautiful in its vulnerability.

Her fingers flickered in delicate, wing-like movements, faster and faster. Time stopped. Minutes became hours, hours mere minutes. Until it all came together. Red, white, yellow, blue. And in a blinding rush of wonder, Harper was suddenly no longer looking at paint on a canvas. She was looking at a face, specifically a mouth. *The* mouth. *His* mouth, and those glorious lips that somehow held the secrets to unlocking a woman who Harper had never realized lived inside her. A woman she rather liked. A woman she'd miss once Tom was gone.

Oh, my God.

The paintbrush slipped from Harper's hand, bounced on her leg and fell to the floor, no doubt leaving a trail of color in its wake. She wasn't sure. She didn't bother looking down. She couldn't, even if she'd tried. She was fixated on the painting, bewildered at how it had gotten there. Had she really done this?

The resemblance was striking, even though she'd used no photograph as reference. She'd needed no picture. This was the face of a man who'd begun to haunt her, to take up residence in her mind as well as her home.

She squeezed her eyes shut tight, but the painting was still all she could see. Tom. His eyes, his nose, his chiseled jaw. And his mouth, that glorious mouth. Strong, silent.

Beautiful.

Just paint, Doc. Paint whatever your heart wants.

There must be some mistake. Her heart didn't want Tom Stone. It couldn't.

She opened her eyes, fully expecting to find a blank canvas

sitting on the easel before her and that she'd imagined the entire experience. But it was still there, awash in color. The soft browns of his hair, the subtle shades of his skin and her very favorite part of his entire face—the delicate indigo shadow that lived beneath the curve of his lower lip. She held that shadow as a secret, a memory her mind visited when she wanted to disappear for a while. There it was, right there, on her canvas, for the entire world to see. Not that she would let anyone get a glimpse of this, but still.

It looked like her secret was trying its best to get out.

Chapter Twenty-Three

IF PRESSED, TOM could have painted a perfect reproduction of the ceiling of Harper's studio. He'd certainly stared at it enough. So many sleepless nights. On this, the night before the big art show, his gaze had been focused on it even longer than usual.

He was now absent the distraction of working on the paintings to occupy his midnight hours. They were finished. All of them. Twenty flowering canvases that would be hung on gallery walls to be scrutinized by people who wouldn't look twice at them if they knew who he really was.

He was nervous. He wanted the show to be a success. Not so much for his benefit, but for Harper's. If the artwork didn't clear him enough money to winterize the boat, he'd figure something out. Without all the studying and painting, his schedule was about to crack wide open. He could walk dogs until he was blue in the face.

But Doc?

If things didn't go the way she hoped, she'd be devastated. Where she was concerned, there was no plan B. Getting promoted to a tenured professor comprised all of her plans A through Z.

He sighed. Lying in the dark and worrying wasn't going to

help matters. He needed to get his mind off things. He needed to somehow get through the night.

He needed to paint.

Just because the art for the show was framed, ready, and hanging on the gallery walls didn't mean he would stop painting. Tom would always paint, even if his every brushstroke went unseen from here on out. It was a matter of survival.

He pushed himself off the bed and flipped on the light. The easel he'd been using for the duration of his stay—Harper's easel—stood empty in the corner.

Damn.

He was out of canvases. Every single one he'd brought with him when he'd moved in had become part of his acrylic garden. He jammed a hand through his hair. It was awfully difficult to paint without a canvas.

On the floor beside the bed, Gunnar stretched and rolled onto his back. He let out a wide doggy yawn and pushed his front legs out perfectly straight. One of his paws hit the closet door, nudging it ajar. Tom shook his head. He'd never understand how it could be comfortable for a dog to sleep with his legs straight in the air like that.

"Crazy dog," he muttered, and walked to the closet to shut the door.

As he pushed it closed, he spotted a stack of rectangular frames. White linen stretched over wood, partially covered with a drop cloth. And it was then that he remembered Harper saying that she always recycled the canvases she used for Art Bar.

He pulled the door open again, wider this time. By his count, there were at least a dozen canvases, all gessoed and ready to be reused. Surely she wouldn't mind if he borrowed one.

He lifted the drop cloth so he could take the top canvas off the stack, but when he got it out, he found it wasn't blank at all. He shook his head, convinced he was seeing things.

He wasn't. Harper had actually painted something. Recently, judging from the appearance of things.

He set the painting on the tray of the easel, straightening it so he could get a proper look. Then he stood there, dumbfounded, staring at the canvas. No, not a canvas—a mirror.

His own face sat on the easel looking back at him. His eyes, his nose. And, by God, his mouth. The focal point of the entire portrait was his mouth. He shook his head. Somehow she'd painted lips that appeared more real than any he'd ever kissed. The detail was exquisite. Worshipful. He couldn't imagine possessing the artistic skill to paint something so lifelike. The rest of his features were slightly out of focus, crafted by what he now knew was an Impressionist hand. It was almost like looking at himself through a misty haze. Except for the mouth, which remained sharply in focus. Realistic down to the smallest detail, drawing the viewer's eye to that place at once. Again and again.

Tom's chest grew tight. The more he looked at the painting, the more the sensation took hold until it became an ache. An ache for the artist.

Don't get carried away. It's just paint.

But it wasn't. He knew it wasn't. It was more than that.

In his wildest dreams, Tom could have never painted something so magnificent, so exquisite in the emotion it evoked. This was art. This was talent. And the mouth on that portrait was the mouth of a man who was adored. Of every*thing*, of every*one* in the world she could have painted, she'd chosen him. And she'd done so with breathtaking devotion.

He reached out and ran a reverent finger over a delicate brushstroke near the corner of his mouth. It was crazy, nonsensical, but he felt that brushstroke. He felt all of them. The feather-soft touch of her bristles, moving over him, creating him, bringing him back. Back to life. Every artistic caress was a kiss he felt deep in the center of his soul.

He was reminded of what she'd said all those weeks ago about Van Gogh's shoes. *Maybe what he was really trying to say was that things that have been damaged by life can still be beautiful.*

That was what this was. This painting. This gift.

This woman.

She'd brought him back, not just with color and canvas. It wasn't a symbolic resurrection. It was real. All this time, he'd thought his education had been about art. And it was, but not the art of the masters, or Van Gogh, or how to paint a pretty picture. Since the moment they'd struck their goofball deal, Doctor Harper Higgins had been educating him in the art of living. That may not have been her intention—in fact, he was certain it wasn't—but that had been the end result.

He was alive.

He was alive and he was in love.

Damn it.

He jammed a hand through his hair and tugged at the ends until he winced in pain. He was in love with her. He had been for a while now. He just hadn't wanted to admit it, to feel it. But now he did. He wanted to feel it all—the bad, the good, and everything in between. How long had he been numb? For far too long.

He was ready now to feel the agonizing ache of being in love—the thrill, the pleasure, the fear, the pain. Every ounce of it. Starting now.

He didn't bother re-covering the canvas, but wadded up the drop cloth and tossed it on the bed.

"Stay." He pointed at Gunner, curled into a black and tan ball of fur.

The dog barely opened his eyes, but Tom wasn't about to take any chances on being interrupted. They were done with that. No more interruptions, no more quick moments of passion followed by longer moments of regret. No more coming together because of chemistry, merely to satisfy the human need to be touched. Tonight he was going to make love, probably for the first time in his entire life.

Satisfied that Gunner had succumbed to sleepy obedience, he left the studio and took the stairs two at a time. He paused for a moment outside the closed door to Harper's bedroom, his hand poised to knock, then thought better of it. It was the middle of the night. Of course she was asleep.

He turned the knob and gave the door a gentle push, so as not to wake her with sound. He aimed to wake her the proper way, the way a woman who was loved should be awakened—with kisses, soft sensual sighs, and the brush of yearning skin on skin.

She rested on her side with her hands tucked beneath her head and her glorious hair spread over her pillow, all those beautiful, blonde locks. He dropped to his knees, twirled of tendril of her hair around his finger and ran his thumb along the stunning curve of her jaw.

Her skin glowed, perfect porcelain, bathed in moonlight that drifted in from her bedroom window. The room was alive with sultry shadows of Prussian blue and perylene violet. Outside, snow swirled and danced against the glass in an elegant flurry of activity in striking opposition to the quiet stillness of the darkened bedroom. It was as if they were in a different place than the rest of the world—protected, sublime, a snow globe where the only threat of blizzard was the one of longing and need that stirred in his soul.

He touched her jaw again, her temple, brushed the hair from her eyes. Her eyelashes gave a quick flutter, like flickering butterfly wings. Then she opened her eyes, and he was instantly lost in their deep, bottle green.

"Tom?" she whispered, not sounding the least bit surprised.

Nor did she seem disappointed to find him there, kneeling beside her bed in the darkest hours of night. A slow, beguiling smile came to her lips, and the sight of it, the realization that she was happy he'd come to her, that she wanted this just as badly as he did, drew a groan from Tom's depths.

She whimpered in response, reaching for him, her fingers gathering in his t-shirt as she pulled him toward her. He stood and pulled the shirt over his head. As he did, Harper rose to her knees and slid her hands beneath the waistband of his pants, pulling them down and taking his erection into her hands.

She looked up at him, and in her eyes, he saw his own impossible, unfathomable desire looking right back at him. It was a sight that gave him more pleasure than any physical touch ever could. He wanted nothing more than for her to feel the way he felt, so full of desire that he was crippled by it. Giving her that gift was his overriding sensual need, the need that kept him awake at night. Every night. It was a need so fierce it had taken over his consciousness and replaced his darkest memories.

He cupped her cheek in one of his hands as she stroked him, never breaking eye contact. In that instant, she was the most beautiful sight he'd ever seen, so beautiful it almost hurt his heart to look at her. She wore a wispy-thin, white nightgown, transparent enough that he could see the outline of her full breasts, trace the rosy hue of her perfect, petal-soft nipples. As she moved her hands over his ever-thickening length, her gown slipped off one shoulder, and he had to take a slow, measured breath to keep from climaxing right then. Her elegant collarbone, her pristine shoulder, the agonizing parting of her lips as she watched the motion of her hands, caressing him—fluid, maddening strokes that nearly drove him back to his knees. He'd never seen such a gorgeous sight. He was struck with the bone-deep urge to paint her, as she'd painted him. He wanted to paint her as she was right here, right now, so he could preserve this moment forever in time and cast her in desire's eternal light.

Then she lowered her head and took him into her mouth and he could only close his eyes because the assault of beauty was just too much to take. He buried his hands in her hair—so soft, like a holy waterfall slipping through his fingers. And as her hands and mouth worked together, he forgot all about paints and brushes, and linen and canvas. He ceased thinking altogether. He was overwhelmed by the assault of sensation. Of pleasure. Pleasure bestowed on him by the perfect woman, down on her knees for him.

Instinctively, his fists tightened in her hair as she brought him closer and closer to the edge. He was torn, drifting helplessly between two shores, wanting to stop her, to slow things down so he could attend to her needs, but at the same time needing release, needing it so badly he saw red. Alizarin crimson swirled behind his closed eyelids. His breathing grew shallow, he heard moaning, and he didn't even know where it was coming from. Then he realized it was him. And just as he approached the ledge, just as he was about fall into the abyss where there was no turning back, he got his wits about him.

"Baby." He groaned. "Baby, I need you to stop."

She released him and looked up with those big, green eyes, shining bright, and the ache returned to his chest—the same ache he'd felt when he'd looked at the painting.

I love her. God, how I love her.

He should tell her.

He wanted to tell her.

"Harper." He cupped her face again and marveled at her beauty. She had the face of an angel. How had it taken him so long to see it? So much wasted time. "I…"

"Tom, no more talking. Not now." She pressed a tender fingertip to his lips to silence him. "Just love me."

Then she removed her gossamer gown, offering him her bed, her beautiful body. And as he slid over her, her words sang to his soul. A silent, winsome tune. Just love me.

I will…if you let me.

SOMETHING ABOUT THIS time was different.

Harper wasn't sure why. She wasn't sure how. She wasn't

sure when it had occurred, but there'd been a shift. The evidence of it was there in the tenderness of Tom's fingers as they slipped inside her. It was there in the way her body responded to the warm, languid, open-mouthed kiss he pressed to her bare belly. It was there in the shuddering sigh that passed her lips as he entered her with his tongue.

The reverence in his movements was palpable. She'd never been touched this way before. By anyone. Under his hands, she felt like a holy relic, an unearthed masterpiece. This was beyond sex, beyond desire. There was magic in his touch—not the desperate aggression they'd always brought about in one another before, but something deeper, more meaningful.

But she was too lost in the pleasure of the moment to examine its significance. As he used his mouth and fingers on her, a fire erupted in her body. It flowed molten through her veins and its flames skittered and danced on her naked flesh. Everywhere he touched, everywhere he kissed. The transcendent sensation started at her center and spread outward to the very tips of her fingers and toes.

It was too much. Too intense, too frightening, too altogether wonderful. She took hold of his hair, simply because she needed an anchor, something to hold her in place. She felt as though she might rise up off the bed at any moment and float right up to the ceiling. Flying—that was what was happening. He was taking her flying. If she went any higher, she was sure she'd be able to reach out and touch the luminous moon.

Her thighs ached. Her breasts ached. Every cell in her body cried out for him, even as he was tormenting her with his mouth and fingers. It was simultaneously too much and not enough.

How was it possible to want someone so much? To crave their touch as if it were oxygen? And how was it that every time he kissed her it was better than before? Dark and dangerous, sweet and tender…she never knew what to expect, and she liked it that way. She was his. All his. Every bit as much as if she'd been branded. But the marks were on the inside rather than the outside, closer to her heart, where they mattered the most.

His tongue moved faster and faster, a relentless assault bringing her to a place she'd never been, a plateau she'd never known existed. She gasped and shuddered, her mind trying in vain to keep up with her body. And then he paused, caressed her thighs and gently blew. The warm air was all it took to push her past the tipping point.

Everything started to shimmer and glow, like she'd been dipped in stardust. She closed her eyes and surrendered to the waves of pleasure, let them wash over her and drag her under. Deeper. And deeper, until she was so far gone, she wondered if she'd ever find her way back.

Her scream pierced the winter's night air—the one and only syllable she was capable of uttering. His name.

Tom.

The word burrowed into her bones, settled in the depths of her. Her body embraced it, as though she'd been waiting for him all along and he'd finally come home to rest.

"I'm here," he murmured, kissing his way up her abdomen. "I'm right here."

Here.

In her house, in her bed, in her life. But for how long? The show was tomorrow. His paintings would sell, every single one of them. She was sure of it. He was a brilliant artist, and more than that, he was a brilliant man. She wanted to see him succeed, and believed he deserved all the success he had coming to him.

But lately, she'd begun to wonder what would happen afterward, when it was all over. Even worse, she'd begun to realize how much she'd miss tutoring him. Somehow, Tom's education had become something different. Something more. During the course of showing him the artists and paintings that she held so dear, she'd shown him her soul.

And he'd seen her. Really seen her.

She would miss being seen. She'd miss the talking, the art, the knowing there was someone waiting for her when she came home at night. She'd miss all the things she'd never thought she'd wanted.

More than any of those things, though, she'd miss *him.*

She couldn't think about the empty place he'd leave behind. Not now. Not when he was gazing down at her with a look that seemed as though it was filled with all the things she couldn't bring herself to say.

She stared up at him, at those eyes that would forever remind her of a Van Gogh sky and at his mouth, the mouth of the only man she'd ever met who'd kissed her soul. No matter what happened, she'd never forget his face. She'd never forget what it felt like to have him look at her that way.

You'll always have the painting.

The painting.

She'd thought she'd been trying to reclaim her talent. That was not what the painting had been about at all. It had been about him. About wanting to hold him close even after he was gone. About remembering him.

Her vision blurred. Suddenly she found herself looking at him through a veil of tears. She blinked them back. She didn't want to cry. This moment was too perfect for tears.

She smiled up at him, the man who'd come into her life and changed everything. The one who'd found a way in, after all those years she'd worked so hard to keep everyone out. The one she wanted to stay. The One.

Just love me. Love me, please.

His mouth came down on hers, gentle and seeking. Then his kiss grew desperate, hungry, and her need for him began to grow again. She wanted him inside her. She wanted him to fill her so completely that all the empty years would fade into a distant memory.

"Now. Oh, please, now," she whispered.

With an excruciatingly sweet ache, he pushed inside her. Slowly, so slowly. She couldn't breathe. She couldn't think. She was suspended in time, precariously balanced in that agonizing moment between wanting him and holding him fully within.

And then he was wholly inside her. She arched into him, wanting to give him everything, every part of herself. Even the parts she'd forgotten existed.

Just love me. Please love me.

She gazed up at him, poised so exquisitely above her, and somehow knew that was exactly what he was doing. Loving her.

Chapter Twenty-Four

HARPER WAS BEGINNING to worry that Tom would never wake up. Sometime during the night, as they'd rested tangled in one another's limbs, his body had finally given up the fight. She didn't think she'd ever seen a more beautiful man than a sleeping Tom Stone.

She didn't have the heart to wake him.

So, she left him there in her bed while she went about finalizing the plans for the show. She talked to Lindsay on the phone. She did her nails. She walked both of the dogs. And still he slept. And slept. And slept.

When late afternoon rolled around, she decided to take one last crack at finding the missing puzzle piece she'd been trying in vain to find for weeks. She had a name. All she needed was an address. At the onset it had sounded like a simple proposition. It had proven to be far more difficult than she could have imagined.

She was running out of time.

But late that afternoon, with only an hour or so to spare, fate smiled down on her. A name popped up on the screen of her laptop. A name that matched the one on the slip of paper she'd been carrying around in her purse. And right beneath that name was an address, and surprisingly, that address was located in the South End.

Jackpot!

She wasn't sure what to tell Tom. She didn't want to ruin the surprise, nor did she want to tell another lie. So it was really for the best that he'd yet to wake. She set the alarm and placed it on the nightstand, along with a note.

Had to run an errand. I'll meet you at the show. xo

She hoped he wouldn't think it impersonal, or worse, that she was abandoning him on his big night. If she could just pull this off, it would mean so much to him. At least she hoped it would. That was the plan, anyway.

She dressed for the art show and slipped out as quietly as she could. When she arrived at the address on the waterfront building, things didn't look right. She checked the slip of paper in her evening bag one more time.

Southard's Wholesale Floral Supply. Owner: Frank Southard.

The addresses matched, but it seemed odd that the place didn't have a sign. Nor did it appear to have a proper door, but merely a lifted garage-style entry with layers of thick plastic sheeting covering the opening.

She lingered on the sidewalk for a moment, debating whether or not to go inside. Honestly, the place seemed a little sketchy. It in no way looked like a florist. She tried to imagine Tom coming here every day and exiting with carefully wrapped bundles of flowers in his arm, and she just couldn't. Then again, a cheery shop overflowing with balloons, flowers and ribbons wouldn't have seemed like the sort of establishment Tom would frequent either.

A gust of wind blew off the harbor. Tiny snowflakes had

begun to gather in the tulle folds of her dress already, and patches of ice dotted the sidewalk. But in the swirl of the winter wind, Harper caught an unmistakable hint of spring's perfume.

Flowers.

She smelled flowers.

This is silly. You've been searching for this place for weeks.

She pushed through the plastic opening and stepped inside.

It was akin to walking into a paint box overflowing with every shade of watercolors she'd ever seen. She immediately found herself surrounded by colorful blossoms—dreamy blues, royal purples, sunshine yellows and every shade of red imaginable. Brick red, fiery crimson, scarlet red with subtle blue undertones, cheerful poppy and a whole range of whisper pinks.

And the fragrance was heavenly and very nearly overwhelming, like she could smell every flower in the world all at once. Her head spun a little.

"Hello, there."

Harper searched for a human face among the flowers. It took a minute to finally see the older man sitting behind a green countertop along the left wall of the room. "Good evening. Your name wouldn't happen to be Frank, would it?"

He set down the long-stemmed rose and florist shears in his hands. "Guilty as charged."

Yes.

Finally. She couldn't believe it had taken so long to find this guy when his shop was right there in the neighborhood.

"I'm sorry. I know this is last minute..." She took a deep breath, nervous all of the sudden.

This man was one of Tom's only friends. Whatever she said needed to be perfect. This wasn't the time to put her foot in her mouth like she seemed to do all the time.

"You're a little dressed up for the waterfront." He eyed her strapless gown and green stilettoes.

On the painterly spectrum, they were brilliant green with a dash of jade.

"On your way to a wedding and in need of some emergency flowers?"

She blinked. *A wedding.* "No. An art opening, actually."

"An art opening. Very nice." He studied her for a moment as she approached the counter. "Wait a minute. You're the girl, aren't you?"

The girl. Harper couldn't readily identify the last time she'd been called a girl. And rightfully so. She was a grown-up. A woman. A doctor. But something about the way he'd said it caused her heart to race. "The girl?"

He nodded, and his mouth curved into the broadest of smiles. "It's you. You're Tom's girl, Picasso's lily."

The flowers. Her heart galloped even faster. "Picasso's lily. I have to say, Frank. You have a way with nicknames."

He shrugged. "Any girl who gets Tom Stone to buy a bundle of Picasso calla lilies is her own kind of masterpiece. Those flowers don't come cheap."

They were on sale.

Right.

Harper smiled and she began to relax. It was theoretically impossible to be nervous around a sweet, elderly man who called her a masterpiece. "Tom thinks very highly of you, sir."

"He's a fine young man. He served in Iraq, you know. He ever tell you about that?" Frank's expression grew serious.

She nodded. "A little, yes."

"Nearly got wiped off the face of planet by an IED. The only surviving member of his unit."

Harper's throat grew dry. She had trouble forcing words out of her mouth. "I knew he'd been seriously injured. I didn't realize he'd lost everyone."

"Don't feel bad. Sometimes the memories that haunt us the most are the ones we find most difficult to talk about." He reached for a lily from a nearby bucket. Ivory, with a deep purple center. *Picasso's lily.* He handed it to her. "Even with those who mean the most to us."

Could Frank possibly be right? Was she the one who meant the most to Tom? Was she his girl?

Tears swam in her eyes, threatening to spill over. He'd lost everyone. His wife. His friends. And he'd very nearly lost his life. No wonder Gunner meant so much to him. That dog was all he had left in the world.

She blinked furiously. She couldn't break down now. She'd come here on a mission, and the show was scheduled to start in less than half an hour.

"Did you know he's an artist?" she asked.

"Tom? An artist?" Frank's eyebrows rose.

Harper couldn't help but be reminded of the night she'd discovered Tom's secret. She doubted Frank could have possibly been as surprised as she was.

"No. No, I didn't."

"He is. He's a painter. A brilliant one." She opened her evening bag, removed one of the cardstock invitations the college had printed up for the show and slid it across the counter. "His work will be featured tonight at a special solo exhibit on the campus of the Boston College of Art. I just know

Tom would be so surprised and delighted if you'd come."

He adjusted his glasses and stared at the invitation. "Those are my flowers."

"Indeed they are." Harper smiled.

Selecting which of Tom's paintings to feature on the invitation had been no easy task. As curator, that job had fallen on Harper's shoulders. She'd been tempted to pick the painting of the Picasso lilies. But in the end, there was really only one choice—the violets.

Frank read the card aloud. "*Nightshade. The paintings of Tom Stone.*"

"He chose that name. Nightshade. Tom paints mostly at night."

Frank shook his head. His eyes remained glued to the postcard. Harper wasn't certain, but she thought she saw the glimmer of tears in his eyes. "I can't believe it. He's been painting my flowers this whole time?"

"Yes, he has."

Frank removed his glasses, pinched the bridge of his nose and blinked. Hard. "Why didn't he tell me? He was in here nearly every day, buying whatever week-old leftover flowers he could afford. Hell, I would have given them to him if I'd known this is what he was doing with them."

Harper reached for his hand and squeezed it. "You and I both know he never would have taken them for free."

She'd been so intent on finding this man in order to surprise Tom, so he would have someone there to support him. She hadn't realized how much it would mean for Frank to see his flowers hanging on the gallery wall. Wasn't it strange how this art show had turned into a gift to so many people? To

Tom, to Frank, to her.

But wasn't that always the way with art? Art was a gift. Always. She'd somehow allowed herself to forget how much meaning the stroke of a paintbrush could carry. And she hoped against hope that it would stay that way. Bringing Frank to the show was a risky proposition. He was one more person who would be there who knew Tom's true identity. Any sane person would see this as a mistake.

"True. He's an honorable guy. It's the soldier in him." Frank nodded, and Harper tried desperately not to think of the myriad ways in which she'd asked Tom to compromise his integrity. Time and time again.

He wanted this, too. He did.

Somehow those assurances didn't make her feel any better at all. What had she done?

"I'd love to come to the show. I wouldn't miss it," Frank said.

Harper exhaled and wondered at what point she'd begun to hold her breath. "That's good news. Really good. I hate to run off, but I'm sort of in charge of the show, and I need to get down there. Here." She offered him the lily he'd handed her.

He shook his head and refused to take it. "That's yours. It's your namesake flower, remember?" He winked.

Picasso's lily. She held the flower close to her heart. "Thank you. Thank you very much."

"Anything for Tom's girl."

Those were the words that haunted her as she left the paint box of flowers behind and hurried to the art gallery. The words that chased her.

Tom's girl.

Despite the ticking clock and the minutes that felt as though they were racing past as the show approached, Harper wanted nothing more than to slow her steps so those words might find her. Because her deepest fears had been realized. She was falling. Falling fast. And she wasn't at all sure Tom's arms would be there to catch her when her world dropped away.

TOM WAITED ON the snowy sidewalk outside the gallery for as long as he could before going inside. He'd been calling Harper for over half an hour and each and every call had rolled to her voicemail. Text messages had gone unreturned.

Where is she, damn it?

The first thing he'd done upon waking was reach for her. Instead of her warm body, his hand had made contact with paper. A note. She'd snuck off and left him a note.

He should have been angry and probably would have been, if not for the fact that he'd actually slept. For almost fifteen hours straight. On land. In a bed.

Harper's bed.

That seemed significant. Significant enough that he wasn't upset with her, just worried.

Since the moment he'd first laid eyes on her, this show was all she could talk about. And now that the night had finally arrived, she was nowhere to be found. He couldn't imagine what in the world could be more important that being here. Now.

He glanced at his cell phone again. Nothing. And the show was scheduled to start in only five minutes. He couldn't wait for her any longer. What was an art show without an artist?

He headed toward the gallery door, all the while reminding himself of the man he was supposed to be. Tom Stone, art expert. Tom Stone, the supposed great-great-grandson of Vincent Van Gogh. Tom Stone, who wasn't romantically involved in any way with the curator of this show.

He had a handle on the first two. It was that last one he was worried about. How was he supposed to stand in the same room with Harper and not think about the way she'd given herself to him last night? Every time he closed his eyes, she was there, her moonlit curves just visible beneath the sheer whisper of her gown. His fingertips remained tangled in her hair, a phantom touch. He was still surrounded by the beauty and softness of her body, he still moved inside her. But more than that, she remained inside him. And he knew without a doubt, that she always would.

The persistence of memory.

He'd never really believed it could work both ways—that his mind and soul could be seized with the memory of overwhelming beauty even more so than a memory of unrelenting pain. He would have bet his life it couldn't happen. But he'd ridden the thin line between life and death before and fate had smiled down on him. This time was no different.

How much longer? How much longer could he defy fate and stars, time and destiny?

A few hours. Right now, that was all he needed. Just a few more hours of pretending. Then all of life would return to its natural state, with or without Harper Higgins.

His head throbbed as he pulled the gallery door open, and he did his best to ignore the voice inside that whispered that a future without Harper would never feel natural.

Now isn't the time.

Everything depended on what happened tonight. He needed to pull himself together and focus.

The entryway to the gallery was dark. His footsteps echoed on the smooth tile floor, and when he turned the corner, he was temporarily blinded by vivid light.

He blinked against the overwhelming assault of spotlight glare illuminating canvases saturated with colors that appeared brighter than possible. Red redder than red. Blue bluer than blue. Peach richer and juicier than any fruit he'd ever tasted.

It took him a full two minutes to realize that the paintings he was looking at were his. It was as if he'd never seen them before. And he hadn't. Not like this. Nothing could have prepared him for the sight of them hanging in that room. All together, perfectly lit, on those smooth blank walls. One right after another in a larger than life garden of color.

As he stood in the center of the room, slowly turning, taking it all in, he realized something. For the first time since embarking on this insane escapade with Harper, it felt real. *He* felt real. No matter his background, no matter his training, he was an artist.

"What do you think?" A gentle voice broke through his reverie. It was the voice he most wanted to hear at that moment.

He turned, and there she was, looking as though she'd stepped out of a canvas herself. His art goddess. She was dressed in the color of violets, hair tumbling and loose, cascading down her back. There was even a Picasso calla lily pinned among those blonde waves he loved so much.

The paintings that had caught him in their spell only moments before faded into the background.

"Doc," he said. "I've been waiting for you."

For so, so long.

"I had an errand to run." She crossed her arms and promptly uncrossed them. She was nervous.

She had reason to be nervous, he supposed. Everything she wanted centered on what happened tonight. All the more reason not to screw things up.

"An errand." He repeated.

He couldn't imagine what could possibly be more important to her than the show. He waited for her to explain.

She didn't. The silence hovered around them, stealing some of the magic from the room.

"What do you think?" she asked, waving a hand at the paintings.

He shook his head. "Words fail me."

"Impressive, isn't it?" Her eyes glowed with pride.

He lowered his voice to a murmur. "It feels almost real."

She came to him, closing the distance between them. "Tom, the art is real. Remember that. These paintings are real, and you painted them."

The door opened and the first rush of people piled in. He could hear footsteps in the entry way and voices bouncing off the walls. And all of time slowed as Harper stepped backward. Away from him. Once again.

Lindsay was the first guest to approach. "Wow, look at this place."

Harper's gaze met Tom's and she smiled.

"Tom, your paintings. My goodness, they're breathtaking."

Lindsay's eyes glittered. She spun around, gasping as she took in one painting, after the next.

It was a good start. Of course, there were dozens more people from the art college scheduled to arrive. Some were among the slow flow of people entering the building. Tom recognized a few faces from the Dada party, Lars Klassen's included.

His jaw involuntarily clenched. He really didn't like that guy. He didn't care at all for the way he seemed to have it in for Harper or for the way he treated Lindsay. Tom wasn't an academic. That much had been made painfully clear. But Lars's obsession with getting ahead didn't seem normal. At least he hoped it wasn't. He hated the thought of Harper existing in that kind of toxic environment.

Get real. Harper can take care of herself.

He knew that, of course. He wasn't sure he'd ever met anyone as capable as Harper, and that included every soldier he'd ever set eyes on. But that didn't mean he liked the idea of her always having to deal with someone so predatory.

He told himself he was making more of things than they really were. They were competing for the same job. Competition was only natural. And, thank God, that would be coming to an end soon. Tonight, if they were all lucky.

"Mr. Stone, good to see you." Dr. Martin appeared at his side and reached to shake his hand. "Congratulations. Your work is remarkable. I'm impressed. Very impressed."

"Thank you, sir."

"Tom, Dr. Martin, if you'll both excuse me. I need to attend to the sales. I've just been told we have buyers who are interested."

Dr. Martin waved her away. "Of course. That's what this

evening is all about, after all. Money for Mr. Stone means money for the college."

"Thank you." Tom nodded at Harper, and she beamed at him before disappearing in the crowd.

Everything was happening so fast all of the sudden. People started coming at Tom from all directions, congratulating him and commenting on the paintings. He shook more hands than he could count.

Faces ran together and names were thrown at him that he'd never remember. Then, in the midst of all the room full of strangers, Tom's gaze landed on a face he recognized.

He blinked, convinced he was seeing things. "Frank?"

No. It couldn't be.

But it was.

Frank Southard, in an art gallery.

"You've been keeping secrets," he said.

You have no idea. "Just one."

"An awfully big one." Frank laughed. "Tom, look at these walls. You did all this?"

"I suppose I did." He glanced around in search of Harper.

She'd probably panic if she knew someone from his real life had shown up at this thing.

"You've no idea how much it means to me to see my flowers up there. Larger than life. Eternal. That's what you've done, son. You've made them live forever." Frank shook his head.

There was a hint of something in his voice that Tom had never heard before, and he decided right then and there that whatever the risk, he was glad Frank had come. He appreciated the paintings in a way no one else ever could or ever would. He needed to be there.

Tom just couldn't figure out how it had happened. "Tonight wouldn't have been the same without you, you know. Thank you for coming."

"My wife, Sarah, is over by the daffodils. Those have always been her favorite. I'd like to introduce you. We wouldn't have missed coming here for the word." Frank laughed. "Of course, we nearly did since I didn't even know about it until your girl showed up earlier."

"My girl?" Competing thoughts swarmed in Tom's head...Harper's errand. The reason she was late.

The lily in her hair.

She didn't. She wouldn't.

He looked up and, toward the back of the room, he spotted her. Their gazes locked. And she smiled a secret smile, one meant only for him.

She had.

HARPER COULD BARELY keep up with the purchases of Tom's art. Every time she turned around, someone was tugging on her arm and waving a credit card in her face. She calmly explained to each buyer that she would mark the painting as sold by placing a circular red sticker on the wall beside it. Once Dr. Martin had said a few words and there had been a congratulatory champagne toast for Tom, the show would come to a close and the buyers could render payment and collect their paintings.

This was the typical way of doing things. Every show the college had hosted during Harper's time on the faculty had been run precisely the same way. Never had she witnessed such an anxious group of art buyers. The paintings were selling faster than she could get the stickers on the wall. And there was no shortage of drama. She'd had to neutralize a few skirmishes on the gallery floor. One of the faculty members had even threatened a local restaurateur to a fistfight over the pink carnations. Harper was fairly certain it was the first time a bouquet of pink carnations, either real or painted, had instigated a physical altercation of any kind. She couldn't be sure, but she would have bet money on it.

Her favorite sale had been the painting of the violets. Of all Tom's pieces, the painting he'd done of those violets on the night they'd first met was the one she held nearest and dearest to her heart. She'd actually fantasized a time or two about buying it herself. If she'd had the cash readily available, and if both of her jobs hadn't been dangling by the thinnest of threads at the moment, she would have done exactly that.

She hated to think of that canvas hanging just anywhere. And luckily, it wouldn't. Frank Southard would be taking it home. He'd approached her and told her he wanted it before he'd even sought Tom out to say hello. She couldn't have been happier to sell it to him.

The rest of the night thus far had been a blur. She hadn't had time to eat a single appetizer or exchange more than a glance or two with Tom. Practically every time she'd seen him, he'd been deeply engaged in conversation with someone anyway—faculty members, art critics, news reporters. He'd looked so calm, so confident. She could hardly believe they'd actually pulled it off. The show was a bigger success than she'd ever imagined.

Still, she didn't allow herself to relax until she'd stuck a little red sold sticker beside the last remaining painting. The hydrangeas. Harper felt unexpectedly wistful as she stuck the red dot on the wall beside the lush, creamy flowers. She would miss being able to look at these paintings whenever she liked. On nights she couldn't sleep, or times when she simply needed to believe in art again, looking at Tom's flowers had always given her a much needed feeling of hopefulness.

Those flowers were the reason she'd started painting again. Those flowers...and the man who'd painted them. It seemed unfair that she would be losing them both at the same time. Her little house that had always seemed almost too small for her and Vincent would feel as empty as a tomb once Tom had moved out. And she wouldn't have so much as a petal to cling to in his absence.

This isn't the end. It can't be. This is a night for celebration.

Celebration. Exactly. She should be celebrating.

"Champagne, miss?" Right on cue, a passing waiter offered her his tray.

"Yes, please." She took one of the slender champagne flutes. "Thank you very much."

"I'll have one of those, as well. My colleague and I need to toast the success of her show." Lars. Of course.

He took a glass without bothering to thank the server. Then he turned his attention to Harper. *Lucky me.*

"Congratulations are in order," he said, extending his free hand.

Harper gave it a wary glance and paused for a moment before taking it.

She was being ridiculous. Paranoid. Everything was going

so smoothly. Didn't every painting have a little red sticker beside it indicating that it had been sold? Dr. Martin was delighted. Her whole department was delighted. The *entire college* was delighted.

They'd done it. She and Tom had fooled everyone. Now was the time to breathe a gigantic sigh of relief.

"Thank you, Lars. Thank you very much." She shook his hand and forced herself to smile.

Actually, she didn't need to force it. The smile was perfectly natural. She was the happiest she'd been in as long as she could remember.

Lars grinned back at her. If he bared his teeth a little too much, Harper didn't notice. At least not until he opened his mouth and spoke.

"Congratulations are truly in order. Everyone is so impressed with the work Tom Stone has done, including myself."

She couldn't quite put her finger on what sounded the alarm bells in her head, other than the fact that he was being nice. Too nice.

She nodded. "He's a rare talent."

His eyes narrowed. "Now, now, Dr. Higgins. Don't sell yourself short. Your job couldn't have been easy."

Paranoia aside, this was feeling creepy. She half expected a forked tongue to come flicking out of his mouth. "Agreed, curating a show can be challenging. But this one went quite smoothly, actually." Then she remembered Archer sitting in a jail cell in New York. "Once the original artist was replaced, of course."

"Is that so?" He angled his head. Somehow, that smallest of gestures was enough to send a chill up and down Harper's spine.

"Mmm hmm." She nodded stiffly and searched the room for Tom. He wasn't anywhere within her line of vision.

The fact he wasn't standing somewhere by himself should have been good news. The show was his event. He should be reveling in the attention and praise he'd worked so hard to earn.

But she needed to get out of this corner and away from Lars Klassen as quickly as possible. If she could only spot Tom and send him a searching glance. Maybe he could come over and rescue her.

Since when do you need a man to rescue you?

She drained her champagne glass.

Lars stepped closer, close enough that she could smell the lingering aroma of the shrimp appetizer on his breath. "How did you do it? How did you manage to trick everyone?"

The champagne flute nearly slipped through her fingers.

Get it together, Harper. He doesn't know a thing. He's just trying to trip you up.

She pasted on a smile. He didn't look like he was fishing for information. He looked confident. Cocky, even. "I don't know what you're talking about, Lars, but I need to go. It's getting late and I need to oversee the sale of the paintings."

He let out an incredulous laugh. "Relax. You'll have all the time in the world on your hands once everyone hears that your boy is a fraud."

She wasn't sure which she found more offensive—Lars calling Tom a boy or a fraud. He was neither of those things. He was honorable, strong, hardworking, sensitive and artistic, all qualities that he'd earned the hard way. Through life. And the agony of war. Not sitting behind a desk in a classroom.

Tom's past, his lack of formal higher education, was one of the things that made him the man that he was. And he was a beautiful man.

She wasn't sure she'd ever thought of Tom's education with such crystal clarity before. What a shame it had taken the likes of Lars to hammer those truths home. "Lars, really. I don't know what you're trying to say—"

He held up a hand to stop the flow of words from her mouth. "Save it. I know the truth. He's a dog walker who learned to paint with discount acrylics on cheap canvases in an Army hospital. He's never even set foot in Amsterdam. You probably wrote all those ridiculous blog posts about him being related to Van Gogh all on your own. Tom Stone is no art expert, no descendant of Van Gogh, and he's certainly no artist."

So seeing Tom walking Buster had been a red flag after all.

She should have been devastated. The first thought in her head should have been about her career. Had Lars told Dr. Martin? If Lars knew she'd lied about Tom's background, he was sure to use that information against her. She would lose her promotion. Maybe she'd even lose her job.

But none of those thoughts were spinning in her head at the moment. Every ounce of her attention was centered on the almost irresistible urge to slap Lars in the face.

How dare he say Tom was no artist? How *dare* he?

She balled her shaky hands into fists at her sides to prevent herself from acting on the notion. She'd already told enough lies, made enough mistakes. It was probably best not to add physically assaulting a colleague to her list of misdeeds. Even a colleague who was a slimy snake.

The thing to do was cut straight to the chase. "What do you want, Lars?"

"What do I want?" There was that sinister smile again. "I want a lot of things. Why don't we start with exposing the truth? Right here, right now. Shall I walk over to Dr. Martin and tell him who the real Tom Stone is, or will you?"

Chapter Twenty-Five

NOT THAT.

Not that.

Anything but that.

If Tom was exposed here, now, he would be publically humiliated. Harper could not allow that to happen, certainly not by her hand. He'd worked too hard for too long. He'd done everything she'd asked of him and then some. He'd memorized every fact, no matter how detailed. He'd moved out of his boat and into her home. He'd gone to the party and wowed everyone in attendance, which was something that had never been part of their original deal. All that, plus he'd painted twenty of the most breathtaking paintings she'd ever seen.

And the entire time he'd been doing those things, she hadn't once thought of the impact it would have on him if their charade were uncovered. All of her thoughts had centered on her job, her future, and her promotion.

Me, me, me.

God, it was disgusting. When had she turned into such a selfish person?

She felt sick to her stomach, like she could vomit into the closest potted plant. "Lars. You can't expose him. You can't. He doesn't like to talk about his time in the military. It's a painful subject. Please understand."

"Of course I can expose him. I can and I will." He pulled a manila envelope out of the inside pocket of his jacket. "I have all the evidence I need right here. Once I saw your boy walking dogs down by the harbor, I knew something was up. I hired a private investigator. The rest was easy."

A private investigator? Wow, he was really going to all lengths to get ahead.

Says the woman who created her own personal, living, breathing Van Gogh…

He thrust the envelope toward her. With trembling hands she opened it. A stack of photographs and papers slid from the manila paper—Tom's military records, a *Washington Post* article about the Combat Paper Project that included a photo of Tom standing beside a piece of handcrafted paper artwork. It was the tank rolling over the flowers that she'd seen hanging in his boat.

Harper squinted at the caption of the photograph. *Army Staff Sargent Tom Stone and the artwork created using paper pulp made from his old combat uniform.*

The tank and flowers were actually his old Army uniform? The one he'd worn in Iraq?

My God.

Frank Southard's voice rang in her head. *He nearly got wiped off the face of planet by an IED. The only surviving member of his unit.*

The newspaper shook in her hands. She folded it back up and examined the rest of the contents of the envelope. There were several images of Tom walking dogs along the South End harbor. Vincent walked alongside him in the two of the photos. There was also a picture of Tom that Harper hardly recognized as him. He had the freshly buzzed hair of a brand new Army recruit, and he wore a starched pair of desert camo fatigues. The name sewn across this young man's chest said *Stone*, and he had Tom's dreamy, blue eyes and those gorgeous lips she loved so much. But this was a Tom she'd never known. There was no tension in the set of his jaw, no heaviness in the lines around his eyes. The faint creases that fanned out from his Van Gogh eyes in this two-dimensional image were true laugh lines. The young Tom Stone had been a more joyful man—one who laughed and probably slept through the night. Every night.

War had changed him. She'd known it had but had never realized quite how much until faced with this image.

Tom Stone. Before and after.

He'd been to hell and back. No more. Enough was enough.

She returned the photos and documents to the envelope and handed it back to Lars. "I'll fix things so that they turn out the way you want them. Dr. Martin is set to give his speech in fifteen minutes. Wait until afterward to make up your mind about exposing Tom." She swallowed around the lump in her throat. "Please."

He regarded her through narrowed eyes. "How are you going to fix things?"

She knew what she had to do. And even though it would put an end to everything she'd thought she'd wanted, she was oddly at peace with her decision. She wasn't sure she'd ever been faced with an easier choice. "I just will. Give me a chance. Tom is an innocent party here. I don't want to see him hurt."

She watched the realization dawn on Lars's face. He knew. She was sleeping with him. It was possibly the only fact his investigator had failed to unearth, but undoubtedly it was one of the most important.

It was also potentially the final nail in the coffin of her academic career. A secret she'd held closer than close. If the fact that she'd fabricated an entire person into existence didn't get her fired from the college, the reality that she was also sleeping with said imposter would surely do the trick.

She didn't care. It no longer mattered anyway.

"You've fallen for your creation." Lars threw back his head and let out a haughty stream of laughter. "How does it feel, Pygmalion? Does your Galatea have lips of cold stone, or upon Aphrodite's blessing, has his mouth turned to warm flesh?"

Pygmalion and Galatea. They were the central characters of Ovid's ancient narrative poem *Metamorphoses*. Pygmalion was a sculptor who fell deeply in love with a statue of a woman he'd carved from marble. He made offerings at the altar of Aphrodite and wished for a bride in the likeness of his *ivory girl*. When he returned home and kissed Galatea on the mouth, he found her cool marble lips had become warm like flesh.

Harper had seen Jean-Leon Gerôme's famous painting of Pygmalion and Galatea at the Metropolitan Museum of Art, where she'd marveled at its beauty—the glorious depiction of the moment when Pygmalion kissed his creation and the metamorphosis began. The rebirth had begun with that kiss, with the transformation of Pygmalion's lips.

She hadn't kissed life into the warmth of Tom's mouth. Life had been there all along. He was no Pygmalion. If anyone had been transformed, it had been her. In changing him into her own creation, she'd been the one forever altered.

"I love him," she said, the words tasting wild and strange in her mouth, like sweet clover honey.

"And I couldn't be happier for you." Lars shook his head. "You've invented him *and* you're sleeping with him. I simply couldn't have asked for a more satisfying turn of events."

Against all odds and all the hopes and dreams she'd thought she'd wanted for herself, even the face of life-changing consequences to come, Harper found she agreed. Falling in love was a satisfying turn of events.

But could she somehow turn the sweet satisfaction of her soul into a breathless happily ever after?

TOM STOOD BETWEEN Dr. Martin and Harper at the front of the gallery while waiters circled the room passing out slender glasses filled with champagne. The time had come for the toast, which would put a close to the evening. The final word of the final sentence of the final page of the book that was the charade of Tom Stone, the artist.

They'd done it. They'd actually carried it out. He couldn't quite believe it.

It had sounded easy enough at first. But once they'd gotten down to brass tacks, and Tom had realized the extent of the education that Harper had in mind, he'd had his doubts. But they'd somehow managed it. Each and every one of his paintings had sold. There were little red dots all over the gallery walls. Once Harper's boss gave his speech, Tom would be handed a check for a dollar amount that could winterize his boat ten times over. Everything could go back to the way it was before.

Then why was he suddenly filled with an overwhelming

sense of loss?

Because you don't want everything to go back to the way it was before.

He didn't want to go back to the boat. He wanted to stay in Harper's home. In her bed. In her life. *She* was his home now.

He took a sideways glance at her. She looked beyond beautiful tonight—hair loose and wavy, dancing on her perfect bare shoulders, exposed by the cut of her gorgeous dress. The dress had a long tulle skirt like something a ballerina would wear. Delicate and dream-like, it was the exact shade of purple as the violets he'd painted. Those fated, tragic violets. The flowers that had started it all.

He'd scarcely seen her tonight. He hadn't even had a chance to thank her for finding Frank and inviting him to the show. In fact, he hadn't seen her at all for the past hour.

In her absence, Lindsay had introduced him to dozens of new faces. Art critics, faculty members from the college who hadn't been in attendance at Lars's party a few weeks ago, newspaper reporters…the list went on and on. And everyone he'd met had said such nice things about his paintings. They'd shaken his hand and congratulated him on his success, and all the while Tom had wished Harper had been the one at his side.

Because she belonged there. The show was as much her success as it was his.

He itched to touch her, to thread his fingers through hers, to pull her into his arms, to kiss her hair. He couldn't, of course. Wouldn't. The last thing he wanted was to ruin her professional reputation.

But, God, how he needed to feel the softness of her skin, as white and pure as one of Frank's expensive lilies.

The waiter stopped in front of him, and Tom took two champagne flutes from his tray. "Thank you."

Then he turned and handed one to Harper.

She reached for it, and the tips of her fingers brushed against his. Contact, at last. Just enough to fan the fire of his need rather than to satiate it.

"Doc," he whispered. "We need to talk."

She nodded. "Yes. Yes, we do."

"Now." He nodded toward the small hallway at the back of the room.

"Good evening, everyone." Dr. Martin tapped the microphone a few times, and the chatter in the crowded gallery subsided.

All eyes turned toward the three of them.

Damn. Too late.

Well, once this final formality was over, they were going to talk. He had things to say to her. Things he wasn't sure she was ready to hear, but things he needed to say nonetheless.

"Soon." She mouthed before turning her attention to Dr. Martin.

Her boss cleared his throat and began. "Tonight is a very special night for the Boston College of Art. We are pleased to honor Tom Stone this evening, the artist behind the fine paintings we've all had the privilege of enjoying this evening."

Dr. Martin raised his glass and smiled at Tom. There was a smattering of applause as everyone sipped champagne in his honor. Tom glanced out at the crowd and spotted Lars Klassen standing against the far wall, his gazed fixed pointedly at Harper.

Tom frowned. He didn't like that look. Not at all.

He stole a sideways glance at Harper. She was looking right back at Klassen. And to Tom's utter confusion, she nodded her head ever so slightly, almost imperceptibly.

Something was going on, and whatever it was couldn't be good.

Dr. Martin's voice echoed off the gallery walls. "Ladies and gentleman, I'd also like to thank our curator, Dr. Harper Higgins, for her hard work on this show. She's done an outstanding job."

Tom clapped, careful not to let his champagne slosh out of its glass.

"I'd like to take this opportunity to make an announcement about Dr. Higgins' future with the department." Dr. Martin cast a questioning glance at Harper, and she nodded in return.

This must be it—the moment when her promotion would be announced. Tom hadn't realized it would happen here, now. But he was thrilled for her.

"As most people gathered here are aware, we have an opening in the Art History department for a tenured professor. About an hour ago, I had a chat with Dr. Higgins and offered the position to her."

Somewhere in his periphery, Tom could see Lindsay bouncing up and down with glee. He almost felt like bouncing up and down himself. He knew good and well how much this job meant to her.

"So, it is with sadness that I announce Dr. Higgins' resignation from the department."

Tom couldn't have heard that right.

Resignation?

That made no sense at all. Everything about the show, all the work they'd done over the past two months, all the late nights, all the deception…everything…had been about Harper getting that promotion.

He turned to look at Harper. She refused to meet his gaze. Her eyes were glued to the floor.

"Dr. Lars Klassen will be appointed to the tenured position, effective immediately. Congratulations, Dr. Klassen."

What?!

The audience applauded politely, even Lindsay, whose eyelashes fluttered a mile a minute.

"No." Tom shook his head. "No, there must be some mistake."

"Tom, stop," Harper said softly.

Tom's head throbbed. Why was she accepting this news so calmly? And why had Dr. Martin said she'd resigned when Tom knew that couldn't possibly be true? Nothing about this scenario was right.

"Doc, say something. This is a mistake." He turned his attention to Dr. Martin, who'd just begun to walk away. Tom grabbed him by the elbow. "Dr. Martin, wait. I don't understand. Harper…Dr. Higgins…didn't resign. And she deserves that promotion."

"I beg your pardon, Mr. Stone?" Dr. Martin frowned and glared at Tom's hand wrapped around his elbow until Tom released his arm. "This is none of your concern."

"Tom. *Stop.*" This time there was an urgency to Harper's voice that he couldn't ignore. "Dr. Martin, I'm sorry. Everything is fine. Just as it should be."

"Very well, then. Good evening. Mr. Stone, you may pick

up your check as soon as Dr. Higgins has gotten it ready." He straightened his coat jacket and brushed away the wrinkles left behind by Tom's grasp, then left the two of them alone.

Harper smiled, but it didn't reach her eyes. Nor could she seem to look directly at him. Rather, her gaze flitted everywhere and nowhere. She was as nervous as a hummingbird. Something was most definitely wrong. Even worse, Harper seemed to have no intention of telling him what that something was.

Tom tossed the rest of his champagne down his throat and handed his empty glass to a passing waiter. "Doc, can I ask what the hell is going on?"

She shrugged. "Of course. I've rethought the promotion, that's all. I don't think teaching is for me."

Then why do you look as though you want to cry? "Are you sure about that?"

"Absolutely." She nodded.

The stricken look on her face made Tom want to hit somebody. He just wasn't sure who, or why.

He reached for her, slipping both of her hands in his. He was struck, as always, by the softness of her skin. Rose petals against his roughness of his world-weary hands. Her coworkers might stare, but what difference did that make now?

"Doc, be real with me. Please."

The crowd milled around them. Happy people, high on art and champagne, chattered away, oblivious to the fact that Tom's world had somehow come together and apart all at once.

Why was she doing this? Last night he'd made love to her with every part of his body and soul. And now, less than twelve hours later, he felt her slipping away.

Was this how things were going to be from now on? Out of

her house? Out of her life? Out of her thoughts, hopes, feelings and dreams? Something altogether uncomfortable—desperation—clawed at his insides.

Harper's eyes shimmered. She blinked, and a crystal tear slipped down her cheek. A perfect, liquid diamond. "Tom. Trust me. It's for the best."

"Harper, here you are." Lindsay burst toward them from a cluster full of tuxedo-clad college professors. Harper's colleagues. Correction—*former* colleagues.

"They need you in the office. And when you're finished, I need to talk to you. Badly." Lindsay jammed her hands on her hips.

"Oh, of course." In a single, slow motion, agonizing heartbeat, Harper slipped her hands away from his. The loss of her touch felt larger than it should, and Tom's soul tripped over the lush forest green of her eyes. "I'll catch up with you later, Tom. Okay?"

She blinked up at him, his tragic, winsome beauty. There was no mask this time, no careful rearrangement of her features. This was Harper Higgins, the real Harper Higgins, in all her raw, honest glory. He'd wanted her to be real with him, and she'd granted him that wish. He just didn't know the whole story yet.

He knew without a doubt that he'd been right. Something had happened. Something she wanted to keep from him.

Trust me. It's for the best.

As she walked away in a swish of violet tulle, Tom couldn't help but wonder how it could be for the best if it made her cry tears that she couldn't explain.

Chapter Twenty-Six

THANK GOD.

Thank God for busy work, for curatorial duties, and the horde of people crowded between the white gallery walls. She couldn't seem to look Tom in the face and lie about why she'd quit her job. And she definitely didn't want him to know the truth. He would feel awful and she didn't want that kind of strain between them.

Secrets...lies...aren't those strains?

Yes. And no.

She'd had no choice. She'd done what she did in order to protect him. Actually, she supposed she'd had a choice, but she'd decided on the only course of action that was acceptable to her. Oddly enough, it had been the easiest choice she'd ever made in her life.

She felt strangely at peace with the decision. An odd sense of relief had overcome her once the words had left her mouth. *I resign.* She'd never seen Dr. Martin so shocked. She couldn't blame him, really. Since the day she'd first set foot on the Boston College of Art campus, all she'd wanted was a tenured position. She would have done anything to get it. Anything, including lie, cheat, and take advantage of a man who'd turned out to be the best person she'd ever met.

She hadn't realized what a toll all of it had taken and just how exhausted, both mentally and physically, she was from it all. The tears behind her eyes were tears of relief. Relief and regret. Relief that it was over, and regret that she'd put Tom through this. Regret that he'd nearly been publically humiliated. Regret for a lot of things.

"Harper." Lindsay grabbed her arm and pulled her closer as they made their way to the gallery's business office. "*What* is going on? All you've talked about for months is the promotion. And now you resign? And *Lars* gets promoted instead?"

"Everything is fine, Lindsay. I promise. It was the right thing to do." Harper gave her a tight one-armed hug.

"What are you going to do?"

The other academics were giving her strange looks as she walked through the crowd, as if she'd suddenly gone completely mad. Maybe she had. But was that really such a bad thing?

The art world was overflowing with stories of madness. The connection between art and suffering had a long, tragic history. Some of the best painters of all time had experienced bouts with mental illness—Michelangelo, Mark Rothko, Paul Gauguin, Francisco Goya and Edvard Munch, to name a few. Georgia O'Keefe suffered an intense nervous breakdown after falling behind on a deadline for a mural she was painting for the Radio City Music Hall. It was only after being hospitalized and taking a two-year break from painting that she was able to regain her love and commitment to her life's work.

And, of course, her favorite artist of all, Van Gogh, was the epitome of the tortured artist. His madness had cost him an ear. And, eventually, his life.

Okay, so maybe those were some rather extreme examples.

Harper had quit her job, not lopped off a body part. But beneath the strain of the charade, beneath the regret, there was a certain wildness stirring in her soul.

She was free. No more competing with Lars. No more shoving information down the throats of students who clearly didn't care that Georges Braque was the first living artist to have his work displayed in the Louvre or that Henri Matisse's painting, *Le Bateau*, famously hung upside down for forty six days in the Museum of Modern Art in New York before anyone noticed. She could devote her time to something she hadn't allowed herself to dream about for years—creating art, rather than talking about it.

She wanted to paint.

"Well?" Lindsay paused outside the door to the business office. "Do you have any sort of plan?"

Actually, she did. "Yes. I'm going to buy Art Bar."

"Art Bar." Lindsay regarded her through narrowed eyes. She wasn't blinking, though, and that was a good sign. "Is it for sale?"

"Not technically. But Peyton has been talking nonstop about being burned out. I think we might be able to reach some sort of agreement." She hoped so, at least.

Peyton had been complaining for months. She was sure they could work something out, fingers crossed.

"But you hate Art Bar."

"No, I don't hate it. Not entirely. There are things I love about it. I love the painting, for one. And the children's classes are a delight. I could add Degas classes for little girls several times a week. I have a few ideas for kid classes, actually."

Shoes.

Like Van Gogh.

The idea had just come to her all of a sudden. She could teach them all about how Van Gogh had painted his shoes, and then the kids could each paint their own. There were all sorts of ways she could encourage children to love art. She could teach about Roy Lichtenstein and they could do comic book paintings, or maybe even portraits of superheroes done in Picasso's cubist style. Her mind was awhirl with possibilities.

"Does Tom know?" Lindsay glanced back in the direction they'd come from.

"Not yet." She bit her lip.

Harper followed her gaze and spotted Tom right where she'd left him, chatting with one of the ceramics professors. He looked distracted and serious, his square jaw firmly clenched, his blue eyes steely and hard as diamonds. They needed to talk. She wanted to make sure he knew she was fine. Everything was wonderful. She just wasn't sure how to convince him she'd come to this decision all on her own, tonight of all nights, and why she'd kept it a secret from him.

TOM HAD SHAKEN the last hand he could take. He'd talked about his flower paintings until he was blue in the face. As blue as the irises his "ancestor" Van Gogh was so famous for.

He shook his head. Was he doomed to forever think in terms of paintings and artists from centuries ago?

Yes. Yes, you are, because that's how she thinks. And she's a part of you now.

He needed to find Harper. He needed to find her and get

to the bottom of what was going on. If she hadn't spent all her time transforming him into a different man over the past two months in order to secure that promotion, then what had all this been about?

He turned in the direction she and Lindsay had gone in, bumping headlong into someone in the process.

"Sorry," he muttered, backing away.

He needed to get his wits about him. Since Dr. Martin's toast, thoughts had been tumbling through his head a mile a minute.

"No worries, Sarge."

Sarge?

Tom looked up and found Lars Klassen staring back at him, his lips curved into a smug grin. Tom knew perfectly well where the smugness was coming from. The creep had just somehow stolen Harper's promotion. But what he couldn't understand was why Lars had just called him Sarge.

"Excuse me?" he said.

"I said no worries." He flashed another arrogant smile.

"That's not all you said." Tom's hands flexed. How easy it would be to pummel this guy into the ground…

Don't. Harper would hate it if you made a scene.

The charade was over. He didn't have to live by Harper's rules anymore. She would no longer be looking over his shoulder, telling him what and what not to say.

But he still wanted to please her all the same, to make her proud, to put a smile on her face.

"Are you referring to the fact I called you Sarge? It's just an expression. Relax." He winked.

And that simple gesture hit Tom like a punch in the gut.

He knows.

"Good evening and congratulations on a successful show." Lars saluted him before walking away.

Not a real salute, only a small movement two of his fingers, but a clear confirmation that he knew everything.

My God.

Tom stood frozen to the spot, unable to move, barely able to think. Lars knew. He'd let the entire show go on undisturbed when he could have told Dr. Martin everything. And instead he'd let everything proceed as planned. But why?

The answer came to him in a moment of blinding clarity. Harper must have stopped him. She'd handed Lars the promotion and quit the department altogether just to get him to keep quiet about Tom's identity.

No wonder. No wonder she'd been on the verge of tears. And no wonder she'd refused to tell him why.

He had to find her.

He took off toward the back of the gallery, pausing to ask the few people he knew if they'd seen her, coming up empty at every turn.

"No idea."

"Try the business office."

"I think she may have left."

Surely she hadn't gone home without him.

It's not your home. You're just staying there, remember? It was always supposed to be temporary.

Well, things changed, didn't they? Just like Harper and her job. If she could choose him over her dreams, that *made* her his home. Not her house, not her bed, but her.

"Tom." Someone tapped him on the shoulder.

He spun around, hoping to see Harper's beautiful face, but found Lindsay standing there instead. "Oh."

She rolled her eyes. "I'm going to choose not to take that note of disappointment in your tone personally."

Tom winced. "I'm sorry. It's just that I've been looking for Harper, and I can't seem to find her."

Lindsay's eyes twinkled. She looked far too happy for someone who would probably be working for Lars Klassen in the near future. Someone needed to introduce that guy to a Starbucks.

"She sent me to come get you."

He glanced around. Still no sign of Harper. The gallery wasn't all that big. "Come get me? Where's she gone?"

"You'll see." She crooked a finger at him. "Come with me."

"Yes, ma'am." He followed her, not that he had much of a choice in the matter.

She led him past the business office, then pushed open a door that had a sign that said *Private. Maintenance Staff Only.* They ended up in a hallway so dark that Tom couldn't see his hand in front of his face, much less Lindsay. He followed the sound of her footsteps and hoped to hell she knew where she was going.

After they'd gone about forty feet, she slowed to a stop. "Here we are."

She heaved open a heavy, metal door that Tom hadn't even realized was there. It creaked on its hinges and scratched against the concrete floor with an agonizing scrape. Then Tom's vision was flooded with a twinkling wonderland of light.

He crossed the threshold and blinked a few times in an effort to adjust to the sudden assault on his senses—the cold bite of air on his face, the sensation of snow flurries falling as soft as feathers against his skin and tiny, glimmering lights everywhere above him. Like stars.

He was outdoors, in some kind of garden surrounded by a low stone wall. The snow-laden branches of the overhanging maple and oak trees glittered with light, bathing the garden in soft golden hues, illuminating the geometric topiaries that lent the atmosphere a distinctive wonderland feel.

He heard the door slam shut behind him and Lindsay was gone.

A voice drifted toward him from the snow-swept shadows. "Hi, Tom."

He took a few steps further, and then he saw her. Harper.

She stood in the center of the garden, surrounded by greenery, the gently swirling snow, and a circle of the most beautiful bronze statues Tom had ever seen.

Each sculpture depicted a pair of dancers, a man and woman with lithe, graceful bodies, pointed toes, and willowy limbs entwined with one another in an eternal pas de deux. The poses varied, from elegant lifts to seductive dips. Exquisite, tortured longing depicted in the green verdigris patina of timeless dancers. As breathtaking as they were, they couldn't begin to compare to the beauty of the woman standing before him.

"Doc." He smiled and moved closer to her. Close enough to see the snow gathered in her hair and the starry reflection of light dancing in her luminous eyes. "Where are we?"

"This is the college's sculpture garden. Pretty, isn't it?" She waved an arm at the nearest dancer sculpture.

Tom's gaze remained fixed precisely where it was. On her. "Absolutely stunning."

She shook her head and laughed. Her glorious hair cascaded down her bare back. Moonlight caressed her shoulders, and snow crystals glittered on the rich violet of her dress. She was a vision, prettier than any painting he'd ever seen.

Because she was real.

And she was his.

He caught her chin between his thumb and finger and tipped her face upward, so she was looking him directly in the eyes. "That wasn't a joke. I'm dead serious. Harper, you are the most beautiful woman I've ever seen."

"Tom..."

"I know what you did," he said, getting right to the heart of the matter.

Wordlessly, she stared up at him. There were no more tears, just a subtle smile and a look he'd seen on her face only a handful of times. It was the expression she always wore when she painted, the one that never failed to take his breath away. But this time, there wasn't a paintbrush or canvas in sight. It was just the two of them, under a snowdrop moon surrounded by dancing art.

She took a deep breath and finally said, "Lars knew. He had a whole file of information about you."

A whole file of information, as if a man's life could be reduced to a stack of papers. "Yeah, I figured that much out. Look, I'll find a way to undo this, to get your job back. There's got to be a way, and I intend to find it."

"But I don't want that, Tom." She shook her head. "I only want you."

Her words washed over him like the gentlest of snowfalls. A blessing. A benediction.

"I want you." She grinned, no timid Mona Lisa smile, but a smile that spoke of pure joy. "I want you, and I want art and painting. I understand now. The purpose of art isn't about history, or color, or composition. It's about the beauty of life and love. And I love you, Tom."

Tom hadn't planned what happened next. Destiny wasn't something to be planned or thought out. It was as simple and natural as a shooting star dancing across the sky, or a snowflake drifting on the night wind. Or a man falling to his knees in reaction to the single most beautiful, significant moment of his life.

He was vaguely aware of the crunch of gravel beneath the fabric of his tuxedo pants. He knew he must be cold, because he could see his breath suspended in a cloud of misty gray vapor. He realized this was something that neither of them had thought they'd ever want or need. But none of those things mattered. The only thing that did was her answer.

He reached for her hands, so delicate, so soft. The hands of an artist. He held those hands as tightly as he could. He had no ring, no real future to give her. He wasn't offering her Tom Stone, the art sensation. He wasn't about to go on living a lie. The only thing he had to offer her was his heart.

"Marry me, Doc," he whispered, the words rising from his soul with aching desire. "I love you. Marry me."

With tears shining in her emerald eyes, she nodded.

He smiled. "Yes?"

She slipped her hands from his grasp and wrapped them around his neck. Then she answered him in a way that surpassed all this wildest expectations.

"Oh God, yes."

Epilogue

Four months later

HARPER HELD THE ladder steady for her husband as he climbed to the top rung.

Her *husband.*

A month had passed since the wedding, and she still got a giddy smile on her face when she thought of Tom as her husband. She wasn't sure she'd ever grow accustomed to it. She'd never wanted a husband, after all. Never thought she needed one. But Tom had changed all that. He'd changed everything.

"Are you sure about this?" he asked, smirking down at her from the top of the ladder. He was teasing her again. Some things never changed.

She rolled her eyes "Yes. Oh God, yes. I couldn't be more sure."

"If you insist." He shook his head and made a tsk-tsk noise as he removed a framed photograph from the wall. "Such a shame. I'm actually quite fond of this picture."

"No, you are *not.*" Harper had despised it since the moment she'd first laid eyes on it. At best, it was silly. At worst, humiliating. He couldn't be serious.

Tom stuck the offensive photo under one of his arms and

climbed down the ladder. Once safely on the ground, he removed the photo and gazed down at it with a bemused expression. "You're kinda cute with a unibrow."

"Give me that." Harper snatched it out of his hand.

That Halloween snapshot of her dressed as Frida Kahlo had tormented her since the day Peyton had nailed it to the wall. Getting it down was Harper's first order of business as the new owner of Art Bar. Co-owner, actually.

"What if I want to leave it up?" Tom asked, clearly joking.

At least she hoped it was a joke. "Then I suppose we'd have our first disagreement as both husband and wife and co-owners of our own painting studio."

So much had changed since the night of the gallery opening. When Tom had heard that she wanted to buy Art Bar, he'd insisted on using the proceeds he'd earned selling his paintings to help with the down payment. He'd never winterized the boat, but that no longer mattered. He spent every night in bed with Harper, no longer plagued by nightmares. On solid ground, he'd found his footing at last, and his unquenchable thirst had finally been sated by the waters of desire. When spring and summer rolled around, they planned to take the boat out and sail up and down the Massachusetts coast. Tom told Harper he wanted to see her standing on the deck, wrapped in a sweater with her fingertips barely peeking out from the sleeves, the sea wind whipping through her hair as the ocean carried them to new dreams. And that sounded perfect to her.

Until then, they had plans for Art Bar. Big plans. Harper had started a children's afterschool program, concentrating on fun and interesting twists on classic masterpieces. Tom planned on teaching lessons in floral painting on the nights he wasn't walking dogs. He'd also been invited to participate in a new gallery show—this time by a contact from the Combat Paper Project, someone familiar with the very real Tom Stone, not his fabricated alter ego. Rounding out the staff at Art Bar was their one and only employee—Lindsay.

Harper couldn't leave her there at the college making coffee for Lars for the rest of her life. She just couldn't. Lindsay was too valuable, too smart for that. So far she'd done an outstanding job taking over the social media and marketing for Art Bar. The class schedule was so full that Lindsay had even offered to teach a few basic painting classes herself.

As it turned out, she wouldn't have been stuck making Lars's coffee if she'd stayed at the college. After only two months as an Associate Professor, he'd been terminated for falsifying his academic background. It seemed that *Doctor* Lars Klassen wasn't actually a doctor at all.

Sometimes Harper wondered if the reason Lars had always been so suspicious of Tom was because he was no stranger to pretending to be someone he wasn't. Not that it mattered now. Tom was no longer pretending, and neither was Harper. They were husband and wife, and they were very much real.

The wedding had taken place in the sculpture garden at the college, under a moonlit sky just like the night Tom had proposed. Frank had provided the flowers—dozens upon dozens of Picasso calla lilies. In a swirl of snow flurries, with only a handful of guests and the bronze dancers as witnesses, they'd vowed to love one another until death did them part. No mention had been made in the vows about eradicating evidence of the Frida Kahlo unibrow. A mistaken omission, perhaps?

"You know what they say about Kahlo's paintings, don't you?" Tom asked, drawing Harper's attention once again to the ridiculous photograph. "*The art of Frida Kahlo is a ribbon around a bomb.*"

She grinned. The man had a memory like none she'd ever encountered before. He still knew pretty much everything she'd made him memorize for the gallery show, and he delighted in peppering conversations with such facts just to make her smile.

She took a step closer to him and slid her arms around his neck. "Who *exactly* said that?" she whispered.

His hands skimmed their way up her back and into her hair, leaving a cascade of goose bumps wherever they touched. "You don't think I know? Because I definitely do."

She purred, leaning into his touch. "I don't know. We might have to make another wager."

"A wager. That sounds fair." He pressed a gentle kiss to the hollow of her neck, nibbled the length of her collarbone and whispered into her hair. "But I'm afraid this time, it's all or nothing. Are you ready to get naked, Doc?"

For him? Yes. Always yes. "We'll see about that. You haven't told me who said it yet."

"The man who said that Frida Kahlo's art is a ribbon wrapped around a bomb was French writer and poet Andre Breton, widely praised as the founder of Surrealism. And I like that image—a ribbon wrapped around a bomb. Beauty and strength, strength and beauty. It reminds me of someone else I know—my lovely, strong wife."

She grinned. "You know just how to compliment me, you charmer."

He shook his head. "Don't change the subject. Am I right,

or am I right?"

"You know you are." She unwound her arms from around his neck and backed away a few inches, just enough space to give her room to unfasten the top button of her blouse. Then the next. And the next. "Well, what do you know? You're right. It was indeed Andre Breton."

His eyes glittered as he watched the deliberate movements of her hands. "Sorry, Doc. I'm afraid you lose. Again."

She undid the final button and let her blouse slip from her shoulders. As it fell to the floor, she couldn't help but think of herself—falling, falling, falling. When would it end, this perpetual fall, and why was she no longer afraid?

Because he will be there to catch you.

He caught her chin in his hand, ran his thumb over her bottom lip in a feather-light touch, and silently mouthed the words, "I love you."

I lose? I don't think so.

This. Right here. This was winning.

"And I love you," she whispered.

Then the words stopped, as she closed her eyes and gave herself up to her prize.

The End

About the Author

Teri Wilson is a romance novelist for Harlequin Books and Tule Publishing, as well as a contributing writer at HelloGiggles.com, a lifestyle and entertainment website founded by Zooey Deschanel and now a division of People Magazine. Teri is the author of UNLEASHING MR. DARCY, now a Hallmark Channel Original Movie. She loves books, travel, animals and dancing every day.

Visit Teri at www.teriwilson.net.

Thank you for reading

The Art of Us

If you enjoyed this book, you can find more from all our great authors at TulePublishing.com, or from your favorite online retailer.

TULE
PUBLISHING

Made in the USA
Monee, IL
05 February 2023